DEBUTANTES &DAGGERS

INCLUDES
REBEL BELLE &
MISS MAYHEM

Rachel Hawkins

speak

"So what does all this mean?"

"It means that you've been given a sacred duty," Saylor said. Her voice sounded different, and there was hardly a trace of Southern accent in it at all. "From this day forward, you will be tasked with protecting the Oracle at all costs. He'll be your sole focus until the day you, like Christopher, have to lay down your life for him."

Saylor reached for my hand, and I gave it to her without thinking. "So, Harper Jane Price. Are you ready to accept your destiny?"

I withdrew my hand. "No, thank you."

Saylor and David both stared.

"I appreciate your offer very much," I continued. "But I'm afraid I have to refuse."

Saylor rose to her feet, an expression somewhere between anger and disbelief spreading across her face. "I'm not inviting you to a garden party, Harper. I'm asking you to accept the role destiny has handed you. I'm asking you to use the powers you've been given."

OTHER BOOKS YOU MAY ENJOY

Anna and the French Kiss	Stephanie Perkins
Bitterblue	Kristin Cashore
The Dark Days Club	Alison Goodman
Fire	Kristin Cashore
Lady Renegades	Rachel Hawkins
The Legend trilogy	Marie Lu
Rebel of the Sands	Alwyn Hamilton
The Season	Jonah Lisa Dyer and Stephen Dyer
The Shades of London series	Maureen Johnson
The Young Elites trilogy	Marie Lu

REBEL BELLE

SPEAK
An imprint of Penguin Random House LLC
375 Hudson Street
New York, New York 10014

First published in the United States of America by G. P. Putnam's Sons,
an imprint of Penguin Group (USA), 2014
Published by Speak, an imprint of Penguin Group (USA) LLC, 2015

This omnibus edition published by Speak, an imprint of Penguin Random House LLC, 2017
Copyright © 2014 by Rachel Hawkins

THE LIBRARY OF CONGRESS HAS CATALOGED THE G. P. PUTNAM'S SONS EDITION AS FOLLOWS:
Hawkins, Rachel, date.
Rebel belle / Rachel Hawkins.
p. cm.
ISBN 978-0-399-25693-6 (hardcover)
Summary: "Seventeen-year-old Harper Price's charmed life is turned upside down when she
discovers she's been given magical powers in order to protect her school nemesis David Stark,
who's an Oracle"—Provided by publisher.
[1. Magic—Fiction. 2. Supernatural—Fiction. 3. Oracles—Fiction.
4. Debutantes—Fiction. 5. High schools—Fiction. 6. Schools—Fiction.]
I. Title.
PZ7.H313525Reb 2014
[Fic]—dc23
2013027102

ISBN 9780147514356
Omnibus edition ISBN 9780451478689

Printed in the United States of America

Design by Annie Ericsson
Interior images courtesy of iStockphoto

3 5 7 9 10 8 6 4

For Aunt Mimi, Aunt Ruby,
Aunt Audie, Aunt Rona, and Aunt Ann,
rebel belles if ever there were ones.

Chapter 1

LOOKING BACK, none of this would have happened if I'd brought lip gloss the night of the Homecoming Dance.

Bee Franklin was the first person to notice that my lips were all naked and indecent. We were standing outside of our school, Grove Academy. It was late October, and the night was surprisingly cool; in Pine Grove, Alabama, where I live, it's not unheard of to have a hot Halloween. But that night felt like fall, complete with that nice smoky smell in the air. I was super relieved that it was cold, because my jacket was wool, and there was nothing more tragic than a girl sweating in wool. I was wearing the jacket over a knee-length pink sheath dress. If I was going to be crowned Homecoming Queen tonight—and that seemed like a lock—I was going to do it looking as classy as possible in my demure pink dress and pearls.

"Are you nervous?" Bee asked as I rubbed my hands up and down my arms. Like me, Bee was in pink, but her dress was closer to magenta and the bodice was covered in tiny sequins that winked and shivered in the parking lot lights. Or maybe that was just Bee. *Unlike* me, she hadn't worn a jacket.

Our dates, Brandon and Ryan, were off searching for a parking place. They had been annoyed that Bee and I had insisted on not showing up until the thirty minutes before the crowning, but there was no way I was going to risk getting punch spilled on me or my makeup sliding off my face (not to mention the sweatiness! See above, re: wool jacket) before I had that sparkly tiara on my head. I planned on looking *fierce* in the yearbook pictures.

"Of course I'm not nervous," I told Bee. And it was true, I wasn't. Okay, maybe I was a little bit *anxious* . . .

Bee gave an exaggerated eye roll. "Seriously? Harper Jane Price, you have not been able to successfully lie to me since the Second-Grade Barbie Incident. Admit that you're freaking out." She held up one hand, pinching her thumb and forefinger together. "Maybe a leeeeeetle bit?"

Laughing, I caught her hand and pulled it down. "Not even a 'leeeeeetle bit.' It's just Homecoming."

"Yeah, but you're going to get all queenly tonight. I think that warrants *some* nerves. Or are you saving them for Cotillion?"

Just the word sent all the nerves Bee could have wanted jittering through my system, but before I could admit that, her dark eyes suddenly went wide. "Omigod! Harper! Your lips!"

"What?" I asked, raising a hand to them.

"They're nekkid," she said. "You are totally gloss-less!"

"Who's 'nekkid'?"

I looked up to see the boys walking toward us. The orange lights played up the red in Ryan's hair, and he was grinning, his hands in his pockets. I felt that same little flutter in my stomach that I'd been feeling since the first day I saw Ryan Bradshaw, way back in the third grade. It had taken me six years from that day to make him my boyfriend, but looking at him now, I had to admit, it had been worth the wait.

"My lips," I said. "I must've wiped off all my gloss at the restaurant."

"Well, damn," he said, throwing his arm around my shoulders. "I'd hoped for something a little more exciting. Of course, no lip gloss means I can safely do this."

He lowered his head and kissed me, albeit pretty chastely. PDA is vile, and Ryan, being my Perfect Boyfriend, knows how I feel about it.

"Hope you girls are happy," Brandon said when we broke apart. He had both of his arms wrapped around Bee from behind, his hands clasped right under her . . . um, abundant assets. Bee was so tall that Brandon's chin barely cleared her shoulder. "We had to park way down the effing road."

Okay, I should probably mention right here that Brandon used the real word, but this is my story, so I'm cleaning it up a little. Besides, if I honestly quoted Brandon, this thing would look like a *Cops* transcript.

"Don't say that word!" I snapped.

Brandon rolled his eyes. "What the hell, Harper, are you, like, the language police?"

I pressed my lips together. "I just think that the F-word should be saved for dire occasions. And having to park a hundred yards from the gym is not a dire occasion."

"So sorry, Your Highness," Brandon said, scowling as Bee elbowed him in the ribs.

"Easy, dude," Ryan said, shooting Brandon a warning look.

Ignoring Brandon, I turned to Bee. "Do you have any lip gloss? I completely spaced on bringing any."

"My girl forgot makeup?" Ryan asked, quirking an eyebrow. "Man, you *are* stressed about this Queen thing."

"No, I'm not," I said immediately, even though, hello, I clearly was. But I didn't like when people used the "S-word" around me. After all, a big part of my reputation at the Grove was my ability to handle anything and everything.

Ryan raised his hands in apology. "Okay, okay, sorry. But, I mean, this is obviously pretty important to you, or you wouldn't have spent over a grand on that outfit." He smiled again, shaking his head so his hair fell over his eyes. "I really hope your tastes get cheaper if we get married."

"I hear that, man," Brandon said, lifting his hand to high-five Ryan. "Chicks gonna break us."

Bee rolled her eyes again, but I didn't know whether it was at the guys or the fact that my outfit was over a thousand dollars (yes, I know that's a completely ridiculous amount for a seventeen-year-old girl to spend on a Homecoming dress, but, hey, I can wear it, like, a million times provided I don't gain five pounds. Or at least that was how I rationalized it to my mom.)

"Here." Bee thrust a tube into my hand.

I held it up to read the name on the bottom. "'Salmon Fantasy'?"

"That's close to the shade you wear." Bee's long blond hair was woven into a fishtail braid, and she tossed it over her shoulder as she handed me the lip gloss.

"I wear 'Coral Shimmer.' That is very different."

Bee made a face that said, "I am only tolerating you because we've been best friends since we were five," but I kept going, drawing myself up to my full height with mock imperiousness, "And Salmon Fantasy has to be the grossest beauty product name ever. Who has fantasies about salmon?"

"People who screw fish," Brandon offered, completely cracking himself up. Ryan didn't laugh, but I saw the corners of his mouth twitching.

"So witty, Bran," I muttered, and this time, when Bee rolled her eyes, I had no doubt that it was at the guys.

"Look," she said to me, "it's either Salmon Fantasy or naked lips. Your choice."

I sighed and clutched the tube of lip gloss. "Okay," I said, "but I'm gonna have to find a bathroom." If it had been my Coral Shimmer, I could have put it on without a mirror, but there was no way I was slapping on a new shade sight unseen. Ryan pulled open the gym door, and I ducked under his arm to walk into the gym. As soon as I did, I could hear the opening riff of "Sweet Home Alabama." It's not a dance until someone plays that song.

The gym looked great, and my chest tightened with pride. I know everyone, even Ryan, thinks I'm crazy to do all the stuff I do at school, but I honestly love the place. I love its redbrick buildings, and the chapel bells that ring to signal class changes. I love that both my parents went here, and their parents before them. So yeah, maybe I do stretch myself a little thin, but it's completely worth it. The Grove is a happy place to go to school, and I liked to think my good example was the reason for that.

And it meant that when people thought of the name "Price" at Grove Academy, they'd think of all the good things I'd done for the school, and not . . . other stuff.

Instead, I focused on the decorations. I'm SGA president—the first-ever junior to be elected to the position, I should add—so Homecoming activities are technically my responsibility. But tonight, I'd delegated all of the decorating to my protégée, sophomore class president, Lucy McCarroll. My only contribution had been to ban crepe streamers and balloon arches. Can you say tacky?

Lucy had done a great job. The walls were covered in a silky, shimmery purple material and there were colored lights pulsating with the music. Looking over at the punch table, I saw that she'd even brought in a little fountain with several bistro tables clustered around it.

I scanned the crowd until I saw Lucy, and when I caught her eye, I gave her the thumbs-up, and mouthed, "Nice!"

"Harper!" I heard someone cry. I turned around to see Amanda and Abigail Foster headed my way. They were identical twins, but relatively easy to tell apart since Amanda always wore her long brown hair up, and Abigail wore hers down. Tonight, both were wearing green dresses with spaghetti straps, but Amanda's was hunter green while Abigail's was closer to seafoam.

The twins were on the cheerleading squad with me and Bee, and Abi and I worked together on SGA. Right behind them was Mary Beth Riley, wobbling on her high heels. Next to me, Bee blew out a long breath before muttering, "Maybe no one will notice if she wears tennis shoes under her dress."

Despite Bee's low tone, Mary Beth heard her. "I'm working on it," she said, glaring at Bee. "I'll get better by Cotillion."

Since "Riley" came right after "Price" alphabetically, Mary Beth would be following me down the giant staircase at Magnolia House, the mansion where Cotillion was held every year. So far, we'd only had two practices, but Mary Beth had tripped and nearly fallen directly on top of me both times.

Which was why I'd suggested she start wearing the heels every day.

"Speaking of that," Amanda said, laying a hand on my arm. Even under her makeup, I could see the constellation of freckles arcing across her nose. That was another way to tell the twins apart; Abi's nose was freckle free. "We got an e-mail from Miss Saylor right before we left for the dance. She wants to schedule another practice Monday afternoon."

I bit back a sigh. I had a Future Business Leaders of America meeting Monday after school, so that would have to be moved. Maybe Tuesday? No, Tuesday was cheerleading practice, and Wednesday was SGA. Still, when Saylor Stark told you there was going to be an extra Cotillion practice, you went. All the other stuff could wait.

"I'm so sick of practice," Mary Beth groaned, tipping her head back. As she did, her dark red hair fell back from her ears, revealing silver hoops that were way too big. Ugh. "It's *Cotillion*. We wear a white dress. We walk down some stairs, we drink some punch and dance with our dads. And then we all pat ourselves on the back and pretend we did it just to raise money for charity, and that it's not stupid and old-fashioned and totally self-indulgent."

"Mary Beth!" Amanda gasped, while Abigail glanced around like Miss Saylor was going to swoop out of the rafters. Bee's huge eyes went even bigger, and her mouth opened and closed several times, but no sounds came out.

"It is not!" I heard someone practically shriek. Then I realized it was *me*. I took a deep breath through my nose and did my best to make my voice calm as I continued. "I just mean . . . Mary Beth, Cotillion is a lot more than wearing a white dress and dancing with your dad. It's *tradition*. It's when we make the transition from girls to women. It's . . . important."

Mary Beth chewed her lip and studied me for a moment. "Okay, maybe." Then she shrugged and gave a tiny smile. "But we'll see how you feel when I'm 'transitioning' into a heap at the bottom of those stairs."

"You'll do fine," I told her, hoping I sounded more convinced than I felt. I'd spent months preparing for my Homecoming coronation, but Cotillion? I'd been getting ready for *that* since I was four years old and Mom had shown me and my older sister, Leigh-Anne, her Cotillion dress. I still remembered the smooth feel of the silk under my hands. It had been her grandmother's dress, Mom had told us, and one day, Leigh-Anne and I would wear it, too.

Two years ago, Leigh-Anne had, but for my Cotillion, I'd be wearing a dress Mom and I had bought last summer in Mobile.

"Babe!" I heard Ryan call from behind me.

As I turned to smile at him, I heard one of the girls sigh. Probably Mary Beth. And I had to admit, striding toward us, his auburn hair flopping over his forehead, shoulders back, hands in his pockets, Ryan was completely sigh-worthy. I held my hand out to him as he approached, and he slipped it easily into his own.

"Ladies," Ryan said, nodding at Amanda, Abigail, and Mary Beth. "Let me guess. Y'all are . . . plotting world domination?"

Mary Beth giggled, which had the unfortunate effect of making her wobble even more. Abigail had to grab her elbow to keep her from falling over.

"No," Amanda told him, deadly serious. "We're talking about Cotillion."

"Ah, world domination, Cotillion. Same difference," Ryan replied with an easy grin, and this time, all three girls giggled, even Amanda.

Turning his attention to me, Ryan raised his eyebrows. "So are we just going to stand around and listen to this band butcher Lynyrd Skynyrd or are we going to dance?"

"Yeah," Brandon said, coming up next to Ryan and grabbing Bee around the waist. "Let's go turn this mother *out*."

He pulled her out onto the dance floor, where he immediately flopped on his belly and started doing the worm. I watched Bee dance awkwardly around him and wondered for the millionth time why she wasted her time with that goofball.

My own much less goofy boyfriend took my hand and started pulling me toward Bee and Brandon, but I pulled it back and held up the lip gloss. "I'll be right back!" I shouted over the music, and he nodded before heading for the refreshment table.

I glanced over my shoulder as I walked into the gym lobby and was treated to the sight of Brandon and one of the other basketball players doing that weird fish-catching dance move. With each other.

Since we'd gotten there so late, most everyone who was coming to the dance was already inside the gym, but there were a few stragglers coming in the main gym lobby doors. Two teachers, Mrs. Delacroix and Mr. Schmidt, were also in the lobby, undoubtedly doing "purse and pocket checks." Grove Academy was really strict about that sort of thing now. Two years ago, a few kids smuggled in a little bottle of liquor at prom and, later that night, got into a car accident. My sister—

I cut that thought off. Not tonight.

It was strange to be in the school at night. The only light in the lobby came from a display case full of "participation" trophies with Ryan's name on them. The Grove was excellent in academics, but famously crappy at sports, even against other tiny schools. I know that sounds like sacrilege in the South, but just like any other expensive private school, Grove Academy was way more invested in SAT scores than any scoreboard. We left the football championships to the giant public school across town, Lee High.

I've been up at school at night a few times, and it's always creepy. I guess it's the quiet. I'm used to the halls being deafening, so the sound of my heels clicking on the linoleum seemed freakishly loud. In fact, they almost echoed, making me feel like there was someone behind me.

I hurried out of the lobby and turned the corner into the English hall, so I didn't see the guy in front of me until it was too late.

"Oh!" I exclaimed as we bumped shoulders. "Sorry!"

Then I realized who I'd bumped into, and immediately regretted my apologetic tone. If I'd known it was David Stark, I would have tried to hit him harder, or maybe stepped on his foot with the spiky heel of my new shoes for good measure.

I did my best to smile at him, though, even as I realized my stomach was jumping all over the place. He must have scared me more than I'd thought.

David scowled at me over the rims of his ridiculous hipster glasses—the kind with the thick black rims. I hate those. I mean, it's the twenty-first century. There are fashionable options for eyewear.

"Watch where you're going," he said. Then his lips twisted in a smirk. "Or could you not see through all that mascara?"

I would've loved nothing more than to tell him to kiss my ass, but one of the responsibilities of being a student leader at the Grove is being polite to everyone, even if they are a douchebag who wrote not one, but *three* incredibly unflattering articles in the school paper about what a terrible job you're doing as SGA president.

And you *especially* needed to be polite to said douchebag when he happened to be the nephew of Saylor Stark, president of the

Pine Grove Junior League; head of the Pine Grove Betterment Society; chairwoman of the Grove Academy School Board; and, most importantly, organizer of Pine Grove's Annual Cotillion.

So I forced myself to smile even bigger at David. "Nope, just in a hurry," I said. "Are you, uh . . . are you here for the dance?"

He snorted. "Um, no. I'd rather slam my testicles in a locker door. I have some work to do for the paper."

I tried to keep my expression blank, but I have one of those faces that shows every single thing that goes through my mind.

Apparently this time was no exception, because David laughed. "Don't worry, Pres, nothing about you this time."

If ever there were a time to confront David about the mean things he's written about me, this was it. Of course, those articles hadn't exactly mentioned me by name. I seriously doubt Mrs. Laurent, the newspaper advisor, would let him slam me directly. But they'd basically said that the "current administration" is more concerned with dances and parades than the real issues facing the Grove's students, and that under the "current administration," the SGA has gotten all cliquey, leaving out the majority of the student body.

To which I say, um, hello? Not my fault if people don't attempt to get involved in their own school. And as for the "real issues" facing the Grove's students? The kids who go here all come from super nice households that can afford to send their kids here. We're not exactly plagued with social problems, you know? Which you'd think David would get. He'd lived in Pine Grove practically his whole life, and not only that, he lived with his Aunt Saylor in one of the nicest houses in town.

Or maybe David's issues had nothing to do with "social injustice" at the Grove and everything to do with the fact that he and I had loathed each other since kindergarten. Heck, even *before* that. Mom says he's the only baby I ever bit in daycare.

But before I could reply, the music stopped in the gym.

I checked my watch and saw that it was a quarter till ten. Crap.

David gave another one of those mean laughs. "Go ahead, Harper," he said, sliding his messenger bag from one hip to the other. I know. A messenger bag. And those glasses. And he was wearing a stupid argyle sweater and Converse high-tops. Practically every other boy at the Grove lived in khakis and button-downs. I wasn't sure David Stark owned any pants other than jeans that were too small.

"Only a few more minutes until your coronation," he said, running a hand through his sandy blond hair, making it stand up even more than usual. "I'm sure you'd hate to miss everyone's *felicitations.*"

David had beaten me in the final round of our sixth-grade spelling bee with that word and now, all these years later, he still tried to drop it into conversation whenever he could. Counting to ten in my head, I reminded myself of what Mom always said whenever I complained about David Stark: "His parents died when he was just a little bitty thing. Saylor's done her best with him, but still, something like that is bound to make anyone act ugly."

Since he was a tragic orphan, I made myself say "Have a nice night" through clenched teeth as I turned to head to the nearest bathroom.

He just shrugged and started walking backward down the hall, toward the computer lab. "You might wanna put some lipstick on," he called after me.

"Yeah, thanks," I muttered, but he was already gone.

God, what a jerk, I thought, pushing the bathroom door open.

If my shoes had sounded loud in the gym lobby, it was nothing compared to how they sounded in the bathroom. Like the dress, they were a little ridiculous, more for their height than their cost. I'm 5'4", but I was tottering around 5'8" on those bad boys.

Looking in the mirror, I saw why Bee had been so horrified by my naked lips. My skin is pale, so without lip gloss, my lips had kind of disappeared into my face. But other than that, I looked good. Great, even. The makeup lady at Dillard's had done a fabulous job of playing up my big green eyes, easily my best feature, and my dark hair was pulled back from my face, tumbling down my back in soft waves and setting off my high cheekbones.

Yeah, I know it's vain. But being pretty is currency, not just at the Grove, but in life. Sure, I wasn't staggeringly beautiful like my sister, Leigh-Anne, had been, but—

No. Not going there.

I unscrewed the tube of Salmon Fantasy, shuddered again at the name, and started applying. It wasn't as pretty as my Coral Shimmer, but it would do.

I had just slathered on the second coat when the bathroom door flew open, banging against the tile wall so loudly that I jumped.

And scrawled a line of Salmon Fantasy from the corner of my mouth nearly to my ear.

"Oh, dammit!" I cried, stamping my foot. "Brandon, what—"

I don't know why I thought it must be Brandon. Probably because it seemed like the sort of moron thing he'd do, trying to scare me.

But it wasn't Brandon. It was Mr. Hall, one of the school janitors.

He stood in the doorway for a second, staring at me like he didn't know who—or what—I was.

"Oh my God, Mr. Hall," I said, pressing a hand to my chest. "You scared me to death!"

He just stared at me with this wild look in his eyes before turning around and slamming the bathroom door shut.

And then I heard a sound that made my stomach drop.

It was the loud click of a dead bolt being thrown.

Mr. Hall, the tubby janitor, had just locked us in the bathroom.

Chapter 2

OKAY. *Okay, I can handle this*, I thought, even as panic started clawing through my chest.

"Mr. Hall," I started, my voice high and shaky.

He just waved his hand at me and pressed his ear to the door. I don't know what he heard, but whatever it was made him turn and sag against the wall.

And that's when I noticed the blood dripping on his shoes.

"Mr. Hall!" I cried, running toward him. My heels slid on the slick tile floor, so I kicked them off. I got to Mr. Hall just as he slumped to the ground.

His face was pale, and it looked all weird and waxy, like he was a dummy instead of a person. I could see beads of sweat on his forehead and under his nose. His breath was coming out in short gasps, and there was a dark red stain spreading across his expansive belly. There was no doubt in my mind that he was dying.

I knelt down next to him, my blood rushing loudly in my ears. "It's gonna be okay, Mr. Hall, I'll go get someone, everything is gonna be fine."

But just as I reached for the dead bolt, he reached out and grabbed my ankle, pulling me down so hard that I landed on my butt with a shriek.

Mr. Hall was shaking his head frantically.

"Don't," he gurgled. Then he closed his eyes and took a deep breath through his nose, like he was trying to calm down. "Don't," he said again, and this time, his voice was a little stronger. "Don't open that door, okay. Just . . . just help me get to my feet."

I looked down at him. Mr. Hall was pretty substantial, and I didn't think there was any way I was lifting him off that floor. But somehow, by slipping my arms under his and bracing myself against the wall, I got him up and propped against the door of one of the bathroom stalls.

Once he was up, I said, "Look, Mr. Hall, I really think I should get help. I don't even have a cell phone with me, and you"—I looked down at the sticky red circle on his stomach—"you look really hurt, and I think we should call 911, and—"

But he wasn't listening to me. Instead, he opened his shirt.

I braced myself for a wound on his stomach, but I wasn't prepared to see what looked like a bloodstained pillow.

With a grunt, Mr. Hall tugged at something on his back, and the pillow slid from his stomach to land soundlessly on the floor.

Now I could see the gash, and it was just as bad as I'd thought it would be, but my brain was still reeling from the whole "Mr. Hall isn't fat, he just wears a fake belly" thing. Why would Mr. Hall pretend to be fat? Was it a disguise? Why would a janitor need a disguise?

But before I could ask him any of this, Mr. Hall groaned and slid to the floor again, his eyes fluttering closed.

I sank with him, my arm still behind his back. "Mr. Hall!" I cried. When he didn't respond, I reached out with my free hand and slapped his cheek with enough force to make his head rock to the side. He opened his eyes, but it was like he couldn't see me.

"Mr. Hall, what is going on?" I asked, the acoustics of the bathroom turning my question into an echoing shriek.

I was shaking, and suddenly realized how cold I was. I remembered from Anatomy and Physiology that this was what going into shock felt like, and I had to fight against the blackness that was creeping over my eyes. I couldn't faint. I *wouldn't* faint.

Mr. Hall turned his head and looked at me, then really looked at me. Blood was still pulsing out of the gash that curved from under his khaki slacks around to his navel, but not as much now. Most of it seemed to be in a big puddle under him.

"What . . . what's . . . your name?" he asked in a series of soft gasps.

"Harper," I answered, tears pooling in my eyes, and bile rushing up my throat. "Harper Price."

He nodded and smiled a little. I'd never really looked at Mr. Hall before. He was younger than I'd thought he was, and his eyes were dark brown. They were beautiful, actually.

"Harper Price. You . . . run this place. Kids talk. Protect . . ."

Mr. Hall trailed off and his eyes closed. I slapped him again, and his eyes sprang open. He smiled that weird little smile again.

"You're a tough one," he murmured.

"Mr. Hall, please," I said, shifting to get my arm free. "What happened to you? Why can't we open the door?"

"Look after him, okay?" he said, his eyes looking glazed again. "Make sure he's . . . he's safe."

"Who?" I asked, but I wasn't even sure he was actually talking to me. I've heard that when people are dying, their brains fire off all sorts of weird things. He could have been talking to his mom, or his wife, if he had one.

Suddenly there was a loud rattle at the door. I gave a thin scream, and Mr. Hall grabbed at the stall door like he was trying to pull himself up.

"He's coming," Mr. Hall gasped.

"Who?" I yelled. I felt like I had stepped into a nightmare. Five minutes ago my main concern had been whether Salmon Fantasy would clash with my pink dress. Now I was cradling a dying man on the bathroom floor while some crazy person pounded on the door.

Mr. Hall managed to get himself into a sitting position, and for one second, I thought we might actually be okay. Like, maybe the wound that had soaked through that pillow wasn't so bad. Or maybe this whole thing was an elaborate prank.

But Mr. Hall wasn't going to be okay. There was a white line all around his lips, which were starting to look blue, and his breaths were getting shallower and shorter.

He swung his head to look at me, and there was such sadness in his eyes that the tears finally spilled over my cheeks. "I'm so sorry for this, Harper," he said, his voice the strongest it had sounded since he'd run into the bathroom.

I thought he meant he was sorry for dying and leaving me at the mercy of whatever was on the other side of that door.

But then he took a really deep breath, lurched forward, grabbed my face, and covered my lips with his.

My hands reached up to pry his fingers from my cheeks, but for a guy who had barely been able to talk a few seconds ago, his grip was surprisingly strong. And it *hurt*.

I was making these muffled shrieks because I was afraid to open my mouth to scream.

Then I felt something cold—so cold that it brought even more tears to my eyes—flow into my mouth and down my throat, and I went very still.

He wasn't trying to kiss me; it was like he was blowing something *into* me, this icy air that made my lungs sting like jogging in January.

Tears were streaming down my face, and I let go of his hands, my arms falling to my sides. By now, my chest was burning like I'd been underwater for too long, and that gray fog was hovering around the edge of my vision again. As the gray spread, I thought of my sister, Leigh-Anne, and how hard it was going to be on my parents if I died, too.

I don't know if it was that thought, or the fact that being found dead in the bathroom underneath a janitor was not how I wanted people at the Grove to remember me, but suddenly I felt this surge of strength. The gray disappeared as adrenaline shot through my system, and I wrapped my fingers around Mr. Hall's wrists and yanked with everything I had.

And just like that, he was off me.

I took a deep breath. Never had I felt so happy to breathe in slightly stinky bathroom air.

For a long time, I just sat there against the stall door, shaking and gasping. I could still hear whatever was on the other side rattling, but it seemed far away for some reason, like it wasn't even connected to me.

I guess it only took about thirty seconds for me to catch my breath, but it felt like forever. I looked down at Mr. Hall. Lying on his back, his eyes staring at nothing, it was pretty clear that he was dead.

Just as I was taking that in, the rattling at the door stopped.

The burn in my chest had faded to a tingle, and there was this jumping feeling inside my stomach, like I'd swallowed a whole bunch of Pop Rocks. My arms and legs felt heavy, and my head was all spinny.

Slowly, I stood up, careful to keep my feet out of the puddle of blood that continued to spread under Mr. Hall. I glanced down at my legs and saw that my panty hose were surprisingly run-free, despite everything that had just happened.

What *had* just happened?

I forced myself to look at Mr. Hall again. The gash in his stomach was horrible, and big, and sure, it looked like a wound from some sort of medieval sword or something, but that was impossible, right? He probably just hurt himself on some scary janitor equipment. I mean, the floor waxer didn't look like it could slice somebody open, but it's not like I'd ever inspected it for danger.

The more I thought about it, the more comforting the idea seemed. It was certainly better than thinking there was a sword-wielding maniac on the other side of the door.

It had just been a rogue piece of machinery. A blade or a belt or something had snapped and cut Mr. Hall open, and that had been the rattling at the door. He hadn't had time to unplug it, and it was probably spinning down the hall right now. I'd get out of here, and I'd go find a teacher and tell him or her, and everything would be fine.

I looked at myself in the mirror. My skin was almost as white as Mr. Hall's, making the Salmon Fantasy look cheap and too bright.

"It's going to be fine," I told my reflection. "Everything is *fine*."

I walked to the door, and as I did, I had to step over that weird pillow thing Mr. Hall had strapped to his body.

Oh, right. That.

Why did Mr. Hall have a fake belly? My brain felt like it was in a blender as I tried to think up a plausible explanation, hopefully one that would tie in with my possessed machinery idea.

Okay, Mr. Hall was younger than I'd thought. And cuter. Why would he be wearing a disguise? Was he in the witness protection program? A deadbeat dad hiding out from paying child support?

And there was something else. Something weird about him.

I looked back at his body, bracing myself against throwing up or fainting, but I didn't feel anything except that tingle in my chest.

It was something about his face, something that had just felt odd when he'd . . . kissed me? Blown on me? Whatever.

I crept back to him, still careful about the blood, then I reached down and touched his beard. My dad and granddad both have beards, and neither of theirs felt like this one.

Sliding my finger around the edge of his beard, just under his left ear, I saw why.

It was a fake. It was a pretty good one, and it was glued on super tight, but it was still a fake.

Then I glanced up at his balding head and saw a fine stubble covering the bare half-moon of his scalp.

So Mr. Hall hadn't been fat, or bearded, or balding.

"Oh, this is some *bullshit*," I whispered. That's when I knew I was seriously freaked out. I never curse out loud, not even in private. It's just not ladylike.

There was no theory I could come up with to explain any of that, no matter how *CSI: Pine Grove* I was trying to be. No, the best thing to do was to get the heck out of the bathroom and find a teacher, or a cop, or an exorcist. I'd take anyone at this point.

I hurried to the door before realizing I'd left Bee's lip gloss in the sink. My brain was still scrambled, and despite the dead body at my feet, all I could think was that Bee loved that ugly stuff, and I had to grab it before it was, like, confiscated for evidence or something. So I ran back to the sink.

It's funny to think about now, because even though that lip gloss had gotten me into this whole mess, that same lip gloss totally saved my life. If I hadn't gone back for it, I would have been at the door when it exploded into two pieces and slammed into the row of stalls with the force of a small bomb.

And if *that* hadn't flattened me like a pancake, I still would have been directly in the path of the man who came running in with a long, curved blade—a scimitar, I was pretty sure I remembered from World History II with Dr. DuPont—held out in front of him.

So thanks to Bee's lip gloss, I was standing frozen by the sink when the sword-wielding maniac came in and my life stopped making even the littlest bit of sense.

In all the dust from the door flying off, it took the man a minute to realize I was there. He had his back to me as he knelt by Mr. Hall's body. I watched, still as a statue, as he reached into Mr. Hall's pockets, but I guess he didn't find what he was looking for because he stood up really fast and muttered the F-word. I couldn't hold it against him, though. This did seem like a dire situation.

Then he turned around, and I'm sure the look of total confusion on his face was reflected on mine.

"Harper?"

"*Dr. DuPont?*"

I didn't get much time to wonder why my history teacher had just killed a janitor, even though I had this whole joke forming about how Dr. DuPont must *really* hate when his trash cans aren't emptied—you know, to make him see me as a person and not just a potential shish kabob. I learned that in the self-defense class Mom and I went to at the church last spring.

But that joke dried right up in my mouth, because Dr. DuPont crossed the bathroom in two strides, and put his sword against my neck.

Chapter 3

Now, this is when it really gets weird. I know, I know, dead janitor in disguise, killer history teacher, how much weirder could it get?

Lots. Trust me.

When Dr. DuPont put that sword—well, scimitar—on my neck, I didn't feel scared, like, at all. Instead, I felt that tingle in my chest again, only this time, it was more like this . . . energy.

I reached out, almost like my hands didn't belong to me, and grabbed the hilt of the sword, just above Dr. DuPont's hands on the handle, and yanked, sliding that lethal blade in the space between my arm and my body.

Dr. DuPont was so surprised he didn't even let go of the sword, which was exactly what I had planned, although where that plan came from, I had no idea. Certainly not from that lame self-defense class, where the only thing I'd learned was how to knee a guy in the groin, and trust me, teenage girls already know how to do that. No, this was a different kind of fighting, one so smooth and powerful that I felt like I was standing outside my body, watching myself pull Dr. DuPont right up to me.

I didn't knee him in the groin, although I didn't rule that move out. Instead I . . . ugh, this is so embarrassing.

I head-butted him.

I know, like a soccer hooligan or something. But it worked. He let go of the sword with one hand and reached up to clutch his probably broken nose.

I'd kept my hand on the hilt, and I used it to pull him past me and slam him headfirst into the wall. Now I had a clear shot for the door, but for some reason, I didn't take it. For one thing, all this ninja-style fighting was . . . well, kind of cool. I had no idea how I was doing it, and I wondered if it was another adrenaline thing, like when I was able to push Mr. Hall off me. But it wasn't just that I was having fun. It was almost like I couldn't leave; like I had to finish the fight until one of us was dead.

See? I told you it got weirder.

I stood there, crouched in my pink dress while Dr. DuPont turned around to look at me with an expression I can only call incredulous (that was the word I had beat David Stark with in the *fifth*-grade spelling bee.)

Blood was caked all around the lower half of his face. Panting, he looked down at Mr. Hall's body, then back at me.

He laughed, but it was an ugly, wet sound. "So he passed it on to you," Dr. DuPont wheezed. Then his bloody lips curved in a nasty smirk. "Well, *bless your heart*," he drawled in a not very nice (if kind of accurate) imitation of my accent.

He moved sideways, toward the stalls, the sword still pointed at me. "I really can't think of a worse choice," he said, still smiling, "than the bimbo who wrote a paper on the history of *shoes* for my class."

Okay, that stung. I'd worked hard on that paper. And it hadn't been on shoes. It had been about how fashion affected politics. And I may like clothes and makeup and shoes, but I am *not* a bimbo. Dr. DuPont could totally bite me. I almost said that, but then I changed my mind. As crazy as everything had gone, Dr. DuPont might take that as an opening to actually, you know, *bite me.*

"Tell me, Harper, are you going to use your new superpowers to strong-arm some boy into taking you to prom? Or maybe become head cheerleader?" Something in his expression hardened. "Not that you're going to live that long."

Then he lunged again, sword high, but I was ready for him. I spun around so my back was to him, then dropped so the sword passed right over my head. With my hands on the floor, I kicked out my left heel. "I already *am* head cheerleader," I said through clenched teeth as my foot connected with his jaw.

Before Dr. DuPont recovered from my kick, I spun in my crouch and used that same leg to knock his legs out from under him.

He cracked his head against the sink as he went down, and I figured that was the end of it.

I stood up and looked down. There was a ragged tear from the hem of my skirt all the way up to the middle of my thigh.

"Oh, *shoot*," I muttered, giving Dr. DuPont's limp body a dark glare.

Then it occurred to me that I should definitely get out of here and find a non-homicidal teacher. Something in me still didn't want to leave, but I shoved that down. Dr. DuPont had said *super-powers*, and talked about Mr. Hall "passing something on" to me. That must have been what that weird blowing in my mouth thing had been. But I could figure out exactly what had happened to me later. Right now I needed to get out of here before Dr. DuPont came to.

My arms and legs were starting to ache. I'd be black and blue tomorrow, I thought, as I scooted around Dr. DuPont, *and* I'd probably missed the crowning, thanks to all this craziness. I swear, if—

I didn't get to finish the thought. Instead, there was a sharp pain at the back of my head that brought tears to my eyes and ripped a short scream from my throat. Dr. DuPont had grabbed a big handful of my thick hair. Yanking so hard that I was surprised I wasn't snatched bald, he used my hair to pull me back and sling me into the sinks.

My right elbow hit the edge of the counter and a wave of nausea spilled over me.

I was still blinking back stars when Dr. DuPont swung a powerful kick to my stomach.

All the air left my lungs, and I crumpled to the ground, gasping and gagging at the same time. My chest was burning again, this time from lack of oxygen.

I lay there, staring at Dr. DuPont's shiny black loafers as he walked over to the corner and picked up the scimitar he'd dropped.

I'm going to die here, I thought dimly. *I'm going to be stabbed to death by my history teacher with some freaky sword, and no one will ever know what happened to me. And my parents will have two daughters who died at school dances, and my mom's eyes will get sadder, and Dad's face will get thinner, and our house will feel even grayer and emptier.*

Now the pain in my stomach had nothing to do with Dr. DuPont's kick. I closed my eyes as tears burned. Dr. DuPont was talking, but I couldn't really hear him. He said something about the wrong place and the wrong time, and then he said this weird word that started with "pal."

Paladin. What was that?

He might as well have been speaking Greek. All I could focus on was the burn in my chest and the aching of my midsection.

He was right in front of me now. I opened my eyes and saw the sword hanging at his side. The end glittered in the ugly fluorescent light of the bathroom.

I turned my head a little so I didn't have to see him raise the blade.

Something pink caught my eye. It was one of my shoes. I remembered taking them off to help Mr. Hall. Apparently, they'd gotten kicked under the sink.

Dr. DuPont was still talking, but I was focused on that shiny pink shoe that now looked so silly in the midst of all this death and destruction. I reached out and pulled the shoe to me. Dr. DuPont laughed. "Afraid of dying without the right accessories, Miss Price? Nice to see you're still a silly bitch, right to the end."

But I didn't want the shoe because it was pretty, or because it was pink. I rolled onto my back, slowly drawing my knees up. It wasn't the most ladylike of positions, but I was going to need leverage. I held the shoe against my chest. I ran my thumb over its heel, remembering my desire to stomp on David Stark's foot in these shoes. It would've hurt.

I fought to keep a smile off my face as Dr. DuPont raised the sword.

In fact, if I had stomped on David's foot hard enough, the heel would've gone right through. It was awfully sharp.

If Dr. DuPont hadn't been a total drama queen and raised the sword with both hands, he might have actually killed me. He certainly wouldn't have ended up giving me the opening he did.

Because while his arms were high over his head, about to bring the sword down, I pushed myself off the floor and into a spin, the high heel clutched in my hands, sharp point out.

The sword was still poised in the air when I came to an abrupt stop and sunk the heel into his throat, right under his jaw. I'd learned about the carotid artery in Anatomy and Physiology, which was turning out to be a *much* more useful class than I'd originally thought, and while I'd definitely been aiming for it, I was still kind of shocked that I managed to hit it.

I guess Dr. DuPont was, too, because his eyes got really wide, and the sword clattered to the floor. He stared at me, his lips opening and closing like a fish, my pink shoe stuck in his neck. I guess it would've been kind of funny if it hadn't been, you know, completely gross and horrifying.

Dr. DuPont reached up and pulled the heel out of his neck. Blood poured from the hole, pulsing out with his heartbeat.

He looked at the shoe for a long time, like he couldn't figure out what it was. Then he muttered, "Pink." The shoe fell from his fingers and he dropped back on the floor, his eyes wide and staring.

The only sound in the bathroom was my breathing and the steady *plink-plink* of the dripping sink.

Reality took a minute to set in, but when it did, it was bad.

I had just killed a teacher. With my shoe.

I ran over and picked up that shoe, wincing at the streaks of red on the heel. I grabbed a handful of paper towels and wiped it off, and my breathing got faster and faster.

"It's okay," I murmured to myself. "It was self-defense. He had a sword."

I scrubbed at the heel, feeling like Lady Macbeth. Self-defense or not, I'd just killed someone. That was bad. That was *really* bad. I looked in the mirror, and saw that other than flushed cheeks and bright eyes, I looked pretty much the same as I had when I came in the bathroom. Well, except for the line of Salmon Fantasy scrawled across my face. I grabbed a paper towel and began scrubbing at my mouth.

Even my hair wasn't that messed up. *I should tell Ms. Brenda that the next time I go in*, I thought automatically. Then it occurred to me that there was no way to tell my hairdresser that her 'dos hold up even when you're kicking the crap out of sword-wielding teachers.

After I was done getting the blood off my shoe and ugly lipstick off my face, I tossed the paper towel in the trash and looked around. Mr. Hall's body was against the stalls, and Dr. DuPont was lying about three feet away. There were big cracks in the tile from where I'd slammed Dr. DuPont's head into the wall, and the bathroom door lay in pieces on the floor, surrounded by a fine layer of grit and more broken tiles.

Without really thinking, I slid my shoe back on and hobbled over to the trash can, where the second high heel lay on its side.

I guess this is the part where I should have started screaming and/or vomiting, but I just felt . . . numb. Certainly not as horrified as someone who just watched two men die (and one by her own hand. Well, her own shoe) should feel.

That weird feeling, like adrenaline times a thousand, was still flowing over me. That was probably what was keeping the nervous breakdown at bay. As I stepped over the fallen door and out of the bathroom, I wondered why no one had come looking for me yet. I mean, I must have been in there for at least half an hour. Then I glanced at my watch and saw that only eleven minutes had passed since I'd bumped into David Stark.

I walked down the English hall, and the farther I got from the bathroom, the shakier my legs felt. I was almost to the gym lobby, close enough to could hear the band's lead singer say, "Okay, in just a few, we'll be announcing Homecoming Queen, so come on up here, ladies."

That's when I felt something in my stomach shift dangerously, and I turned and ran back down the English hall.

As my heels clattered down the hallway—

Oh God, oh God, don't think about your heels, don't think about your shoe sticking out of his neck!

I realized I should have run down the history hall because

there was no way I could go back in the bathroom with Mr. Hall and Dr. DuPont.

But it was too late now.

Then I remembered that—hello?—there are two bathrooms in the English hall, so I ran into the boys' room across the hall from the girls'.

As I barreled through the door, I heard a startled male voice squawk, "What the hell?" but I didn't even glance at the figure standing by the sink. I ran straight into one of the stalls, actually thankful it didn't have a door.

I had barely hit my knees before everything that was in my stomach came up.

"Holy crap," I heard Sink Guy say, and then he was there in the stall with me, lifting the heavy mass of hair away from my face and neck. It felt so good, and it was such a nice thing to do that I wasn't even embarrassed that some random guy was watching me, Harper Jane Price, SGA president, head cheerleader, Future Business Leader of America, and soon-to-be Homecoming Queen, puking my guts out in the boys' bathroom.

I felt shaky and hollowed out when I was done, but better. Lots better.

"Here," Sink Guy said, handing me a bunch of damp, cool paper towels. I took them gratefully and pressed them against my sweaty face. At the same time, the mystery guy laid a few more of the paper towels against the back of my neck. He was still holding my hair back.

My face buried in the paper towels, I reached up and flushed the toilet.

"Thank you," I murmured into the wad of wet towels.

"No worries. So are you knocked up?"

I looked up and found myself glaring into David Stark's blue eyes.

Of course.

"No," I said, trying to get to my feet in the narrow stall without flashing my panties at him. He reached down and took my elbow to help me. "I was joking," he said. "If there's ever been anyone *less* likely to be on *Teen Mom* than you, I've never met her." He sounded sincere, but I still shook him off.

I walked out of the stall and over to the sink, where I rinsed my mouth out about twenty times. When I was done, David reached into that stupid messenger bag of his and pulled out a tin of Altoids, wordlessly handing me a few.

"Thanks," I said again, hating that I'd had to say "thank you" to David Stark two times in as many minutes.

He just shrugged, but he was looking at me in that weird, almost predatory way he has. With any other guy, that look would mean he was trying to get in my pants, but I doubt David even thinks about those kinds of things. He only gets that look about the stupid school paper, and I knew he was trying to sniff out a story about why "Pres" was tossing her cookies in the boys' room the night of the Homecoming Dance.

"I know you weren't drinking," he said. "Not after—" He broke off awkwardly before clearing his throat. "So, food poisoning?"

"No," I said again, "It's just that they're about to announce Homecoming Queen, and I'm nervous. Stage fright."

I thought it was pretty good as far as excuses go, but David just laughed. "Yeah, right. Pres, you'd make out with a spotlight if you could figure out how. It's gotta be something else."

That hungry look was back in his eyes, and it suddenly occurred to me that the reason I'd thrown up was literally across the hall. My stomach and knees turned to jelly. It was a miracle that David hadn't noticed the broken door to the girls' room when he'd come in here. There was no way he was going to miss it when he left. And David was the smartest person I knew; he was the only thing currently standing between me and valedictorian. David had seen me going toward the girls' room, and when he saw the two dead bodies in there, he'd put two and two together.

And he would *love it*. He'd write a bazillion articles for the paper chronicling my downfall, and the eventual trial, and he'd win awards for it. Do they have a Pulitzer for high school papers?

"Well, whatever is up with you, I suggest you get over it so you can collect your crown," he said, turning to leave.

"Wait!" I cried, grabbing his arm. How could I keep him from going out there?

"What?" he snapped, clearly pretty irritated.

"Um . . . I just, uh, I just wanted to say thank you. Again."

David stared at me like I'd just started speaking in tongues, but after a moment, kind of patted my hand and said, "Yeah, you're, uh . . . no problem."

Then he pulled open the bathroom door. I stayed, frozen, waiting for him to shout or something when he saw the destruction across the hall.

But all I heard were the soft squeaks of his tennis shoes as he walked away.

Oh my God, had he missed it again? Looked like valedictorian was in my grasp after all!

But then, when I walked out of the bathroom, I saw why David hadn't seen anything: There was nothing to see.

The bathroom door was in place and in one piece.

Chapter 4

EVERYTHING after that is kind of a blur, mostly because I was pretty sure I was going insane. I know I walked into the bathroom and didn't even feel all that surprised to see that it was empty, with no sign of the two dead bodies that had been in there just—I checked my watch—six minutes ago. The walls were fine, no cracks or big craters roughly the size of Dr. DuPont's head. I even checked the trash can for the bloody paper towel I'd used to clean my shoe.

The trash can was empty.

That's when I made this weird, high-pitched sound that was kind of a sigh and kind of a gasp. I'm pretty sure I would have had a complete nervous breakdown right then and there if David Stark hadn't poked his head in and said, "Uh . . . Pres? You gonna hurl again?"

I turned to look at him, and the smirk fell off his face. "Holy crap," he said, crossing the room and grabbing my arms. "Harper? What's wrong?"

I saw my reflection in the mirror, and totally understood why he looked genuinely freaked. My eyes were huge and glassy and my skin had gone gray. Not that I really cared. I mean, I'd gone crazy. I was crazy.

For some reason, that thought was way more upsetting than the idea that I'd turned into some sort of superhero who'd killed evil Dr. DuPont with my shoe. That had been traumatizing, I guess, but it had also been . . . well, kind of cool. Like something out of a comic book. But going insane? That was *real*.

"Harper?" David said again, giving me a little shake.

I think I would've caved then and the whole story about Mr. Hall and Dr. DuPont would've come tumbling out in a series of sobs and shrieks. But luckily, Bee chose that moment to push the bathroom door open.

"God, there you are!" she exclaimed, and her voice reverberated off the tile walls, hurting my ears. Behind her, Amanda, Abigail, and Mary Beth crowded into the bathroom, too.

Then they saw David, and all of their normally pretty faces twisted into sneers. I wasn't the only one who didn't like David's editorials.

One of Bee's best qualities was loyalty, but it sometimes had an ugly way of showing itself, especially where David was concerned. "What are you doing in the girls' room, paper boy?" I wondered if I'd ever looked at David like that.

"Are you stalking Harper?" Amanda asked, folding her arms over her chest.

David wasn't holding my arms anymore, and he certainly wasn't looking at me with concern. His usual scowl was back in place. "Yeah, that's it, Amanda," he said, trying to shove his hands into the pockets of his skinny jeans. "I'm a stalker. And what a charming and unique insult."

Amanda rolled her eyes, which was her standard response when she didn't have a comeback, and Bee looked at me. "Whoa, Harper, what's wrong?"

"I think she's sick," David said, stuffing his hands in his pockets, his eyes focused on a spot somewhere over my head.

"Probably because she's been talking to you," Abigail snapped back.

"Abigail," I said, but David just laughed. "Lovely talking to you ladies," he said as he walked out the door.

"Did he do something to you?" Bee asked as soon as he was gone.

I laughed, but it sounded, um, crazy, so I stopped. "No. I just . . . I think I'm coming down with something. He was checking on me. It was nice, actually."

Mary Beth wobbled up to my side and frowned. "Probably only because he wanted something. I don't trust David Stark as far as I could throw him."

That's when I finally noticed the crown dangling from Bee's fingers, the rhinestones shining dully in the florescent lights. "Is that . . ." My voice came out squeaky, so I started over. "Is that the Homecoming Queen crown?"

She looked down like she had totally forgotten about it. "Oh, yeah! Duh. That's why I came to look for you. You totally won!"

She squealed and threw her arms around me. I kind of

hugged her back, but mostly I was just thinking, *I missed it. I've wanted this for years, ever since Leigh-Anne won it two years ago, and I missed it because I was having a schizo freak-out in the bathroom.*

Bee didn't seem to notice that I was less than enthusiastic. "We looked for you, like, everywhere when they called your name."

"Everywhere?" I parroted.

"Well . . . everywhere in the gym. So then Ryan said I should just go up there and, like, accept it on your behalf, so I did, and then I remembered you'd gone to the bathroom, so I came to find you!"

Pursing her lips, Bee tilted her head to one side. "Seriously, Harper, what's wrong? You look really bad. No offense."

I rubbed my hands over my face. "I told you," I said from behind my fingers, "I started feeling sick." I put my hands down and tried to smile brightly, but I had a feeling I looked demented. I *felt* demented.

Bee was still squinting at me when Abigail took the crown from her hands. With a big smile, she reached up and plonked the crown on my head. "Well, there you go, Your Majesty!"

I turned and looked in the mirror. My face was still gray, my eyes were still huge, and the crown looked fake and stupid. Plus it was crooked.

I burst into tears.

All four girls wrapped me in a group hug, and at first I thought they were comforting me, that somehow they understood that I'd had a terrible night, and that I had thought I'd killed a guy, but actually, I was just going insane, and seeing that *effing* crown on my head had been the final straw.

But then Abigail squealed, "Oh, sweetie, I know! It's, like, a dream come true!"

"What do you know about schizophrenia?" I mumbled against Ryan's mouth.

He raised his head, his eyes hazy, his hand still hovering around the hem of my dress. "Huh?"

We were sitting in his car, parked in my driveway. It was after midnight, but still bright in the car, thanks to the truly obscene amount of security lighting my parents have. Somebody tried to break in a few years back, and ever since then, my dad has been more than a little paranoid. But, I mean, if we didn't have this big brick, ivy-covered house that pretty much screams, "HI! THE PEOPLE WHO LIVE HERE ARE TOTALLY LOADED! PLEASE TAKE SOME OF THEIR STUFF! THEY'LL JUST BUY MORE!" he wouldn't have to worry so much.

My crown was on the floorboard. I'd taken it off as soon as we'd left the school, even though Ryan had joked that he expected me to wear it 24/7 from now on. And then Brandon had made a joke about how I should wear it during sex, and said something about properly "saluting" the Queen, which, A) didn't really make that much sense, and B) was dumb anyway.

"It's just something I was thinking about," I said to Ryan now. "Didn't you write a paper on it for AP Psychology last year?"

Ryan blinked. In the dim light of the car, his hazel eyes were nearly black, and he'd loosened the hunter green tie around his neck and shed his suit coat. Normally, seeing Ryan all rumpled and disheveled sent a little thrill through me, but tonight, I was way too preoccupied to appreciate his hotness.

He slid off me and back into the driver's seat, running his hand through his hair. "Um . . . yeah. Well, I mean, to be honest, I used one of Luke's freshman psych papers." Luke was Ryan's older brother, currently off at the University of Florida. When I frowned, Ryan gave me one of those lopsided grins that usually made me smile in return. "Is this about the Committee for Academic Honesty?" he asked. "Because I'd hope dating the committee chairwoman, like, exempted me from that."

"No, it's nothing to do with CAH," I said, rubbing my eyes. "I just . . . wait, Ry, you used someone else's paper? For an *AP class?*"

He sighed and leaned forward, folding his arms on the steering wheel. "It was right in the middle of basketball season, and I didn't have time to write a paper on crazy people. And it wasn't anyone, it was Luke, and since we're brothers, that makes that paper, like, half mine anyway."

He was joking, and I wanted to laugh, I really did. I rolled my lips inward, trying to stop the next sentence from coming out, but it was no use. "Ryan, playing basketball on quite possibly the worst team in Alabama is not going to get you into a good college."

"Oh God," he muttered, slamming his head back against the headrest.

"However," I continued, hating myself, but, as usual, totally unable to stop, "cheating in an AP class will most definitely keep you *out* of Hampden Sydney. Colleges take academic honesty very seriously."

He snorted, but didn't look up. "Can we not do this right now, Harper? I know you're perfect, but—"

"I am not perfect," I muttered, crossing my arms and settling back into my seat. I had hallucinated killing my teacher with a shoe. That would probably do a lot more to keep me out of a good college than Ryan's stolen paper.

"Yeah," Ryan said, raising his head, "you are. Or at least you try to be. I mean, I love you, but why do you have to be queen of everything? Why can't you just . . . *chill?*"

Last year, my mom took me to see a therapist after she found me making decorations for the Spring Fling at three in the morning. Dr. Greenbaum said that my "obsessive need to overachieve" was due to a "fear of being out of control" and that, like Ryan said, I needed to chill. Only she used some fancy term for "chill" and also suggested I start taking Lexapro to help facilitate said chilling. I managed to get out of the meds by wearing blue jeans and a T-shirt to my next therapy session, where I drew pictures of myself crying in a tornado. That seemed to make Dr. Greenbaum happy and she decided I didn't need the drugs after all. And the next time I did school stuff in the middle of the night, I just did it in my closet with the door locked. Honestly, what is wrong with this country when striving for excellence means you need antidepressants?

But then I remembered I actually *was* crazy now.

"Forget it," I said to Ryan. "I don't want to fight about this again. I'm just having a really rough night."

"Are you bummed you missed the crowning ceremony?" he asked, leaning down to pick up my tiara.

Leave it to my Perfect Boyfriend to give me the perfect out. Of course Ryan would assume I was bummed about missing the crowning.

"Yeah," I said, trying to look more wistful than freaked out. "I know it's stupid, but . . ."

"Hey," he said softly, "It's okay to feel disappointed. Here." He took the crown and gently placed it back on my head. "Harper Jane Price, I officially crown you Homecoming Queen." Then he leaned forward and kissed me. It was a sweet, soft kiss, and one for its own sake, and not as a prelude to something else.

That was one of the many great things about Ryan. Just a few minutes ago, we'd been fighting, but once I'd said I was sorry, he was over it. I could be a champion grudge-holder. Briefly, an image of David Stark flickered in my brain, but I pushed it away. David had been nice to me tonight—well, nice for him—so maybe it was time to bury the hatchet. Besides, it was creepy to think about David while I was kissing my boyfriend.

Ryan pulled away, and I smiled at him, laying my hand on his cheek. "You are the greatest boyfriend ever, you know that?"

He shrugged. "Pretty much, yeah." He scooted closer and kissed me again, but this time, it was definitely a prelude to something else; something I was most definitely not in the mood for.

Gently pushing at his shoulders, I said, "It's been kind of a crazy night. Can we maybe . . . not?" I hoped I sounded regretful and not irritated.

Ryan sighed, ruffling the hair that flopped over his eyes, but then he turned to me and smiled. "Sure." Then he glanced down and frowned. "Oh, crap, babe, I'm sorry."

"For what?"

He reached out and touched my leg. "Your skirt. I must've accidently ripped it."

I felt the hysterical tears/laughter start to rise again as I looked to where his finger was slowly running up and down the tear in my skirt. The tear I'd made when I'd kicked Dr. DuPont.

But it was impossible to have that tear, since the whole thing had been in my head because I was crazy now.

Right?

But . . . . a little voice whispered in my head, if it had all been imaginary, then why did I still have that Pop Rocks feeling in my chest? Why did I still feel a tremor running through all my muscles, like I could tear off Ryan's car door if I really wanted to?

"Oh, don't worry about it," I said, trying to sound normal even though all I really wanted to do was run inside the garage and try to lift my dad's SUV. You know, for scientific purposes.

We made out for another ten minutes or so, but neither my head nor my heart were particularly in it. Ryan could probably sense that, but he didn't say anything. Finally, he walked me to my door, gave me one last kiss, and then I was breathing a sigh of relief as his taillights disappeared down my drive.

But I didn't go inside. Instead, I sneaked around the back of the house to the tall wooden fence that surrounded our backyard—if you could call the half acre of landscaped gardens a "yard." The fence was eight feet high and covered in thick, thorny pyracantha bushes. Leigh-Anne had dared me to climb it once when I was six. I'd gotten maybe a foot off the ground before the thorns tore up my palms. I still have a thin white scar at the base of my right thumb. Needless to say, I'd never made another attempt to scale the fence.

But now I stood in the dark, my heart pounding in my ears, and a shivery feeling coursing through me.

Just try it, I thought.

It wasn't real, the larger, more sensible part of my brain screamed. *There were no bodies! No collateral damage! Not even a freakin' paper towel!*

I looked down at the tear in my skirt. Sure, it was possible I'd been kicking and punching at thin air because I'd finally gone full-on schizoid. *But*, I thought, *what if . . .*

I was done thinking. I slipped off my pink, teacher-killing heels, threw them over the fence, and felt my muscles tense.

And then I jumped.

Chapter 5

I GRABBED the top of the fence, my hands tangled in the pyracantha bushes, my feet dangling off the ground. Okay, so far, no proof of my superhero-ness. Sure, it had been a great jump, but I was a cheerleader; jumping was not new to me. At least I'd missed the thorns this time.

I took a deep breath. Whatever happened next meant I'd know for sure whether or not what had happened tonight was real. Either way, I figured, life was about to get pretty different.

Slowly, I curled my legs up to my chest and lowered my forehead to the top of the fence. Then I pulled with all the strength in my arms until the top of my head was resting on the gate. My arms didn't even tremble as they held all my body weight.

I uncurled my legs and pushed until I had both arms fully extended and both legs straight up in the air. My dress fell down over my head, so if any of our neighbors were up and about, they saw more than just me going all Russian gymnast on our fence.

Then I brought my feet down to rest on the top of the fence by my hands, so I was basically doing the world's most extreme backbend, a move I'd never been very good at despite all of my years of cheerleading. But now I did it with no problem, feeling like my body was almost out of my control, the same way I'd felt fighting Dr. DuPont. Planting my feet, I let go of the fence with my hands and pulled my torso up so that I was standing, looking down into the garden, my dress falling back down around my knees.

"Well," I murmured, "that answers that."

But just for good measure, I did a front flip off the top of the fence.

I landed in our pool, which was kind of bad planning on my part. I'd jumped just a little too hard and overshot the small patch of grass between the fence and the ridiculously huge expanse of aqua water. Of course, on the bright side, I'd also missed slamming into the concrete patio.

I came up out of the super chilly water not even caring that my new, really expensive dress was ruined. There was a huge smile on my face.

I was a superhero.

"HARPER JANE!"

The smile fell from my face instantly. Oh, crap.

Mom stood just inside the back door, wearing a robe and pajamas. She must have been right in the kitchen to have made it outside so quickly, but Mom had never waited up for me before. Why did it have to be the one night I was diving off the fence?

But Mom must've missed that part of the show because all she said was, "What on earth are you doing in the pool?"

As I hoisted myself up the ladder, she came rushing down the steps of the deck, her bare feet slapping on the wood. "I'm fine," I told her, climbing out of the chilly water.

"You clearly are not," she fired back, whipping off her robe and throwing it around my shoulders. "You're practically blue, and your dress is *ruined*. Have you lost your mind?"

"No," I said, pulling the lapels of the robe closer around me. It was warm and smelled like Lancôme lotion and coffee. "I just decided to come in through the back door so I wouldn't bother you and Daddy. I wasn't looking where I was going, and I tripped." I gave her what I hoped was a sheepish smile and nodded toward my heels which, thankfully, had landed on the pool deck. "Stupid new shoes, you know how it is."

But Mom wasn't an idiot. She frowned at me. "And, what, you just . . . didn't see the pool?"

I glanced over at it, noticing that all the underwater lights were on. It gleamed like a giant turquoise jewel in the darkness of the backyard. There was no way anyone could miss it.

"Mom—"

But she already had me by the shoulders, turning me to face her. "Harper, have you been drinking?"

"*No*," I said, reaching up to squeeze one of her hands for emphasis. "You know I wouldn't do that. I promise."

Mom watched me for a long time. There were new wrinkles around her eyes, and in the dim, greenish light of the pool, she looked almost sickly. All the euphoria that had just been coursing through me seemed to drain out. I had almost been killed tonight. I pictured Mom, sitting at the kitchen table in her robe, waiting for me when I was never coming home, and suddenly, the whole superhero thing didn't seem so great.

"I'm *fine*," I told her again, reaching out to hug her before remembering that I was soaking wet. "Just . . . distracted and clumsy."

I wasn't sure how convinced she was, but she finally smiled and tucked a piece of wet hair behind my ear. "Okay. But you might want to work on that, or Mary Beth won't be the only one taking out an entire row of debutantes."

Relieved, I laughed. "She'll get better."

Mom and I walked back into the house, and I saw that the coffeepot was on and nearly empty. "How long have you been up?" I asked. It wasn't even midnight yet, and that was my curfew.

"Awhile," was all Mom said, but then, from the doorway, I heard Dad say, "She hasn't been to bed yet."

Dad's hair—what little he had left—was sticking up and his eyes were blurry with sleep. As he shuffled into the kitchen, I smiled at his familiar plaid pajama pants and University of Alabama T-shirt. "Why are you soaking wet?" he asked.

"She fell in the pool," Mom explained. Unlike her, he seemed to take that in stride. "Gotta be more careful, kiddo," he told me, walking up to Mom. He put a hand on the back of her neck, pulling her toward him to kiss her temple.

I guess I should be icked out that I have parents who are obviously still so in love—and to be honest, sometimes, I am—but there was also something . . . comforting about it. I thought of

Ryan, wondering if we got married, would we be like this in twenty years?

"So did you win?" Dad asked, and it took me a minute to remember what he was talking about.

"I did," I told him. "But I left the crown in Ryan's car."

Dad squinted. "That doesn't sound like you. Hope you weren't *distracted*. Do I need to get my shotgun?"

"Ew," I said as Mom nudged him with her elbow.

"I don't think any firearms will be required to get Ryan and Harper down the aisle one day," she said, winking at me.

Mom loved Ryan, especially since he'd been so great after everything with Leigh-Anne.

"So now that she's home, will you finally get some sleep?" Dad asked Mom.

The lines around her eyes deepened as she smiled. "Sure will," she said, but rather than heading back to her own bedroom, she walked me up to mine.

"You're sure you're all right?" she asked, hovering in the doorway.

"I will be once I take the hottest shower in the world."

Mom smiled again, but it was faint and kind of sad. And then her eyes drifted to my open closet, where my Cotillion dress was hanging in its plastic bag. "It's such a gorgeous dress," she said softly. "I just wish . . ."

I held my breath, waiting for the tears. But this time, Mom gave a tiny shake of her head and said, "Anyway. You'll be beautiful. Oh, and Miss Saylor called tonight. There's an extra—"

"An extra rehearsal on Monday, I know." Twisting behind me, I reached for the dress's zipper. "Amanda and Abigail told me."

Mom crossed the room, helping me unzip. "You know I think Cotillion is a wonderful thing, but sometimes I wonder if Saylor doesn't take it a little bit too seriously. Before she took it over, the girls had maybe three practices for the entire thing. Now it seems like you have three a week."

Last week we'd had four, but I didn't say that to Mom. "Miss Saylor just wants it to be perfect."

Mom pursed her lips, and for a second, it was like she was Old Mom again. The mom who laughed more, who had a weakness for gossip, who didn't wait up for me before it was even my curfew. "Pine Grove's Cotillion has been going on for nearly a hundred years, and there was never one hiccup until Saylor Stark took it over. Do you know how much mistletoe she makes the Junior League pay for? I tried to tell her that just because our town's Cotillion takes place a month before Christmas, there's no need to re-christen Magnolia House 'Mistletoe Manor.' That stuff is *expensive*."

Saylor Stark, with her gorgeous clothes and her silver hair and her impeccable manners, was kind of my hero. I mean, I put up with her nephew because I liked her so much. But it was nice having old, gossipy Mom back, so I nodded in sympathy. "She's also really strict about where we stand. That's what all the rehearsals are about. Making sure we're all standing in a perfect circle."

"Ridiculous," Mom said on a sigh. "Anyway, go take your shower and get some rest."

"Will do!" I said brightly, waiting until she shut the door to drop my grin. As soon as I heard her footsteps heading downstairs, I shimmied out of my wet dress and dashed into the shower. Once I was out, I threw on some flannel pajamas, snatched up my laptop, and headed into my walk-in closet. There was little chance of my mom coming back, but I didn't want to freak her out any more than I already had tonight. I was *not* going back to Dr. Greenbaum.

The first thing I did was Google "superhero," but that just got me a bazillion way too detailed Wikipedia entries on Marvel comics. A search for "Mr. Hall, janitor, Grove Academy" turned up absolutely nothing, which wasn't too surprising. What *was* surprising was that a search of "Michael DuPont, history teacher, Grove Academy" brought up only his faculty page on the Grove Academy website. That was weird. All of the Grove faculty are super accomplished; most of them are former college professors, and Googling any of them brings up either a book or paper they've published, or a lecture they've given at some academic conference. But there was nothing for Dr. DuPont. Almost like he hadn't existed before he came to the Grove last year.

Chill bumps broke out all over my body, and I reached up to pull a fluffy pink robe from a hanger. Wrapping it around me, I thought back to my fight with Dr. DuPont. He had called me something, some weird word I'd never heard before. "Pal" something.

I typed "superhero pal" into Google, but that just brought up some truly disturbing Batman/Robin fan fiction. So I tried "warrior pal." That got me a bunch of World of Warcraft sites. I sighed, scrolling down, about to give up when a word caught my eye: "Paladin."

That was it. That was the word he'd used. I clicked on the link and a definition popped up. "Paladin: an honorable knight; defender of a noble cause."

"Laaaaaame," I whispered. I much preferred superhero.

An hour later, I'd read pretty much everything the internet had to offer on the subject of Paladins and I was more confused than ever. The word was used to describe everything from high officials in the Catholic church to French knights to a class of warrior you could use in—ew—role-playing games.

But even with all the definitions, one thing remained the same. Paladins were warriors and protectors, charged with safeguarding a specific person or place.

That didn't sound particularly super. I slumped against the wall of my closet, pulling the robe tighter around me and burying my chin in it. Shouldn't I get to fly? Or at the very least, shoot laser beams out of my eyes?

Feeling like a complete moron, I stood up and focused as hard as I could on my closet door. No matter how hard I stared, no laser beams. I even tried muttering "laser" under my breath, but nothing.

That done, I gave a few experimental hops, trying to see if I could levitate even for a second. When that didn't work either, I briefly considered trying to jump out the window, but then I remembered Mom's expression when she'd found me in the pool.

So no lasers, no flying, but superstrength and an ability to kick some major ass. That was something.

I sat back down on the floor of my closet and turned to my computer. I had a couple of tabs open, and when I went to close the one about superheroes, a boldface paragraph caught my eye: "Perhaps the most defining characteristic of the superhero is a willingness to sacrifice for the good of others, even to the point of laying down his or her own life."

A shiver went through me. Mr. Hall had done that, apparently. And I knew that whole spiel about great responsibility coming with great power, but *dying* . . . that didn't seem worth a few measly superpowers. Even laser beam eyes weren't worth getting gutted by a scimitar-wielding history teacher.

But, I reminded myself, technically Mr. Hall hadn't been a superhero. He'd been a Paladin, and that was . . . different, right? And what—or who—had been his noble cause?

What was mine?

The next morning, I woke up early and drove to the library, checking out a bunch of DVDs. I spent the rest of the weekend holed up in my room with all three *Spider-Man* movies, the new *Superman*, and *X-Men* 1–3. I already owned *Batman Begins*, so I watched that, too.

Bee and Ryan both called my cell, and while I talked to Ryan, telling him I wasn't feeling so hot, I let Bee's calls go to voice mail. I felt awful doing it, but it was too risky to talk to her. Lying—okay, not *lying*, exactly—to Ryan was one thing, but Bee was tougher. She'd bought my whole "I got sick" thing Friday, but I'd been lucky. Normally, her Best-Friend Sensor was a lot more finely tuned than that. Besides, it might be too tempting to spill everything, and until I had a better handle on what was going on, that didn't seem like the best idea.

So I dedicated myself to my mission, and by the time Monday

morning rolled around, I had definitely figured some stuff out. First of all, I had gotten totally screwed on the "origin story" front. All superheroes have origin stories, like how Bruce Wayne's parents get killed and he goes to Tibet or whatever, and Superman is an alien, and Spider-Man had that radioactive spider. Me? I kissed a janitor in the school bathroom. Also, from *X-Men*, I learned that the people who seem to know what the eff is going on usually come find you, take you to a secure location, and tell you . . . well, what the eff is going on. So the way I saw it, some organization had clearly sent Mr. Hall to the Grove to protect something or someone. And Dr. DuPont had clearly come to the Grove to take that thing/kill that someone. And then that shadowy organization had fixed the bathroom with . . . um . . . magic or something (okay, so I wasn't clear on everything) so no one would know what happened.

Now, all I had to do was go to school and act normal and wait for them to find me.

Easy. Provided no one else tried to kill me, of course.

Usually, Ryan drove me to school, but when I called him Sunday night, I told him I was going to drive myself Monday.

"Okay," he replied, a little hesitant. "Is . . . Harper, is everything okay? I mean, I've hardly heard from you this weekend; you said you weren't feeling great . . ."

"I'm fine," I assured him. "It's just supposed to be really pretty tomorrow, and I haven't driven my car in, like, forever."

There was a pause, and I waited for Ryan to suggest I just pick him up instead. But then he sighed. "Right, I get that," he said at last. "No problem."

Still, when I hung up the phone, I couldn't shake this feeling that there *was* a problem. I pulled out my day planner, and on my list of weekly activities, added, "Spend more time with Ryan."

Seeing it written down made me feel better and I reminded myself that it wasn't like this was forever. As soon as I understood what had happened Friday night, I could move past it and get back to my normal life. Easy.

Monday *was* gorgeous, one of those perfect fall days that are kind of rare in Alabama. I drove to school with my windows down, the cool autumn air blowing my hair around my face. Now that I knew I wasn't crazy, I felt a lot better. Being a superhero, or Paladin, or whatever, seemed like a natural extension of the stuff I already did. I mean, didn't I work my butt off to make the Grove a safe and fun place to be? Whatever was at the Grove that needed protecting, chances were I was already protecting it.

As I pulled into the sweet parking place I had by virtue of being SGA president, my good mood swelled. The school looked so beautiful under the bright blue October sky. The Grove was made up of four redbrick buildings with a large courtyard in the center. There were stone tables and benches in the courtyard where seniors ate lunch when the weather was nice. The trees surrounding the cluster of buildings were stunning shades of red and orange and gold, and when the bell tower chimed the half hour, I thought my heart might burst with pride.

I got out of the car, smoothing my hair and readjusting my green headband. Even though the Grove didn't have uniforms, we did have a really strict dress code that ensured everyone always looked nice: no jeans, no T-shirts, definitely no shorts. Today, I had worn one of my favorite outfits, a turtleneck the same green as my eyes, and a plaid skirt with brown knee-length boots and tights. I looked awesome and I knew it.

In fact, I thought it was my awesome outfit that was making people stare at me as I made my way from the parking lot. Then I noticed that they were . . . staring.

That's when I realized that the starers were all holding a bunch of papers stapled together—the school newspaper.

Clutching my books and tossing my head back, I forced a big smile and approached the nearest group. They were sophomores, so they were still a little scared of me. All three immediately went to hide the papers behind their backs.

"Hi!" I said brightly, hugging my bag tightly to my chest.

"Hi," they chorused back. The one in the middle reminded me a little bit of Bee, all fluffy blond hair and big dark eyes, and I was sure I'd seen the other two around campus. Yes, the one on the right—a tall redhead wearing a skirt just a little bit too short—had tried out for cheerleading last spring.

None of the three met my eyes.

"So, is there something in that paper that I should know about?" I asked, trying to sound friendly and jokey. "It's not a hideously unflattering picture of me after cheerleading practice, is it? Or me shrieking at the SGA?"

Translation: I am head cheerleader and SGA president, and I could destroy you all if I wanted to. And that's not even bringing my superpowers into it. I had never used my popularity for evil before—but I'd never been gaped at either. So I figured there was no harm in putting a little of the fear of God into these girls.

The girl on the left cracked first. She was tiny and had white-blond hair, and her blue eyes were huge as she looked up at me. "It's just the . . . uh, special Homecoming edition of *The Grove News*."

My smile froze in place. Surely, he wouldn't have.

"Can I see it?" I asked, still grinning, still upbeat.

The one who looked like Bee shook her head ever so slightly at the tiny girl, but she was already handing me the paper. I took it with trembling hands.

My worst fears were confirmed.

There, on the front page of the special Homecoming edition of *The Grove News*, was a huge, albeit blurry, picture of me leaning on Bee, clearly sobbing my eyes out, as we made our way out of the girls' bathroom. It looked like it had probably been taken with a cell phone, and the headline read, "It's Her Party and She'll Cry If She Wants To?" Under the picture of me and Bee, there was a smaller caption: *Homecoming Queen misses crowning under mysterious circumstances.* My eyes darted over the rest of the article as my heart started pounding. ". . . *hiding in the boys' room . . . violently ill . . . tension between the 'Queen Bee' and her underling, Bee Franklin . . . this reporter . . .*"

By now, I had sort of started hyperventilating as my eyes zeroed in on the byline in bold letters.

David Stark.

Who I was now going to *murder*.

Chapter 6

IT WASN'T just the humiliation of having the entire school know that I was puking and crying in the bathroom during Homecoming, or the veiled insinuations that I'd been sick because I was pregnant or on drugs. It was that the school probably already knew that Mr. Hall and Dr. DuPont were missing. And sure, that bathroom had looked spotless, but it's not like I'd done a sweep for DNA. For all I knew, the police were in Headmaster Dunn's office right now, with big folders full of evidence that two men had died in the girls' bathroom last Friday, and asking if anyone was displaying any "strange behavior." And, oh, look! Here was a convenient picture of me sobbing around the girls' bathroom.

"Are you okay?" the tall sophomore asked. "You look kinda . . . purple."

I snapped my head up and smiled, or at least pressed my teeth together in the semblance of a smile. "I'm fine," I said, but my voice was way too loud. "This is just a silly misunderstanding between me and David. Can I keep this?"

"Sure," the shorter girl who'd handed me the paper said.

"Thanks so much!" I turned around and headed straight for Wallace Hall.

Before I'd gone more than a few steps, I heard Ryan call my name. He was jogging over from the parking lot, a bunch of papers crumpled in his hand. "Hey!" he said once he'd caught up to me. One hand cupping my elbow, he leaned down, studying me. "Are you okay?"

"Of course," I said, trying to look more okay and less homicidal.

"Why didn't you tell me you were sick Friday night?"

"It was nothing," I insisted, shifting my backpack to my other shoulder. "And I didn't want to make a big deal about it. Honestly. This is just another one of David Stark's jerk moves. I can handle it."

Ryan clenched his jaw, looking up toward Wallace Hall. "What is that dude's problem?"

"He's a jackass."

Not taking his eyes off the building, Ryan shook his head. A muscle worked in his jaw and he shoved the sleeves of his dark blue sweater up his forearms. "No, it's more than that. He's always been like this with you, ever since we were little. Back in middle school, I thought maybe he had a thing for you, but—"

"First of all, I highly doubt that. Secondly, sometimes people are just . . . I don't know, born mean or something."

Glancing back down at me, Ryan gave a half-smile. "Maybe. Want me to go kick his ass?"

Ryan was joking; I think the closest he'd ever been to a fight was watching UFC with his brother on Saturday nights. But as soon as he said it, it was like someone had punched me in the stomach, an almost overwhelming sense of *wrongness* washed over me. "No!" I yelped, and Ryan startled.

"Whoa, Harper, I was kidding." He held both hands up in mock surrender. "I'm a lover, not a fighter."

That weird, nauseous sensation subsided, and I rubbed my temples. "I know, sorry. Anyway, let me go talk to David, and I'll see you at lunch, okay?"

"Sure you don't want me to go with you?" An auburn curl fell over Ryan's forehead as he ducked his head to meet my eyes, concern all over his face.

But the idea of him coming with me to see David sent my stomach roiling again. I managed to give a little laugh. "No, I've got this."

Ryan dropped a kiss on my cheek and gave my elbow one last squeeze. "You always do."

He headed across the quad, broad shoulders held back, long legs striding across the grass, and I turned back to Wallace Hall. I don't know what I looked like, but it must have been pretty scary, because everyone was quick to jump out of my way. Most of them were holding papers, though, so they probably all thought I was about to have a nervous breakdown right in front of them. Which actually was a good thing. After that weird thing with Ryan, a lot of my anger had died down. Hearing people whisper behind my back powered it right back up.

As I pushed open the heavy door, I mentally called David Stark every bad word I could think of.

By the time I reached the journalism lab, it felt like sparks were exploding from my head. There were a few articles taped to the door, and even in my rage, I saw that almost all of them had David's byline. Gritting my teeth, I stepped inside.

Thanks to all of the computers lining the back wall, the classroom felt a lot warmer than the hall. No one was working at the computers now, and there were only three people in the room. David was sitting on a desk, laughing with two other newspaper staffers, Michael Goldberg and Chie Kurata.

I'd planned out this whole speech in my head amidst all the bad words—yay, multitasking!—about how what he'd done was not only personally offensive to me, but demoralizing and degrading to the school, because when we make one of us look bad, we *all* look bad. And honestly, how did he expect to get away with this kind of crap? He had to have written the article and printed up the paper over the weekend. That meant he'd done it behind Mrs. Laurent's back, and that had to be a detention-worthy offense at the very least.

But something about seeing him sitting on top of a desk, eating yogurt and laughing with his friends made me snap. I could feel my face get red, and this intense, trembly feeling rose up from the middle of my chest. My intelligent and calm speech flew right out of my head.

"WTF, David?" I asked, storming into the room and throwing the paper on the nearest desk.

He at least had the good grace to look chagrined. "Harper—"

"No!" I said, or at least I meant to say. It came out a little shriek and Michael flinched and looked at his feet. Chie, a pretty, petite Asian girl who'd transferred to our school just this year, raised her eyebrows so high they disappeared underneath her heavy black bangs.

David stood and put his hands up in front of him in the universal sign for "calm the heck down."

But there was no stopping me now. "Why would you do this?" I gestured angrily at the paper. Just over David's head, there was a poster featuring a typewriter and the quote "Journalism Is History on the Run," and I made myself stare at that rather than meet his gaze. Man, laser eyes really would've come in handy now.

He sighed and ran a hand through his hair. He was always doing that, which is why he usually looked like he'd been electrocuted by fourth period. "It was a valid story, Pres," he finally said. "Something was definitely wrong with you that night and I think the student body of the Grove has the right to know if their golden girl is hiding something."

"No, they don't," I fired back. "What was going on that night was none of your business!"

"I was involved that night too, Harper."

"Um, you held my hair while I puked. I don't think that exactly makes you a major player in the night's events, David."

"You held her hair?" Chie asked. She had slid down into one of the desks, twisting around to face us.

He glanced over at her, his mouth turning down with impatience. "Yeah, but that's not the point."

He turned back to me, and he didn't look even a little bit sorry anymore. "When I see a story that affects the school, it's my journalistic duty to report it."

I laughed. "Your *journalistic duty*? Look around you, David." I snatched up the paper from the desk, gesturing around the tiny, hot room with its posters of famous dead journalists and lame quotes. "You write for the tiniest school paper ever. This"— I rattled the paper—"is a glorified newsletter. You don't even send it to a real printer. You just print copies off the secretary's computer! Don't you get it? No one wants you to dig up corruption in the SGA, or uncover health violations in the cafeteria, or write nasty stories about a girl who works hard to make the Grove an awesome place for everyone, even total jackasses like you. I can't believe you would do something like this when—"

I broke off. I was breathing hard, and the paper was crumpled in my hand. Michael had gone to one of the computers, his back to us, but his shoulders tight and his ears nearly as red as his hair. Chie was still sitting in her desk, stunned. Truth be told, I felt kind of stunned, too. I mean, I hardly ever lost my temper, and I'd certainly never done it in public. But here I was, panting, sweaty, my hands smudged with ink. My face was on fire, and I could feel some of my hair sticking to my cheeks and neck.

Was this part of being a Paladin/superhero? Was I like the Hulk, only sweaty instead of green? What was wrong with me?

Okay, I mean, obviously I was freaked out that David's little exposé might get me, um, *thrown in jail forever*, but my anger seemed to run deeper than that. What had I been about to say to him? *I can't believe you'd do something like this when . . .*

When you were nice to me that night.

That's what I had been about to say. I was angry because David Stark had hurt my feelings. I took a deep breath and dropped the paper onto the nearest desk. Then I carefully smoothed my hair away from my face and willed my blood pressure back to a non-stroke level. I straightened my shoulders and looked at David with haughty disdain.

"Anyway," I said, "I expect a printed retraction and apology in the next issue."

David folded his arms over his chest and grinned, clearly deciding to battle haughty disdain with snarky nonchalance. Well, his posture was snarky nonchalance at least, but his eyes were practically burning. "Expect it all you want, Pres. I stand by that story."

If I hadn't already been so rattled, I wouldn't have said what I said next. But David had pushed so many of my buttons that I just smirked back. "Retract it, or I am going to file a formal complaint with the school board."

The grin faltered.

"It would be the second one, right? Didn't someone on the debate team file in September after you accused him of cheating?" I rolled my eyes upward, like I was trying to remember something. "And didn't your aunt say something like if you got one more demerit, she was making you resign from the paper? I seem to recall her mentioning it to my mom at Cotillion practice."

The look of naked fear that skittered across his face made me feel sick. So did the sound of my voice. I sounded so much like Leigh-Anne.

He made me do it, I told myself. *You're not a mean girl, but he made you be one.*

David recovered quickly, but his grin was ugly now. "Fair enough, Pres. Next issue."

"Thank you."

I cleared my throat and picked up my book bag. As I turned to go, David called out, "Harper?"

"What?"

He took a minute, like he was trying to decide if he should say whatever it was he wanted to say. I wondered if he felt like I had, like he didn't want to say something hateful, but I'd made him.

"You know, all the articles aside, I actually thought you were better than this," he finally said. "Nice to know that you *are* just another high school bitch."

Maybe it was that his words were so close to what Dr. DuPont had said right before he nearly murdered me. Maybe it was because a little part of me felt like David might be right. Or maybe it was because I just really didn't like to be called names. Whatever the reason, my right hand shot up to slap David Stark across the face. I didn't even consider my new superpowers, and if those new powers would mean David's head would go flying off.

But it didn't matter. Half an inch from David's cheek, my hand stopped in midair. And it wasn't because I had some crisis of conscience, either. It was like my hand hit an invisible wall right by his head.

He had flinched in anticipation of the slap, but now he opened his eyes and looked at my palm as it hovered next to his face. I wasn't sure which one of us looked more surprised.

I drew back my hand a little, then pushed it forward again. Again, my hand stopped like there was Plexiglas between my hand and his head.

I tried the left hand, making David raise his shoulders and shut his eyes again, but the same thing happened, so now I was standing in front of him with my hands poised on either side of his face.

This time when he opened his eyes, he looked at my hands in confusion. "Um . . . Harper? Are you gonna hit me or not?"

I stood there, looking at my hands and at his face between them. I still really wanted to hit him, but it was obvious that I wasn't going to be able to.

So I dropped my hands and raised my chin. "No, I'm not." I let my tone say, *Because I am totally a better person than you* and hoped he hadn't noticed the fact that my hands didn't seem to work when it came to slapping his face.

"Ooookay," he said slowly, and I heard someone stifle a giggle behind him, so I had a feeling this bizarre little story would run right next to my apology next week.

"I'll see y'all later," I mumbled, grabbing my book bag and trying not to run out of the room.

The bell rang as I ran down the hall, passing the bathrooms. There was no police tape across the doors, so that was a good thing. As I turned the corner to go down the history hall, I glanced in Dr. DuPont's room. Mrs. Hillyard, a substitute teacher

I'd had a few times, was standing at the front of the class. All the stuff in the garden had pretty much convinced me that my fight with Dr. DuPont had been real, but I was still super relieved to see Mrs. Hillyard. There had been a tiny (okay, not that tiny) part of my brain that had been terrified of coming to school and finding Dr. DuPont and Mr. Hall there like nothing had happened.

But they were definitely gone and I was definitely a super-hero . . . er, Paladin. Hadn't that thing with David proved it? If I was guardian and protector of the Grove, I couldn't just run around slapping people in the face. My body actually wouldn't allow it; that's how good I was now.

Or maybe it was just David.

That thought leapt into my brain and I stopped in my tracks. Hadn't the Paladin definition said that we were guardians of places or *people*? But why would David need a Paladin unless there was some group dedicated to removing the world of self-righteous jerks, in which case I was *totally* on the wrong side?

Then it occurred to me that there was a pretty easy way of fig-uring out if it was just David I couldn't hurt or people in general.

I looked around until I saw Brandon by his locker. "Bran!" I called, waving him over. I kind of felt bad about doing this ex-periment on Brandon. It felt like slapping a puppy. A dumb, per-verted puppy, but a puppy nonetheless.

Brandon looked as concerned as he was able to. "Hey, Harper. You okay? The paper said you were sick Friday night, and Bee said she didn't hear from you this weekend, and—"

"I'm fine," I said with a wave of my hand. "Food poisoning. Anyway, would you mind if I tried out an, uh, experiment on you?"

His face brightened and he gave me a look that I guess was supposed to be sexy, but was vaguely stupid instead. "Does this experiment involve nakedness?" he asked, leaning one shoulder against the lockers.

"Brandon, your best friend is my boyfriend. And *my* best friend is *your* girlfriend."

He shrugged, flipping his hair out of his eyes. Brandon's hair was a few shades darker than Bee's, more gold than blond, and while I guess he was attractive in a clean-cut jock kind of way, I'd never go for his type. Too many muscles, too few brain cells. "And?"

Well, at least now I wouldn't feel bad about hitting him. I raised my hand and brought it down on his cheek with a really satisfying SMACK.

He yelped and a bunch of people in the hall turned to stare.

"Sorry!" I said. "You, um . . . there was a bug. Okay, see you later, bye!"

I dashed into my first period class, my hand stinging and my mind whirling. Normally, first period AP European History was my favorite class, but that day, I didn't even take notes. I spent most of the time wondering why I'd been able to slap Brandon and not David. If I was Paladin for the Grove, I shouldn't have been able to hit any of its students.

I wrote in my notebook, *"B said offensive thing, so could be hit as he is jerk."*

That made sense. But then I wrote, *"D also said offensive thing—called me bitch. But could not hit."*

Then under that, *"But you were a bitch to D, so deserved it, so D not jerk, so could not hit."*

Hmmm . . .

Clearly, I needed a test subject, someone totally innocent. If I couldn't hit him or her, then I was right, and it was my job to protect the Grove. If I could . . . ugh, I did not want to think about that.

I glanced around until my eyes landed on Liz Walker. She was sitting one desk over and up from me. I had several classes with her, but we weren't exactly friends. She ran with a group some of us called "the churchy people." Other, less-nice people called them "the Jesus freaks." Basically, if I were looking for one of the nicest people at the Grove, Liz was it.

So that's why I *did* feel bad when I fished a pen out of my bag and chucked it at her, figuring that if I were Paladin of the Grove, it would stop about an inch from all that shiny blond hair.

It didn't.

I flinched as the pen smacked Liz right in the back of her head. She gave a startled cry and whirled around, hand on her head, eyes full of not-so-churchy anger.

"Harper?"

My teacher, Mrs. Ford, was looking at me with total confusion. "Harper," she said again, "did you just . . . did you just throw a pen at Liz?"

Now the whole class was looking at me. I turned on my best smile and said, "Oh my gosh, no, Mrs. Ford! I was just . . . um . . . writing really fast because there was so much information to take in, and I had, like, some lotion? On my hands? Anyway, the pen flew out of my hand and hit Liz." I turned to Liz. "Really sorry about that. Total accident."

"It's okay," Liz said, but she was scowling and rubbing the back of her head.

Mrs. Ford was watching me like I had just sprouted a second head, but she eventually shrugged and said, "Well, be more careful."

"Will do!" I chirped. Then I turned back to my notebook, my heart pounding and my mouth dry. Holy crap.

I had a noble cause, all right. But it wasn't Grove Academy.

It was David Stark.

Chapter 7

I SPENT the next three classes pretty out of it. For the first time in history, I took absolutely no notes. I just sat and stared and thought.

Mr. Hall had been protecting David. Dr. DuPont had been trying to kill David. I now had to protect David. Other people would probably try to kill him. But why? I mean, yes, David Stark was annoying, but that didn't make him worth *killing*. And if Mr. Hall had been protecting him, had he chosen to? Because I sure as heck hadn't chosen this. What would happen if I just . . . didn't? Or could I pass the powers on to someone else?

By the time the bells rang for lunch, one thing was abundantly clear to me:

I needed my mentor-person *right now*. I had figured out as much as I possibly could, so it was time for my Giles or my Professor X or whoever to get here and start explaining.

I slung my bag over my shoulder and started heading to lunch when it occurred to me that it wasn't like my Giles/Professor X could just come sashaying into the cafeteria amidst a hundred teenagers. No, I'd have to be on my own.

The problem was—where? The Grove was so small that there were very few places without students lurking. I stood on the steps of Wallace Hall, looking down at the courtyard, which was already filling up. Any minute now, Ryan, Bee, and Brandon would be here. I looked over to Nash, the building that housed the cafeteria and the fine arts classrooms—and the only building on campus that even *I* had to admit was ugly, all short and squat—and saw Bee coming out the door, a Styrofoam box in her hand. Amanda, Abigail, and Mary Beth were all surrounding her, and she was looking over her shoulder and laughing at someone behind her. Brandon, probably, which meant Ryan wasn't far behind.

For a second, I thought about going over to meet them. I even started down the steps. But when I got to the bottom, instead of heading across the courtyard, I found myself turning left and heading for the chapel that was in the very back corner of campus. Of course! The chapel was only used for assemblies, so it was deserted most of the time. Plus, the back of it faced the woods. If ever there were a perfect place to wait for superhero instructions, that was it.

The chapel was actually really pretty, and it was a shame that we didn't use it very often. It was built out of pale gray stone, and there were stained-glass windows running down each side. As I walked around toward the back, I decided that at the next SGA meeting, I would definitely bring up ways we could use it more. Maybe something at Christmas. Provided I would still *be* on SGA. What if my Professor X person said I had to quit all my extracurricular stuff? Or what if I had to leave school altogether?

If I had powers, would I have to go to some other school for kids who had them, too? Were there any other kids who—

I came to a sudden stop as I reached the back of the chapel. There, sitting on the steps where I'd planned on waiting for my mentor-person, was David Stark.

"Ugh, no!" I cried without really thinking. I'm pretty sure I even stamped my foot.

David's blue eyes widened. "Harper?" he mumbled around a mouthful of sandwich.

"What are you doing here?" I asked, pushing my shoulders back.

He swallowed and stood up, dusting his hands on his pants. He opened his mouth like he was going to say something, but before he could, he suddenly winced, pressing his fingers against his temple.

I immediately took a step forward. "What's wrong?"

David blinked a couple of times, fingers moving against his forehead. "Headache. I've had one for like a week now. Probably spending too much time in front of the computer." Reaching into his pocket, he pulled out a tiny packet of aspirin. As he tore it open with his teeth, he glanced over at me. "Anyway, that's why I'm here. Lunchroom was too loud. So what are *you* doing out here, Pres? Why aren't you eating lunch with your court?"

Darn it, why hadn't I thought up a reason to be out here in case I bumped into anyone?

But then the perfect excuse came to me. I looked down and scraped the dirt with my boot heel. "I just couldn't deal with all the questions about that article you wrote. I was embarrassed."

David watched me for a long moment and I studied him right back. I wanted to see something, anything, that would make David Stark look like someone who needed to be protected by supernatural bodyguards, but he seemed to be a normal high school boy, albeit one with truly terrible fashion sense. Today he was wearing worn-out corduroys with a bright green T-shirt and a too-small navy blazer.

Who are you? I thought. What the heck is so important about David Freaking Stark?

He laughed, startling me. I was so used to David scowling that it was kind of weird to see so many of his teeth. "God, you're the worst liar I have ever seen," he said. "First the whole stage fright thing, now this 'I was embarrassed' act . . ."

"I *was* embarrassed!" I shouted back, but he just kept on laughing. I picked up a small rock and tossed it at him, but it came to a skidding stop six inches from him, and dropped back to the ground. Luckily, David was so caught up in laughing at me that he didn't notice. I'd known it wasn't actually going to hit him, but still, it felt good just to throw something. Then I remembered my Professor Giles X could be watching me right now, and probably wouldn't approve of me slinging rocks at the guy I was clearly supposed to protect.

"I just don't see why the eff that's so funny," I muttered, just in case that person was listening. At least they'd know I'd had just cause.

David's laughter trailed off and he looked at me with genuine curiosity. "Why do you do that?"

"Do what?" I tucked an errant strand of hair back into my headband.

"Say 'eff' or 'G. D.' Why not say the actual words?"

I heaved a sigh and glanced toward the woods. If my Professor Giles X was out there, there was no chance he was coming now. So much for alone time.

I turned back to David. "I just don't think it's . . . necessary to use those words in polite company when there are so many perfectly good euphemisms."

David stared at me. "Dear God, what planet are you from?"

I threw up my hands. "Forget it, okay? I wouldn't expect you to understand anyway. Just like you don't understand why the Grove is important to me, or why I might not want my personal issues blasted all over your stupid newspaper, or why I might have wanted to eat lunch by myself for once."

Oh God, I was doing it again, that shouty, kind of scary thing I seemed to do whenever I had to talk to David for more than five minutes. I needed to go. This idea had obviously been a bust, and there was still plenty of lunch left to hang out with Ryan.

Speaking of whom . . . I pulled my phone out of my bag and saw that, sure enough, Ryan had sent me a text message five minutes earlier. "Where R U?" Then another one from three minutes ago. "R U OK?"

"I gotta go," I said, but David caught my arm before I got very far.

This close, I could see the faint blond stubble on his chin, and when he opened his mouth, I noticed the tiniest chip in his front tooth. "Harper, look, I just want to say . . . earlier today, that whole thing with . . . what I called you, and—"

"No problem," I said, waving my hand, my eyes still on my cell phone as it started blaring "Sexy Back," Ryan's ringtone (he had picked it himself). I didn't really want to answer it when I'd be seeing him in just a few minutes. Plus I didn't want to lie to him in front of David, giving him even more ammo against me. I could just hear him. "Why did you lie to your boyfriend about where you were? Why are you really out here? Did you by any chance murder Dr. DuPont?"

Okay, so that last one was a long shot, but I was not in the mood to deal.

I looked at David, not even trying to hide my irritation as "Sexy Back" finally stopped. "It's fine, okay? I shouldn't have said that stuff about the school board and your aunt. I'm . . . I'm sorry."

My phone started ringing again. Ryan must've been really worried. "Now, I really have to go."

But David wasn't letting go so easily, not of the subject and not of my arm.

"Fine, but what was up with you not hitting me? It didn't look like you didn't want to, it looked like you *couldn't*."

Great, so he had noticed that. "David, look, we can talk about this later, but my boyfriend is looking for me, and I have to go—"

"Harper?"

Oh, *shoot*. I turned just as Ryan rounded the corner. He was holding his cell phone in one hand, a look of total confusion on his face.

"Ryan," I said, trying to make myself smile. I guess I thought if I just smiled a lot, Ryan wouldn't think there was anything unusual about me arguing behind the chapel with David.

But Ryan wasn't even looking at me. He was glaring at David, towering over him by at least four inches. "What the hell is going on?"

David dropped his hand. "Nothing, man," he said to Ryan. "We were just talking about the paper. That's it."

Ryan was looking between us, an unfamiliar expression on his face. It took me a second to realize that he was angry. More than angry, really. He was furious. And Ryan *never* lost his temper.

"Why can't you just leave her alone?" he asked David. Ryan's jaw was clenched, and I'd never seen his hazel eyes look that cold. "I mean, other than being better than you in every class, what has Harper ever done to you?"

David must have been as weirded out by Angry Ryan as I was, because for once, he didn't have a smartass response. His skin went a little pale, and I could see the whites around his blue eyes. "Look, I'm sorry. You're right, I've been a dick, but I swear to God, I wasn't bothering her. I was sitting here first, and she just—"

"Save it," Ryan said, holding up a hand. "Whatever your little war on Harper is about, it's over. I don't want you to write one more damn word about her. I don't want you to talk to her. I don't even want you to *look* at her."

I knew that Ryan was trying to protect me, and maybe I should've been thrilled to watch my boyfriend go all alpha male for me, but instead I felt . . . irritated. "Ryan, I told you I could handle this."

"But you haven't," he fired back, his voice unnaturally loud in the quiet behind the church. The breeze had died down, and there wasn't even the rustle of leaves. It was hard to believe that only a few hundred feet away, kids were eating lunch, talking, laughing. "This guy is a jerk, and you've just taken it for years. I get that you're sucking up to his aunt, and that you want to be nice to people, Harper, but damn. You don't have to be a doormat."

"I'm not sucking up!" I said, just as David moved forward, saying, "Take it easy, Ryan—"

And then everything exploded.

Ryan, sweet Ryan, who had never purposely hurt anyone, shot a hand out to push David away, and suddenly, it was like a screen dropped in front of my eyes. I could see Ryan's hand hit David's chest, saw David stumble back as his glasses flew off.

I saw his head hit the edge of the stone steps of the chapel, blood erupting from underneath his sandy hair. I saw his blue eyes roll up until all I could see were the whites.

Then the vision vanished.

I was moving before I even really knew it, just like with Dr. DuPont. My hand shot out and caught Ryan's wrist, his hand just inches from David's chest. I yanked Ryan's arm down as my knee came up, catching him in the stomach. While he was bent over from that, I leaned down and put my shoulder into his chest and, still holding his arm, flipped him over my back. All six feet three inches, two hundred pounds of him.

He landed on his back. As he landed, I straightened up and put my foot on his throat, pressing down slightly. My fingers were tight around his wrist, and some inner knowledge told me that if I pulled up and twisted in a certain way, I'd break it, along with a few bones in his hand.

And if David hadn't shouted my name, I probably would have.

It was like waking up from a dream. I looked down and saw Ryan's wide, panicked eyes, my boot against his neck. I saw the shocked look on David's face.

"What the hell?" Ryan squeaked, and I immediately dropped his arm, stumbling a few steps back.

Getting superpowers was supposed to be a good thing. You helped people. You didn't nearly twist your boyfriend's hand off.

David was leaning down, helping Ryan to his feet, but all I could do was stand there, numb. That feeling I'd had when I was fighting Dr. DuPont, like I wasn't even in control of my body. *Then* it had been cool. But this? So out of control that I'd hurt someone I loved? That was terrifying.

"Pres?" David asked hesitantly. Both he and Ryan stood there, waiting for me to say something. Dozens of excuses ran through my mind. New energy drink. New, high-tech cheerleading moves. But in the end, no words came out of my mouth, and I just did the easiest thing I could think of.

I ran.

From behind me, I heard someone call my name, but whether it was Ryan or David, I didn't know.

Or care.

I didn't stop to get my bag, which meant that I couldn't drive home, but I knew I had to get out of there.

Stopping just outside the gates, I looked left, then right. The Grove was located in one of the town's nicer neighborhoods, full of tree-lined streets and big houses. My own house was a good three miles away and to the left. So I turned to the right.

I had no idea where I was going, so I figured I'd keep walking until my mentor found me, or the cops came after me for assaulting Ryan.

A cool breeze ruffled my hair and blew my skirt against my legs as leaves skittered down the sidewalk. I didn't realize that I'd started crying until the wind cooled the tears on my cheeks.

"It'll be okay," I mumbled out loud, adding talking to myself to the list of crazy things I'd done today. Not that I cared. "It'll be okay," I said again, louder this time, and the more I thought about it, the more convinced I was that it really would be.

All right, so my superpowers had flipped out on me and nearly made me hurt Ryan. But he and David were the only people who had seen it. Ryan loved me. He'd forgive me as soon as I came up with a reason for what happened. Preferably one that didn't sound completely insane.

And David . . .

If there had been any doubt in my mind that David Stark was involved in whatever was going on with me, it was gone now. I'd flipped Ryan to keep David safe. And something told me that if Ryan hadn't been joking about kicking David's ass earlier, I would have done that ninja thing on him then, too.

But why? That was the thing that didn't make any sense. Okay, it was one of the many, many things about this that didn't make any sense, but it was definitely the most pressing. The *why* would lead to the *who* and the *how*. And that meant I didn't have time for this middle of the sidewalk pity party I was currently throwing. I had to get back to the Grove, and I had to talk to—

Suddenly, pain slammed into my chest, like someone punched me in the sternum. It was so intense that I gasped. Then, as quickly as it had come, it was gone, leaving behind a heavy pressure that made me wonder if my lungs had been replaced with bricks.

I stood there, my hands clenched at my sides, sucking in deep breaths. I had felt this way before.

Right before Dr. DuPont burst through that bathroom door.

"Pres?"

The pain had crowded so much of my mind that I hadn't heard David's Dodge pull up alongside me, which meant I had been *really* out of it, because that thing had to have a hole in the muffler or something.

"Oh God, *seriously?*"

"Look, let me give you a ride home, okay? It isn't safe for you to be walking here by yourself."

The heavy feeling intensified. "Um, David, hate to break it to you," I said, trying to sound normal even though my breathing was speeding up, "but this isn't exactly a rough neighborhood. I think I can avoid getting raped and murdered on someone's croquet lawn, okay?"

He leaned across the passenger seat and for the first time, I saw that he looked genuinely worried. Maybe even a little scared. "Harper—" he started to say.

I stepped down from the sidewalk, and leaned forward, my hands resting on the open passenger window. "What's wrong?"

"It's *that car*." His eyes darted to his rearview mirror and I turned to look over my shoulder. About a hundred yards away, a black car with tinted windows idled at a stop sign. I figured the suffocating feeling in my chest had something to do with it, and *that* meant it was probably not filled with good guys.

"The car was outside the school when I left," David said in a voice barely above a whisper, like the people in the car could hear us. "It's been following you."

Adrenaline started flooding through my system as I turned back to David and said, "Get out of here. Now. Drive—"

But before I could finish, the black car revved its engine with a roar that drowned out David's crappy Dodge.

And then it was racing straight at us.

Chapter 8

It wasn't like I had a lot of time to think about what to do next, so I went with instinct.

I dove through David's open passenger window and scrambled onto his lap.

I know, I know. Between that and the head-butting, I was going to get my southern belle title revoked. But I knew what I needed to do, and it was faster to drive the damn car myself than try to explain it to David. And I knew he couldn't move into the passenger seat in enough time. That black car would be on us in seconds.

David made a sound that was somewhere between shock and outrage as I grabbed the wheel and placed my foot on top of his on the accelerator.

The Dodge rattled, and squealed, and thunked, but, thank God, it lurched forward just as the black car's front grille kissed our bumper. The shock was still enough to send me flying painfully into the steering wheel, and David into my back.

"What the hell?" David yelled in my ear.

My eyes still on the street, I reached down with one hand and unfastened David's seat belt. "Scoot!" I hollered over the clunking of the car and the rush of wind pouring through the open passenger window.

We were hurtling down the oak-lined avenue, branches forming a leafy arch overhead. My hands were slick with sweat as I clutched the steering wheel, and my calf muscle was already aching from how hard I was mashing David's foot on the gas pedal. There was still a trace of that disconnected feeling I'd had when fighting Dr. DuPont and Ryan, like I wasn't completely in control of my body, but this time, I was definitely feeling more there, if that makes any sense.

I glanced in the rearview mirror and saw that the black car was only a few feet behind us. We'd gotten a head start, but they were driving a much better car. Already, the Dodge was shuddering like its frame was about to fly into pieces, and we were only going seventy miles an hour.

Then it occurred to me that we were going seventy miles an hour on a street where the speed limit was twenty-five. I sent up a quick prayer that there were no little kids riding bikes anywhere nearby, and pressed my foot down even harder.

David gave a grunt of pain as my heel dug into his foot. "Sorry!" I yelled. "But come on! Scoot!"

I could tell he was trying to get out from under me, but the only way to do it quickly (and so I could maintain our speed *and* my concentration) would be to actually put his hands under my butt, lift me off him, and slide. Instead, he was trying to slide out from under me without touching my butt, or hips, or really any area that could be considered inappropriate.

That wasn't going so well. It's not like I weigh very much—I'm maybe a buck ten—but David is a slight guy, and I was pretty firmly wedged onto his lap. While I appreciated this rare show of chivalrous behavior, now was not the time for David to worry about my delicate sensibilities.

Especially since I'd just realized this was a dead-end street.

"Scoot, scoot, SCOOT!" I yelled at David.

"I AM SCOOTING!" he shouted back.

Then he looked out the windshield and saw the same thing I had: the large grove of trees at the end of the street that we were headed straight for. At seventy-five miles an hour.

He used three different versions of the F-word, and before I knew it, his hands were on my butt and he was sliding into the passenger seat. I landed on the nubby seat with a grateful sigh. Now the steering wheel wasn't pressed into my chest, and David's bony knees weren't cutting into the back of my thighs. Cheap upholstery had never felt so good.

David was several inches taller than me, so I had to slide down a little to maintain my pressure on the accelerator, but we never swerved or dropped our speed.

"Thank you!" I said, but David didn't seem to hear me. He was running a shaking hand over his paper-white face and mumbling to himself.

"Buckle up!" I shouted.

That he heard. I buckled my seat belt, too, and then looked over at him as the trees got closer and closer.

"Why are you smiling?" he shouted, terror all over his face.

I was smiling? I could see my reflection in his glasses, and he was right. I was smiling kind of big, actually. And then I realized why. Because even though this was scary and dangerous and so, so illegal . . .

It was fun. I felt in my element and in charge. I'm always happiest when I'm excelling at something, and, to quote one of those World of Warcraft websites I'd stumbled onto, these bad guys were about to get *pwned*.

The smile turned into a laugh as I gripped the steering wheel tight in my left hand and reached down with my right.

"I've always wanted to do this!" I shouted.

The end of the street was only a few dozen yards away. The black car was right behind us.

I pushed down as hard as I could with both feet on the brake pedal, and at the same time, I jerked the emergency brake up and spun the car hard to the left.

And it worked! Okay, so it wasn't a total success. The black car was so close to us that it hit us as we spun, crunching in the back door on my side. David gave a low groan, but whether that was for his car or the fact that we had been literally seconds from death, I wasn't sure.

The rear of the car fishtailed, taking out at least three mailboxes as I righted the Dodge and sped off in the opposite direction, back toward the Grove. I had an idea.

I glanced in the rearview mirror and saw the black car had done a similar spin and was now following us again, although we had a much bigger lead this time.

It wasn't going to last long, though. I could see sparks shooting up from the rear tire. It had probably gotten crunched along with the back door. The Dodge also seemed to have trouble shifting into fifth gear, and I heard a grinding sound that couldn't be good. I only hoped I had enough time . . .

We shot down the street, the car wobbling now and much harder to control. We passed one house where a woman in a flowery shirt and hot pink capri pants dropped her garden hose and stared at us in openmouthed shock. I cringed. Mrs. Harris, who was in the Junior League with my mom. I really hoped she hadn't recognized me.

We passed the Grove, and I was super thankful there was no one loitering outside the gates.

"Two more miles, two more miles," I muttered to myself. The Dodge was only going around fifty miles an hour now, and the black car was gaining on us.

Another sound caught my attention over the rushing wind and dying car. "Sexy Back" was playing somewhere. Somewhere nearby.

I looked around until I spotted my book bag at David's feet. "You got my bag?"

By this point, David was huddled against the passenger door, staring at me with naked horror. He shook his head, like he hadn't understood the question before blinking a few times and saying, "Oh . . . um, yeah. I thought you might need it."

"Why did you follow me?"

David looked over his shoulder at the black car. "Huh? Oh, well . . . I wanted to, uh, ask you some more questions about what the hell is going on with you." He turned back around and wiped his glasses on the bottom of his T-shirt. "Of course, *I* thought you were on drugs. I didn't realize you were actually an assassin or something."

He was lying, I could tell. Maybe it was a Paladin thing, or maybe I was finally seeing through him the way he always seemed to see through me.

"Bull," I said.

"What?" He looked at me with wide eyes.

"Bull," I repeated. "You didn't want to ask me more questions about the paper. Why did you follow me?"

"I'm not lying!" he insisted, glancing behind him again.

"Yes," I said calmly, even as the black car got closer, "you are. Why did you follow me?"

The black car thumped our bumper, but I wasn't worried anymore. We were only a few houses away now.

"Because you were crying!" David shouted, his voice cracking with fear, and, I thought, anger. "You were upset and I felt bad about the stupid article, and then that weird shit happened with Ryan, and even if I don't always agree with the things you do at school, you do try and you didn't—"

He broke off and sagged against the seat, closing his eyes. "I just . . . I don't like crying girls, okay?"

We were quiet for a second while I took that in.

"That was very nice of you, David," I finally said. "Now hold on because I'm about to drive into a fence."

"Yeah, okay," he muttered, his eyes still closed. "You do that."

Then his eyes shot open. "Wait, what?"

My house was there on the right, and I swung the Dodge straight through our fence.

We crashed through with enough force to rattle my bones and shatter the windshield into roughly a million spiderweb cracks. But that was okay. I didn't need to see now.

I kept pulling the wheel to the right, which meant that I missed our pool, driving David's car straight to the back corner of our yard.

The black car wasn't so lucky. Not only did it hit the water, it had been going so fast that it hit it with all the force of driving into a brick wall. I could hear the splash, and as I looked in the rearview mirror, I saw the huge wave that came out of the pool.

The Dodge came to a shuddering halt, bumping against something solid that I thought might be my mom's new birdbath.

Whoops.

I put the car in park and turned it off, plunging us into silence. Well, not total silence, since I was breathing pretty hard and David kept mumbling, "Please don't let us be dead, please don't let us be dead."

"David," I said, reaching over to grab his arm. He reached over with his other arm and covered my hand with his.

"Pres?" he said, opening his eyes, which still looked very wide and very blue in his pale face. "We're not dead," he said, almost like he was talking to himself. "How did we not get dead?"

I smiled at him and squeezed his arm. "Because I'm awesome."

He stared at me and his smile got bigger and brighter as the fear drained out of his face. "We're not dead!" he said, like he just now got that we were still sitting in his gross—and now completely busted—car instead of playing harps in the sky or whatever.

I was smiling back, my grin probably exactly as crazy as his. "We're *so* not dead!"

He laughed and the sound was so full of relief that I found myself laughing, too.

He turned to me, still grinning. I was grinning back when he reached out, grabbed the back of my neck, and pulled me to him.

Chapter 9

For one horrifying second, I thought he was going to kiss me. I wasn't really sure how I'd react if he did. I mean, I knew that if he kissed me, it would be a kiss of the "I am so glad I am not dead that I would kiss a flesh-eating zombie were it sitting in this car beside me" variety more than the sexy "I only write mean articles about you because I am secretly in love with you" type.

But it was only a hug. And if I maybe spent a second or two thinking that he actually smelled really nice, or that he was much more solid than he appeared, so what? I was traumatized by all the car chasing/nearly dying.

Luckily, it didn't last long, but when I pulled back, I noticed that my heart was pounding and there was this weird fluttering sensation.

Butterflies.

No, I thought to myself. Near-death flutters of anxiety. That's all.

Then I noticed that David was staring out the shattered windshield, looking as weirded out as I felt.

Oh my God, what was wrong with me? I could barely muster

up the enthusiasm to make out with my own super hot boy-friend, and I was . . . oh dear God, was I blushing? Ugh.

Ugh ugh ugh.

Yup, the car chase had clearly addled my brain.

I was about to say something mean to David, you know, to restore equilibrium, when his eyes got big and he blurted out, "Bad guys in the pool!"

Huh? Was that like thinking of baseball when—OH! Right!

I pushed open my door and leapt out into my yard, taking deep breaths, hoping the cool air and sight of people drowning in my pool might get my hormones or whatever back under control.

I had knocked over Mom's birdbath. It lay in three big pieces right under David's bumper. And then, of course, there was the giant hole in our fence. But those were really the least of my problems. This biggest issue was the black Cadillac currently sinking into my pool.

No sound came from the car, and there didn't appear to be any activity inside, so I guessed the impact had knocked out the driver and any passengers he or she might have had.

David was standing next to me, watching the car as the aqua water bubbled and churned around it. "So are we, um, are we gonna let them drown?"

I was glad he said that. We.

I had killed Dr. DuPont, and I didn't feel bad about that. I couldn't. He had been seconds from killing me when I jammed that shoe into his neck. But whoever was in that black car . . . well, I didn't know what they'd wanted. My gut told me they had been bad guys, but that still didn't make me feel great about letting them drown in my pool.

I was also more than a little worried about explaining this whole thing. All evidence of my fight with Dr. DuPont had mysteriously vanished, but I wasn't sure how whoever had worked that particular mojo could cover *this* up. I expected our neighbors to start congregating in the street any minute now, like they did when the power went out.

David gave a huge sigh and ran his hands over his hair. "Well, this is weird. And awful."

"Yup." My skirt had gotten twisted around my hips somewhere in all of this, and I started straightening it. Anything to avoid looking at the pool.

"Who are you?" David asked me for the second time that day. "International assassin? Ninja? Vampire slayer, maybe?"

I lifted my head. "No, I'm a—"

There was a slight popping sound from the pool, and David and I both turned our attention back to the water.

Which was now empty.

And with one loud crack, the hole in my fence was suddenly gone. I didn't even have to look behind me to know that the screech of metal was David's car repairing itself. In just a few seconds, all evidence of the insane car chase, the crash, all of it, was gone. Then the only sound in my backyard was the singing of birds and the rustling of the leaves.

"That really happened," David said softly. "All that shit, it . . . disappeared, right? I didn't hallucinate that?"

My adrenaline seemed to vanish as completely as the Cadillac, and it was all I could do not to collapse in a heap on the grass. It was one thing to see the aftereffects of stuff disappearing. It was another to see an entire car—with people inside—poof out of existence.

"Yeah," I replied. "That happened."

"Do you know why?"

When I turned to him, David was still staring at the pool, the fingers of his right hand pressed against his temple again.

"No. But . . . David, something seriously weird is going on."

The hand at his temple moved up to tug on his hair as David made a sound that was part sob, part laugh. "You think? Jesus, Harper. You . . . you flipped Ryan Bradshaw like a pancake. You drove a car like Jason Bourne. And then this . . ." He waved his hand at the water. "I don't . . . I mean . . ." His words trailed off and he sank down into a crouch, eyes still fixed on the pool.

Walking over to him, I pulled at the shoulder of his jacket. "Okay, I get that it's weird, and while I totally respect the need for a PTSD moment, we really need to talk."

His eyes moved up to my face, still kind of unfocused. "About what? Why bad guys are chasing you, and why freaking *magic* is apparently real?"

"I actually think the bad guys might be chasing *you*, but yeah."

David staggered backward, and sat down heavily on the grass. As he did, he nearly overturned Mom's statue of two little girls reading on a bench, but I was able to grab it before it fell.

His sleeves, too short as usual, fell back from his thin wrists as he rested his elbows on his knees, hands tugging at his hair. "Hold up, what? You think those guys were after *me*? Why?"

"I don't know. Do *you* know why?" I towered over David, my shadow falling on his body.

Dazed, David shook his head. "I can't—"

And then I saw it. Something flickered across his face and he flinched.

"You do know," I said, yanking him to his feet. "David, what is it?"

He swallowed heavily. "Nothing. It's nothing."

At that moment, I really hated that my superpowers prevented me from shaking the crap out of him. I settled for balling my fist up in the front of his shirt and pulling him down to meet my eyes. "David, look around you. This? *This is crazy-sauce.* And if you know anything that could help me figure out why I'm suddenly Wonder Woman, I need to know it right. Effing. Now."

I actually said the word that time, and David's eyes went so wide I wondered if that had shocked him more than the disappearing Cadillac.

But he never got a chance to answer me.

"Yoo-hoo!" a voice called out from the other side of my fence, and David and I both went still.

"Is that?" I hissed.

"My Aunt Saylor." He gulped.

The back gate swung open, and suddenly Saylor Stark was standing there, a pair of Chanel sunglasses pushed down her nose as she took in the sight of me, shaking and sweaty, clutching the front of her nephew's T-shirt.

"Oh my," she said, and two syllables had never contained so much dismay. "What exactly is going on here?"

David and I practically leapt apart as Saylor moved into the yard, her high heels sinking slightly. The late afternoon sunlight flashed on her silver hair as well as the silver and turquoise jewelry around her neck. Other than a slight grass stain on the hem of her beige trousers, she looked as immaculate as ever.

"I was over at Anne Beckwith's, and I *thought* I saw your car tearing down the street, David James Stark," she said, pushing her sunglasses back into place with one finger. "But I told myself, 'Of course not, Saylor. David would never drive so irresponsibly. Besides, he's meant to be in school right now.'"

She turned her head to me. "As are you, correct, Miss Price?"

"Yes, ma'am," I said feebly. "I . . . I felt sick, and David offered to drive me home."

I couldn't see her eyes behind her dark glasses, but I had a feeling they were very cold. "Really?" she said. "How odd. Because right after I had the thought that David would never, ever drive his car in such a manner, I noticed that *he* was not the one behind the wheel."

Oh God. Of all the people to see me doing my Dale Earnhardt, Jr., impression, it had to be Saylor Stark.

"She asked to drive it," David said, speaking up for the first time. He still seemed a little out of it, and his voice wasn't as strong as normal, but he was still good at thinking on his feet. "She'd never driven one like it before, so she, uh, wanted to."

As one, the three of us looked over at David's pathetic Dodge. Even without its fender and back door mangled, it didn't exactly scream, "DRIVE ME."

Maybe David wasn't that great at thinking on his feet. And

why did he even own a car like that, anyway? Saylor surely could've afforded something nicer. It was probably a point of pride with him, like his weird thrift shop wardrobe.

"I'm sorry, Aunt Saylor," he continued. "I shouldn't have ditched school, but Harper, uh, was sick. And you're always going on about good citizenship."

I tried not to let surprise show on my face. That was actually a pretty good save. Certainly better than "chicks really want to get behind the wheel of my Stratus." And the fact that he'd been able to do it after nearly getting killed *and* dealing with what appeared to be magic was impressive.

"Good citizenship doesn't have to come at the cost of your own morals, David," Saylor snapped. "You know better than to skip class, and I am very disappointed in you. And of course, we haven't even gotten into the completely reckless way you two were driving. I think you and I will be having a long talk when I get done with Cotillion practice this afternoon, young man."

Saylor's gaze swung back to me. "Speaking of, Miss Price, if you're feeling so ill, maybe you'd better sit today's rehearsal out."

"But we're supposed to practice the prayer today," I said, blinking. "I'm leading the prayer."

Her smile was brittle. "I'm sure Miss Franklin will do a fine job filling in. And maybe by Wednesday's practice, you'll be feeling more yourself."

Sick for real now, I could only nod. Behind my parents, Saylor Stark was the last person in the world I wanted to disappoint. And there was no mistaking that tone. Not only had she caught me skipping class, I was skipping class *with her nephew*, whom I had clearly sucked into my downward spiral. If she knew that I'd also made him an accessory to what *might* have been murder . . .

And that's when it hit me. David was Saylor's *nephew*. He had lived with her his whole life. If people wanted to kill him, surely Saylor would know why. But how exactly did you go about asking something like that? *Hi, Miss Saylor, are y'all by any chance in the witness protection program? Or hiding from wizards?* She wouldn't just take the prayer away from me after that. She'd kick me out of the entire Cotillion. Maybe even out of the entire *town*.

As she dusted imaginary dirt from her slacks, I watched Saylor, trying to see if there was any sign that she knew why David and I had been speeding down the street. But between the huge sunglasses and Saylor's Perfect Southern Lady ability to repress any and all emotions, I couldn't tell.

David, shaking off his daze, moved toward his aunt. "Let Harper do the stupid prayer," he said, sounding a bit more like himself. "This isn't her fault."

Saylor's head shot up. "First of all, you will not call the Cotillion prayer 'stupid.' Secondly, you should be at school right now, not drag racing down Ivy Lane. Thirdly, I have told you that you need to be more careful. And going a hundred miles an hour in a car that is on its last legs is hardly careful. What if you'd had another one of your headaches?"

David scowled at her. "My headaches are no big deal," he said, but Saylor held up her hand.

"We are not having this argument in Miss Price's backyard. You're coming with me."

He flung one long arm out toward his Stratus. "My car—"

"You can pick it up in the morning. Harper, I'm sure your parents won't mind if David leaves his vehicle here."

The way she said it left no doubt that refusing was not an option. "It's fine," I said. "And honestly, it's still another few hours until practice, and I'm sure if I took a quick nap and had a sandwich, I'd be fine, too." I ended with a little laugh, as if by sheer force of will, I could make her see the funny side to all of this.

That smile again, the one that felt like a threat. "I'll see you on Wednesday, Harper," she said, and I could practically hear a gavel go down. I'd been found guilty of Unladylike Behavior, Nephew Endangerment, and, if the look she shot my boots was any indication, Improper Footwear.

And if she ever found out about Ryan . . . oh God, *Ryan*. I had to call him. I had to explain. "Say good-bye to Harper, David," Saylor trilled as she began making her way toward David's car, moving on the balls of her feet to keep her heels from sinking again.

David's eyes met mine, and I could tell the shock was definitely wearing off. He was getting that same predatory look he'd had at the Homecoming Dance. "Tomorrow. You and me. *We need to talk*," he said in a low voice.

I couldn't help but roll my eyes. "Duh. But . . . I need to smooth things over with Ryan before I'm seen having sneaky conversations with you. So let me find you tomorrow, okay?"

"Pretty sure ninjas and magic and dead guys trump your boyfriend's insecurity," he hissed, leaning in closer.

"And pretty sure *you* now know I could kick your behind, so why don't you let *me* handle this?" I whispered back. That wasn't true, of course. If David hadn't been rattled, he would've remembered this morning, when I hadn't even been able to slap him. But at least I got a little satisfaction out of seeing him go pale.

"Fine," he said through clenched teeth.

"Thank you," I huffed back.

"David!" Saylor called again, and this time, there was a definite edge to her trill.

"Tomorrow," he said again, pointing at me.

"Tomorrow," I agreed.

Chapter 10

"So ARE you mad at me about yesterday?"

I gave a shuddery sigh as I slid into the passenger seat of Bee's car the next morning. Thank God, she'd made a Starbucks run before coming to pick me up. I took a scalding sip of my latte, then nearly choked on it.

Bee always got me a skinny vanilla latte. This was a triple espresso that was so strong, I was surprised my teeth hadn't melted. Then I noticed how rigidly she was sitting in her seat, and that the rap music she liked was especially aggressive today.

For a second, I sat there, trying to figure out why I *would* be mad at Bee. I'd spent the night tossing and turning, worrying about why Ryan wasn't answering my calls. I must have called him at least ten times, but he'd never picked up. And when I hadn't been worrying over that, I was thinking of Saylor Stark, the look on her face when she'd seen me grabbing her nephew. God, what if she'd heard me use the F-word?

Then I remembered. Bee had done the Cotillion prayer for me yesterday, and she'd sent like three texts last night that I hadn't responded to.

"Of course I'm not mad at you," I said, but I must not have sounded very convincing.

"You seem like you are. Harper, you always answer my texts. And a couple of people said you had a big fight with Ryan yesterday and ditched school."

My heart stuttered in my chest at that. Oh God, had Ryan *told* someone what happened? Did the entire school know I'd flipped him like a freaking omelet?

But no. No, if Ryan had told anyone, it would have been Brandon, and Brandon would've told Bee, and Bee definitely would've mentioned that first. I tried to keep my sigh of relief quiet before replying, "I told you, I was sick."

I reached out to turn the radio down, but Bee slapped my hand. "No touching my tunes until you 'fess up. Were you really sick, or did you have a fight with Ryan?"

"I was sick," I insisted again. "Remember the night of the Homecoming Dance? I . . . I must have some kind of bug."

Bee frowned. "Something was definitely up that night," she murmured, and for the first time, I noticed that while she might have been asking if I was mad, she was the one who seemed pissed.

"What's that supposed to mean?" My brain was racing. Oh my God, had Bee put Mr. Hall's and Dr. DuPont's disappearance together with my pukeage?

A muscle worked in Bee's jaw, and finally she spit out, "Mary Beth was going home for her free period yesterday, and she said she saw David Stark coming out of your backyard. She said he looked really weird, and then later, she saw Ryan leaving school, and he was super upset, and . . ."

She trailed off and my fingers tightened around my coffee cup. "Go ahead."

"Mary Beth said that you and David have always been kind of . . . sparky. So she thinks there's something going on with the two of you."

I frowned at the "sparky" bit. David and I did not have . . . sparks. What we had was a feud that had been running since we were both in diapers. Something Bee of all people should have understood.

"Is that what you think, Bee?" I asked.

She shrugged. Today, Bee was wearing a huge pair of sunglasses that seemed to hide half her face. Her hair was done up in a high ponytail, and I could see a muscle twitch in her cheek, like she was grinding her teeth. "Explains a lot. Like why you've been so freaking weird lately."

Then she glanced at me. "Explains what was going on in the bathroom the night of Homecoming."

It was way too early in the morning for this conversation, I decided, drinking a little more espresso. It still tasted like battery acid, but I needed the caffeine. I already had a slight headache.

"I'm not going to pretend to understand why you suddenly have a thing for David when you have *Ryan Bradshaw* as a boyfriend," Bee continued, yelling over the music. I went to turn it down, but she pushed my hand out of the way. "What pisses me off is that you didn't tell me about it."

"There's nothing to tell!" I shouted. "I'm not cheating on Ryan, I don't have a thing for David, and I was *sick* yesterday. That's it! Not fighting with my boyfriend, not pregnant, and not any of the other hundreds of things you and Mary Beth probably guessed while y'all were talking behind my back. Oh, and by the way, David was at my house with his aunt. I'm guessing Mary Beth left out that little tidbit."

Guilt, or maybe hurt, flickered over Bee's face. "Do you think I'm a total dumbass?"

My head was pounding, and my face felt hot. "Right now, yeah, I do!"

Bee whipped into a parking place and braked so hard that I jerked forward in the seat.

She pushed her sunglasses up to glare at me. "I caught the two of you in the bathroom and you burst into tears."

"That was actually a little *after* you found us," I muttered, but she was on a roll.

"I know you want everyone to think you're perfect, but you don't have to pretend with me." She thunked her head back against the gray leather, and a few girls walking by shot curious glances at the car. "Or at least I thought you didn't."

She slumped back into her seat, shaking her head. "I tell you everything," she said softly. *"Everything."*

I put my drink back in the holder and took her hand. "Hey," I said softly. "I tell you everything, too. I promise." Guilt tasted more bitter than the espresso, but I told myself that it wasn't technically a lie. After all, I wasn't lying to her about Ryan and David. Not really. Still, for just a second, I thought about how nice it would feel to tell someone—someone who loved me, someone who wasn't David Stark—about what was going on.

But it was too bizarre, and for all I knew, it might also be dangerous. Until I had a better idea of who was after David and why, the best thing I could do was keep things as normal as possible.

So I leaned forward and said, "Ryan and I did have a little argument yesterday, but it was nothing. We'll be fine. I plan on making up with him as soon as I see him today. And there is nothing going on with me and David Stark."

She swiveled her head to face me. Bee's eyes had always been both spooky and beautiful, almost startlingly dark against the peachiness of her skin and the wheat blond of her hair. Now, they were narrowed and wary. "Promise?"

I held up my hand. "Pinky swear."

After a pause, she giggled and hooked my finger with hers. The little silver ring Brandon had gotten for her—complete with a pink cubic zirconia that we will not talk about—dug into my skin. "Pinky swears are sacred, you know."

"I do," I said, sitting up primly. "So I don't use it lightly."

Her grin turned into something like a leer. "So when you and Ryan make up, is it gonna be hot?"

Rolling my eyes, I disentangled our pinkies. "Perv."

That sorted, we got out of the car. Then, out of the corner of my eye, I caught sight of David standing outside Wallace Hall, waving at me. He was wearing a bright purple argyle sweater over a white button-down and jeans, so he wasn't exactly inconspicuous.

As subtly as I could, I flicked my hand at David behind my

back. I knew we needed to talk, but with Bee on high alert where he was concerned, now was not the time.

"I can't believe we still have a sub in history," Bee said, snapping my attention back to her.

"Oh, is, uh, Dr. DuPont out?" I asked, trying not to imagine him standing in front of me, my shoe sticking out of his neck.

"Apparently," Bee said, nodding across the courtyard. Mrs. Hillyard, the substitute teacher from yesterday, was hurrying up the steps into Wallace.

"But Dr. DuPont was a jackass anyway," she added. "Didn't he give you a hard time?"

You could say that. "Oh, not really," I replied, just in case there were undercover police officers hiding in the bushes or something. "I actually kind of liked him."

"Liked who?" Brandon asked, coming up to join us. "Me? Because I can tell you one thing, Miss Harper here is not a fan of the Bran Man."

"And I'm not a fan of you calling yourself that," Bee muttered, even as she let him take her hand and swing it.

"No, I'm serious!" Brandon insisted, flicking his blond hair out of his eyes. "Yesterday, she full-on smacked me in the middle of the hall. For no reason!"

"Oh, I'm sure," Bee said sarcastically.

"It's true," Brandon insisted before shooting me a sideways look. "Is that why Ryan's out today? Did you smack him around, too?"

That was way too close to the truth for comfort. Frowning, I asked, "He isn't here today?"

"Not yet," Brandon said, nodding toward the parking lot. Sure enough, Ryan's car wasn't in its usual spot. Heart sinking, I did my best to look concerned, but not panicked.

"Maybe he's running late," I offered.

David chose that moment to walk over to us, and next to me, I felt Bee stiffen a little.

"Harper, can I talk to you for a sec?"

"The bell's about to ring," I said to David, hoping he heard that as *Friend Time, not right now.*

He frowned. "We really need to talk about yesterday." He had gotten my message, and now he was sending one of his own: *I don't care.*

"What happened—" Bee asked, but I was already tugging her away.

"Your apology was more than sufficient," I called breezily over my shoulder. "We're fine."

I could feel David glaring at my back, but I kept pulling Bee toward the school. Yes, yes, David might be my noble cause, but Bee was my best friend. There was a chance I'd already screwed up the boyfriend thing. I didn't want to screw up what I had with Bee, too.

"You sure you don't want to talk to him?" she asked once we'd walked through the front doors.

"Positive," I replied. "I told you, it's nothing more than the usual me and David Stark Mutual Disdain Society thing acting up again."

Bee pulled her lower lip between her teeth, stopping just in front of the main office. I thought she glanced back outside toward the parking lot and Ryan's empty spot. But all she said was, "See you at lunch?"

"Absolutely!" I chirped, doing my best to ignore David as he stormed past us.

Nothing happened the rest of the morning, but that didn't stop me from jumping every time the bell rang. I also went out of my way to avoid the English hall, wondering if I'd ever feel safe at school again. There were no Pop Rocks in my blood, and there was no summons to the headmaster's office to talk about Dr. DuPont, but I stayed on edge. Ryan's absence didn't help. Was he hurt, or too freaked out to even look at me?

By the end of first period, I'd made up my mind to call him, one more time. Cell phones were a major no-no during school hours, but I decided to risk it in the bathroom.

I'd just turned down the corridor when a hand shot out of the nearby janitor's closet and hauled me into the dark.

Chapter 11

WITHOUT MAKING a sound, I went to slug my attacker, only to have my hand freeze in midair.

Of course.

"Are you insane?" I hissed, batting David's hand away. It didn't touch him, obviously, but it still made me feel better.

"I told you we'd talk today," he whispered.

"Right. Talk. Like normal people, not . . . skulking around in broom closets."

"Skulking? Really?" David raised his eyebrows, and even in the dim light, I could see the smirk forming.

"First of all, I'm not taking crap about word choice from the guy who uses 'egregious' in every article he writes. And secondly, this"— I gestured to the cluttered shelves, the cleaning products, the damp mops—"definitely warrants the use of skulking."

Rubbing his hand over his eyes, David heaved a sigh. "Fine. We're skulking. And since the bell rings in five minutes, we need to skulk fast. Tell me everything."

I shifted my weight from one foot to the other. "It's . . . kind of long. And intense. And not something that can be spilled between classes in the janitor's closet."

"Try," David said, his teeth clenched.

Frowning, I put my hands on my hips. "Fine. On the night of the Homecoming Dance, a janitor passed some kind of superpower on to me before he died. Then I killed Dr. DuPont with my shoe, but when I came back to the bathroom, everything had disappeared and I thought I was going crazy, but then those bad guys chased us yesterday, and they also disappeared, so I'm not crazy, but there's something *super* crazy going on, and I think it's connected to you since I'm totally incapable of hurting you. That's why I couldn't slap you the other day even though, trust me, I really, really wanted to."

I took a deep breath. "So there. That's the fast version. Any questions?"

David stumbled backward, sitting down hard on an upsidedown bucket, then shook his head. "I . . . I think my brain actually shut down," he said. He braced his elbows on his knees, leaning forward with his steepled fingers covering his mouth.

"After yesterday, I thought whatever you said, I'd be good. I mean, dude disappeared. And my car magically repaired itself. I should be unshockable, you know?"

David still wasn't looking at me, so I knelt down in front of him as gingerly as I could, trying not to touch the ground or accidentally flash him. "I know," I told him. "It sounds insane. It *is* insane."

His eyes fixed on mine. "You killed someone," he said, his voice barely audible. "With a shoe."

"He had a sword," I fired back and then, to my shock, David burst out laughing.

"A sword. Our history teacher attacked you with a sword in the bathroom and you killed him." He dropped his head into his hands, only to raise it a second later. "Wait. You said a janitor passed these powers on to you. A janitor who died. Mr. Hall?"

Surprised, I nodded. "Yeah. Had you noticed that he was missing?"

But David was pressing his face into his hands again, moaning. "Oh my God, oh my God."

"What?" When he didn't answer, I tugged on his sleeve. Apparently that much I could do. "What do you know about Mr. Hall?"

When David lifted his face, he was pale. "He rented the little house at the back of our property."

I rocked back on my heels. "Mr. Hall *lived* with you?"

"Not with me, but more or less in my backyard, yeah. He . . . he took off a few days ago. Or at least that's what my aunt thought. I even asked her if we should, like, report it or something, but she said he was a grown man, he could come and go as he pleased."

Now David's skin had taken a bit of a greenish cast, and I grabbed one of the extra buckets, just in case. "I was at school Friday night, working on the paper," he said, almost like he was talking to himself. "Dr. DuPont . . . do you think he was after me, and killed Mr. Hall when he got in the way?"

"I don't know," I told him. "But that makes sense. And you're sure nothing like this had ever happened to you before?"

Briefly, he was the old David again. "Are you asking me if I'm sure no one has ever tried to kill me before, Pres? Trust me, nothing like this has ever happened."

"That you know of."

That wiped the smirk right off his face. "Oh God. You're right. If you hadn't told me, I never would've known about Friday night. Mr. Hall and Dr. DuPont and you and swords . . ."

He trailed off, and for a long moment, he sat there, totally quiet, twisting his fingers and breathing. Then he glanced back up at me, he nodded. "Okay. Processed. Now what do we do?"

As bizarre as it sounds, I wanted to . . . I don't know, hug him. He'd taken all this weirdness and done the same thing I'd managed to do with it: take it in, feel crazy for a little bit, and then deal.

Maybe David Stark wasn't completely useless.

"When Dr. DuPont tried to kill me, he called me a 'Paladin.'"

"Like Charlemagne," David said, almost to himself.

"What?"

Shaking his head, David said, "Charlemagne. He was this French king—"

Irritated, I cut him off with a wave of my hand. "I know that. I was in AP European History, too. But what does he have to do with Paladins?"

"He had a group of knights called Paladins. I don't remember anything about them having superpowers, though."

Well, that was something, at least.

As briefly as I could, I filled David in on what I'd learned about Paladins so far. When I finished, he nodded. "So you think I'm your noble cause."

"I really hope you're not, but it's looking like that's it. Which is why, yet again, I'm going to ask you if there's anything you can think of, any reason people would care about you enough to want to kill you. I know you write annoying articles, but if I haven't wanted to murder you yet, I don't know why anyone else would."

He gave a little snort of laughter. "Fair enough. But I'm telling you, Harper, there's nothing. I'm just . . . a guy."

But he was flexing his fingers, and I knew there was something he wasn't telling me.

"David," I told him, reaching out to touch his knee before I thought better of it. "Seriously. Whatever it is, no matter how random you think it might be, you need to spill, and you need to do it *now*."

His blue eyes blinked behind his glasses, and for a second, I thought he was going to give me the brush-off again. But then he sighed, tipping his head back to study the ceiling. "It's so stupid I can't believe I'm even going to tell you. But . . . the debate club thing. The article saying that Matt Hampton had stolen the other team's questions . . ."

I nodded. That had been a pretty big deal a few months back. David had snuck the article into the paper after hours, which had seriously pissed off Mrs. Laurent. But not because it was underhanded. The match David was talking about? It hadn't even *happened* yet. That debate had been scheduled for the Saturday after David wrote the article.

He didn't have any excuse for why he'd made it up, and I honestly think he'd have gotten expelled if it hadn't been for his aunt's influence. I still couldn't believe Mrs. Laurent let him stay on the paper, but I guessed that could be chalked up to Saylor, too.

"I know everyone thinks I wrote that article to be a dick or whatever. But the thing is, Pres, when I wrote it . . . it was like I was sure it had happened. I knew it. I couldn't tell you how or who told it to me, but I was positive it had happened. I never would've written it if I hadn't been."

I took that in. "Okay. So maybe you . . . I don't know, dreamed it. I've had dreams that seemed completely real, and—"

But David was already shaking his head. "No, I've always had weird dreams. Like, seriously intense, crazy dreams. I even talked to Aunt Saylor about taking me to the doctor for it, but she said vivid dreams ran in our family."

"Huh," I said, filing that away for later. David didn't seem to notice.

"But this wasn't like those. This was something I . . . I knew."

"So you thought something was true, and it ended up not being true. That's not exactly a superpower, David. And certainly not worth chasing you down over."

David drew his legs up, pressing his heels against the edge of the bucket as he rested his elbows on his knees. "That's what I thought. That maybe too many late nights had finally gotten to me."

I found myself nodding in sympathy.

"But then, the day after the academic hearing, Matt Hampton caught me in the bathroom. Tossed me against a wall and asked who had told me about the questions. He had stolen them, Pres,"

David said, his expression grave. "He was going to use them. But . . . hadn't yet."

Okay, that was a little more interesting. "So you . . . you can see the future?"

David rolled his eyes. "Okay, it sounds really stupid when you say it like that."

"David, we're huddled in a supply closet talking about killer history teachers and superpowered knights. Telling the future, honestly, doesn't make it any weirder. In fact, it makes it some-what clearer. At least now we know why someone might want to kill you."

David snorted. "Yes, my ability to not predict debate club out-comes is incredibly impressive."

The bell rang. It startled both of us, and we shot to our feet. Kneeling down, I'd been a few inches below David, but when we stood up, we were suddenly way too close, and I found myself stumbling backward away from him.

Once again, my chest tightened, and there was that weird fluttering sensation that was like butterflies. But it couldn't be butterflies. I did *not* have butterflies over David Stark.

But he backed up, too, a weird look on his face. Then he cleared his throat. "Okay," he said. "I'll check out Mr. Hall's house today. See if there's anything there. What are you planning on doing? Other than keeping people from killing me." His eyes wid-ened. "Oh man, how are you supposed to do that? Mr. Hall lived with us and worked at the school. We can't be that . . . that . . . *close* all the time."

I nodded in agreement. "And logistics are the least of it," I muttered, thinking about Ryan and Bee, both of whom had reasons to want me and David to spend less time together. Then something else occurred to me. Mr. Hall had died defending David. Bled out on the bathroom floor from a giant *scimitar* wound. Was I expected to defend David to the death? *My* death?

Something must have shown on my face because David squinted at me. "What?"

I shook my head. We could get into how far my protective services extended later. "Whenever you're in danger, I can sense it. There's this . . . jumpiness and pain and stuff. I can't exactly miss it. Besides, this town's not that big, and we only live a few blocks apart. And I am here at school every day. As for the rest of it, we'll . . . I don't know. Once we figure out what's going on, maybe we can figure out some way to stop it."

"Good plan," he said, even as he gulped nervously. "Look, you said the internet didn't yield much in terms of answers. But if this Paladin thing is ancient, maybe we should use . . . I don't know, older sources."

"By which you mean books?" I asked, quirking an eyebrow.

"Exactly." Now that some of the color was returning to his face, he looked more like the David I was used to. "When the debate club thing happened, I checked out a book from the library about . . ." He trailed off and cleared his throat a little. "Um, you know, people who see the future and stuff. Here."

He reached into his backpack and pulled out a thin black book, handing it to me. *They Saw the Future!* was emblazoned on the cover in bright purple foil.

I studied it for a second, pressing my lips together. "It's like you *want* me to make fun of you."

Scowling, David went to take the book back, but I held it out of reach. "No, you're right. There might be something in here. It's better than nothing."

David didn't look much happier, but he nodded. "Right. I've marked some of the pages I thought were the most interesting. Plus we can go to the library this afternoon and—"

"No," I said automatically. I'd already been caught spending one afternoon with David Stark. If we got caught two days in a row, even if it was in an unsexy place like the library . . .

David scowled, and I hurried on. "I only mean not *today*. I have . . . family stuff."

I wasn't sure David was going to accept that for an answer, but in the end, he gave a terse nod. "Okay. Maybe this weekend then."

Today was Tuesday. Surely by Saturday, things with me and Ryan would be sorted out. "Saturday is fine," I said, bending down to scoop up my backpack. "And that was a good idea. The book thing."

"Maybe the next time you pay me a compliment, you can try not to sound like you're about to hurl." He smirked, a tiny dimple appearing in one cheek.

I rolled my eyes.

"Okay," he said, going to open the door. "I'll pick you up at around nine on Saturday."

I shook my head. "I'll pick you up. One ride in that deathtrap you call a car was plenty, thanks."

"You know, it actually wasn't a deathtrap until someone decided to drive it down a residential street at roughly a bazillion miles an hour."

"To save your life," I threw over my shoulder as I left the closet.

Luckily, David had enough sense to let me leave first. Also luckily, I only got one girl looking at me as I shut the door behind me. I gave her my brightest smile. "Wanted to make sure everything was spick-and-span in there!"

Chapter 12

I DROVE past Ryan's house on the way home that afternoon. His car was there, but I didn't have the guts to go up to the house. Instead, I went to the library. Maybe I could find out some of this stuff on my own, and then I wouldn't need any more alone time with David.

Except you're supposed to protect him, I reminded myself as I searched the shelves. *That will probably require plenty of alone time.*

Unless there was some way out of this whole thing. With that thought in mind, I grabbed two different biographies of Charlemagne. Between those and *They Saw The Future!*, maybe I'd figure *something* out.

Mom and Dad were both at work when I got home from the library, and aside from Bee texting me a few times, my phone was depressingly quiet, and I was, well . . . depressed. It seemed almost impossible to believe that yesterday, I was driving to school, happy and excited about my newfound superpowers. And now, after only a few days, I'd already killed a man (possibly more than one, actually, if the pool thing had worked), jujitsued my boyfriend, and made Saylor Stark, the one woman I lived to impress, think I was some kind of hot-rodding skank. And now David knew about them. David, who practically made a habit of ruining my life, knew the biggest secret I'd ever had.

To keep my mind off all of that, I paged through the books. Unfortunately, they were about as helpful as the internet had been. The Charlemagne book mentioned Paladins, naming them as some kind of elite bodyguard force for the king. There was even a picture of them, looking entirely too skinny to be badass killers. As I studied the reproduced painting, I was at least grateful that their lame burgundy suits no longer seemed to be the official uniform. Burgundy washed me out, and velvet made me itch.

Other than that, there wasn't much there. The book referenced the Paladins guarding the king, but it never mentioned noble causes or superpowers, so it seemed kind of useless. After all, I was pretty sure David Stark wasn't a king.

But that thing with the debate club, no matter how stupid he thought it was, had to be important. It wasn't like whether or not the debate club cheated was a major, world-changing event, but still. If David could see the future, no matter how small or insignificant those visions seemed to be . . . yeah, that might be something people would kill for.

Tossing that book aside, I picked up *They Saw the Future!* It was one of those Time-Life books they used to sell on TV. I was pretty sure my Aunt Jewel had a few, but I'd never seen this one before. I opened it up, scanning the chapters, muttering their titles aloud. "'Visions of Doom,' 'Seen Too Late,' 'Dreams of Destiny' . . ."

David had put a little Post-it flag beside that chapter in the table of contents.

He'd marked another one, too. "Oracles." I flipped the book to the page listed, snorting with laughter when I saw the picture taking up most of the page. It was a scantily clad girl, wearing what appeared to be a large, transparent handkerchief, her head thrown back, her eyes closed. "Okay, you weren't marking this one for the information," I murmured, but when I turned the page, I saw that David had actually put more flags on the pages not featuring half-naked ladies.

"'Historically, Oracles came into their power in their teen years,'" I read next to one marker. "'The visions often did not reach full potency until the Oracle was between eighteen and twenty years of age.'"

I turned another page, and found more little paper flags. "'The original Oracles at Delphi were controlled by five men known as the "Ephors," elected men who served as a sort of Parliament. Oracles were strictly female.'"

"Well, there you go then," I said quietly. Unless David had a secret bigger than the debate club thing, it was looking like we could dismiss any chance of him being an Oracle.

But then another flag caught my eye. "Oracles were greatly prized commodities, and it was rumored that most of the great leaders of the world—Genghis Khan, Elizabeth I, Charlemagne—all had Oracles at their disposal."

The hair on the back of my neck stood up. David wasn't a girl, that was for sure, but I knew Paladins were connected to Charlemagne. And if Oracles were, too . . .

I reached out for the Charlemagne book, flipping it back to the page on Paladins, my eyes scanning for anything about Oracles. There was nothing, but once again, I found myself staring at the illustration of the Paladins in their fancy little uniforms. Their fancy, burgundy uniforms embroidered with gold thread in the shape of—

I grabbed the psychic book again. There, over the picture of the half-naked Oracle, was a little symbol, like a skinny figure eight, turned on its side. It was the same shape embroidered on the Paladins' uniforms.

"Holy crap," I muttered under my breath.

"Harper?"

Startled, I looked up from the book. Ryan was there. Standing in my doorway. And he was smiling at me.

Okay, so the smile was kind of tentative, and he seemed a little . . . wary, hovering there by the door, but still. He was *here*.

I immediately pushed myself into a sitting position, shoving the books away and wishing I was wearing something a little more flattering than my sweats and one of his old basketball T-shirts. But his expression softened when he saw "Grove Academy Raiders" scrawled across my chest. "I wondered where that shirt ended up," he said, lips lifting. There were shadows underneath his eyes, and his wavy hair seemed a little poufier than normal. It was the closest I'd ever seen Ryan to looking "rough" since the time he'd had the flu sophomore year.

"Oh my God, Ryan, I am so sorry about yesterday," I blurted out. "I was afraid you were going to hit David, and I don't know, get suspended or something, and I . . . freaked out. Did I hurt you?"

Sighing, Ryan came in and sat on the edge of my bed. "I really wish I could say no, because it kind of hurts my masculinity to admit my tiny girlfriend kicked my ass."

"I didn't kick it so much as *throw* it," I said, wanting him to laugh. *Needing* him to laugh.

And he did. Kind of. It was more a huff of breath than his normal laugh, but I would take it. "Where did you learn how to do that anyway?" he asked. His eyes searched my face, and I twisted my fingers in the bedspread.

"Self-defense class. I guess I took it a little more seriously than I thought." Lifting my head, I tentatively moved my fingers closer to his. "Is that why you weren't at school today? Because I hurt you?"

Ryan shook his head. "I was a little sore, yeah, but I . . . I needed some time to think." Hesitantly, he reached out and took my hands between his. His hands were warm and big, dwarfing mine. "Harper, believe it or not, the kung fu isn't really what I wanted to talk about. I mean, it's part of it, but . . ." He paused, looking down at our joined hands. "I just . . . things are weird with us."

"No, they're not," I said immediately, and when he quirked an eyebrow, I sighed and rolled my shoulders. "Okay, yes, the past few days have been a little intense, with Homecoming and all, and Cotillion coming up, and the, uh, flipping you bit."

Ryan shook his head, a tiny crease appearing between his

brows. "No, it's been going on a lot longer than the past few days."

Okay, now I was confused. Sure, my superpowers had been throwing things off since Friday, but before that, everything with me and Ryan had been fine. Better than fine. We were happy.

"I'm not blaming you," Ryan was saying. "You had a really rough year with—with your sister and everything, and I know getting college stuff together is freaking you out—"

"No, it's not," I said, and the corners of Ryan's mouth turned down.

"And that's another thing. Lately, it's like I can't say anything without you contradicting it."

"I don't—oh. Sorry."

Ryan ran a hand over his hair, ruffling it. "I love you," he said at last. "You know that. But it's . . . it's like we're speaking two different languages most of the time. Harper." He tugged on my hand. "If there's something going on with you, you can tell me, okay?"

For a second, I really thought about telling him. I wasn't sure how I was going to spin it, exactly, but there had to be something I could say. Some way of letting him know it definitely wasn't *him*, it was me. And then a funny expression crossed his face. "Is it David Stark?"

Maybe it was because the question was so unexpected, or maybe because it *was* David Stark—in a way—but whatever the reason, my reaction was . . . not great.

I made this kind of spluttering sound that was kind of like a laugh, but mostly involved me nearly spitting all over Ryan. "W-what? What would David Stark have to do with anything?"

"You guys seemed pretty . . . intense yesterday," Ryan said, dropping my hand.

"Yeah, we were *intensely arguing* over him writing that stupid article," I said even as I had a sudden vision of me and David, laughing in his car. Hugging. God, we had *hugged*.

Now Ryan was frowning. "But you're always arguing with him. Or talking about him. Or competing with him. And sometimes I wonder how you can be so obsessed with someone you supposedly hate."

"I'm not obsessed," I corrected before I could stop myself, and his mouth tightened. "Forget it," I said quickly, rising up on my knees to scoot closer to him. "I promise you, David Stark is . . . nothing to me." And he wasn't. I mean, he may have been some future-telling guy I was supposed to protect, possibly unto *death*, but other than that . . .

Ryan seemed less than convinced, so I leaned forward and pressed my lips to his. He hesitated for a second, but then, finally, he kissed me back. As his hand slid up to tangle in my hair, I moved forward, still on my knees. Ryan's other arm tightened around my waist, and I sank into the kiss, trying for a few seconds to turn my mind off.

It was nice. I know you're probably supposed to use words like "hot" or "amazing" to describe your boyfriend kissing you, and we've had plenty of make-outs I could describe that way, but "nice" was good, too. Comforting. Stable.

When we pulled apart, Ryan had that happy, glazed look that told me all thoughts of David Stark and my ninja moves and basically anything else had been obliterated.

Smiling, he leaned forward, pressing his forehead to mine. "So we're good?" he said, and I realized we hadn't really talked about anything. He'd brought up stuff, I'd denied it, and then we'd made out for a little while. It was becoming something of a pattern.

But that probably means we're good at conflict resolution, I thought.

"We're better than good," I told him, smiling back.

Still rubbing one of my hands, Ryan glanced down. "So what were you reading so intently it made you use a four-letter word?"

Before I could stop him, he picked up *They Saw the Future!* Both of his eyebrows went up as he studied the Oracle. "Whoa."

I snatched the book back, half shoving it under my bed. "Doing some research. Essay on ancient Greece for a college application thingie."

I'd been so happy to see Ryan that for a few minutes, all thoughts of Paladins and Oracles and whatever the heck was going on with me and David Stark had fled my brain. But looking at the picture reminded me that while things may have been better in Boyfriend Land, the rest of my life was only getting twistier.

Chapter 13

THANKS to a little more making out, Ryan seemed willing to let the subject drop, and I think he'd totally forgotten about it by the time we heard the garage door opening. "Your mom," he said, moving back.

"Yeah, we better get downstairs." Mom loved Ryan and I think she already thought of him as her son-in-law, but that still didn't mean she'd be okay with the two of us alone in my bedroom.

We made it to the living room before she came in, both of us striking nonchalant poses, me on the couch, him in my dad's chair. "Har—oh, you have company," Mom said as she came in the living room. She glanced back and forth between us and decided no rules were being violated. "Excellent!" she said. "Four hands to help me with groceries."

Once we'd helped Mom unload the car, Ryan decided to head home. After one last kiss, he drove away, and I went back into the kitchen. As I did, I spotted the space where David's car had been yesterday. He'd gotten it this morning, apparently—I'd left the gate unlocked for him, but I hadn't seen him. Still, it reminded me that while things with my boyfriend might be okay for the time being, things with the Starks definitely were not.

But I had an idea. While Mom put groceries away, I rummaged around in the pantry, grabbing flour, some spices, and a can of crushed pineapple. Dumping those on the counter, I fished out a mixing bowl and some measuring cups and went to work.

"What are you doing?" Mom asked, setting the paper bags of food on the counter.

"Making a cake," I replied. I measured out a tablespoon of vanilla as Mom walked over to the bowl, taking in the assembled ingredients. "Hummingbird cake? Fancy. Who's the lucky recipient?"

"Miss Saylor." Reaching in one of the drawers, I pulled out the biggest spoon I could find.

Mom gave me a careful look. She knew what hummingbird cake meant. "And what did you do that requires a 'sorry I screwed up' cake?"

I was already lucky the school hadn't called Mom and told her about me skipping class, so I decided to keep it as simple as possible. "David and I had a thing the other day."

Mom heaved a sigh. "Harper . . ."

"We weren't fighting," I quickly added, earning me a snort of laughter.

"That's a first, then."

"We had a disagreement, that's all. Miss Saylor saw us, and I thought a cake would smooth things over a little bit." Which it would, hopefully. And it would give me a good excuse to go tell David about the connection I'd made between Paladins and Oracles.

With a rueful smile, Mom walked over to the fridge and pulled out the eggs and sugar for me. "Well, in that case, let me help. You're a good baker, but you're not the best one in this family."

Mom cracked the eggs in a separate bowl while I lifted two bananas out of the fruit basket on the counter. We fell into a comfortable silence as she whisked and I mashed. And then, when I leaned over to scrape the bananas into her eggs and sugar mixture, Mom gave a little chuckle. "Do you remember how bad Leigh-Anne was at baking?"

I watched her out of the corner of my eye as I started to stir. It wasn't that I didn't want to talk about my sister, but I never knew how it would go. Sometimes, Mom could look at pictures of her and tell stories, and it was fine. We'd smile or laugh, and then move on to some other topic.

Other times, her voice would get tight, and her lip would tremble, and then the tears would come. And even though I knew it was awful of me, when she got like that, all I wanted to do was run away. To ignore it.

But there were no tears in Mom's voice now. "Yeah," I said carefully. "The baking soda brownies."

Mom's chuckle turned into a real laugh. "Yes! Oh God, I knew I should've tasted them before we started wrapping them up for the bake sale."

Now I smiled, too. "Yeah, but even though they were terrible, Leigh-Anne sold all of them, remember? Said they were special 'vitamin brownies' and that's why they tasted so bad."

"And then you told her she shouldn't lie at a church bake sale," Mom added, holding the mixing bowl as I dumped the wet ingredients into the dry.

"Right." I nodded. "But she said the more brownies she sold, the better it was for the church, so God would understand."

We both laughed again, and then that silence fell, this time a little heavier than before.

"That's the Leigh-Anne I wish people would remember," Mom finally said. Her voice wasn't tight, and her lips were steady, but sadness clung to every word. "I wish people could focus on her, not . . . not how she died."

I wanted that, too. More than anything. But Leigh-Anne's death hadn't only been a nuclear bomb going off in the middle of my family. It had been a scandal. A source of gossip. The pretty and popular Homecoming Queen getting drunk on prom night, wrecking her car, killing herself and nearly killing her boyfriend? It wasn't something people would easily forget.

They wouldn't forget no matter how much Mom wished, or how hard I tried to make up for my sister's one stupid decision. Not that I thought running SGA or organizing charity bake sales could wipe out the memory of that night. But maybe I could . . . I don't know, reset the balance.

Clearing my throat, I turned away and grabbed a few cake pans from the cabinets. I focused on pouring the batter, waiting for Mom to leave the kitchen and go up to her bedroom, the way she almost always did when we started talking about Leigh-Anne.

But to my surprise, she started unwrapping the packages of cream cheese for the icing. "I hope Saylor appreciates all the trouble you're going through."

"It's not that much trouble," I insisted, sliding the cake pans into the oven. "I've been meaning to make hummingbird cake for The Aunts for a while now."

At the mention of The Aunts, Mom rolled her eyes affectionately. "Well, don't let them know you gave their cake away to Saylor."

The Aunts were actually my great-aunts, but since my grandmother—their sister—had died when I was a baby, they'd kind of adopted me as a granddaughter by proxy. They got together at my Aunt Jewel's house every Friday afternoon to play cards, and I usually tried to stop by, but between school and Cotillion, I'd been too busy lately. It had probably been nearly a month since—

Suddenly, what Mom said registered. "What do you mean? Don't The Aunts like Saylor?" They'd never said anything to me about her, and trust me, if The Aunts weren't crazy about someone, they didn't exactly keep it a secret.

Mom shrugged as she started to whip the cream cheese and sugar together. "Saylor's monopoly on all major town events has never sat well with them. Especially since she's still a relative newcomer and a Yankee."

Now I rolled my eyes. "She's been here for nearly eighteen years, and she's from *Virginia*."

"You know The Aunts don't consider Virginia the South." Triumphantly, she pushed the bowl of icing toward me. "Can you take it from here?"

"Sure, thanks," I replied, but my mind was still on The Aunts. I didn't know why I hadn't thought of it before. If there was something weird about the Stark family, they would know it. They knew everything. Seriously, why had I wasted any time searching the internet when I had them? I made a mental note to stop by Aunt Jewel's on Friday—and to buy more cake ingredients.

Mom and I chatted while the cakes baked, and once they were done, I stuck them in the fridge to cool and went to my room to make myself a little more presentable. That accomplished, I headed back to the kitchen to find Mom frosting the cake for me.

"You're seriously going to take this to Saylor tonight?" Mom asked, nodding to the microwave clock. "It's nearly seven."

"Which is perfect timing," I insisted. "After dinner, but before people start getting ready for bed."

Mom looked up, a strange expression flitting across her face.

"Harper, you know . . . you don't have to prove anything. Not to me, or Saylor Stark, or this entire town. You could just—"

"Chill?" I suggested, thinking of Ryan.

Mom didn't laugh. "I worry about you. You've always taken things so seriously, and—" She broke off with a little laugh. "While I'm proud of all you've accomplished, it's not like the fate of the world depends on dance decorations or when you bring people cake. Or Cotillion."

I tried to shrug that off. Again, what was wrong with a little dedication? But Mom's words seemed to lodge somewhere inside my chest. She was right that the *whole* world didn't revolve around what I did at the Grove, but she also didn't know about David. About whatever I *was* now. What if the entire fate of the world did depend on me taking this cake to Saylor Stark?

With that thought in mind, I decided to pick out one of Mom's nicer cake plates. Just in case.

"I promise, once Cotillion is over, I'll start dropping some things. I'll need to focus on college stuff by then anyway."

Mom didn't seem particularly comforted by that, but she helped me move the cake onto the holder. "I hope Saylor appreciates all of this."

Sighing, I lifted the cake. "You and me both."

Chapter 14

DAVID'S HOUSE was only a few blocks from mine, so it didn't take long to get there. People who aren't from the South imagine we all live in these big plantation houses like in *Gone with the Wind*, but the truth is, those are few and far between. And if you *do* see one of those big wedding cake houses, chances are it was built in the past fifty years.

But Saylor Stark's house was the real deal. Built in 1843, it was the oldest house in Pine Grove. According to The Aunts, it used to have a name. Ivy Hall, or Moss Manor. Something silly like that. The name had even been worked into the iron of the giant double gates. But Saylor had had new gates made when she moved in, something that, again according to The Aunts, was a supremely bad idea. "Houses are like boats," Aunt May had sniffed. "They should always keep their original names."

I didn't know about all that, but I did know that the Stark house was one of the prettiest I'd ever seen. It wasn't as grand and imposing as Magnolia House, but it was pretty in its own way. There was a wide front porch covered in ferns and white rocking chairs, and lamplight spilled out of the big windows lining the front of the house. Ivy crept up one brick wall, and the curving driveway was made, like the one at Magnolia House, out of crushed shells rather than gravel. I parked behind Miss Saylor's Cadillac, and, gingerly taking the cake, headed up the brick steps to the front door. I was about to ring the doorbell when I heard Miss Stark say, "Done with that paper."

"I can't," David replied. I'd heard that tone of voice before. I didn't have to see David to know that he was clenching his teeth and scowling.

"You can and you will," Miss Saylor fired back. "No more late hours, no more riding around in fast cars with girls—"

"Oh my God," David groaned. "Like Harper Jane Price is some kind of bad influence on me."

"I want you to stay away from that girl," Miss Saylor said, and I nearly reeled.

That girl?

Since when was I someone people called That Girl? That Girl didn't wear pearls. She wasn't SGA president. She didn't volunteer her time on teen counseling hotlines. I was most definitely *not* That Girl.

"I don't know what's going on with you," David said, his voice getting louder. I had the impression that was because he'd moved closer to the front door. "But since when do you care where I go or who I spend time with?"

"I have always cared," she replied. "But I worry about you. I'm your aunt, David; that's allowed."

"Whatever," David replied, and I cringed. Saylor Stark didn't seem like the kind of woman you could say "whatever" to. "I'm nearly eighteen, and the last time I checked, that means I get to see who I want to see and go where I want to go. And right now, I'm going to the library."

Wait, what?

Suddenly, the front door swung open.

Shoot.

David took a step forward, nearly bumping into me. His eyes widened as he pulled himself up short. "Whoa, sorr— Pres?"

And now Saylor was peering around his shoulder, and there I was, holding a stupid cake, which suddenly seemed less like a peace offering and more like a really bad idea.

"I was bringing this by to say sorry for yesterday. To both of you," I added as Saylor moved forward. "You know, for the . . . the car driving and the recklessness, and the—the grabbing . . ."

With my free hand I started making this clutching gesture. I was talking about grabbing David's shirt, but it looked like I was milking a cow.

Or worse.

My face red, I thrust the cake at David, who nearly stumbled backward. "Anyway, it's hummingbird cake, and I know that's your favorite, Miss Saylor, so . . . enjoy!" Ugh. It wasn't like me to be this . . . awkward. And then, to make matters worse, I tripped a little in my hurry to get back down the steps and out of there as quickly as I could.

But I'd barely gotten to the driveway before Saylor called, "Harper!"

I turned around. "Yes, ma'am?"

Saylor waved her hand at me, diamonds catching the street-lights. "Have you eaten dinner yet?"

My palms were sweaty and I did my best to discreetly wipe them on my skirt. "No, ma'am."

"Well, neither have we. I made chicken and dumplings. Why don't you come on in and eat with us. Then we can try out this lovely looking cake."

In all the years I'd known the Starks—and that was basically all my life—I'd never actually been inside their house. The temptation to see inside . . . well, I couldn't resist.

"That would be nice, thank you," I said, walking back up the steps. As I did, I noticed a set of wind chimes hanging from the porch roof. They were silver and shiny, and there was something weird about the shape of them. Musical notes?

Before I could look any closer, Saylor had an arm around my shoulders, guiding me into the house. It smelled a lot like my Aunt Jewel's house—that comforting combination of scented candles, coffee, and something cooking. But that was where the similarities ended. While Aunt Jewel's house was neat and full of light and space, the Stark house was so full I found myself nego-tiating around couches and ottomans. Every room was full of furniture, vases, picture frames, weird little porcelain statues of farm animals. It was like she'd raided every garage sale between here and Mobile.

Thankfully, Saylor's dining room was the one room that wasn't overstuffed, and I took a deep breath as Saylor gestured to one of the chairs around a long wooden table. "Sit down, honey," she told me. To David, she said, "Give me a hand."

While they disappeared into the kitchen, I sat down and took in Saylor Stark's dining room. Like the rest of the house, it seemed slightly . . . crowded. Even the wallpaper was busy, covered in a pattern I couldn't quite make out. There was a heavy curio cabinet in the corner, filled with all kinds of knickknacks, and more pictures on the wall. I scanned the faces, wondering if any of them were David's parents. Most of the pictures did seem to be of young, shiny-haired, smiling people, but none of them actually looked like David.

Frowning, I leaned forward, trying to see more clearly. But before I could, David came back in, a small stack of plates and some silverware in his hands.

"We need to talk," I whispered quickly, darting a glance at the door to the kitchen. "After dinner. I think I found out some—"

"Here we are!" Saylor trilled, carrying a steaming pot. After sitting it on a terra-cotta trivet in the middle of the table, Saylor took the seat at the head of the table, David to her left, me to her right. The smell from the pot was mouth-watering, and I suddenly realized I'd been so nervous about Ryan that I hadn't eaten lunch.

"My aunts make chicken and dumplings," I offered. "My mom tries, but she can never get them quite right."

Saylor gave me an indulgent smile. "The secret is white pepper. I bet your aunts know that. Which reminds me, I need to call your Aunt Jewel. Can't have Cotillion without her famous punch!"

I tried to hide my shudder. I loved Aunt Jewel, but her punch— a truly dreadful concoction made from white grape juice, ginger ale, Hawaiian Punch, and practically a pound of sugar—made my teeth hurt. Still, I nodded at Saylor. "She'd like that. And actually, speaking of Cotillion—"

But before I could say anything else, Saylor held one manicured finger up to her lips. "We can talk about that later. Let's say grace first."

She reached out her hand and took mine, lifting her other hand to David. He took it and then held his other hand out to me.

I laid my palm in his.

When I was eleven, my family was visiting my uncle's farm and Leigh-Anne dared me to touch an electric fence. It had been stupid, but I did what my big sister asked. The shock had blown me off my feet and made my whole arm numb for nearly an hour.

What happened in Saylor Stark's dining room felt a lot like that. Power surged through me, and every nerve in my body screamed. Saylor's rings felt almost unbearably hot against my skin, and for one dizzying second, I thought I could smell something burning.

A screen dropped in front of my eyes, just like that day behind the church with David and Ryan. But this time, I couldn't make any sense of the images. Girls in white dresses, a pool of red liquid on a hardwood floor. Chunks of glass—no, *ice*—flying through the air. And over the hum of whatever power was linking me and the Starks, the sound of screams. So much screaming.

Almost as suddenly as they'd begun, the images stopped, and suddenly, my hands were at my sides and I was staring at Saylor's dining room table, my breath sawing in and out of my lungs.

"What—" I said, but Saylor was already getting up, moving so quickly her chair slammed into the wall, scuffing a black mark into the wallpaper.

"David!" she cried, and I turned to see that he was slumped on the floor, head in his hands. I thought the lights were reflecting off his glasses, but then I realized that that wasn't it. His eyes were solid white.

As Saylor crouched next to him, cradling his head, David began to speak. "The night of the swans," he muttered. "Power restored, a new era rises, but one must fall. One must give everything. Night of the swans . . ."

"Shhh," Saylor murmured, smoothing his hair away from his face.

My own face still felt hot and when I glanced down, I saw that all the hairs on my arms were standing up.

David's eyes fluttered shut, and with a sigh, he sagged against the carpet. As he did, Saylor gently pulled her hands back and rocked on her heels.

Saylor Stark had always been one of the most beautiful women I knew, but now, she looked old and almost . . . haggard. And her eyes, when they studied my face, might have been the same warm blue as David's, but they were steely and hard and full of something I didn't have a name for.

"You're our new Paladin," she said, and despite all the awfulness of what had just happened, relief so intense it nearly took my breath washed over me. After all this time waiting for my Professor X, it was Saylor Stark. We were going to be fine.

"Well." Saylor rose to her feet. "We are totally effed."

Chapter 15

SHE SAID the actual word. Saylor Stark said the F-word.

From his place on the carpet, David started to stir. "What happened?" he muttered, trying to sit up. As soon as he did, he flinched, lowering his head back into his hands. "Did I have a stroke? Is that why I think you said what I think you just said?" he asked Saylor.

"You know," I said, ignoring David. "You know what I am."

She didn't answer. Instead, she walked into the kitchen. I heard the rattle of ice, then a cabinet opening and closing.

David still sat on the carpet, knees drawn up to his chest.

"Are you okay?" I asked, sliding out of my chair and onto my knees. The thick carpet scraped my skin as I edged forward.

"No," he replied. "I feel like my head is about to explode."

I moved a little closer to him. He looked so pale and wretched that I was tempted to smooth his hair back the way Saylor had. Instead, I fisted my hands in my skirt. "I know that was intense, but hey—your aunt knows what's going on. That's awesome, right? We can get some answers."

David raised his head. His pupils were so huge his eyes looked almost black. "Actually, Pres," he rasped out, "my aunt being in on this makes it a hell of a lot weirder."

Saylor came back in, holding a small glass full of a dark amber liquid. She sat down at the table, threw back the drink, and then looked at the two of us again.

Then she got up and made another drink.

Once that one was down, she finally said, "I'm not really your aunt, David. If that makes things easier for you."

David went very still, and for a moment, everything was so quiet, I could hear the ticking of the grandfather clock in the hallway.

Then she turned to me. "I thought it might be you. I knew that Christopher was gone, I . . . I felt him go. And then you and David both looked so shaken up yesterday that I wondered if maybe . . ." Sighing, she set her glass down. I stared at the perfectly set table, the silverware still in neat rows, napkins folded, and fought the urge to burst into hysterical giggles. Or tears.

Shutting my eyes, I tried to focus. "Christopher?"

David murmured, "Mr. Hall. That was his first name." When I opened my eyes, David was still looking at the ground, arms encircling his knees.

Saylor tipped her head back. The light from the chandelier caught her earrings, sending scattered rainbows across the shiny surface of the dining room table. "What happened?"

I told her about the night of the Homecoming Dance as briefly as I could. When I was done, a single tear trickled out from under Saylor's closed eyes. "It's my fault," she murmured. "I knew the wards needed to be stronger the closer we got, but I couldn't think of a way to do it. And I hoped . . ." She opened her eyes then, focusing on David. "I hoped," she said again, and then she was standing up.

I half expected her to go make another drink. Instead, she wandered to the window, hands braced on her lower back. "I'm guessing you two will want the whole story, then."

David was still grayish, but when he rose to his feet, there was steel in his voice. "You think? If you're not my aunt, then who the hell are you? Why do I live with you?"

Saylor took a deep breath. "Technically, I kidnapped you."

I felt David jump at that, and wasn't sure anything had ever been more painful than watching him try to think of some way to respond. "My parents?" he asked, his voice strangled.

"Dead," Saylor replied, blunt. "Murdered by the same people who are after you now."

She dropped her head, pinching her nose between her thumb and forefinger. "I'm messing this up. There's so much to tell you, and I don't even know where to start. Christopher would've been better at this, Christopher was—" Saylor broke off. "It doesn't matter. The point is you're an Oracle."

"But that's impossible," I said. "Everything I read said that Oracles are always girls."

Saylor whipped her head around to me. I think for a second, she'd forgotten I was there. "You've already started researching this?"

"A-a little," I told her, standing up. "Dr. DuPont used the word Paladin, so I started there. Then when I talked to David, he mentioned his . . . his dreams, and we started putting things together."

The look Saylor gave me was part pride, part appraisal. I'd seen it before at Cotillion practice. "Clever girl," she said in a low voice. "Maybe you'll be better at this than I thought."

Then she heaved another sigh and came back to the table, bracing her hands on it. "But what you read was wrong. There *can* be male Oracles, although there's only been one besides you, David. In the eighth century, there was one named Alaric, and—"

David gripped the back of a chair, his jaw set. "I don't want a history lesson," he ground out. "You're telling me you're not my aunt, my parents are dead, and I'm an *Oracle*. The eighth century doesn't really mean shit to me right now."

"David," I said, tugging his jacket.

"It's all right," Saylor said, her eyes still on David. "You have every right to be upset. More than upset. But we are running out of time, and now that there are . . . ," her gaze flicked to me, "unforeseen complications, I need you to listen. I need you to understand. I don't need you to forgive me right now, but please. Hear me out."

David paused, nearly vibrating with anger and energy. But eventually, he sat.

Saylor closed her eyes briefly and then continued. "Unfortunately, Alaric was nowhere near as powerful as all of the women who came before him were. His visions were muddy, unclear. More what could be than what *would* be."

"That seems . . . lame," I said, going back to sit in my chair.

"That's a word for it, yes," Saylor replied. "And the problem is, you can't have more than one Oracle at once. One has to die for another to be born."

Dumbly, I nodded. "So if you get stuck with a dud Oracle—"

Saylor cut me off with a wave of her hand. "You have to kill it in order to bring forth the next one. But obviously Alaric wasn't about to let himself be killed. Instead, he attempted a . . . well, a ritual on himself. One that would make his powers increase tenfold so that his visions would be clearer."

"Did it work?" David's hands were still wrapped tightly around the top of his chair, but his shoulders weren't up around his ears anymore and some color had returned to his face.

Saylor patted at her hair, leaning back. "It did. But it worked too well. Alaric didn't just improve his visions. He gained new powers. Alarmingly strong ones. At that time, Alaric . . . I suppose you could say he belonged to Charlemagne. And Charlemagne had set up a cadre of knights to protect Alaric that he called the Paladins. But until Alaric did his ritual, they were just ordinary men. After the ritual, Alaric was able to make them . . ." She trailed off, her eyes moving over me. "Well, you. Not just knights, but supernaturally gifted warriors, all of them loyal to Alaric to the point of death."

I swallowed, not liking the sound of that.

Saylor sat forward in her chair a little, hands clenched in front of her. "But the ritual had an unintended side effect. That much power, it's . . . it's more than a human brain can handle. It more or less burned Alaric up from the inside, twisting him into something evil. Charlemagne eventually ordered him executed."

"But he had a whole posse of bodyguards with superpowers," David muttered, sinking into his chair.

Saylor nodded. "Exactly. Between Alaric's powers and the

dozens of Paladins guarding him, it took over a hundred men to kill the Oracle. An entire village was destroyed in the process, and there were only two Paladins left when it was all over."

"So once Alaric was dead, what happened?" David asked. His mouth was still set in a hard line, but his eyes were curious.

"A group of powerful men met and decided that the Oracle should no longer belong to any one ruler. She—and they were only ever women after Alaric—should be kept safe somewhere, guarded. The two remaining Paladins volunteered for the task."

"Okay," I said slowly. I really wish I'd brought some paper and pens. This seemed like a situation where a chart could help. "So what are you then?"

The corners of her mouth turned up. "When Alaric took Charlemagne's knights and turned them into Paladins, he also took Charlemagne's two court magicians and gave them powers as well. Granted, they only got a fraction of the magic that Alaric possessed, but it was enough. They called themselves Mages. And that, Harper, is what I am."

In the silence that followed, I heard a car drive down the street and the distant hooting of an owl. "So you're a witch?" David finally asked, the tips of his ears red.

Saylor smoothed an imaginary wrinkle from her pantsuit and gave a dismissive sniff. "That is an ugly word, David Stark. Mages don't ride around on broomsticks or conjure up things. We use potions, minor spells to assist the Oracle and the Paladin in their work."

"So there's one Oracle," I said, flinging a hand out toward

David. "And now there's one Paladin." I pointed at myself. "How many Mages are there?"

"Two, usually," Saylor answered, fiddling with the edge of a placemat. "The Ephors—those are the men who took charge of the Oracle—believed in keeping things traditional. Since there were two original Paladins, two original Mages, they've always tried to maintain that balance. You said the bathroom was spotless after the fight with Christopher and Dr. DuPont, right?"

When David and I both nodded, Saylor said, "That was alchemy." Then she frowned. "Incredibly dangerous alchemy, though. That spell is a sort of temporal shift. It returns the setting to what it looked like before the trauma. Cara never would've tried something like that."

When David and I both asked, "Who?" Saylor waved a hand. "The other Mage when I was with the Ephors. She was old then, though, and that was nearly twenty years ago. They must have someone new."

David, who had been worrying at one of his fingernails, dropped his hand. "A temporal shift. Why doesn't that make the people that got killed . . . undead?"

Saylor turned her glass over and over in her hand. "I told you, our powers are very limited. Control over the human body and soul . . . that's very far beyond us. Fixing a gate or a broken section of tile in a bathroom is one thing. Erasing something as permanent as death is . . ." She broke off, pushing her glass away. "In any case, the main purpose of the Mage is to serve as a kind of . . . battery, I suppose, to the Oracle. That's what happened tonight. When the three of us joined hands, you finally got the burst of power you needed."

And we'd seen David's vision, too. Except even now, it was fading from my mind, like trying to remember a dream. What had David said?

I glanced over at him and saw that he also appeared to be deep in thought. But before I could ask any more questions, Saylor stood up.

"Which leads us to now. And to you. Both of you. Eighteen years ago, we were living in Greece. That's where the Ephors keep the Oracle, Paladin, and Mage. We'd had the same Oracle for . . . oh, years. Since before I was called. And when she died, she gave us one last prophecy. That the next Oracle born would be a boy. So they ordered Christopher to kill him. You," she said to David.

I took a sip of my lemonade. The ice had melted, and it tasted bitter now, but my mouth was so dry I didn't care.

"When an Oracle dies, she always gives the place and time where the new one will be born. Christopher and I were sent to get you."

For the first time, shame washed over Saylor's face. "Alchemy." She fumbled in her pocket, bringing out a small blue jar of lip balm. "This is a salve. A potion that lets the Mage do minor mind-control spells. I compelled your mother to hand you to me. She did it with a smile."

I thought the back of the chair might crack under David's hands, but he didn't say anything.

"We were halfway back to Greece when I realized I couldn't

do it," Saylor continued, tears in her voice. "Christopher couldn't, either. We'd made a vow to protect the Oracle, no matter what. And so we . . . we stole you."

She stood up again, brushing at her slacks. "Mages don't have particularly powerful magic, so we try to steal it whenever we can find it. Back in the 1800s, there was a witch who lived in this town. I don't know why, but for whatever reason, she threw up wards all over the place. Makes it hard for anyone to get in if they mean to do harm. So it seemed like the perfect hiding spot."

Saylor busied herself with some of the knickknacks on the sideboard, picking up a porcelain shepherdess and putting it down beside a Swarovski hedgehog. "And of course, I made sure I got on every committee I could, the more excuse to put up extra protection symbols. I even put one on you," she said, pointing to David's arm. Startled, he pushed up the sleeve of his T-shirt, and sure enough, there was a tiny scar on his arm, almost like a birthmark, in that same shape of a figure eight on its side.

"But then," Saylor said, "I guess you figured that out. Still, they worked. Oh, the first year, there was a man the Ephors sent who got through, but Christopher sorted that out, and I put up that ugly statue in the park. After that, there were no more incidents until recently."

My brain actually ached. I didn't know that was possible.

I rolled my neck, hoping that might help. "So why now, then? Why after nearly eighteen years are all your spells and wards not working?"

Saylor gave a rueful smile. "They were only ever a Band-Aid. The closer we get to Cotillion, the weaker they'll become."

David's head shot up. "Cotillion?"

"Night of the swans," I said, suddenly remembering. "That's what you said when you had your little"— I waved my hand— "fit."

"Vision," Saylor corrected while David shrugged his shoulders, uncomfortable.

"What's happening the night of Cotillion?" It was stupid, I know, but as soon as I said it, a weight seemed to settle in my chest. Cotillion. The night I'd been looking forward to for so long, and now even *it* was part of this insanity?

Saylor went to take another sip of her drink, but it was empty. I didn't drink alcohol, but I felt her pain as she frowned at the ice cubes in her glass. I could use a drink, too. "Before the last Oracle died, she not only gave us the location of the new Oracle, she also named a specific night when the new Oracle would be tested. At the end of this test, the Oracle would either be the most powerful Oracle yet, or . . . or he would be dead."

That word—*dead*—seemed to hang in the air around us. David dropped into a chair, his hands clutching the knees of his pants as he slumped forward.

Saylor reached out, to touch him, I think, but her hand only hovered a few inches in front of him before she drew it back. Clearing her throat, she continued, "So that's why I took over Cotillion and moved it to that night."

"Why not cancel it altogether?" I shifted in my seat. "Take David out of the country that night or something."

But Saylor just shook her head. "Certain events, they're like fixed points in time. Destined. This is one of them. David has to go through this test, whatever it is, and nothing can stop it. All we can do is . . . be prepared."

"So what does all this mean?" I finally asked. My voice sounded dry and unused, and my mind was racing, trying to process all of this. Magic, and Greece, and stolen babies . . . it was like my life had suddenly turned into a really bad soap opera.

"It means that you've been given a sacred duty," Saylor said. Her voice sounded different, and there was hardly a trace of Southern accent in it at all. "From this day forward, you will be tasked with protecting the Oracle at all costs. He'll be your sole focus until the day you, like Christopher, have to lay down your life for him."

Saylor reached for my hand, and I gave it to her without thinking. "So, Harper Jane Price. Are you ready to accept your destiny?"

Chapter 16

I WITHDREW my hand. "No, thank you."

Saylor and David both stared.

"I appreciate your offer very much," I continued. "But I'm afraid I have to refuse."

Saylor rose to her feet, an expression somewhere between anger and disbelief spreading across her face. "I'm not inviting you to a garden party, Harper. I'm asking you to accept the role destiny has handed you. I'm asking you to use the powers you've been given."

But I was already shaking my head. "No. No, this is not my destiny." Heart hammering, I could feel blood rushing to my face and I knew that my chest and neck must be splotchy. "I have my own life, and things . . . things I want to do. I can't follow him"— I flung my arm out at David—"and keep him safe forever. What am I supposed to do about college? Or—or getting married and having kids and—"

Breaking off, I took a deep breath and held up my hand. "You know what, no. Forget it. It doesn't matter, because I'm not going to be a Paladin."

Saylor rolled her lips inward, eyes narrowing. It was an expression I'd seen on her face dozens of times, usually when Mary Beth was screwing up at Cotillion practice. "It's not something you get to decide," she said. "You already *are* a Paladin. The moment Christopher passed his powers on to you, you accepted this responsibility."

"But I didn't," I fired back. My throat was tight, and I could feel the tears pricking my eyes. Great, splotchy *and* I was about to be snotty. "This was done to me. I didn't choose this. And so now, I'm choosing *not* to do it."

I looked down at David who was still sitting on the floor, watching me. "I'm sorry," I told him. "I obviously don't want you to die. I mean, I know I've said that I did a few times, but I didn't really mean it. And it was only when you were being especially provoking, so—"

"Harper."

I turned back to Saylor. "No," I said again, but she continued like I hadn't spoken.

"This isn't something you can walk away from." Saylor's back was ramrod straight, shoulders tense under the bright coral of her jacket. "Do you know how important Oracles are? Wars have been fought over them. And now the Ephors are coming after David again, and I don't know what they want to do with him."

"You can do magic!" I shouted back and despite all of it, there was some tiny part of me still horrified I'd shouted at Saylor Stark. But I shoved that down and kept going. "You can make wards to protect him, and—and make things disappear. You don't need me."

Walking forward, Saylor gripped my arms, tight enough to hurt. "We do," she insisted, giving me a little shake. "There have to be three, Harper. Three people, working together. The Oracle, the Paladin, and the Mage. One part of that missing . . ."

"And what?" I asked, my gaze flying back to David. He was standing now, but his face was blank and I had no idea what he was thinking.

"It won't work," Saylor said, and for the first time, I saw how desperate she really was. Her voice went softer even as her grip got tighter. "Harper, Christopher and I risked everything to save David. We did not get this close to lose him now."

I struggled out of her hands. As I did, my eyes fell on the wall behind her and all of those skinny sideways figure eights, the symbol of the Paladin. Something surged in my blood, but I shut my eyes. No. No, I was not doing this. I was walking away. I *could* walk away.

But standing there, shaking with some power I couldn't even name, that seemed easier said than done.

I thought of my mom and dad. Of Ryan and Bee and all those college brochures in my desk at home. And the shaky feeling started to recede.

Taking deep breaths through my nose, I tried to get myself under control. "Tell me why," I said at last. "Tell me why it's so essential that I give up my whole life to keep David safe."

Saylor blinked and took a step back from me. "He can see the future, Harper. The only person in the entire world who can. Don't you think that's worth protecting?"

Rubbing my hands over my face, I fought the urge to scream. "Yes, but not at the expense of *my* life."

There was the lip roll again. "And what is it you plan on doing with your life that's so important, Harper? Is it more important than ensuring the safety of the only Oracle?"

"Yes."

We both turned to look at David. His hands were shoved in his pockets, his gaze on the floor. "Harper's life is important, Aunt—" He broke off, shaking his head. "And she's right. She can't just follow me around forever. That's not fair to her. Or to me. I mean, I might actually want to get a girlfriend at some point, and no offense, Pres, but I think you might salt my game a little. Wait, do I have to be celibate, too?"

Saylor rolled her eyes. "David, take this seriously."

Even from a distance, I could see the steeliness in David's eyes as he took Saylor in. "I am. Trust me. And that's why I'm saying this whole thing is crazy. Paladins and Oracles and ancient Greece . . ." Sighing, he lifted one hand to rake it through his hair.

"You keep doing—what did you call them? Wards?—and I'll try really hard not to tell the future anymore, and Harper will go back to her regular life of committees and dances and being a pain in my ass."

Saylor opened her mouth to reply, but David held up his hand. "You said the three of us have to work together. Well, it's two against one here. This?" He made a circle with his finger between the three of us. "This isn't happening. And now if you ladies will excuse me, I'm going upstairs and taking some aspirin."

With that, he turned and walked away. Saylor and I listened to his heavy tread on the staircase, both of us jumping a little when his door slammed.

Dropping into the nearest chair, Saylor covered her face with one hand. "I meant what I said, Harper. There's no walking away. From the moment you entered that bathroom, your fate was sealed. His, too." She picked up her head and nodded in the direction of the stairs.

I didn't answer her. Instead, I took my keys from where I'd laid them by my plate. The chicken and dumplings had coagulated into a beige blob and I wondered how I'd ever thought they looked appetizing.

"Thank you for dinner," I told her even though I hadn't eaten a bite. "Also, I think—" My voice broke, so I cleared my throat and tried again. "I think it would be best if I pulled out of Cotillion this year." I wasn't sure how I was going to explain that to my parents, but I also knew that I wanted no part of whatever was going to happen that night.

Saylor's gaze stayed steady on me. She might not have been related to David by blood, but her eyes were nearly the same shade of blue. For a second, I thought she was going to try the sales pitch again. Instead, she gave a little nod. "I understand."

My knees were shaking as I went to leave the dining room. I was just to the doorway when Saylor said my name again.

"Yes, ma'am?" I asked, turning to face her.

"Thank you so much for the cake," she said, and in that moment, she was the Saylor Stark I'd known my entire life, all perfect silver hair and straight white teeth. "You're a doll."

Chapter 17

I spent the next few days avoiding David. Or maybe he spent them avoiding me. Either way, I hardly saw him, and when our paths crossed, both of us were quick to look the other way. Once, as I watched him cross campus, his shoulders up around his ears, I felt a twinge of . . . something. At first, I thought it was maybe the beginnings of that gut-wrenching pain that meant he was in trouble. But it wasn't that. I think it was sympathy. Or pity. As hard a time as I was having wrapping my brain around *Saylor Stark* being some kind of witch, David must have been having it a million times worse.

But I'd done the right thing in walking away from them. From all of it. No matter how awesome I thought superpowers would be, they weren't worth giving up my life for.

Still, as I perched on a stool in my Aunt Jewel's kitchen that Friday afternoon, I couldn't stop thinking about how worried David looked every day, how just that morning, someone had slammed a locker in the hallway, and he had nearly jumped out of his skin.

It was true, what I'd told Saylor; I didn't want David to get killed by bad guys, obviously. But I still couldn't see how it was even feasible for me to watch over him forever.

So why did I feel so bad?

"Harper, a bird is going to land on that lip if you keep pokin' it out," Aunt Jewel said. She sat at the table with her two sisters, my Aunts May and Martha. The three of them were doing what they did every Friday afternoon—playing cards and smoking. Since I wasn't married, I didn't get to play with them, and smoking was out until I was widowed.

Not, I thought as I fanned the smoke away from my face, that that was ever going to be an issue. Smoking was so seriously gross.

"I'm not poking out my lip," I replied, even though I was pretty sure I had been.

Aunts May and Martha were twins, but seeing them with Aunt Jewel, the three could have easily been triplets. All of them had the same iron-gray hair, permed within an inch of its life, and all three wore the same type of brightly colored elastic-waisted pants, usually paired with floral sweaters, or, like today, holiday-appropriate sweatshirts. Aunt May's had a turkey on it, while Aunt Martha was wearing pumpkins. Aunt Jewel had what appeared to be a giant pie stitched on the front of hers.

Sipping sweet tea, I watched them play rummy and insult each other. "Martha, I know you're not going to take that ace," Aunt May said as my Aunt Martha did just that. May scowled as she flicked ash into an ugly clay dish I'd made for that purpose at summer camp seven years ago.

"You are evil, Martha," she said, drawling her twin sister's name out so that it sounded more like "Maawwtha."

Aunt Martha gave a smug smile and arranged her cards. "Harper, baby, do you hear your Aunt May being ugly to me?"

"Don't drag Harper into this," Aunt Jewel said as she laid down another card. She was the eldest of The Aunts, and the other two tended to listen to her. "We never get to see her, and now the two of you are going to spoil her visit by fussin'."

I hid a smile behind my glass. Actually, sitting in Aunt Jewel's cozy, yellow kitchen, watching the three of them argue with each other, was one of my favorite things. They could get downright nasty over cards, but there was never any doubt that they were sisters who loved one another.

I wondered if I could ever think of the word "sisters" and not feel a steady ache in my chest.

I sat my tea on the counter behind me. "I'm fine," I told them. "Also, Aunt May, if you pick up that four Aunt Martha discarded, you can get a run."

Jewel and Martha groaned as, hooting, Aunt May scooped up the card. "You should come by more often, Miss Harper," she said.

Aunt Jewel began gathering the cards back up, and Aunt Martha looked over at me. "Speaking of, what brought you by today, sweetie? Not that we're not thrilled to see you, of course, or that we aren't pleased as punch to have a hummingbird cake"— she nodded toward the heavy glass platter on the counter—"but you're usually so busy."

"Too busy," Aunt May chimed in. "Girls today have so much going on. School, and sports, and dances, and committees . . . it's too much!"

"Don't say that," Aunt Martha told her, lighting another cigarette. "Our Harper is responsible and has a good sense of community. What's wrong with that? And least she's not one of those Teen Moms."

The other aunts clucked in sympathy. A few months back, Aunts Martha and May—they lived together—had gotten a satellite dish and discovered the joy/horror of reality TV.

"Or one of those crackheads, like on that show where they make people feel bad about taking drugs," Aunt Jewel offered. "Did you see the episode with the girl who did something called huffing? With the cans of cleaning—"

I hated to interrupt, but once they got going on car crash TV, they might never stop. "I have been busy," I broke in. "And that's kind of what I wanted to talk to y'all about."

All three of my aunts put their cards down and swiveled in their chairs to face me. There were few things they loved more than people coming to them for advice. It helped that they were really good at it. "It's about Cotillion," I said, and Aunts Martha and May exchanged a look, while Aunt Jewel exhaled a cloud of smoke.

"That Cotillion," Aunt Martha spat out. "I suwannee." That was her way of saying "I swear." Aunt Martha belonged to that generation of ladies who thought any type of swearing—not just saying the bad words—was not the thing to do.

"You don't like Cotillion?" I asked, surprised. All of them had done it, and so had my grandmother, my mom, my sister . . .

Besides, The Aunts lived for tradition and propriety. Cotillion should be one of their favorite things ever.

"We did," Aunt Jewel said, stubbing out her cigarette as she stood. Ladies never smoked unless they were sitting, after all. "Until that woman took it over."

More grumbling. I scooted forward on the edge of my stool. "Saylor Stark?"

Aunt Jewel rolled her eyes. "Such a silly name."

"Before she came, Cotillion was held in the spring. Which is when it's *meant* to be held," Aunt Martha said, laying her hands in her lap. "Girls are supposed to come out in the spring; everyone knows that. That's why it used to be called the Chrysalis Ball."

"And now it's what? The Mistletoe Ball?" Aunt May asked. She gave a derisive sniff. "That doesn't even make sense. Unless she has y'all running around kissing people."

"She would," Aunt Jewel muttered, plucking a piece of lint from the pie emblazoned across her chest.

"Who ran it before?" I asked.

"Cathy Foster," Aunt Jewel answered promptly. "And she did a lovely job of it, too. I never understood why she handed it over to a stranger."

"I never understood why Saylor Stark was so bound and determined to be in charge of Cotillion, anyway," Aunt Martha said. "Apparently, she'd run one back in her hometown in Virginia."

Another round of frowns and clucking. "The whole thing was odd," Aunt May mused, leaning back in her chair. "Cathy loved running Cotillion, and as far as I knew, she planned on passing it on to her daughter. Then Saylor Stark showed up, had one lunch with her, and suddenly, *she* was in charge."

"Same with the Pine Grove Betterment Society," Aunt Martha reminded her. "I thought Suzanne Perry was going to run that until the end of time. But it was the same thing. Saylor Stark marches her behind over to Suzanne's house with a rum cake, and suddenly she's in charge of the PGBS, too."

I fidgeted on my stool, thinking about my conversation with Saylor. She'd called herself a Mage, but it seemed like "witch" was just as good a term. And she'd obviously used some kind of power on Cathy Foster and Suzanne Perry. And now that I knew why she'd taken over all of those things, my beloved Cotillion included . . .

"Do y'all know anything else about the Starks? Anything . . . I don't know, kind of odd? Out of the ordinary?"

Aunts May and Martha exchanged another glance as Aunt Jewel got another glass of sweet tea. "Whole family is strange if you ask me," she said, frowning. "Saylor appearing in town like she did, with that brand-new baby. And buying up Yellow-hammer."

Right, that had been the name of the Starks' house. I knew it was kind of dumb.

"When we were growing up, people used to tell ghost stories about that house," Aunt May mused. "They said a witch lived there a long time ago. Or something like that." She waved her hand, raining ashes down on Aunt Jewel's yellow gingham table-cloth. "Of course, you can't swing a possum without hitting a haunted house in these parts, so I'm sure it was nothing."

Aunt Martha shook her head. "I always thought it was odd that she didn't have a husband. I'm telling you, I don't think that boy is just her nephew."

"Hush, Martha," Aunt Jewel admonished. She went back to the table and began dealing cards again. "I'm not Saylor Stark's biggest fan by any means, but no matter who she is to that boy, she's done the best she could by him. And he's turned out nearly as smart as our Harper!" Leaning forward, Aunt Jewel gave me a shrewd smile. "You're still going to whup him for valedictorian though, right, baby?"

I smiled back. "Absolutely."

They started to play again, and while I was already about to go into a diabetic coma, I poured myself some more tea anyway. "Are there any other weird things that've happened here in town? Not only related to the Starks, but . . . I don't know. People seeing things. Stuff disappearing, like . . . magic kind of stuff?"

All three of them exchanged a look this time, and then Aunt Martha very gingerly put her cards down. "Harper, have you been doing the huffing?"

"No," I said, setting down my glass so fast that tea sloshed out onto the counter. I reached behind me for a paper towel and continued. "I was just wondering. For a research project. I'm doing a—a paper on local superstitions."

Mollified, The Aunts resumed their card game. "Oh, well, in that case, of course there have been odd things," Aunt May said.

"There's that window in the courthouse that supposedly shows a man's face if the sun hits it the right way."

"And they say the choir loft at First Baptist is haunted," Aunt Martha added, pulling out another cigarette from her pack. "Although I think it's just pigeons up there, and the janitorial staff isn't doing their job."

"You know, sweetie, now that you mention things disappearing, there *was* that man years back," Aunt Jewel said, not looking up from her cards. "Real particular. Several people saw him lurking around town, dressed all in black, very suspicious. He was renting a room over at Janice Duff's boardinghouse. One night, Janice hears this awful ruckus up there, and when she goes in, she swears up and down that she saw him dead on his bed with a big sword in him."

My neck prickled as Aunt May nodded. "That's right. I talked to her about it the next week at church. She said it wasn't a regular sword either, it was one of those big curvy ones. Like in the old movies about sheikhs. What do they call those things?"

"Scimitars," I croaked, my mouth dry.

"That's right, a scimitar. Anyway, she calls 911, havin' an absolute fit, but when the police get there, the man was gone."

"And more than that," Aunt May said, discarding a five of clubs. "There was no trace he'd ever been there. No blood, no clothes, no suitcase. Bed made up all pretty and everything."

"Most everybody thought Janice was having a nervous breakdown. Happens when some women go through"— Aunt Martha dropped her voice to a whisper—"The Change."

My hand was shaking as I poured myself another glass of tea.

This time, I was pretty sure it wasn't from the sugar. Closing my eyes, I took a deep breath and hoped The Aunts wouldn't notice.

Not my problem, I tried to tell myself.

Aunt Jewel picked up a discarded card, and then turned a bright smile on me. "Anyway, does that answer your question, baby?"

I swallowed. "Sure does."

Chapter 18

"I'M PREGNANT."

"Huh?" Looking up from the pair of shoes I'd been pretending to study, I turned to face Bee. "What did you say?"

"Finally!" Bee said, tossing her head back with an exaggerated eye roll. "I said your name three times already, and when that didn't grab your attention, I decided to go dramatic."

Smiling, I tossed one of those little stockings you get to try on shoes at her. "Well, it clearly worked. I take it you are not actually carrying Brandon's spawn, then?"

Bee snorted and lifted one foot, turning her ankle so that I could admire the shoe from all angles. "No, thank God. My mama would kill me. Now what do you think of these?"

We were at the Pine Grove Galleria, our typical Saturday-afternoon destination. Today's trip was especially important since we were picking out our shoes for Cotillion. Or Bee was. I hadn't worked up the nerve to tell her I'd quit Cotillion yet, but since we were already on our third store, I was going to have to do it soon. I just wasn't sure how to break it to her in the middle of Well Heeled. The store was relatively deserted and I didn't see anyone we knew; the only other customers were a little girl, who was probably around ten, and her mom. Still, I was beginning to wish I'd just said something in the car on the way here.

Dutifully, I continued to inspect the white high heel she'd slipped on. "Pretty," I told her.

Bee frowned. "But not perfect."

"I . . . don't you think they're a little high?"

Sighing, Bee slid her foot out of the shoe and put it back in the box. "Probably. I'm good in heels, but I don't want to pull a Mary Beth."

Next to us, the little girl was trying to talk her mom into buying her a pair of red sparkly ballet flats, but the mom was holding her ground. "We're picking out *church shoes*, Kenley," she said, exasperated, and I had to hide a smile.

Bee stood up and reached out, picking up a strappy sandal. She ran her fingers over the jeweled straps. "This is pretty. It would look good with your dress. Doesn't it have sparkles?"

I tried to keep from sighing longingly. Yes, my dress had sparkles. Subtle ones, but sparkles nonetheless. And a little bustle and a short train, and about a hundred silk-covered buttons . . . and I would never wear it.

I'd been trying to work up the nerve to tell Bee all afternoon. First, I'd sworn I'd say something on the ride to the mall. And when we'd walked inside, I had been all set to say, "Actually, Bee, I've decided not to do Cotillion this year."

Now we were on our third store, and I knew it was now or never.

I took the shoe from Bee's hand and set it back on the shelf. "It would look good, but . . . I'm, um, not doing Cotillion after all."

Bee's mouth dropped open a bit, but no sound came out. Turning away from her, I moved over to a display of scarves. I'd never worn a scarf in my life, but I made a big show of pulling one out and examining the pattern.

"Why not?" Bee asked from behind me.

I put the first scarf back and pulled out another, and once again thought about telling Bee the truth. *I can't do Cotillion because I have superpowers, but they suck. Because something is going to happen there that night that I don't want to be involved with.*

But I couldn't say any of that. So instead, I played the one card I'd promised myself I would never, ever play. "Leigh-Anne," I said. "It's . . . too hard. Thinking about the year *she* did it . . ."

Bee didn't say anything for a long time, and I wasn't sure I had ever felt worse than I did at that moment. Damn it, I'd given up the whole Paladin thing. So why was it still messing up my life?

Bee appeared at my elbow. "Okay," she said, tucking her hair behind her ears. "Then I won't go either."

I dropped the scarf. "Bee, you can't—"

"I can," she said, even as she threw one last lusting look at the shoes. "We always said we were going to do Cotillion together."

Bee may have been the only person on earth more excited for Cotillion than I was, but she gave me a brave if entirely fake smile. "It'll be fine. We'll do, like, one of those anti-prom proms, only it'll be an anti-Cotillion Cotillion. We'll wear black dresses and hang out at my house watching bad movies and drinking bad punch."

"It'll be hard to find worse punch than my Aunt Jewel's," I said, and Bee's smile got a little more real.

"We'll manage," she said. Then she stopped to pick up the scarf, placing it back on its shelf. "Now let's go to the food court and eat our weight in Cinnabon."

"You are the bestest best friend in all the world," I said, looping my arm through hers.

"I know," she said, squeezing my arm against her side. "And you in no way deserve me."

I didn't. Not even a little bit, and the truth of that lodged in my throat so that all I could do was squeak, "Yup."

As we made our way through the mall, Bee and I chatted about Ryan and Brandon, and it could have been any other Saturday, if it weren't for the constant gnawing of guilt. Staying away from the Starks was the best thing to do, which meant staying away from Cotillion. I didn't want to ruin that for Bee, but it wasn't like I'd asked her to give it up.

Suddenly, Bee came to a stop, pulling me up short, too. "Oh."

"What?" I asked, following her gaze. And when I saw what she was looking at . . .

"Oh," I echoed.

Mary Beth was standing in front of the Starbucks in the food court, sipping an iced coffee and smiling up at Ryan.

He was leaning against the wall, hands in his back pockets, and he was smiling down at her. There was even . . . head-tilting.

My boyfriend was leaning and head-tilting at another girl. And not any girl. Mary Beth Riley, who practically had a neon sign flashing "TAKE ME NOW, RYAN BRADSHAW!" over her head.

"Is she chewing on her straw?" Bee asked quietly, and I narrowed my eyes. She was. She was *totally* chewing on her straw and smiling and head-tilting and—

Before I could think it through, I was walking over to the Starbucks, Bee trailing a few steps behind. "Ryan!" I called, smiling broadly.

He swiveled his head at the sound of my voice, but there was no guilt in his face. Mary Beth, however, jumped a little.

"Are you following me?" I asked him, coming in close to slide my arm around his waist. "I told him Bee and I were doing some shoe shopping today," I informed Mary Beth, who gave me a sickly smile.

"Actually, no. I was here to pick up my tux. Check me out, renting a full six weeks early."

"You're a good boyfriend," I conceded. And he was, which was why I couldn't stand idly by and let other girls chew straws at him.

A thought occurred to me. Ryan said he was picking up his tux for Cotillion. Ryan was supposed to escort me to Cotillion, and while the night wasn't as big a deal for guys as it was for girls, I knew Mrs. Bradshaw was on the committee at Magnolia House. She expected her son to go. And if I wouldn't go with him . . .

Bee must have been thinking something similar, because she turned to Mary Beth. "Do you have an escort for Cotillion?"

A sudden flush spread up Mary Beth's neck. "Not yet," she answered, and I saw her gaze flit to Ryan.

I moved in a little closer to him. Okay, this Paladin thing had already derailed my life enough. Turning Saylor Stark down was supposed to mean getting my life back, not ruining Cotillion for my best friend and handing my boyfriend over to Mary Beth Riley.

Bee glanced over at me, a little smile tugging the corner of her lips. "Bummer. I mean, it seems like all the decent guys at school are taken, and really, what are the chances of someone suddenly becoming available?"

The great thing about best friends is that they know you really well. And the terrible thing about best friends is that . . . they know you *really* well. Bee knew that the thought of Ryan taking Mary Beth to Cotillion was killing me. And what better way to get me to change my mind about Cotillion than to dangle that possibility?

I met Bee's eyes. "You know what? After we grab some food, why don't we go back to the store and get those shoes? The more I think about it, the more I think they *would* be perfect with my dress."

Bee grinned. "I think that sounds like an excellent idea."

I watched Mary Beth watch Ryan, longing all over her face. And I remembered that while Ryan might not have seemed guilty, he had been leaning. Exactly the way he used to lean against my locker door back in ninth grade. No, there was no way I was letting this happen. Operation Get My You-Know-What Together was starting now.

So I smiled at Bee, hugged my boyfriend, and said, "Me, too."

Chapter 19

THAT MONDAY, I found myself back at Magnolia House. Saylor's eyes had widened a little when I'd walked through the door, but she hadn't said anything, other than, "Good afternoon, Harper. I trust you'll be ready to take over the prayer again?"

I had, and it had gone well. Unfortunately, the rest of the practice was going less smoothly.

"Oh, for Heaven's sake, Miss Riley!" Saylor snapped yet again.

As Mary Beth stammered out apologies, I rubbed my ankle and tried not to grimace.

Cotillion practice had only started half an hour ago, and this was Mary Beth's third fall. The first one had been before we'd even put on our heels, and the second one had nearly taken out the potted fern by the bay window, but this third one had been on me.

As usual.

Normally, I stuck up for Mary Beth when she stumbled, but after the stuff at the mall with Ryan, I was feeling less than charitable.

I was also feeling slightly unsettled. David was currently

slumped in one of the tiny velvet chairs in the sitting room, his legs out and crossed at the ankle. Even though I couldn't see his face behind the Kurt Vonnegut paperback he was holding, I had a feeling his expression was somewhere between boredom and disdain. It was the first time I'd been this close to him since that night at Saylor's, and even though I was doing my best to ignore it, it was almost like I could feel this thread stretching between us.

"Ladies," Saylor said, clapping her hands. "I realize you're all very busy and preoccupied, but Cotillion is one of the most important nights of your life. It's when you present to the world both the kind of woman you are and the kind of woman you would like to be."

"I am the kind of woman who would like to be done with this shit," Mary Beth muttered. She'd taken off her heels and they dangled from her fingers, bumping my shoulder blades. I rolled my back irritably, hoping she'd move them away. And stop talking. That also would've been nice.

Saylor didn't give any indication she'd heard Mary Beth. I'm pretty sure if she had, we would have seen Magnolia House's first murder. Instead, she clasped her hands in front of her and turned her gaze on me. "For example, Miss Price. What kind of woman do you want to be?"

The question threw me, and I suddenly realized that this was a test. Apparently, walking away from Paladin-dom wasn't going to be that easy.

I knew the things I wanted to *do*—make my school better, go to college, become the second female governor of the state of

Alabama—but I had a feeling that wasn't what Saylor was looking for. "I . . . I want to be a good woman," I said finally. "One who does the right thing, not only for her community, but for herself. Who follows her heart even if it's not the most popular thing to do."

There were a few giggles behind me. I knew how lame that answer had sounded, but it was true. Doing the right thing didn't seem like all that much, but look at Leigh-Anne. Look at what doing one wrong thing had cost her. Lame or no, that was my answer. And I hoped Saylor heard what I was really saying.

Across the room, I caught a little glare of light. I realized David had lowered his book, and was watching me, his lips pressed in a thin line. I wondered if he thought I was talking about him.

"That was a lovely answer, Miss Price," Saylor said. Her voice sounded . . . different. A little lower, and without those clipped tones she usually used. Then she gave a little shake of her head and clapped again.

"All right, now we're going to practice descending the staircase accompanied. On the actual night, your escort will lead you down these stairs. There is a trick to walking gracefully on the arm of a man, and luckily, my nephew, David, has graciously volunteered to assist us."

"If by 'graciously volunteered,' you mean 'was threatened and coerced,' then yes, I did," David said, unfolding himself from that tiny chair.

A muscle twitched in Saylor's jaw, but she let the remark pass.

"Go ahead and line up at the top of the staircase," she said, pulling that little blue pot of lip balm out of her pocket. "Oh, and Mary Beth, if you could come down here for a moment."

"Ugh, what now?" Mary Beth sighed, but she went.

"Remember, girls," Saylor called as David loped up the stairs, passing Mary Beth. "You are to lay your hand gently on the forearm, not loop your arm through his. This is Cotillion, not a square dance."

"I actually think square dances are less shameful than this," David muttered at the top of the stairs. Still, he held his arm out gallantly to Elizabeth Adams, keeping his spine straight and shoulders back. As they made their way down the staircase, I watched Saylor and Mary Beth. They had gone into the alcove by the front door, and Saylor was talking to her while holding her hands and looking into her eyes.

Once Elizabeth was at the bottom of the staircase, David jogged back up to take Abigail Foster's arm, then, once she was done, Amanda's, then Bee's. There was only one other girl between me and Bee: Lindsay Harris. According to The Aunts, every girl in town had done Cotillion when they were young, but now, fewer and fewer girls did it every year. It was becoming one of those traditions that some people thought was a little too old-fashioned, a little embarrassing.

Once Lindsay was safely at the bottom of the stairs, David came up to me, crooking his elbow. "Shall we?"

But before I could rest my hand on his forearm, Saylor called, "Actually, David, I'd like for Miss Riley to go first."

"Sure," David said, shrugging and raising his eyebrows.

I was left to hover there awkwardly as Mary Beth walked back up the velvet-covered stairs, her white heels still hanging from her hands. When she reached the top, she took a deep breath, slid the heels on, and took David's arm.

David made his way down the steps as carefully as if she'd been made of glass, but he shouldn't have bothered. Mary Beth didn't just walk. She floated. She glided. She practically levitated down those stairs.

As she passed me, I got a hint of rose, and then they were there at the bottom of the steps. With a little squeal, Mary Beth clapped her hands and bounced up and down on the balls of her feet. Even David seemed impressed.

Magic. Whatever Saylor had done to the lady who'd run Cotillion before, or the former head of the Pine Grove Betterment Society, she'd done it to Mary Beth, too. If you asked me, it seemed like kind of a waste of something so super powerful, but if it kept me from being trampled, I guess it was all for the good.

No reason to feel bad about ditching my Paladin duties, then. What would it matter if the occasional guy broke through Saylor's wards? Maybe she'd already made them stronger.

Now that Mary Beth had finally made her first successful run down the stairs, it was my turn again. David offered his arm, and I laid my palm as lightly as I could on his sleeve.

"We need to talk," he said in a low voice as we started to descend.

"We don't," I replied through clenched teeth.

I could feel his forearm tense under my hand. "Except that we *do*."

From her position at the bottom of the staircase, Saylor watched the two of us. Anyone observing would've thought she was making sure we were moving at the right pace while using the appropriate posture. But I knew better.

So when David turned to me again once we were done, I hurried off to the little powder room off the main foyer.

Like everything else in Magnolia House, it was done all in shades of burgundy and green. A tiny wicker table by the door held a basket of scented lotions and a small bowl of potpourri, and there were tiny framed pictures of Magnolia House throughout the years on the walls. It wasn't actually an antebellum house—they'd built the place in the thirties—but it was still a pretty exact replica of the big places that had once filled Pine Grove. They even kept antique furniture in the bedrooms upstairs.

I was studying one of the pictures when I realized what else was covering the walls—dark green wallpaper with a familiar pattern. My vision swam with skinny golden figure eights. My hands started shaking as I turned on the little gold faucet shaped like a swan. I splashed my face with cold water and was taking a deep breath when the door suddenly opened and David was standing there.

He went to shut the door, but I pushed past him before he could. Or at least I tried to. Even though my hands only shoved against the air half a foot from him, David still got out of the way, letting me into the hallway.

"No more skulking," I hissed, shooting a glance back at the main foyer. This corridor was nearly blocked by the main staircase, so David and I were partially hidden. "We don't have anything to talk about. Not anymore."

David made a move toward me. I thought he was going to grab my arm, but then he seemed to think better of it. "I need to talk to someone about this," he said, and there was almost something pleading in his voice.

Since I'd never heard David Stark plead for anything ever, I hesitated. Then I remembered how desperate I'd been to tell someone, anyone, about what had happened with Dr. DuPont.

So I stepped back a little farther into the shadows. "What is it?"

Sighing, David tugged at his hair before reaching into the pocket of his jeans. "This." He handed me a crumpled piece of paper, and I saw that it was an e-mail.

"This is the third one of these I've gotten this month."

From the foyer, I could hear Saylor announcing the next rehearsal, and I knew I didn't have much longer before I'd be missed. As quickly as I could, I scanned the e-mail.

Dear Mr. Stark: We here at the University of West Alabama are pleased to inform you that you have been selected for our Distinguished Student Scholarship. Recipients of this scholarship must first submit to an in-person interview with a representative from the university. We would be happy to schedule this interview at any time that is most convenient for you. Kindly contact us so that we might set up a time as soon as possible.

Underneath that there was a phone number and a name, Blythe Collier.

Handing him the paper, I glanced over my shoulder. "Okay, what's so weird about that? That's a legit scholarship. I've heard of it."

David leaned close enough for me to see my reflection in his glasses. "Yeah, it's legit, but you have to *apply* for it, Pres. They don't *offer* it to you. And there's no interview for it."

I flexed my fingers. "So someone might be trying to lure you out of town."

"Maybe." He was a little sheepish as he shoved the paper back into his pocket. "I know it sounds stupid—"

"David, you're really going to have to stop saying that. And look, I admit, maybe this is a bit fishy, but why tell me? Why not tell Saylor?"

Snorting, David tugged at his hair. "Can you blame me for not trusting her right now, Pres? She's lied to me my entire life. She's not even my actual aunt."

His voice rose on the last word, and I touched his arm. "Shhh. I know. But . . . she's in this with you. I'm not."

David looked down at me. "I'm not asking you to go full Paladin on this. But I . . ." He broke off and sighed. "God, I might actually choke on these next words. I trust you. And I wanna check this out, but I'm not stupid enough to go check it out myself, and I think I might . . . need you."

No. No. Tell him no. You are not his Paladin and this is not your issue anymore.

But I watched David chew a thumbnail, his skin pale. His other hand, shoved in his pocket, jangled change nervously, and he looked more freaked out than I'd seen him yet. That had to be the only reason I heard myself say, "E-mail her. Make an appointment. And I'll . . . I'll go with you."

Chapter 20

"THIS IS ridiculous. You know that, right?" David glared at me as he slid into the passenger seat, fastening his seat belt. "You could've come up to my house. Or I could've gone to your house. Basically, there were at least three options that didn't involve me walking three blocks from my house and you dressing like Carmen Sandiego."

I adjusted my sunglasses and pulled my hat a little farther down. "I'm not . . . look, you were the one who didn't want your aunt to know we were doing this. And I think it would be better if people didn't see us together." Especially since I'd begged off hanging out with both Ryan and Bee, telling them I was studying for the SATs.

David settled into his seat and immediately reached out to flip the radio on. My finger itched to push his hand away—I could be as bad as Bee when it came to people touching my radio—but music was probably better than awkward silence or bickering.

The drive out of town was pretty. Fall had come to Alabama in full force, the leaves orange, gold, and red. Overhead, the sky was that pure, impossible blue that only happens in the fall, and if I rolled down the window, I knew I'd smell wood smoke.

Nearly every other house we passed had some kind of Thanksgiving decorations in the window or on the mailbox. I counted three papier-mâché turkeys, two cling-form Pilgrims, and at least half a dozen cornucopias. Pine Grove definitely went all out for the holidays.

It wasn't until we were about a mile out of town that David finally turned down the radio. "We're going to feel really stupid if this is a totally legit scholarship offer, aren't we?"

I glanced over at him. "I won't, but you should. Who turns up to a scholarship interview in skinny jeans and a *Doctor Who* T-shirt?"

Reaching down, David slid the seat as far back as it would go before resting his heels on the glove compartment. "You mean like you did? Because there are few things less conspicuous than a teenage girl rocking a sombrero."

"It's not a—forget it. My choice of headgear is not the important thing. We need to figure out what we're going to do once we get there. I mean, if this *is* an attempt to lure you out of town to kill you or kidnap you or whatever, we should be prepared."

David shifted in his seat. "Isn't that your area?"

Uncomfortable, I shrugged. "I guess so."

Silence fell over the car again.

"Are you going to kill him?" David finally asked. "Or her?"

That was my job, right? Or it would be, if I were actually going to be a Paladin. Which I *wasn't*.

"We can question whoever it is," I said. "See how many of them there are, what their plans are."

"You heard Saylor. Their plans are probably to kill me."

"Yeah, but maybe we could get more of a sense of why. Is it the whole 'boys make crappy Oracles' thing, or is there more to it? For example, maybe you've been writing horrible articles about other people."

Snorting, David wrapped his arms around his knees. "No, you're the only person I torture in that particular way."

Why do you? I suddenly wanted to ask, but I bit back the question. David and my tangled personal history wasn't the issue here.

"Have you had any more . . . you know?" I lifted one hand off the steering wheel and wiggled it. "Visiony things?"

"Prophecies? No. Nothing since that night."

I made the turn into Merlington, driving down an oak-lined street. "Well, that's part of it, right? Being a boy means not having great visions." Overhead, the trees cast shadows on the car, covering David's face in dappled sunlight.

David shrugged. "Unless I do some kind of crazy spell on myself that makes me Mega Oracle."

I turned to look at him, nearly running a stop sign. "You wouldn't do that though, right?"

David dropped his feet from the dash, pulling at the hem of his T-shirt. "Seeing as how I wouldn't even know where to start on something like that, let's go with no."

He wasn't looking at me, but something in his voice wedged

under my skin like a splinter. "But even if you did know how," I said, "you . . . you wouldn't, right? I mean, you heard what Saylor said. That spell gave Alaric awesome visions and power, but it also fried up his brain and ended with lots of dead people."

David sighed, scrubbing a hand up and down the back of his neck. "Yeah, I got that part. Still, it sucks having visions that are so half-assed, you know? And no matter what Aunt—" He stopped, dropping his hand back to his lap. "I'm never going to stop doing that, am I?"

"You can still call her your aunt, David," I said, surprised at the gentleness in my voice. "I mean, she did raise you."

He made a noncommittal sound in reply before settling back in his seat. "All I'm saying is, being able to see the future but not really see the future is frustrating as hell. I get why someone would try a spell like that."

We drove past the big brick sign reading "The University of West Alabama," and I turned down the narrow street leading to campus. The library was at the end of the road, rising out of the bright green lawn like some kind of medieval church. I could already make out the stained-glass windows. "Well, the next time you start thinking like that, try to remember that Alaric ended up dead thanks to that spell."

David turned to me as I pulled into a parking space. In his glasses, I had to admit, I did look a little Carmen Sandiego-ish, so I tugged off the hat. "Okay, before we go in, anything else I should know?"

Unbuckling his seat belt, David dropped his gaze. "No."

"You are the worst liar in the entire world." As I shifted the car into park, a couple of girls walked past the car, long hair blowing in the breeze. Other than them, I didn't see anyone else in the parking lot.

"I'm not lying," he said, but I waved him off.

"Look, I know we're not exactly best friends, but we *have* known each other more or less since the womb. Remember in second grade when you spilled all the blue paint, and tried to say you hadn't? You're making the exact same face."

David rolled his eyes. "And what face is that?"

I jutted my jaw out and gave my best David scowl. "Kinda like this," I said through clenched teeth, and he gave a surprised laugh.

"Okay, I do *not* look like that. That looks like . . . I don't know, Dick Cheney."

"No, this is totally how you look when you lie," I insisted. "You did it with the blue paint and you're doing it now."

David's grin slowly faded and his fingers fiddled with the edge of his T-shirt, pulling it up over his bicep a little. Since when did David Stark have biceps? How did you get any muscle tone when all you did was type and be annoying?

"Trust me, Pres," he answered as he opened his door. "That's it. No more to tell."

He wanted me to trust him, and Saylor wanted him to trust her, and I just wanted this whole thing over with.

So why are you here? a little voice whispered inside my head. Instead of chasing that thought, I got out of the car and hurried after David.

He was looking at his phone. "Okay, so the appointment is in ten minutes on the second floor of the library. Which would be . . ." He pointed to the large Gothic building. "Here."

I stared at it, waiting to feel that sudden tightness in my chest that told me David was in danger. But there was nothing but the breeze brushing my hair into my face and the slight chill of early November. No vise around my heart, no Pop Rocks.

"Should we go in?" David asked, and I nodded.

Walking inside, the familiar old building smells of mildewed carpet and burnt coffee assaulted my nose, but other than that, everything felt . . . fine. Normal. Maybe this *was* a routine scholarship interview.

The office David had been told to go to was on the library's second floor. As we made our way up the stairs, everything was completely silent except for the squeak of David's sneakers on the stone floor. "Do you feel weird?" he asked.

I shook my head. "No. I feel . . . weirdly unweird, actually."

Slanting me a look, he gave a half-smile. "Only for us would unweird *be* weird."

It was easy enough to find 201-A. It was the first office right off the stairs, and when David knocked on the door, a pretty, petite brunette opened it, smiling at us. There were deep dimples on either side of her shining white teeth, and despite the imminent danger we might be in, I couldn't help wondering where she'd gotten her lipstick. That was a seriously gorgeous—ugh, no. Focus.

"Hi, there!" she said brightly. "David?"

It was hard to imagine anyone looking less like an assassin, especially since she was decked out in a pink and green Lilly Pulitzer dress.

David startled slightly, and I wondered if he was thinking the same thing. "Yeah," he finally said. Then, clearing his throat, he tried again. "I mean, yes, I'm David Stark."

The brunette reached out and shook his hand. "I'm Blythe," the woman—girl, really—said, pumping David's hand enthusiastically.

Then her eyes slid over to me. "Oh!" she said. "You brought a friend!" The dimples deepened, and she leaned forward with a conspiratorial wink. "Or is this your girlfriend?"

Rude, I thought, but then I realized we hadn't exactly come up with an excuse as to why I was here with David.

David slung an arm across my shoulders, and I automatically slid my arm around his waist. Seeing as how we were standing a few feet apart, I'm not sure if any two people have ever held each other more awkwardly.

"Yup," I said. "Girlfriend."

"So my girlfriend," David agreed, and I would've dug my fingers into his ribs if I'd been capable of it.

But if Blythe noticed our extreme awkwardness, she didn't acknowledge it. "Well, y'all come on in!" she said.

Once her back was turned, David glanced over at me. I knew what he was thinking. How could a girl who appeared to speak only in exclamation points possibly be a hired killer?

"I have to say, David, we have heard so many great things about you," Blythe said, going over to her desk. As she riffled through it, she added, "Oh, and could y'all shut the door, please?"

David turned to do that while Blythe kept talking. "You do not even know the trouble we've had trying to get in touch with you."

His hand still on the doorknob, David turned back to Blythe. "Yeah, you guys have sent a bunch of e-mails."

Blythe gave a light, trilling laugh. "Oh, trust me, it's been a lot more extensive than some e-mails." Suddenly her face brightened as she found whatever it was she'd been looking for.

"Oh, here we go!" she said chirpily. She was holding a letter opener, one that looked far longer and far sharper than necessary for opening mail.

For a second, all I could do was stare dumbly at the blade, wondering why I wasn't feeling the chest tightening and the Pop Rocks, and all of that.

Blythe planted one foot on the edge of the desk, launching herself up and over, and I realized why I hadn't felt like David was in danger.

She was lunging for *me*.

Chapter 21

Like it had that night with Dr. DuPont, my body started moving before my mind had time to catch up. David shouted, but I was already bracing myself, throwing up an arm to deflect the blow. Blythe landed on me, hard, and I felt something icy arc along the skin below my elbow. Then the ice turned into searing heat, and I saw a flash of red. *Oh my effing God*, I thought, almost from a distance. *She stabbed me. A girl in Lilly Pulitzer stabbed me.*

Gritting my teeth against the sudden blossom of pain, I reached up with my other hand, trying to grab her wrist, but she moved faster than I'd anticipated, snaking out one foot to hook around my ankle and send me crashing to the ground.

As she did, I managed to grab the hem of her dress, yanking her off balance, too. We fell together, my head thwacking the base of one of the chairs. I saw stars, and then another flash of silver as the blade darted at my throat. Without thinking, I grabbed at the letter opener, my palm closing around it. I could feel metal cutting into my skin, but the agony was nothing compared to the adrenaline and fear racing through me. Above me, Blythe had her teeth bared in a snarl. Sweat dotted her forehead and her upper lip, and strands of hair came loose from her pony-tail to cling to her cheeks. Her face was pale, dark eyes huge in her head, and I realized that despite her being the one with a weapon, she was scared. Terrified, even.

Blythe might have had the element of surprise on her side, but she wasn't a Paladin. I gripped the blade even harder, forcing her hand away from my throat. Red rivers were running down my forearm now, but I didn't care. I'd deal with the pain later.

I decided to go with the same move that had surprised Dr. DuPont. Jerking my head forward, I smacked my forehead as hard as I could against her nose. The letter opener dropped to the floor as Blythe raised both hands to her face with a watery cry. Pushing myself up on my elbows, I went to shove her off me, but before I could, there was a crash and the sound of breaking glass.

Blythe slid off me, boneless, and collapsed on the floor. Behind her, David stood clutching the remnants of the desk lamp. His eyes were wild and he was practically panting.

Wincing, I pushed myself up, taking care not to put any pressure on my injured hand. Now that the fight was over, the pain was even worse. I only had to glance at the gash bisecting my palm to know it was going to need stitches. Even as I stared down at Blythe, I was wondering how I could explain this particular injury to my parents.

"Jesus," David said, looking down at the blood dripping from my hand and arm. "Are you okay?"

When I stared at him wordlessly, he amended, "I mean, obvi-ously you're not, but . . . are you going to be?"

"I-I think so," I told him, but to be honest, I felt a little faint. Not from the blood loss and the pain—although they were part of it—but from how close that blade had been to my throat. How all my supposed superpowers hadn't counted for much when someone got the jump on me.

There was a little white cardigan hanging from the back of Blythe's chair, and I grabbed it, wrapping it as tightly as I could around my bleeding hand. The wound in my arm still hurt, too, but it wasn't as deep and it had already stopped bleeding.

"Why didn't you feel anything?" David asked. "Isn't that part of your whole deal? Like with the guys in the car?"

Staring down at Blythe, I shook my head. "Seems like I only feel that when someone's after you. She was trying to kill *me*."

David blinked. "So . . . your superpowers don't help you defend yourself, too? That seems kind of unfair."

It seemed a heck of a lot more than kind of unfair to me, but I didn't say that to David. "Give me that lamp. Or what's left of it," I said. When he did, I ripped the cord out of the base, then nodded at Blythe, who was beginning to groan a little. "Help me get her in a chair."

Once we did, I threaded the cord through the slats in the back of the chair, tying her hands tightly behind her back. Blythe stayed unconscious through the whole thing, blood dripping steadily from her nose, leaving bright red splotches next to all those little pink and green daisies on her dress.

"I can't believe no one heard all that," David said, gesturing to the blood on the carpet. Frowning, I looked up from the cord.

"Yeah, me neither. There aren't many people here, but you would think someone would've heard me nearly getting murdered."

Chewing on his thumbnail, David was still staring at the letter opener. It was lying on the carpet, edge gleaming in the fluorescent lights. "This is insane," he said at last.

I gave the knot one last tug and sighed. "Yes. As has been established."

Now that I was certain she was pretty securely tied to the chair, I stepped back next to David and studied our captive.

"She seems . . . younger," he said at last. "I thought she was too young to work at a college before, but now that I really *look* at her . . ."

She was young. Barely out of her teens, I'd guess. I looked at her crooked nose, wondering if I should feel guilty. But then I thought of her leaping over that desk, blade in hand.

Nope. No guilt here.

Moaning, she started to stir. "What are we going to do?" David whispered.

"Question her," I replied. My blood continued to drip steadily on the beige carpet, and underneath the fluorescent lights, David looked greenish. Outside, the leaves of a giant magnolia tree beat softly against the window.

"We can't . . . are you going to kill her?" I didn't think it was possible for David to look any more wretched, but as he turned to me, hands clenching and unclenching at his sides, I was worried he might throw up.

And I didn't know how to answer him. I honestly hadn't

thought about that. Meet this chick, question her, get a little more info on what was going on—that had been my whole agenda. But David was right, it wasn't like we could just leave her here. And she *had* tried to kill me. Before I could think through that any further, Blythe's eyes fluttered open.

They rolled around in her head for a second before coming to land on me. "You are a heck of a lot tougher than you look," she said, her voice thick.

I folded my arms over my chest. "Who are you?" I'd seen enough movies to know this was the part where the bad guys usually laughed and started spitting in people's faces, but the girl nodded at her name tag.

"Like it says on the freaking pin. Blythe." There was no hint of a Southern accent in her voice now.

"Yeah, right," David muttered next to me, but I ignored him.

"I don't mean your name." I'd only ever interrogated one person—a freshman cheerleader named Tori Bishop. Of course then, I'd been asking about some car wash money that had gone missing, not my potential murder. Still, I figured the technique would be basically the same. Clenching my jaw, I narrowed my eyes at Blythe. "I mean . . . what are you? You're not a Paladin—"

Blythe snorted and then winced. "Obviously. And since I'm clearly not an Oracle"— she jerked her head at David—"why don't you use the process of elimination?"

"You're a Mage," David said, mimicking my pose. "Like my— Like Saylor Stark."

Blythe surged against the cords holding her, eyes suddenly

fierce. "No, I am nothing like Saylor Stark. I do my damn job. I am loyal to the people who gave me this power."

"The Ephors?" I asked as David said, "How long have you been a Mage?"

We glared at each other, and Blythe's gaze flicked back and forth between us. The corner of her mouth lifted in a smirk, cracking the dried blood under her nose. "Which one of you am I supposed to answer first?"

After a moment, David rolled his eyes. "Her," he said, gesturing toward me. "Answer her first."

But instead of answering, Blythe kept looking at the two of us. "How old are you guys?"

"Seventeen," we answered in unison, and Blythe made a kind of gurgling chuckle. Seriously, I never wanted to break someone's nose again, even if they *were* trying to stab me. It had some majorly gross aftereffects.

"Me, too," she said. While she'd seemed young, she hadn't looked *that* young. David glanced over at me, and although telepathy wasn't part of the Paladin-Oracle bond, I still knew what he was thinking: *How effed up is this?*

Tightening the cardigan around my hand, I stared Blythe down. "You haven't answered my question."

Heaving a sigh, Blythe leaned back in the chair. "Yes, the Ephors," she said, and while she didn't add "you idiot," it was clearly implied. Then she looked at David. "And as for your question, about six months."

"How do they find you?" I found myself asking. Suddenly, I was really regretting not asking Saylor more about all of this. It would've been nice to know that Mages could be just as homicidal and dangerous as Paladins in their own way.

Blythe looked up at me, tilting her face. "You know those tests you take in school? The things that judge aptitude for certain careers?"

"I worship those tests," I said, leaning back against one corner of the desk.

A lock of hair had fallen into Blythe's eyes, and she huffed out a breath. "Me, too. There are questions woven into that thing that alert the Ephors to people who have Mage potential."

David stepped back a little, nearly tripping over a jar of pens. It must have fallen during the fight with Blythe. Righting himself, David rubbed one hand over his mouth, studying Blythe. "But a Mage's power can be passed on, right?"

Sighing, Blythe rolled her neck. "Yes, but it helps to find someone with a few natural abilities if you can. If the Ephors have time, which they did in my case. The Mage before me knew she was dying for months. Plenty of time to prepare."

Over Blythe's head, David and I locked eyes. That was an interesting little fact. I wondered if it worked the same way for Paladins. But before I could ask, Blythe jerked her head in my direction and said, "Now would the two of you get on with the killing me part already?"

"We're not going to kill you," I heard myself say, and when Blythe looked up at me, eyebrows raised, I hastily added, "I mean, not yet. So long as you tell us what we need to know."

The letter opener was near the door, so I picked up the nearest weapon I could lay hands on: a stapler.

I lifted it, going for "menacing." I admit it lacked a certain elegance, but hey. It was worth a shot.

David placed his hand on my arm and pushed it back down. "What?"

"Just . . . that's embarrassing for all of us," he replied.

Blythe gave another one of those laughs that made me shudder. "This is such a freaking mess," she muttered before fixing me with her dark eyes. "You don't even know what's really going on here, do you? What's your name, Paladin?"

"Harper Price," I said, good manners automatically kicking in over sense.

"Do you want to give her your address, too?" David muttered, but Blythe's gaze stayed on me.

"Well, listen to me, Harper Price. Me, the people I work for . . . we don't want to hurt David. We want to *help* him."

I opened my mouth, but David replied before I could say anything. "Help me?" His voice was tight with anger, and he reached up to tug at his hair, never a good sign. "You killed the man who was sworn to protect me."

"That wasn't me—" Blythe said, but David acted like she hadn't spoken.

"You tried to run me over," he said, eyes wide behind his glasses. I could see a flush creeping up his neck.

Scowling, Blythe struggled a little against the cords. "Okay, that *was* me, but technically I was after *her*—"

"And then, to top it off, you lure me out of town and try to stab Harper right in front of me."

By now, David was nearly shouting, and again, I wondered

why no one was running in. Surely we'd made enough noise to bring someone up here. I mean, this was a library, for goodness' sake.

"If you're trying to help me, why would you—or the people you work for—do any of that crap?" David rocked back on his heels, waiting for an answer, and I would've felt sorry for Blythe had it not been for the whole stabbing thing. Being on the other end of a David Stark Glare was a truly unpleasant thing.

Blythe sat up as straight as the cords would allow, leaning forward. "Because," she said, clenching her teeth, "those people—that janitor, your so-called aunt—they were holding you back, David. You have a destiny, and I'm here to help you fulfill it."

Chapter 22

THERE WAS a pause. In it, I could hear the ticking of the little clock above Blythe's desk, but nothing else. No sounds from downstairs, nothing from the parking lot outside. Finally, David took off his glasses and scrubbed a hand up and down his face. "I am so effing sick of that word," he muttered, and I found myself nodding. "Destiny" was not my favorite word these days either.

"The Ephors wanted to kill David," I told Blythe. "Because of his . . . boy parts and stuff."

David lifted his head at that, and I think he mouthed, *Really?* at me, but I was watching Blythe.

She held my stare, grinning, and between the blood, her ridiculously young face, and the Lilly Pulitzer, it was more than a little unsettling. "So you're not totally ignorant, then. Awesome. Yes, at first the Ephors thought that David's 'boy parts' would make him a bad Oracle. After all, the only one they'd ever had didn't exactly work out for them."

"Alaric," David said, polishing his glasses on the bottom of his shirt.

"The very same," Blythe said with a little nod. "So you can

imagine why they were very anti–boy Oracle for a while there. But"— Blythe's smile went from slightly unhinged to smug, but still seriously unhinged—"that was before they found *me*."

David still had his glasses dangling from his fingers, but at that, he put them back on and squinted at her. "What does that mean?"

"No offense or anything, but Saylor Stark has nothing on me as far as the alchemy game goes," Blythe said, settling back into the chair. For the first time, I honestly believed she was seventeen. "I mean, Saylor can do a mind-control potion on what? One, two people at a time, max? I've got this whole *freaking* library under my thumb right now." Smirking, she tried to cross her legs, but the way we'd tied her to the chair made that impossible. She settled for bringing her knees tighter together. "I got a job here as a volunteer, and every Friday, they do this big potluck thing. One potion in a batch of brownies, and bam. I have an of-fice, an official e-mail account . . ."

My hand was starting to feel a little numb, so I loosened the cardigan around it. As I did, I saw Blythe's gaze flick to her sweater, a tiny frown creasing her brow. "So that's why no one came up here when we fought," I said, getting it at last. "Alchemy."

Tearing her eyes from her blood-soaked cardi, Blythe nodded. "I didn't want to be disturbed."

"So what does your badass alchemy have to do with David?" I asked, looping the sweater around my hand again. Blythe grimaced.

"I liked that sweater," she said, and while I could appreciate an attachment to clothes, I was quick to snark back, "I liked my hand."

Blythe rolled her eyes. "You were the one who grabbed the knife."

As she said it, some of the adrenaline started to wear off, and a wave of nausea swept through me as I remembered the blade so close to my throat, the blinding pain of wrapping my palm around it. How close to death had I actually been? Moments, definitely. And for the second time in my life. Third if you counted the car chase.

I was pretty sure Paladins weren't supposed to feel scared or sick, but that was fine. I wasn't *really* one. Was I?

That wasn't something I wanted to think about right now, so I scowled at Blythe. "Answer my question," I said. "What does your . . . magic or whatever have to do with David?"

David had moved across to Blythe's desk, and he leaned back against it, bracing himself on his hands as he waited for Blythe to answer. That put him a little bit behind her, and I could tell she was trying to look at him out of the corner of her eye.

"Boy Oracles can be just as awesome as girl Oracles. Heck, they can be *better*." Behind her back, she flexed her fingers. "And—look, can y'all loosen these things? I can't feel my hands."

David made a move forward, but I held up my hand. "Answers first."

The look Blythe gave me was weirdly approving. She shrugged and continued, "If you know the right kind of alchemy to use—which, hi, I do—you can . . . I don't know, like, *supercharge* him. Make it so that he can see further into the future. And more. And it's not even that difficult of a spell, really. Some alchemy requires, like, lizard innards and stuff, but this is just saying some—"

"We know about the spell," I interrupted, clenching my hands at my side. "It made Alaric insane and ended with a whole bunch of people dead and a whole village destroyed."

Disgust flickered over Blythe's cherubic face. "Because he wasn't a Mage. The spell itself isn't bad. It was just that Alaric didn't know what the heck he was doing. I would. I mean, I *do*. And there's so much you could do once the spell was in effect."

"Like what?" David asked, and even though she couldn't look right at him, Blythe swiveled her head in his direction.

"Come with me and I'll show you," she said, her voice lower than before, almost like a purr.

David straightened a little, and I saw him swallow hard. "Um . . . no. Thank you," he said, and it was all I could do not to roll my eyes. Boys, honestly.

"Okay, so the Ephors want David all Super Oracle. Got it. That really doesn't sound all that bad, I guess."

Blythe's eyes narrowed as David startled. "Pres?"

I kept going. "And of course, once they have a Super Oracle, it makes total sense that they'd want to kill, you know, *the person sworn to protect him.*"

Gripping the arms of Blythe's chair, I leaned down, getting in her face. "Oh, wait, except it doesn't make sense at all. If you guys want David to be more powerful, why kill Mr. Hall? Why kill *me*?"

For the first time, Blythe seemed unsure. She dropped her gaze, and David stepped forward, coming to stand behind me.

"Because the spell is dangerous," he said softly. "Why else would Harper need to be out of the way?"

My head shot up. Saylor had said that spell ended up destroying Alaric. As David's Paladin, would I need to protect him from that?

Blythe's big brown eyes widened in appreciation. "No," she said, shaking her head. "It's not—well, there is a *slight* danger element, maybe. But, hi, crossing the freaking street can be dangerous. And like I said, Alaric wasn't a Mage. He wasn't *me*. So it wouldn't *be* dangerous. Just because he screwed up the spell doesn't make it a bad spell. Just a bad . . . spellcaster."

I might have bought that if her gaze hadn't slid from David to the bright splash of blood—mine or hers, I wasn't sure—on the carpet. "I would do it right."

My head ached, and my hand and arm were still stinging, and I felt this weird desire to curl up on my bed and cry. Or sleep. Instead, I tightened my hold on Blythe's chair. "So that's the test David has to face at Cotillion? You're going to do some spell on him that will either soup up his powers, or turn him into a crazy person."

From behind me, I heard David make some kind of noise, but I didn't turn around to face him. One problem at a time.

The dried blood around Blythe's face cracked and flaked when she smiled. "Look, I am trying to help you guys out. Just . . . just go with it, okay? Don't fight me, don't try to stop me. David will have awesome powers, the Ephors will have an Oracle again, and we can all be buddies. The three of us, working together, kicking ass, taking names . . . all that."

"We already *have* a Mage," David said, coming to stand beside me. I could feel him trembling, but his voice was steady. "Saylor Stark."

Blythe blew a breath out, ruffling her bangs. "Who can maybe do a couple of weak mind-control spells. Boring. I'm offering you everything. All the power you could ever want."

Flexing his fingers, David just watched her.

I shook my head. "Okay." Setting my hands on my hips, I faced Blythe. "Interrogation over."

It might have been the bad lighting, but I thought her olive skin went a little pale. "So this is the part where you kill me, huh?"

I should. Everything in my blood was urging me to kill her. Somehow, I knew that if I gripped her head the right way, jerked her neck just so, she'd be dead in less than a second. No blood, no fuss, and almost no pain at all. But even as my fingers curled into my palms, as cold sweat trickled down my back, I knew I couldn't do it. Self-defense was one thing. This felt like . . . murder. Besides, there was something else I could do with Blythe.

"We need to take her to Saylor," I told David. "She'll know what to do." I wasn't a hundred percent sure that was true, but I was positive that *I* sure as heck didn't know what to do.

David must've felt the same way because he shoved his hands in his pockets and rocked back on his heels. "Yeah. We definitely need an adult."

It wasn't that funny, but the whole afternoon had been so stressful that I burst into giggles. Surprised, David rocked back farther, but, after a second, a slow grin spread across his face.

"Wait, are you two really a thing?" Blythe asked, making David's grin disappear.

"No," he said quickly, and I shook my head so hard it was a wonder I didn't sprain something. "No," I echoed. "No, no, no, no. Vast worlds of no."

I think Blythe would've said something sarcastic in reply, but David didn't give her the chance. "We need to get you out of this building without anyone seeing it. You have anything for that?"

Blythe slumped in her bonds, dimples vanishing, big brown eyes going dull. "If I say no, are you going to staple me to death?"

David bent down and picked up the letter opener, tossing it to me. It was slick with blood—*my* blood—but I still caught it easily with my good hand. "No," he told her. "If you say no, Harper gets her turn with that."

It was a tone I'd never heard David use, and considering how long I'd known him, that was saying something. He sounded steely and grown-up, and threatening. Almost like someone who could be a superpowered . . . something.

But this was *David Stark*. The only threatening thing about him was his toxic level of obnoxiousness.

Still, it worked on Blythe. She jerked her head toward her desk. "Top drawer. Bottle of nail polish. Dab a dot on all of us, we're as good as invisible."

I moved to the drawer, and pulled it out before something occurred to me. "David, why don't *you* get it?"

He crossed the room in a couple of strides and rifled through the open drawer. When I didn't double over in pain, I gave a little nod. "Okay, it's safe."

Blythe was watching me from under her bangs, her brown eyes sparkling. "Smart girl. But, honestly, if I had some kind of deadly potion, wouldn't I have used that on you instead of a letter opener?"

David snorted, turning the bottle of nail polish over in his long fingers. "She has a point, Pres." As I snatched the bottle from him, he reached up to smooth his hair, making him look . . . well, he was never going to be entirely presentable, but at least *better.*

After dotting the back of all of our hands with the nail polish, David and I managed to untie Blythe, get her out of the chair, and tie her back up without her attempting to murder me. We navigated her down the stairs, and sure enough, even though we passed several people, no one so much as glanced in our direction. It was eerie.

We were at the car before David asked, "Why don't Mages have potions that can kill people?"

I wasn't sure if Blythe's expression of disgust was for the question or for the way I kind of manhandled her into the backseat. "We're not that powerful. A little mind control, some temporal disturbances . . . those we can pull off. Anything to do with human life is a little trickier. But I'm working on it, trust me."

"Is that how you survived the car crash into my pool?" I asked her, but Blythe just fidgeted on the seat, trying to tuck her dress underneath her.

"I actually poofed out of there before the car hit."

"You can just 'poof' out of places?" David leaned his forearms on the roof of the car, looking in at Blythe. "Can you also just poof into places?"

I handed David the keys—my hand still hurt too much to think about wrapping it around a steering wheel—and slid into the passenger seat, buckling my seat belt. "David, maybe *don't* give the tiny psychotic witch ideas, okay?"

As David pulled out of the parking lot, I leaned back and closed my eyes, taking a deep breath through my nose. *We'll take her to Saylor. Saylor will know what to do.*

The more I repeated it, the better I felt. In fact, as David got closer to Pine Grove, I was feeling almost . . . proud. My first real mission as a Paladin, and I had captured the enemy, learned something about the other side's plans, and managed not to get too horribly injured. Of course, I'd still need to go to the hospital. My hand would need stitches, which meant coming up with a good excuse for my parents. But when I slid the sweater sleeve off my hand, I could see that the wound was already beginning to heal. It was puckered and red and ugly, but mostly closed. I turned my hand back and forth, marveling at it, and David glanced over.

"Whoa," he murmured, and I nodded.

The "Welcome to Pine Grove" sign loomed in the distance, and I actually smiled a little bit. Yes. Today was definitely one for the win column.

David must've felt the same, because as we sped into town,

he looked over at me and said, "You know, Pres, this was actually . . . I don't want to say fun because of the attempted stabbing, but—"

"No," I said. "I get what you mean. We did good work today. And once we get her—"

I turned to the backseat, ready to face Blythe's sullen expression and found myself staring at . . . nothing.

The backseat was empty.

Chapter 23

THE CAR shook and shimmied as he slammed on the brakes and swerved off the road. Throwing it in park, he turned around in his seat and joined me in staring slack-jawed at the spot where Blythe had been. "How?"

"She's a Mage," I offered, too stunned to think of anything else. Saylor had said their magic was pretty low-level. Making yourself disappear was not what I considered low-level magic.

David made a sound that was somewhere between a laugh and a groan, and lowered his forehead to the seat.

"She wasn't kidding about her alchemy game, was she?" he asked, his voice hoarse.

As I looked at the empty backseat, all I could see was Blythe leaping over that desk, Mr. Hall bleeding to death on the bathroom floor. They weren't trying to kill David, they were trying to kill *me*, and I had let one of my would-be assassins go. One who had way more power than I'd prepared for, at that.

After a beat, David turned to me. "You wanna drive around for a little bit?"

Wordlessly, I nodded. David turned my car down one of the side streets leading toward Pine Grove Park, and we drove until we reached the little hill above the playground.

We sat in silence while watching kids scampering over the brightly colored playground equipment. A little girl climbed up the same slide where, when we were eight, I'd shoved David off the ladder. Or had he shoved me? I couldn't remember. And there, on the swing set, a boy sat on the swing where Ryan had given me my first kiss.

Shutting off the ignition, David leaned forward on the steering wheel. "She wants you dead," he said.

I looked at my hand again. "Yeah, I got that."

He let out a heavy sigh, dropping his forehead to the steering wheel. "So what do we do now?"

I wished I had an easy answer. I wished I could pretend none of this was real, and that everything could go back to the way it was. But now there was a lot more on the line than my social life. My actual *life* was at stake here, and while the idea of hiding under the covers, preferably until Rapture, was appealing, it didn't seem to be an option.

Sitting up straight, I pushed my hair away from my face, gathering it into a loose knot. David's backpack was at my feet, and I fumbled through it until I found a notebook and a pen. Skipping past a bunch of sketches at the front—which, hey, were actually pretty decent. I stopped, looking more closely at a few. There was Chie, his friend from newspaper, her dark hair curling around one ear, hand playing with her bangs. And there was Bee, laughing. Bee did this thing when she laughed of tipping her head all the way back, mouth open and teeth flashing. David had captured it perfectly, and I couldn't help but smile.

I flipped to another page, and there was me. I took up nearly the whole sheet of paper, standing next to a wall of lockers, my head slightly down, face in profile. I was smiling, but my shoulders were tense and I was clearly twisting my ring around my finger.

Clearing his throat, David pulled the notebook back and flipped to a blank page. "I like drawing people," was all he said before once again placing the notebook back in my hands.

Something seemed to have settled over the car, something heavy and weirdly tense, like the air before a storm.

"When did you draw—" I asked, but David tapped the blank paper in front of me.

"So what was all that stuff Blythe said?"

Taking the hint, I nodded and picked up a pen. "Okay. So the Ephors want to do a spell that makes you Mega Oracle." I jotted that down. "And they're doing it at Cotillion."

David was studying me over the rims of his glasses. "Are you . . . making a flow chart?"

"Shut up. Also, why is it that prophecies are always so vague and mystical? I mean, would it kill you to be able to say, "Oh, the bad guys are coming on *this* day at *this* place and they're going to do *this* thing? 'Night of the Swans,' honestly . . ."

A ghost of a smile flittered across David's face. "I'll try to make things more specific the next time I have terrifying visions of the future, Pres."

I caught myself smiling back before returning my attention to the notebook. "But now we know what this test you have to face is. She's going to try the spell on you. So all I have to do is keep that from happening."

David nodded, but he didn't seem any happier. "Unless she kills you first."

I swallowed around the sudden lump in my throat. The cold sweat was back, too. You know, if the universe is going to give you superstrength and superspeed and fighting skills you never had, it should also give you some kind of anti-fear power.

"Saylor has wards up all around town to protect you, right? Well, we'll see if she can whip up some for me, too." My voice was light as I said it, but the hand holding the pen shook a little, and David was still frowning.

"You're serious," he said after a moment. "You really want to do this. Be my Paladin. Fight the forces of evil during your Cotillion."

I laid the pen on the notebook and met his eyes. "It's the only choice. These people want me out of the way—"

"Dead," David interjected, and I scowled at him.

"Yes, dead." I tucked my hair behind my ears. "Why do you keep bringing that up?"

"Because I want you to get it," he snapped back, his hands squeezing the steering wheel. "Because the idea of someone—anyone—*dying* for me makes me feel sick, and the thought of *you* dying for me is . . ."

Breaking off, he squeezed the steering wheel again, fingers flexing almost convulsively. "Pres, this is real. It's real, and it's scary, and it's so messed up, I don't even know where to start. You could die. I could die. People are actively trying to hurt us. And I feel like we both need to . . . acknowledge that. Use words like 'dead' instead of cutesy euphemisms."

Cold sweat was still prickling all over my body. Outside the car, on one of the benches, a harried young mom in jeans and a black turtleneck called out something to her kid, probably "Be careful!" My own mom had sat on that same bench, saying the same thing to me.

I thought of Mom's tired smile, of her sad eyes, and the big hole that Leigh-Anne had left in our house. If something happened to me . . . Blinking against the stinging in my eyes, I picked up the pen and started to write again. I would have to make sure nothing *did* happen to me.

"You're right," I said, and David didn't say anything for a long time.

Then, finally, "It hurt you to say that, didn't it?" Out of the corner of my eye, I saw him lean back in his seat.

"The words nearly choked me, yeah."

He snorted, and I went back to writing. "So, yes, people want me dead. They might do a spell that makes *you* dead. Happy now?"

David reached around the headrest to stretch his arms. "Will you start saying the real F-word with more regularity, too?"

"Don't push it," I replied, as outside, a gust of wind sent dead leaves rattling against the car. Cotillion was only three weeks away. Three weeks didn't seem like nearly enough time to plan for something this big. Heck, last year's Spring Fling had taken me over two *months* to prepare.

Glancing up from my notebook, I took in David as he slouched in his seat. Once again his hair was all mussed and his glasses were slightly crooked, and he was obviously thinking over something pretty hard. His brow was furrowed and his fingers drummed against the steering wheel.

"What are you fretting about so hard over there?" I asked him.

He worried at his lower lip for a moment before answering. "Remember when I told you about those crazy dreams I always had?"

"Yeah."

"Well . . . one of them was about you."

My heart thudded heavily in my chest, but I made my voice as light as I could. "Ew. So don't want to hear about that."

Now he did smile, but only a little. "No, not like that. You asked me the other day why it was that you and I could never seem to get along. And, I mean, yes, part of it was competition."

"Egregious," I muttered, and now his smile was a little wider.

"Felicitations," he replied, and some of the tightness in my chest eased. "But part of it—" He broke off and thumped his head back against the steering wheel.

"God, this is so dumb." He sat up again, his eyes on the ceiling. "When I was like five or six, I dreamed that you killed me."

"Okay," I said slowly, and he swiveled his head to look at me.

"I always knew a dream was a stupid reason not to like you. But now . . . Pres, apparently I can see the future. What if—"

I cut him off with a wave of my hand. "No. Saylor said you were only now starting to come into your powers. You probably didn't even have them when you were five."

He nodded, but his knuckles were white around the steering wheel. "Only . . . you weren't angry in the dream. Neither was I. It was like we were both . . . sad. I woke up crying and everything."

The hairs on the back of my neck prickled. Even as he said it, it was like I could see it. Me and David, staring at each other, tears streaming down both of our faces. There was something in my hand . . .

But wait. No, there was no way that could happen.

Making a fist, I pulled my arm back and swung at his face with everything I had. David gave a startled cry and flattened himself against the other side of the car, but the punch never landed. Instead, my fist came to a halt six inches from his nose.

"See?" I said, and relief washed over his face.

"Right." David gave a shaky laugh. "You can't hit me."

"I can't so much as pinch you," I replied. "So killing you? Totally off the table. Now let's drop that, and get back to the real problem, namely this."

I thumped the notebook with my pen, dismayed to see that everything Blythe had told us didn't even take up a whole page. "You need to call your Aunt Saylor."

"She's not—"

"I know, I know." Lifting a hand, I waved him off. "But you know what I mean. We need to talk to her as soon as possible and tell her what happened. Call her and tell her to meet us—" I checked my watch. It was only a little past one in the afternoon. Hard to believe it had only been a few hours since we set off for Merlington. "Tell her to go to Miss Annemarie's Tearoom."

David already had his phone out, but he paused, lifting both eyebrows. "And you want us to talk about this in Little Old Lady Land why?"

Miss Annemarie's was a Pine Grove institution. A tiny room filled with china, chintz, and more ceramic cats than anyone should ever own, the tearoom catered almost exclusively to senior citizens. It was one of The Aunts' favorite places to go for lunch, but today was Saturday, and they only went on Wednesdays.

"I want to talk this out in a neutral area," I told David. "And, no offense, but ever since that night, your house gives me the creeps."

He nodded, sympathetic. "Yeah, I get that."

"Plus, everyone at Miss Annemarie's is ancient, so there's less chance of being overheard."

"Good thinking." David went to dial, but before he did, stopped, ducking his head a little so he could meet my eyes. "So we're really doing this. You're going to fully accept Paladin-hood or whatever."

The way I saw it, my only foolproof way of getting out of this thing alive was getting rid of Blythe and ensuring the spell didn't happen at Cotillion. It had taken the Ephors seventeen years to find her; who knew how long they'd have to search for a new Mage? Besides, no Blythe, no spell, no need to kill David's Paladin.

But all I said to David was, "Harper Jane Price doesn't quit. Ever."

David's lips quirked. "Yes, I believe I've picked up on that over the years."

He turned back to his phone, punching in Saylor's number. As he talked to her, making plans to meet in a few minutes, I watched the kids playing and tried to tell myself I wasn't making a huge mistake.

Chapter 24

"YOU SHOULD TRY the oolong," Saylor told David as she unfolded her menu at Miss Annemarie's. As I'd anticipated, the tearoom was nearly empty, with the exception of two women sitting by the front window, both of them easily in their eighties. Outside, the wind had picked up, and gray clouds moved swiftly across the sky. Miss Annemarie's was situated in the town square, right next to the jewelry shop where The Aunts bought all my Christmas and birthday presents. In the middle of the square, there was a statue of one of the town founders, Adolphus Bridgeforth. David was glaring at Saylor over the top of his menu. "I hate oolong," he told her. "It tastes like leaves."

"It *is* leaves," I noted, opening my napkin over my lap.

"Touché," he muttered, a faint smile hovering on his lips.

Saylor was watching David, and the look on her face wasn't quite sadness and it wasn't exactly longing, but it was some mixture of the two. Then she folded up her menu, slid the corner of it under her saucer, and folded her hands on the table, fingers clenched.

Her diamonds winked in the light from the tiny lamp in the

center of the table, and now her expression was as placid as all the china cats dotting the restaurant. Seriously, Miss Annemarie could give Saylor a run for her money in the glass knickknacks department. "Well," she said at last. "I assume the two of you had a reason for bringing me to Miss Annemarie's."

I squirmed a little bit in my rose-patterned damask chair. I'd made my chart and I thought I had a good idea of what I wanted to tell Saylor, but there was no escaping the fact that David and I had kind of screwed up today. Even though I knew Saylor wasn't the person I'd thought she was, old habits die hard, and I hated the thought of disappointing her.

Maybe David picked up on that, because he leaned over the table, and in a very low voice, said, "Something happened today."

Saylor didn't move, but her eyes flicked to my hand. We'd stopped on our way back into town to get bandages and antibiotic cream for my cut, and the majority of my palm was swathed in gauze. "I can see that."

As quietly and quickly as he could, David told Saylor about Blythe, pausing only when Miss Annemarie tottered over to take our orders. When he was done, Saylor sat very still, her face totally blank. But her hand was clutching her fork so hard, I was afraid she might actually bend the metal. "And the two of you decided to tackle this by yourselves why exactly?" she asked, voice syrupy sweet, eyes blazing.

I took a sip of ice water, stalling for time, but David already had an answer. "Because I don't trust you," he said. "Her," David added, gesturing to me with a teaspoon, "I trust."

Miss Annemarie reemerged with our food—chicken salad for me and Saylor, a club sandwich for David. As she set it down on the table, Miss Annemarie smiled at me. "How are your aunts, Harper?"

"Fine, thank you," I said, hoping that would be enough. I loved the old ladies in my town, but dear God, they could *talk*. And Miss Annemarie didn't show any signs of quitting. "And your parents?"

"Also fine, thank you, Miss Annemarie."

The old woman sighed and shook her head, chins wobbling. "They've been so strong after your sister passed. Such a tragedy."

I forced a tight smile. "They have, yes."

"I'm keeping y'all on my prayer list," she murmured, patting me on the shoulder before shuffling back to the kitchen. Now the two women by the window were looking over at us, squinting like they were trying to recognize me. *Yes,* I wanted to say, *I am Leigh-Anne Price's sister. Yes, that Leigh-Anne, the Homecoming Queen who wrapped her car around a tree when she was totally smashed.*

"You okay?" David asked in a low voice.

Clearing my throat, I speared a mayo-coated grape with my fork. "Yup. Now, back to what we were saying about Blythe. She told David that they didn't want to kill him anymore; now they want to do a spell on him. Apparently it's the same one—"

I didn't get to finish. Saylor's hand was shaking so badly she nearly dropped her tiny cup of oolong.

She put it back in the saucer amid a clatter of china. "Alaric's ritual."

"That's the one," David said around a mouthful of club sandwich. "But Blythe said it only went so badly with Alaric because he wasn't a Mage. She thinks if she tried it—"

"Don't even finish that sentence, David Stark," Saylor snapped. Outside, the wind blew harder, rattling the big window, and all three of us jumped. "Didn't you hear what I said the other night? That ritual drove Alaric mad. It resulted in the deaths of hundreds. It turned him into a monster."

Saylor laid her hands flat on the table, and I could see they were trembling slightly. "No matter what this girl said, it's the ritual itself that's dangerous. Alaric had to be put down like a dog. And you said this Blythe girl was . . . what was the term you used, David?"

He swallowed before answering, "Super psycho bitch batshit."

Saylor's upper lip curled. "Ah, yes. Charming. And only seventeen, right?"

When we both nodded, she closed her eyes and took a deep breath. "The temporal shifts, the vanishing spell . . . those are things Mages just don't do. They're too dangerous, too risky, too . . . big. And she's using them all over the damn place. What must they be thinking, using someone so young to attempt something so insane? And *why?*"

I shook my head. "She claimed she could do it better than Alaric, and that David and the Ephors could work together afterward. Apparently surviving this ritual is the test David has to face the night of Cotillion."

"Which I'm still in favor of just skipping altogether," David said, dumping three packets of sugar into his cup.

Saylor stirred her tea with more force than was probably necessary. "I told you, there is no skipping it. This event is preset. Destined."

David and I both groaned a little at that word, but I had to admit, it made sense. "Think of it this way," I told David, tossing my hair over my shoulder. "At least we know when it'll happen. We have a set date to prepare for."

If the way David glowered at his tea was any indication, he wasn't exactly buying that, but he gave a little shrug. "Okay."

I shot a look over at the old ladies by the window, but they were deeply involved in their crème brûlée and not paying any attention to us. "Miss Saylor, could you get back to that part about putting Alaric down like a dog?" I glanced over at David. He wasn't looking at me, but was tracing little patterns on the tablecloth with his fork. "You said almost all of his Paladins died protecting him. So who killed Alaric?"

Saylor was quiet for so long that I didn't think she was going to answer. And then, finally, "The other two Paladins."

David's fork stopped moving on the table, snagging on the gingham. "How? If their 'sacred duty' is to protect—"

"Alaric was a danger to himself in that state." Saylor reached out, her hand hovering over David's for a moment before she pulled it back. "Which meant the inherent contradiction in that overrode the Paladins' instinct to keep him safe."

Lowering her head, Saylor pinched the bridge of her nose. "If we were at my house, I'd be able to show you. I have books, illustrations, things you'll need to see."

Giving up the pretense of eating—my mouth was too dry, my

stomach too jumpy—I pushed my plate away. "Well, we're not at your house. If I'm going to do this, I need to do it . . . my way."

"There is no your—" Saylor said, but she broke off as the front door to the tearoom rattled open, bringing another puff of wind and the smell of rain. As her eyes widened, I heard a familiar voice say, "Jewel, honestly, no soup is worth going out on a day like this."

My heart sank as I heard Aunt Jewel reply, "Oh, hush, it's not even raining."

"Yet," Aunt May snapped.

Turning slowly in my chair, I took in my aunts, all huddling in the doorway of the restaurant. The three of them were all dressed in nearly identical black slacks, orthopedic shoes, and bright sweaters. Aunt Martha saw me first, her eyes widening in pleasure. "Oh, look, girls!" she trilled. "It's Harper Jane!"

Smiling weakly, I raised my hand in a little wave as they started to bear down on me. As they did, the front door opened again, and there, right behind The Aunts, was my mom.

Chapter 25

MOM LOOKED toward The Aunts and, finding them, saw me. Her brow wrinkled in confusion. "Harper?" she said, walking toward the table. Compared to the aunts in their party-colored sweaters, Mom looked a little wan in her silky cream blouse and tan slacks. Her hair, a few shades lighter than mine, was mussed from the wind.

"Mom!" I said, trying my best not to sound guilty.

"Hillary, you didn't tell us Harper would be here, too," Aunt May said. Mom shook her head. "I . . . didn't know she would be. You did say you were going out with Bee today, didn't you, Harper?"

It wasn't really a question; Mom knew exactly what I'd said. Still, I wondered why she looked so befuddled. I mean, she'd caught me having lunch in Miss Annemarie's Tearoom with Saylor and David. It wasn't like she'd found me smoking crack in an alley.

"Plans fell through," I told her, wrinkling my nose like "What can you do?" "But then I ran into Miss Saylor, and she asked me out to lunch with her and David."

Next to me, David lifted his hand in greeting, and Saylor picked up her teacup, taking a swallow. Only seconds ago, she'd been rattled and freaked out. Now she looked like she always did: cool, collected, Queen of Pine Grove.

"It was so sweet of Harper to join us," she said. "Boys never really appreciate this place."

No one under seventy-five really appreciated Miss Annemarie's, but Mom nodded. Still, that crease between her brows didn't ease.

"Why don't we pull a table over?" Aunt Jewel asked, tugging at the hem of her purple sweater. "I'm sure Annemarie won't mind, and then we can all have lunch together."

"No!" I said, way more sharply than I should have. The crease between Mom's brows deepened, and even Aunt Jewel seemed surprised.

"We're about to finish up here," Saylor covered smoothly. I saw The Aunts and Mom drop their gazes to our nearly full plates. "And, Harper, didn't you say you were meeting Miss Franklin after lunch?"

"I did," I said, nodding. "So . . . I wouldn't want Miss Annemarie to go to the trouble of bringing a table when we're about to leave."

Mom was intent as she watched me. It reminded me of when I was little and she was checking me to see if I was sick. I half expected her to lay a hand on my forehead. "All righty then," said Aunt Jewel, clapping her hands together. "Y'all finish your lunch, and we'll go grab a table. Your Aunt May is absolutely perishing for Annemarie's crab bisque, else we'd be eating at Golden Corral like we usually do on Saturdays."

Cursing Aunt May's sudden highbrow craving, I got up and gave each of them a quick hug. "I'll stop by later this week," I promised, breathing in The Aunts' familiar scent of Youth Dew, hairspray, and smoke.

When I got to Mom, she hugged me back, but concern was still stamped all over her face. "Harper, are you sure you're—" She gasped then, grabbing my hand and lifting it to her face. "What on earth happened to you?"

Gently as I could, I took my hand back, fighting the urge to hide it behind my back. "I broke a glass this morning. Stupid. But it's fine! The bandage makes it look worse than it is."

I think Mom would have asked more questions if Aunt Jewel hadn't leaned over and taken my hand, inspecting it over her glasses. "Did you put peroxide on it?"

The Aunts would pour peroxide over a severed leg; it was their cure-all.

"Yes, ma'am."

Sniffing, Aunt Jewel gave me my hand back. "Well, then you'll be right as rain. Now come on, let's get a table before May dies of soup deprivation."

They steered Mom toward a table in the corner, and I sat back down, taking a deep breath. Once I was sure my family was out of earshot, I leaned into Saylor. "That's why we have to do things my way. I have a family here. Friends. A life. I have to keep those things. I have to make it through this as—as normally and inconspicuously as possible."

Saylor raised one perfectly groomed brow at me. "And how exactly do you plan to 'inconspicuously' stop this Blythe from doing a spell on David at Cotillion?'"

"I'll . . . figure it out," I said, shooting a glance at my mom and The Aunts. Aunts May and Martha were arguing over the tea list, and Aunt Jewel was regaling Mom with a story that apparently required a bunch of hand gestures. Watching them, a wave of affection washed over me. "There has to be a way to keep me not killed, keep David un-bespelled, and still live my own life."

If Saylor Stark were the type of woman who chewed her lip, I think she would have at that moment. As it was, she tapped her teaspoon against her saucer. "I'll put up more wards around the town, wards geared specifically toward you. Of course, that won't do you any good the night of Cotillion, if David's vision is anything to go by. And you have to train with me. At my house, every day."

"Train how?" I asked, thinking again of Blythe and the letter opener. What training would've prepared me for *that*? "Do you know how to fight? I mean, no offense, Miss Saylor, but you *aren't* a Paladin. And you don't exactly seem like the . . . fighting type."

Saylor leaned back in her seat, raising one silver eyebrow. "You're right, I'm not a Paladin. But I worked next to one for nearly thirty years, and I was there with Christopher when he trained under the Ephors. Now, if that isn't good enough for you, you're welcome to go to the judo classes at the community center."

Chastened, I poured another cup of tea. "I'm sorry. I'd . . . I'd love to train with you, Miss Saylor, but every day—"

"We only have three weeks," Saylor interrupted, sitting up straight. "And that is not nearly enough time to get you ready for something like this."

"Trust me," David said. "If anyone can handle pressure, it's Pres."

I appreciated his vote of confidence, but Saylor was right—three weeks was nothing.

On the other hand, three weeks was *nothing*. I could do this. I could find some way to balance my regular life with my Paladin responsibilities. Maybe all those other Paladins gave up their lives to protect Oracles, but they probably weren't as good at organizing and multitasking as I was.

"I can do that," I told Saylor, and as I said it, I realized that I could. I just had to be careful with scheduling and do, as Bee would say, a leeeeeettle bit of lying. And, I resolved, it was also time to start telling a leeeeeeettle bit of the truth to someone. "But I'm going to do it my way."

Saylor's brows drew together. "What does that mean?"

"It means we're in trouble," David said, but when he looked at me, he was grinning.

Chapter 26

ON MONDAY, I put my plan into action. Bee, Ryan, Brandon, and I were having lunch in the courtyard underneath one of the big oak trees. Ryan leaned against the trunk, long legs stretched out in front of him. Brandon had Bee in his lap, and if Headmaster Dunn saw that, they'd both end up with detention, but I refrained from mentioning it. Next to me, Ryan nudged my hip with his.

"Harper?"

"Hmm?"

Smiling, Ryan balled up the rest of his sandwich, tossing it at the nearest trash can. It bounced off, of course, and I made a note to remind him to pick it up later. "You are a million miles away," he said, snaking an arm around my waist and pulling me closer.

"It's nothing. Thinking," I said, ducking my head and laying it on his shoulder. I was usually against PDA of any kind, but after neglecting Ryan all weekend, I felt like I owed him a little extra demonstration. He must've appreciated that, because he pressed a kiss to my temple.

"You're always thinking," he said, more affectionately than accusatory. "And I'm always wondering what about."

I lifted my head. "We've known each other for eight years, been dating for two, and you don't know what I'm thinking?" I was teasing, but Ryan, still smiling, shook his head.

"Never," he said. "No idea what goes on in that giant brain of yours."

I wasn't sure why the words stung, but they did. He was still grinning guilelessly, his hazel eyes bright, his auburn hair tumbling over his forehead, and he was still so handsome it made my chest tight.

So he didn't know what I was thinking. Ever, apparently. Big deal.

I snuggled in closer, and said, "I have a lot going on right now."

From Brandon's lap, Bee giggled. "You always have a lot going on, Harper. It's, like, your thing. When you die in a hundred years, they'll probably write on your gravestone, 'Here Lies Harper Price—Damn It, She Still Had Stuff to Do!'"

Ryan and Brandon laughed, but I couldn't stop the shiver that ran through me. A hundred years or three weeks? And damn it, I *did* still have stuff to do. Starting now.

"Hey, guys?" I said to Brandon and Ryan. "Could I talk to Bee alone for a sec?"

"Sure," Ryan said, automatically rising to his feet.

"Are you going to talk about your periods or something?" Brandon said, frowning.

"You're disgusting!" Bee shrieked, slugging him in the shoulder.

Even Ryan frowned with distaste. "Dude, really?"

Brandon grabbed Bee by the waist, lifting her with him as he stood up, pressing a smacking kiss to the side of her neck. Once she was on her feet, Bee's cheeks were red, her blond hair a fuzzy halo around her head. "Go," she told Brandon, playfully shoving at him.

The boys loped off, and Bee and I watched them go. Shaking her head, Bee sighed. "I don't know why I put up with him."

Me neither, I thought. But I needed Bee on my side for what I was going to say next, and ragging on her boyfriend was not going to accomplish that.

Once the boys were out of sight, Bee turned to me, sympathy in her big brown eyes. "Look, you and Ryan are perfect together," she said. "Don't worry about that."

I blinked at her. "What?"

Tucking her hair behind her ears, Bee tilted her head. "Isn't that what you wanted to talk about? Ryan saying he never knows what you're thinking? I know how you can obsess over stuff like that, but it doesn't mean anything. Brandon probably doesn't even know I *have* thoughts."

Impulsively, I reached out and wrapped my arms around Bee, squeezing her tight. "That wasn't what I wanted to talk about, but your best friend skills are seriously off the charts."

Laughing, Bee hugged me back. "I try."

We pulled apart, but I held on to her elbows, keeping her at arm's length. "Ryan and I are fine, promise," I told her. "But I actually needed to tell you . . . kind of a secret."

Bee chewed on her lower lip. "I thought we didn't have secrets from each other. Wasn't that what the pinkie swear was about?"

I linked my pinkie with hers again. "It was, and it is. That's why I'm telling you this now. But, I'm warning you, it's . . . weird."

Bee's pinkie tightened around mine. "I can handle weird, Harper."

Seriously hoping that was true, I tugged her to sit down next to me under the oak. "It's about Saylor Stark . . ."

A few hours later, once school was out, Bee and I stood on the Starks' front porch. She stared up at the house, her eyes wide, mouth slightly agape. "You're totally serious about this?"

Ringing the doorbell, I nodded. "One hundred percent."

We could hear the bell echoing throughout the house, and as it did, Bee straightened her skirt self-consciously. "But . . . Saylor Stark? Seriously?"

"Seriously," I replied. The door swung open, and David stood there, dressed in a yellow sweater and his green corduroy pants. He looked like he should be on PBS, talking to a puppet about the alphabet. Still, I had to admit, yellow was a good color on him. It brought out the gold in his hair, and—

I stopped myself. *The gold in his hair?* Since when did I care about David Stark's hair except to note when it was trying to escape from his skull? These past few days were clearly messing with my head.

"Hey, Pres," David said, and then his gaze swung to my right. "And . . . Bee. You're here. With Harper. At our house."

His brows practically disappeared as he turned back to me. "You . . . brought Bee to—"

"Training, yeah," I said quickly. While David stared at me like I'd grown a second head, I breezed past him, pulling Bee after me. "I couldn't keep everything a secret from *everyone* forever, so I let Bee in on what's been going on."

Now David's jaw was hanging open slightly. "You told her—"

"That Saylor is training me and you in martial arts, yes." I moved into the foyer, heading toward the back of the house.

"Martial . . . arts," David repeated slowly, closing the door behind him.

It was stupid. Ludicrous, even, the idea that Saylor Stark was some kind of secret kung fu master, teaching me and David the ancient art of hand-to-hand combat, but I had to tell Bee *something*. It would give me an excuse to be around the Starks, *and* it would get Bee on my side. When I'd told her, I hadn't had to fake my blush or the embarrassment that colored every word.

"That's . . . super bizarre," Bee said once I'd finished.

"Now you see why I've been so secretive about it. I mean, learning to kick people in the head and stuff? It's not exactly how people see me."

Bee had pulled a long strand of hair over her lips and mouthed it thoughtfully. "I get that, Harper, but this just . . ." She shook her head, blond hair moving over her shoulders. "It seems so not you."

"I know it does, but I wanted something that was different. Something for me. Leigh-Anne was a cheerleader, and Homecoming Queen and did Cotillion, and this just felt . . . mine."

The words spilled from my lips almost too easily, and surprised, I realized that's because they were . . . kind of true. I was enjoying this. All right, maybe "enjoying" was a strong word, but as soon as I'd committed myself to helping David, to fully being a Paladin, a kind of rightness had set in.

And maybe that's what Bee saw on my face, because she made a clucking noise and reached out to briefly squeeze my hand. "You could use something that's all yours. Although I have to admit, this is not exactly what I would've expected. But I guess it's a good thing to learn? And it *will* look stellar on your college apps."

After that, it had been no problem persuading Bee to help me keep this a secret from Ryan. She totally got why I'd be embarrassed if he found out, and she'd sworn to carry my secret to her grave.

What I hadn't expected was for her to ask to tag along. All I'd wanted was to give her something slightly close to the truth so there would be at least one person kind of in on what was going on. But no excuse had rushed to my lips, and so now here I was, reporting for my first day of Paladin training with Bee Franklin at my side.

David was clearly biting his cheek, and his eyes were bright. "Right, yeah, my . . . my aunt teaches martial arts. To me and Harper. Which is why we've been hanging out a little more."

Bee gave a delicate snort. "Seems like a dangerous thing, teaching the two of you how to kick ass. What if you end up murdering each other?"

David and I exchanged a glance. "Risk we're willing to take," he said at last. "Let me go get Aunt Saylor. She's gonna need to, uh, be prepared for this."

David went into the kitchen, and Bee glanced around. "Miss Saylor's house looks exactly like I imagined." I remembered thinking the same thing when I was here last. It seemed like an entire millennium had passed between that day and this one, so it was hard to believe it had been almost a month.

Saylor bustled out of the kitchen, hands clasped in front of her, all smiles, all business. "Miss Franklin! What a surprise." That last bit was directed at me, but I gave her a little shrug. *My way.*

"So Harper has told you about our little secret," she continued, waving us toward the French doors leading to the balcony.

"She did," Bee said, her eyes taking in every nook and cranny of the house. "And to be honest, I think it's great, Miss Saylor. A young lady today should be able to protect herself."

Behind Saylor's back, I stuck my tongue out at Bee and mouthed, *Suck-up.*

She gave a shameless grin and followed us out into the backyard.

I don't know what I'd expected. Some yoga mats. Maybe a punching bag. And Saylor did have those things. But she also had three dummies set up on stands. Against one of them, there was a sword at least as long as my leg, and Bee stared at it, mouth agape.

"Oh, wow. Y'all are . . . hard-core."

"Yes, yes," Saylor said, bustling over to the sword and picking it up. "This is for . . . inspiration. We obviously don't want to involve weapons. At least not yet."

"Yet?" Bee asked, but Saylor was already heading back into the house with the sword. "Now," she said when she came back.

"One of the things Harper has been learning is how to stay on her guard so attackers can't surprise her."

"Right," Bee said, nodding like that was a totally normal thing for Saylor to be teaching me.

And I have to hand it to my best friend. For the next hour, she watched Saylor Stark throw various things—knives, pots, and more ceramic lambs than any one woman should own—at me from various directions while I was blindfolded, and at no point did she run away screaming, calling us all crazy people. She sat in the grass, legs folded, serenely watching the president of the Pine Grove Betterment Society lob a knife at the Homecoming Queen.

"Good job, Harper!" Bee called out when I batted the knife away, striking the hilt with the side of my hand. "Way to hustle!"

It was the exact same thing she shouted at Brandon when he practiced basketball, and for some reason, it made me smile. Same when, after I spun away from a particularly heavy china cat tossed at my midsection, Bee launched into one of our cheers, complete with shaking her fists like there were pom-poms in them.

After I'd deflected enough things, Saylor finally called it quits. We were both sweating and breathing hard, Saylor from throwing, me from the tension of spending an hour trying not to get whacked.

"Good job, Harper," Saylor told me, untying the blindfold. "And you, Miss Franklin. You were very . . . supportive."

Bee stood up, dusting off the back of her pants. "Thank you, Miss Saylor." Then she nodded her head at the sun porch. "I thought you were training David, too. Why didn't he get stuff thrown at his head?"

David, who was leaning on the French doors, arms folded over his chest, said, "I've already passed this stage. Have my dodging-stuff badge. Belt. Whatever."

I shot him a look, and his chin trembled with the effort of not laughing.

But Bee accepted that. "Okay. Well, that was . . . interesting. Thanks so much for letting me watch, Miss Saylor."

"Any time, honey," Saylor cooed, even as she gave me a glare that plainly said, *Never again.*

"Are y'all done now?" Bee said.

"I have a few more things to go over with Harper, but it's more theory than training." Right. Saylor had wanted to show me the spell Blythe was planning on doing.

"In that case, I'll go ahead and skedaddle," Bee said.

"I'll walk you out," I told her as I wiped the sweat from my face with an embroidered towel that smelled like lavender.

Once we'd gotten to the driveway, Bee turned to me. "Right, so that's kind of nuts," she said.

I grimaced. "I know."

"But," she added, screwing up her face, "it's also kind of awesome. You looked so fierce, all—" She lifted her hands, doing a few chops and slices that I guess were an imitation of me deflecting stuff.

"Shut up," I said, laughing as I batted her hands down.

"Seriously, I get why you're keeping this secret, but . . . I don't know, I'm proud of you. Homecoming Queen, debutante, President of All the Things, *and* a secret ninja. Best best friend ever."

"Harper!" Saylor called from the porch. "Are you coming?"

Sighing, I gave Bee a quick hug. "No rest for the ninja," I said. "And thanks, Bee. For not thinking this was *too* weird."

Her cheeks flushed a little, and she glanced down. "To be honest, Harper? I didn't believe you. That's why I wanted to come today, to, like—"

"Call my bluff?"

Nodding, Bee pulled her sunglasses down from the top of her head. "Which makes me the *worst* best friend ever."

"No," I said quickly, shaking my head. "I've been out of it lately; I understand."

"Harper!" Saylor called again, her voice a little sharper this time.

"Go," she said, giving me a friendly shove. "Get your ninja on."

I reached out to link my pinkie with hers. She squeezed it back. Smiling sheepishly, Bee ducked her head, blond hair swinging over her collarbone. "I forgive you for being a bizarre combination of totally perfect and totally weird."

I laughed at that, and as Bee drove off, my heart felt lighter in my chest.

Chapter 27

THAT WEEKEND, I finally had a date with Ryan. Between training with Saylor, preparing for Cotillion (both the normal and the supernatural parts of it), and keeping up with all my regular stuff, I hadn't exactly been a model girlfriend. Hence tonight's date, which included a movie of his choosing and, since his parents were at their lake house for the weekend, some alone time at Ryan's place. I actually couldn't remember the last time we'd . . . been alone, and I told myself it was anticipation making my hands tremble as I brushed my teeth that evening, not nerves.

When I came downstairs, Mom and Dad were both sacked out on the couch, watching some true-crime TV show. "Hey," I said, pausing in the doorway.

Dad's arm was around Mom's shoulder and both of them had their feet propped up on the coffee table. Even their ankles were crossed the same. "Hay is for horses, Harper Jane!" Dad called out, and I rolled my eyes, but smiled.

"Fine. Good evening, parental types."

Mom looked over her shoulder at me. "You look pretty. Where are you off to?"

Preening a little, I smoothed my fitted sweater over my stomach. "Date night with Ryan. I'll be back by midnight."

There was a splash of light across the pale blue of the wall as Ryan's car pulled into the driveway, and I was already turning to meet him at the door when Mom said, "Ten."

I paused, sure I'd misunderstood her. "Ten what?"

"Ten is when you need to be home. The movie starts at what? Seven? That's plenty of time to get back."

Dad kept his eyes on the TV, but his fingers were drumming on Mom's shoulders. "Um . . . seriously?" My purse was on the end table nearest the couch, and I twisted to grab it.

Mom's eyes met mine, and I could swear there were hollows under hers, new wrinkles in the corners. "Yes, seriously. Ten o'clock, Harper."

Outside, Ryan's door thumped shut, and I could hear his steady tread coming up the front steps. "It's always been midnight," I insisted, hating how petulant I sounded, but . . . I had plans for tonight. Boyfriend maintenance plans. And I hadn't had to be in that early since middle school.

The doorbell rang then, and I cast a quick look toward the front door. "Mom, my curfew has always—"

"I don't care what we've always done," Mom snapped, her voice slightly shrill. "I'm your mother, and tonight, I want you back in this house by ten. Is that clear?"

Ryan had better manners than to press the doorbell again, but

I could practically feel him out there waiting for me. Too bad he wasn't the only one I clearly needed to spend more time with. Knowing that snottiness wouldn't get me anywhere, I nodded. "Okay," I said, doing my best to seem okay. "See y'all at ten."

Mom sagged back onto the couch, relief obvious on her face. Dad, too, seemed to relax a bit, lifting his hand in a wave. "Be safe, kiddo."

I brooded the entire way to the theater. Pine Grove only had one, and it only showed two movies at a time. I'd let Ryan pick tonight—I almost always chose what we saw—and of course, he'd gone with the action film. I'd rolled my eyes, pretending to be exasperated, but really, I wanted to see it, too. I had plenty of moves in my Paladin arsenal, but it wouldn't hurt to add a few more.

We already had our tickets and had stepped into the lobby when I told Ryan about Mom's new curfew. Frowning, he shoved his hands in his back pockets. "Whoa. Okay. I just . . . I kind of wish you'd told me that before we'd come here."

The lobby reeked of burnt popcorn and spilled Coke, and it seemed even more crowded than usual for a Saturday night. The place was always full—when you only have one movie theater in your town, that happens—but tonight it was packed, and I suddenly felt a little claustrophobic. "Why?" I asked Ryan as someone bumped into me from behind.

Rolling his shoulders, Ryan stepped a little closer to me. "Because if I'd known I was only going to have a few hours with you, there are a lot of other things I'd rather be doing than watching a movie."

Maybe it was that unexpected bout of nervousness I'd felt about that very thing earlier. Maybe I was still irritated with my mom and looking for someone to take it out on. Or maybe I was honestly a little pissed off at Ryan. "So, what, if you'd known you'd have to choose between a date and fooling around, you would've chosen the latter?"

"Whoa, Harper." Ryan lowered his voice and looked around us. "Keep your voice down." Only a few yards away, our old Sunday school teacher, Mrs. Catesby, was buying a box of Junior Mints, and I should have been horrified at the thought that she might have overheard me, but I wasn't. Not even a little bit.

Ryan, on the other hand, was. "That's not what I'm saying. I'm saying that I've hardly been alone with you since when? Before Homecoming?"

"I've been busy," I insisted, and Ryan rolled his eyes at me.

"Yeah, I know. With school and Cotillion and whatever other stupid shit is more important than your boyfriend."

I could not believe this was happening. I was fighting with my boyfriend in public. Across the way, I could see Abigail and Amanda, huddled near the ladies' room. They saw me, too, and as they lifted their hands in greeting, Mary Beth emerged from the bathroom. Her eyes landed on Ryan first, and there was no mistaking the . . . it wasn't even lust, it was honest to God *love,* or at least a very deep case of like.

"Don't call the stuff I do stupid," I told him, this time pitching my voice near a whisper. I tried to keep my face blank so the other girls wouldn't be able to tell we were fighting, but they were already heading this way.

"I'm sorry," Ryan blew out on a long breath. "But, God, Harper, sometimes I feel like your whole life is a checklist, and I am way down at the bottom. And, you know, every once in a while, you throw me a bone to keep me happy."

I flinched at that, hard. Not only because it was insulting, but because it was way too close to the truth. "You're not at the bottom," I said, and then Abigail, Amanda, and Mary Beth were there, and I was frantically blinking back tears and faking a huge smile.

"Hi, girls!" I said with forced brightness.

"Hey, Harper," Mary Beth replied, but her eyes were on Ryan. "Are you guys . . . okay?"

"We're fine," Ryan and I said in unison, too quickly. Abigail and Amanda exchanged a look, and I stepped closer to Ryan, slipping my arm through his. His forearm was like a rock under my fingers, and I could still feel the tension humming through him. Even though he was smiling at the girls, I knew they could sense it, too.

There was an awkward silence before Abigail said, "Is Ryan trying to drag you to that stupid *Hard Fists* movie?"

"Grooooosssss," Amanda drawled. "I hate stuff like that. Ryan, be a good boyfriend and take your girlfriend to *The Promise*. Y'all can sit with us."

"Mandy," her twin said, elbowing her in the side. "They probably want to sit alone at the movies."

Mary Beth swallowed, and her shoes must have been really fascinating for all the attention she was paying to them.

"Oh, please," Amanda said, delicately picking out a piece of popcorn and tossing it in her mouth. "Like Ryan and Harper are the make-out-in-the-theater type. That would be like . . ." She screwed up her elfin face. "My parents doing that or something. No offense, guys."

I waved her off, but under my other hand, I could swear Ryan got even tenser. More people were coming in the door now, and as I moved closer to Ryan to avoid the crush, he stepped the tiniest bit away. Ignoring that as best as I could, I held on to his sleeve tighter. "Actually, I want to see *Hard Fists*."

Amanda and Abigail both snorted in disbelief, but Mary Beth's lips lifted in a little smile. "It does look kind of badass," she offered, and Amanda and Abigail swung identical frowns at her.

"Ugh, no, it does not, Mary Beth. All that violence and blood and . . . bleh." Amanda shuddered.

"Maybe you need a Y chromosome to properly appreciate the amazingness of *Hard Fists*, Amanda," Ryan said. Then he nodded at Mary Beth. "Or maybe you just need to be a cool chick like MB here."

MB? Since when did Ryan have a nickname for Mary Beth? It wasn't like anyone else called her that.

Mary Beth's face flushed, and while I thought pink was supposed to look terrible on redheads, she actually looked really pretty with a little color in her cheeks. And there was a softness in Ryan's grin as he looked down at her that I recognized. He used to smile at me like that.

For once, the pain in my chest had nothing to do with David

or danger or magic. This was straight-up teenage angst, and it *hurt*. I mean, fine, if he suddenly liked Mary Beth, whatever, but did he have to do it in front of Amanda and Abigail?

Wait a second. Whatever? My boyfriend was smiling at a blushing girl, and I was embarrassed because my friends were watching?

Standing there in the theater, with what felt like my entire town hemming me in, I let that thought sink in. I wasn't hurt that Ryan might have a thing for someone else. I was scared of what that might make other people think about *me*.

That was . . . effed up.

Suddenly, the lobby was too hot and the smell of popcorn was making me slightly nauseous, and all I wanted to do was go home. What would happen if I turned around and walked out? Would Ryan come after me, or would he shrug and go watch the "badass" *Hard Fists* with MB? And why didn't that thought make me want to tear MB's pretty auburn hair right out of her head?

"Harper?" Abigail asked, laying a hand on my arm. "Are you okay?"

I hadn't realized I was staring at the floor, my eyes tracing the golden concentric circles stamped on the grubby navy carpet. Lifting my head, I did my best to smile, but from the look on Abi's face, I wasn't pulling it off. "Yeah," I said, "it's just hot in here."

"It is," Abigail agreed. "I mean, look at Mary Beth, she's practically a tomato."

Mary Beth's cheeks *were* more red than pink now, and Amanda tried to disguise a giggle as a cough.

Tired of this, tired of them, I tugged on Ryan's sleeve. "In that case, we better go ahead and get into the theater before we all boil to death out here."

I took a step forward and as I did, I looked up into the crush of people waiting to get their sodas and Gummi Bears. I could recognize nearly every face, either from school or church. And then Matt Sheehan, a senior at the Grove, stepped aside, and I found myself staring into a very familiar—and very crazy—pair of brown eyes.

Blythe.

Chapter 28

I FROZE, my hand still on Ryan's sleeve. My heart was somewhere south of my knees, sweat immediately prickling my brow. The crowd shifted, a group of preteen girls sliding in front of Blythe. When they moved on, she was gone.

Rising up on tiptoes, I frantically searched the lobby, looking for some trace of her. "Who are you looking for?" Ryan asked, lifting his head to glance around, too.

"Did you see a girl?" I said, still scanning the mass of bodies moving through the theater.

"I . . . see lots of girls," Ryan replied, bemused.

"No, a specific girl. A tiny one with brown hair and dimples."

"Lauren Roberts?" Abi asked, naming a girl in our math class.

"No," I told her, twisting to look behind me. "But like her. About that height, same hair. Like Lauren Roberts with a major case of crazy eyes."

She could be *anywhere*. She was short enough to pass through the crowd unseen, and damn it, *I* wasn't tall enough to see over all these people.

"Does this chick owe you money or something?" Ryan joked, finally sounding like himself again. But I was too panicked to be happy about that.

The glass doors opened, and as they did, I spotted a few people leaving the theater. I caught the briefest glimpse of a long brown ponytail, and then the door swung shut. It might have been Blythe, but I couldn't be sure.

Whirling on Ryan, I grabbed his arm again. "I'll be right back. Go on into the theater and I'll find you in a few minutes."

"Whoa." Ryan flipped his hand, fingers encircling my wrist. "Where are you—"

I tugged out of his grasp, forgetting about my superstrength, so instead of taking my arm back gently, I more or less wrenched it from him.

Surprise, hurt, and more than a little bit of anger all warred on his face, but I didn't have time to worry about that right now. Blythe was here, and I had to find her before she found me.

"I'll be right back," I said again, then dashed out the front doors of the theater before Ryan had the chance to say anything else.

The November night was cold and clear, and my breath puffed out in front of me as I stood on the sidewalk, looking left, then right. The theater took up one whole side of the square; the other three sides were taken up with little boutiques, Miss Annemarie's, the jewelry store, and Pine Grove's sad attempt at a coffee shop, the Dixie Bean. Other than the theater, the rest of the square was relatively deserted, since most of the shops closed around five. Miss Annemarie's and the Dixie Bean were probably the only things open, but there was no one on the sidewalks, and no sign of the little group that had just left the theater.

I jogged across the street, heading for the center of the square. The statue of Adolphus Bridgeforth, one of the founders of Pine Grove, glowered down at me. The Pine Grove Betterment Society, led by Saylor, had raised the money for it about five years back. I knew that if I looked closely, I'd see wards etched into the stone base. Saylor had been very thorough where David's protection was concerned.

Next to him, the little fountain splashed away merrily, the night wind blowing a few stray droplets on me. Every nerve in my body felt tense and coiled, the hair on the back of my neck standing up.

You're a Paladin, I reminded myself. *You have all kinds of kick-ass abilities and she doesn't.*

But then I remembered how easily she'd gotten the jump on me before.

To Adolphus's right, there was a little flower garden surrounded by a tiny white picket fence. A bronze plaque on the fence said that the garden had been planted by the Pine Grove Betterment Society just last year. Sure enough, as I got closer, I could see tiny golden wards on all the fence posts.

Giving another quick glance around to make sure no one was looking, I reached down and, easy as picking a flower, plucked a stake from the fence. The hole glared at me accusingly, and I slipped the pointed piece of wood behind me as I backed away from the center of the square. I hated vandalism more than anything, but I needed a weapon. Besides, Saylor had put that fence up, so when you thought about it, the fence was practically mine.

In a way.

Keeping the stake low at my side, I headed back toward the theater. There was a parking lot behind it. Maybe that was where Blythe had gone. As I hurried in that direction, a tiny voice in my head kept up a running commentary. *So if you find her, you're simply going to stab her to death with a piece of wood in the parking lot? And hope no one sees? Because tiny girls getting staked behind the Royale Cinema seems like something people would notice.*

But if I got rid of—no, *killed*, I needed to say killed—Blythe now, all of this ended. No Cotillion showdown, no chance of my whole town being wiped out, no chance of David dying. This was my chance.

Or it would have been, if she had been in the parking lot.

There were a few people straggling in, but both of the movies had already started, so the parking lot was more or less empty. Still, I kept my stake hidden at my side as I walked the rows of cars, ducking down to look under them, even peering in the windows.

No Blythe.

When I got to the last car on the row, I sighed, nearly letting the fence post drop from my hand. This was stupid. It probably hadn't even been her. Maybe the stress of the past few weeks was finally catching up with me, and I was going crazy *in addition* to becoming a Paladin.

I should go back into the theater, find Ryan, and figure out some way to salvage this evening. The fence post clattered to the ground, and I turned back to the theater.

And suddenly I heard the sound of running feet. As I whipped around, I could have sworn I saw brown hair disappearing around the corner, back toward the square.

Dropping to my knees, I scrambled for the fence post. Not caring who saw me dashing through downtown Pine Grove wielding a damn stake, I took off after her. My boots clicked hard on the pavement, and I could hear the wind and my own blood rushing in my ears.

Was there a flash of movement over by Miss Annemarie's? I ran in that direction.

But just as I reached the tearoom, the door swung open. I didn't even have time to register that someone was coming out of that door before plowing directly into him.

Something warm splashed all over me, and for one horrifying, dizzying moment, I thought I'd plunged my stake into an innocent person's heart. But, no, I'd managed to lower it at the last second, and I could hear the wood clatter harmlessly to the pavement. As for the hot liquid currently seeping into my cashmere sweater, from the smell, it was the crab bisque that my Aunt May was so fond of.

My breath was sawing in and out of my lungs, burning with the sharp night air, as I stumbled back from . . . David.

Bisque was dripping from the front of his tweed jacket, the crushed plastic container still clutched against his chest. He looked down at himself and then back at me. "Pres? Is this some kind of Paladin thing? Was the soup poisoned or something?"

I didn't answer; I was too busy looking for Blythe, but there was no sign of her. She was gone.

Dropping my hands to my knees, I bent forward, taking deep breaths, trying to slow the slamming of my heart.

"I thought you had a date tonight," David said, and I don't know why that's the thing that did it. The tears that had pricked my eyes earlier suddenly came back full force, and to my absolute horror, I burst into tears.

"Whoa, whoa, Harper," David said, the plastic container tumbling to the sidewalk. He gripped my arms, holding me slightly away from him and ducking his head to look into my face. "What happened?"

"I was on a date, but Ryan and I got in a fight, and he likes Mary Beth—*MB*—I think, but it's like I don't even *c-care*, which makes me a-a horrible person, and then I saw Blythe, or I thought I did, and I vandalized a *fence*, and now we smell bad, and that s-s-soup wasn't poisoned, I just ran into you, and—"

I didn't get any further before David carefully wrapped his arms around me. He held me like I was a bomb he was afraid was seconds from going off, keeping our bodies as far apart as he could while still technically hugging me.

"It's okay," he said, patting my back once. He apparently decided that was a good move because he did it a few more times. And the weird thing was, it *was* kind of a good move. I lowered my forehead to his tweed-covered shoulder and let myself be patted until my tears slowed to a trickle. A few weeks ago, if you had told me that being held in David Stark's arms was one of the nicest things I'd ever feel, I wouldn't have laughed at you. I would've been too busy choking on my own horror.

But leaning against him, crying into his stupid tweed, I thought I could maybe stay there forever. It was such a relief to be able to sob and have someone know all the reasons why.

Once I was calmer, I lifted my head to find David watching me with an expression I'd never seen before. Before I had time to figure it out, he reached behind him and opened the tearoom door. "Well, I'm going to need another order of soup to go, so why don't we go inside and have a cup of tea. Tea fixes stuff, right?"

I looked back across the square at the theater. Ryan was in there, waiting for me. Or sitting next to Mary Beth and not worrying about me at all. Besides, I smelled like crab.

So giving one last glance to the theater, I nodded and followed David inside.

Chapter 29

DAVID AND I sat at the same table in the corner where The Aunts and my mom had had lunch last week. Miss Annemarie brought us a stack of napkins along with our tea, and we both did our best to blot the bisque from our clothes. As we did, I told David about Blythe.

Taking a sip of his tea, he mulled that over. "So you think she was following you just to, uh, mess with you?"

I dropped a sugar cube into my Earl Grey. "I guess. If she was even there. And it's okay, you can say the F-word."

To my surprise, David shrugged. "I don't know, I've kind of become fond of the euphemisms. The other day, I said 'mother trucker' when I dropped a book on my toe, and I have to admit, it was every bit as satisfying as the actual curse."

"See? I told you there were acceptable alternatives."

Raising his teacup in a salute, David inclined his head. "You were right." Then he widened his eyes in mock surprise. "Hey! Saying that didn't even burn my tongue! We're making progress, Pres."

I tossed one of the crumpled-up napkins at him. "Ha-ha."

He tossed the napkin back, but there was a smile playing around his lips.

I sipped my tea, feeling the warmth of it in my toes. The tearoom was always so overstuffed and tacky during the day, but at night, it felt cozy. There were tiny lamps in the middle of all of the tables, and we were the only people in the place. Everything smelled pleasantly spicy—well, everything except me and David—and the atmosphere was almost . . .

No, I wasn't going to say romantic. There was nothing romantic about Miss Annemarie's Tearoom. Or David Stark for that matter.

"What?" David asked. He was frowning slightly, the dim light making shadows underneath his cheekbones. There was the lightest smattering of freckles along the bridge of his nose, and I wondered why I'd never noticed those before.

I looked at him, eyebrows raised. "You shook your head," he said. "What were you saying no to?"

"Oh." I took another sip of tea so that I wouldn't have to answer right away. "I was thinking how crazy this night has been."

Leaning back, David stretched his arms over his head. "Yeah, I was planning on *eating* crab bisque tonight, not being doused in it."

"Oh, please. That jacket cost you what? Two bucks at Goodwill? I will never get the smell out of this sweater."

David reached down and gripped the lapels of his jacket, straightening it. "Hey, I like this jacket."

"That makes one of us," I replied, tucking my hair behind my ears.

David and I had been snarking at each other since we learned how to talk, but tonight, our barbs seemed less pointed. I wouldn't go so far as to call them affectionate or anything, but there was a definite lack of sting.

"We need to tell Saylor about tonight," I told David.

He was turning his teacup around in his hands, steam drifting up to fog his glasses. "I will, when I get home."

Silence stretched between us. Not awkward, really, but heavy somehow. Laden with something I couldn't name. "I'm sure he doesn't like her," David said.

"What?"

"Ryan," he clarified before draining his cup. "You said you think he likes Mary Beth. I bet you're wrong."

"Oh, right. That." Now that the moment had passed, I felt my cheeks flame at the memory of how I'd vomited up all of my feelings out there on the sidewalk. I should've just told him Blythe freaked me out. There was no need to drag my personal life into all of this.

"Don't get me wrong, Mary Beth is . . . well, she's not objectionable or anything, but she's not . . ."

My hands were tight around the teacup, the heat radiating on my palms. "She's not what?"

David tugged at his lapels again before leaning back in his chair. "You."

The lamplight shone on David's glasses, but behind them, his eyes were very blue and intent, and then I suddenly couldn't meet them anymore.

Thank God for Miss Annemarie, who chose that moment to

waddle over to the table, a plastic bag in hand. "Here you go, sweetie," she told David, handing him the soup. "Try to be more careful with this batch. I'm closing up now, so this is your last chance."

"Oh, r-right," David said, fumbling slightly with the bag. "Thanks, Miss Annemarie."

Our tea was gone, so we both got to our feet, thanking Miss Annemarie again. "Don't mention it," she said with a wave of her hand. "It's nice to have young people in here at night for once. Most of the other kids, they all go somewhere fancy on their dates. Like Ruby Tuesday."

I waited for David to insist we weren't on a date, but he gave Miss Annemarie a little smile and a nod. I didn't say anything either, and as weird as it seems, it was like by letting Miss Annemarie think it was a date, it had somehow . . . become a date.

I shook my head again. Crazy thought. Stupid.

After the warmth of Miss Annemarie's, the square seemed even colder. I shivered a little as the breeze made my still-damp sweater cling to my body.

"Here," David said, handing me the takeout bag. "Hold this."

I did, and he slipped out of his tweed, revealing an actually halfway-decent button-down dress shirt underneath. He slid the coat over my shoulders before taking the bag back.

"Thanks," I said, a little awkwardly. I never thought I would be grateful for the scent of crab bisque, but as I pulled the coat tighter around me, I was glad that was all I could smell. I felt weird enough as it was without adding nice boy smell to the mix.

David and I walked down the sidewalk, our arms a few inches apart.

"Do you want me to drive you home?" he asked as we passed the antique store.

"I should probably get back to the theater," I said. "Ryan . . ."

I let that trail off, and David shoved his free hand in his pocket. "Right. Ryan."

We had reached David's car by now, but both of us were sort of hovering beside it. "So," he said.

"So."

David rocked on his heels, frowning slightly. "Is it me, or are we being weird?"

I laughed, nerves making it sound high and thin. "We are being weird. Which is saying something for us."

Grinning, David let his shoulders drop a little. "Okay, good. It's only . . . I should've said something to Miss Annemarie about us not being on a date, but—"

"No," I rushed in to say, slipping my arms into his jacket. "That would've been awkward, too, and probably bad manners to correct her."

"Right!" he said, a little too loud. "It would've made her feel bad, and we don't want to do that. Not when she's made me delicious soup. Twice."

"Exactly," I said, feeling like my voice was a little too loud, too.

His mouth lifted in a half-grin, revealing a flash of teeth and making me realize for the first time that David Stark had surprisingly nice cheekbones. "You actually look pretty good in tweed,

Pres," he joked, reaching out to straighten the lapel of my—his—jacket.

"No one looks good in tweed," I insisted, going to push his hand away. But as I did, our skin touched, and the little pulse that went through me had nothing to do with prophecies or magic.

David must have felt it, too, because his eyes suddenly dropped to my mouth. I saw him swallow.

Oh my God, David Stark wants to kiss me. In public. In the middle of the street.

I waited to be horrified by that thought, but for some reason, horror wasn't coming. Neither was awkwardness or being freaked out or any of the other perfectly acceptable reactions to David Freaking Stark wanting to kiss me.

Instead, I felt myself swaying forward a little on the balls of my feet. But before anything profoundly stupid could happen, a car drove by, some country song blaring out the windows, and David and I stepped away from each other.

My heart was pounding, and I shoved my shaking hands into the pockets of the jacket. "Okay," I said at last. "So I'm going to go back to the theater, and you go home and eat soup and talk to Saylor about Blythe, and I'll see you Monday."

David wrapped one hand around the back of his neck, rubbing the back of his head so that even the hair *there* stood up. "Monday," he repeated, jangling his keys in his pocket. "And speaking of, do you think Bee could maybe sit out on training that day?"

I raised my eyebrows. "Probably. Why?"

He shrugged, sheepish. "I thought you and I might try something. Something prophecy related," he quickly added.

"Right, of course," I said, like it hadn't even occurred to me he could be talking about anything else.

"Awesome," he said. "So Monday."

"Monday," I repeated, and just when I was afraid we were going to stand there echoing each other all night, David finally gave a little wave and got in his car.

As he drove off, I started walking back to the theater, my head so full it ached. So much for a normal Saturday night.

The idea of searching a crowded theater for Ryan was more than I wanted to deal with, so once I got back to the Royale Cinema, I took a seat on one of the padded benches in the lobby and waited. I thought about Ryan sitting in the dark, maybe next to Mary Beth, and tried to summon up some kind of righteous indignation. Here I was, trying to keep this entire town safe, trying to save my own freaking life, and my boyfriend was sitting in the movies with another girl.

But righteous indignation wouldn't come. Neither would devastated betrayal or hurt disbelief. Mostly, I wanted the movie to be over so I could go home and wash the crab bisque out of my hair.

Finally, the doors opened and people began spilling out into the lobby. Ryan was there, but there was no sign of Mary Beth. His eyes roamed until they found me. Crossing the room in long strides, Ryan looked a little relieved, but also fairly irritated.

"There you are," he said, standing in front of me. "I texted and called you like a hundred times."

Rising to my feet, I fished my phone out of my pocket. Sure enough, I had about a dozen missed calls. I'd forgotten that I'd put the phone on silent.

"Have you been here this whole time?" Ryan continued, folding his arms over his broad chest.

"No," I said, but before I could get any further, Ryan frowned.

"Why do you smell like an aquarium? And what are you wearing?"

Oh, crap. I'd forgotten to give David back his jacket. "Someone spilled soup on me," I said, which, hey, was pretty close to the truth. "So that's why I didn't want to go in. Because of the smell."

"And the jacket?" he asked. "Did you knock down a random professor and steal it?" He was smiling a little now. I'm sure the sight of me, bedraggled and covered in soup, was amusing.

And then his smile faded. "I've seen that jacket," he said slowly, eyes moving over me. "That's . . . David Stark has a jacket just like that. I remember the stupid elbow patches."

Ugh. Why hadn't I given the damn coat back? "Yeah," I said lightly. "He was the one who spilled the soup on me."

Ryan's expression was stony. "So you ran out of the place looking for some girl, and then you found David Stark, but he spilled soup on you in the middle of Pine Grove Square, and gave you a jacket?"

"Yeah," I said on a nervous laugh. "Pretty much. Weird night, huh?"

Heaving a sigh, Ryan glanced behind him. "Weird. Sure."

We hardly said anything on the drive home, and when he

pulled in my driveway, Ryan didn't even shut off the car. "I'll call you tomorrow," he said, and all I could do was nod and tell myself he wasn't kissing me good night because I smelled like a Red Lobster.

When I walked through the front door, it was 9:45. Mom and Dad were exactly where I'd left them, although Dad was now asleep, his head tilted back, softly snoring. Mom sat up as I closed the door. "You're early."

"Movie wasn't very long," I said.

Mom clearly had more to say, but I jogged up the stairs before she had a chance. I'd desperately wanted a shower, but once I was in my room, the idea of getting undressed was exhausting to me, so I just slumped down on my bed, bisque, tweed, and all.

It had been one week since I'd sat at Miss Annemarie's and told Saylor Stark that I could be a Paladin and a regular girl. That nothing had to change.

"Nothing does," I muttered to myself. So tonight had been bad. And odd. And, I thought, remembering sitting across from David in the lamplight of the tearoom, unsettling.

But it was one night. And we only had two more weeks of this left before Cotillion.

I could do this. I *would* do this.

I drifted into sleep, David's jacket still wrapped around me.

Chapter 30

"AGAIN," Saylor said, her tone of voice exactly the same as it was during Cotillion practice. But this time, instead of walking down a flight of stairs in heels, I was practicing sword fighting. Also in heels.

To tell the truth, whacking things with a sword felt really good today. Ryan hadn't called on Sunday, and then at lunch, Amanda and Abigail had been talking about *The Promise* and how good it was. "I still can't believe you missed it to see something called *Hard Fists*," Abi had said to Mary Beth.

Mary Beth had darted a glance at me as Amanda elbowed her twin, and I pretended to ignore all of them. I also ignored the stab of guilt that pierced my chest when I saw David in the halls. I had not almost kissed him, I reminded myself. He had almost kissed *me*, and if he had, I would have pushed him away and made all sorts of shocked sounds, and not kissed him back, even a little bit. I was positive of that.

Then, when I got to Saylor's, I'd been treated to a lecture on how possibly chasing Blythe had been foolish and irresponsible.

So yes. Smacking things with sharp metal felt good. Or it had for the first hour at least.

"I don't see why I have to practice so much," I said, wiping sweat from my forehead with the back of my hand. It was a chilly day, but the sun still beat down on me, and I'd been getting quite a workout. The sword was heavy in my hand, and my muscles ached. Still, the dummy I'd been slicing looked a heck of a lot worse.

"Practice makes perfect, Miss Price," Saylor trilled.

"I know that. Heck, I practically *invented* that. In fact, if I decided to do something so low-class as get a tattoo, it would probably be that. What I mean is"— I took another swing at the dummy—"is that I don't have to practice this. You said that when Mr. Hall passed his powers on to me, he also passed on his knowledge. And the knowledge of every Paladin before him."

I swung the sword in an arc over my head, going in to slice the dummy up under the ribs. "I don't have to practice. I can . . . I don't know, do this."

Saylor gave a long suffering sigh and took another sip of sweet tea. "And all of that is true. But practice never hurt anyone. And while your brain knows all of these things, your body is still unused to them." She nodded at the dummy. "Hence the practice. Now again."

"Why swords anyway?" I asked even as I did what she said. Spinning, I hit the dummy in the neck, then pulled the sword out and dropped into a low spin, whacking the flat of the blade against its legs. "They're not exactly the most convenient weapons.

Shouldn't I have"— I grunted as I brought the sword down with both hands—"a gun?"

Saylor poked at the ice in her glass with a bright pink straw. "Modernized weapons won't work for Paladins."

I swung around, the sword making a slight *zing* in the air. "Like, we're not supposed to use them or—"

"The original magic that created Paladins didn't take things like guns, or grenades, or—or rocket launchers into account. Therefore, you can't work with those nearly as well as you can with a sword."

I took that in, turning the hilt of the sword over in my hands. "Okay. But a rocket launcher sounds a lot more useful than a sword."

It took another fifteen minutes, and my thighs and calves had joined my shoulders in screaming, before Saylor said I could quit. I wanted to fling the sword to the ground and sink into a lawn chair next to her, but instead, I put the sword back in the house and wheeled the dummy back onto the patio.

When I did sit down, Saylor rewarded me with one of her rare grins. "Good girl."

She handed me a bottle of water, and I gulped half of it down. "You're doing well," Saylor said as I drank. She frowned, her eyes narrowing behind her sunglasses. "Unfortunately, I'm not sure that it'll be enough."

I lowered the bottle. "What do you mean?"

"You're learning quickly," she acknowledged. "But what the Ephors are intending . . . I never thought I'd face something like that with an untrained Paladin at my side."

"I didn't exactly expect to spend my Cotillion battling the forces of evil, either," I reminded her, and the frown deepened.

"I understand that, Harper. But . . ." She sighed. "As successful as you've been, to be honest, I have no idea how to . . . to train a Paladin. I never had to before. We all have our roles. David is the Oracle, I'm the Mage, and Christopher was the Paladin."

"We'll be okay," I said, wondering how I managed to get the words out without choking. "We'll get through Cotillion and then . . ." I trailed off.

It wasn't like I hadn't thought about what came after Cotillion. Whatever this big prophecy was, it would be settled. But David would still be an Oracle (or dead). I would still be a Paladin (or dead). Right?

Saylor was watching me. "Harper, do you fully comprehend what being a Paladin means?"

I sat up a little straighter in my chair. "Right now, it means making sure crazy Blythe doesn't kill David and inadvertently make a crater where our town used to be."

"But do you understand what that means giving up?"

Now I really didn't want to look at her. I got up out of the chair and started doing the stretches she'd shown me. "Once Cotillion is over, I won't have to give up anything," I said. "Blythe will be gone—dead—the spell won't have worked, and I can get back to normal life."

"Harper, this *is* your normal life now. No matter what happens at Cotillion, you are a Paladin, linked to me, linked to David. Forever. And that means that eventually, you'll sacrifice everything," Saylor said. She didn't insist it. Didn't say it with force, like she was trying to make me believe it. It was a fact.

I faltered, nearly losing my balance. Taking a deep breath, I moved into another stretch. "I don't believe that," I said. Overhead, the sun was so bright, the sky a steely blue.

Suddenly Saylor was standing in front of me. We were nearly the same height, so she was looking right into my eyes. "I don't have a family," she told me evenly. "Or a home. Even my name isn't real. That's what I gave up to keep David safe. Myself. It's what Christopher gave up, too. And it's what you'll give up as well, whether you want to admit it or not. My every waking moment is dedicated to keeping that boy alive."

My arm was very heavy as I lowered it. Everything in me felt heavy. "I don't want that," I said, hating how . . . petulant I sounded. But I couldn't help it. "After Cotillion, what will he even need protecting *from*? The Ephors want to kill *me*, not him."

"Harper, remember what I said about the Paladins protecting Alaric from himself."

As though I'd forgotten about that. "That's not going to—"

"Hey," David called, and Saylor and I both jumped. He was standing inside the back door, watching us. "Did I miss the sword show again?"

He said it jokingly, but somehow I knew he'd overheard us.

I hadn't seen David since Saturday night, and I gave a small sigh of relief. Standing in Saylor's backyard, wearing a sweater that was two sizes too big and jeans that were a size too small, he just looked like David. I wasn't noticing his hair or his eyes or his hands. Whatever that had been between us had clearly been a fluke of the hug and the lamplight and him actually acting like a decent human being.

Still, when he said, "Pres, you wanna come upstairs and work on that thing with me?"

Saylor's eyes narrowed a bit. "What thing?"

"Project for the newspaper," I said. "Can't let major supernatural happenings get in the way of journalism, right, David?"

"Yup," he said with a little nod.

"I thought you weren't on the paper, Harper," Saylor said, sounding unconvinced.

"I'm not," I told her, grabbing my coat from the back of a lawn chair. "But David and I are trying to work together more at school. You know, so no one gets suspicious of us hanging out."

Saylor's blue eyes moved from David to me and back again. "All right," she said. "Don't be too long. I still have a few more things to go over with you before we're done for today, Harper."

"Aye aye," I replied, giving her a tiny salute.

David headed for the stairs, and I followed. We were about halfway up when he stopped and turned back to me, lifting his eyebrows. "'Aye aye?'" he whispered, his mouth lifting in a crooked grin, and . . . oh.

Suddenly, the fluke felt a lot less fluke-y.

Hoping the light was dim enough to hide my blush, I muttered, "Shut up," and pushed past him up the stairs.

Chapter 31

DAVID'S ROOM was a lot like I'd pictured.

I mean, not like I'd ever spent a huge amount of time thinking about David Stark's room, but if you'd asked me to describe it, I think I would've been pretty dead on. There was the totally sensible wooden-framed bed, complete with a blue comforter. There was a matching desk piled high with notebooks and computer stuff, and not much on the walls except for a few maps. I paused in front of one of them.

"Where is this?" I asked.

It wasn't a continent I recognized. David looked up from gathering a pile of laundry. "Oh. Um, that's Middle Earth."

I could've sworn he was blushing, but in the interest of working together, I decided not to give him a hard time about it. Instead, I nodded and moved over to the bookshelf. There was a corkboard posted above it with a few newspaper articles pinned to it, and three photographs. Two were nature shots—a tree that I thought was the oak in Forrest Park, and the pond behind Grove Academy—but one showed David sitting on a stool in front of a blue backdrop. There were three other kids in the photo. I recognized all of them from the newspaper staff. Chie, the pretty Asian girl I'd seen hanging around David, was leaning on his shoulder.

"Are you guys a thing?" I asked, tapping the picture. It suddenly occurred to me that I knew next to nothing about David's social life. He'd always hung out with the same handful of kids in school, all the same kids that were on the newspaper staff now. And since David and I had basically declared ourselves mortal enemies in preschool, our circles didn't overlap often. But I never saw him at school dances or at the movies or anything. I'd certainly never seen him with a girl. But Chie *had* looked weirded out about him holding my hair when I puked at Homecoming.

"Huh?" he asked, squinting at the picture. "Oh, no. We're friends. That was . . . goofing off with the camera in newspaper."

"I think she likes you," I said. He gave a noncommittal grunt in reply, shoving his laundry basket into the closet.

Since that was a dead-end street, I crouched down in front of the bookcase. Like mine, it was overstuffed, but whereas I'd at least made an attempt at organizing titles, David had books shoved in every which way and stacked on top of one another.

There were a bunch of fantasy novels, and classics, as well as several biographies of journalists. I picked up a book about Ernie Pyle and started thumbing through it. "So you're really into this whole newspaper guy thing."

David pushed the closet door closed. "Yeah. I always thought that's what I'd do for a living one day."

I put the book back and turned to face him. "You still can."

He snorted, leaning back against his footboard. "Yeah, I'll

be one heck of a journalist. I can predict the stories before they happen."

I wanted to say something encouraging. Something like, "Hey, you still can! So what if you might be a supernaturally powered crazy dude!"

But even I couldn't fake that much pep. "We'll work it out," I said.

David looked at me, and there was that expression again, the one he usually got right before he wrote a terrible article about me. "You really believe that, don't you?"

I walked over to his desk and sat in the chair. "The only alternative is to sit here and whine about it, and I don't think that's going to accomplish much. Now. What is it you want to try?"

David rubbed his hands up and down his thighs. "I want to try to have a prophecy."

Confused, I sat up straighter. "Don't we need Saylor for that? She's your battery or whatever."

David shook his head. "I don't want her to know about this. And I think . . . I think just the two of us ought to be enough to get some kind of vision. It's worth a shot, at least."

I wasn't exactly opposed to the idea. Some hint of what was coming could be helpful. But I still didn't get why David was so set against telling Saylor.

He must've read that in my face because he sat on his bed, propping his elbows on his knees. "I know I have to trust Saylor again. Eventually. And I will."

I didn't know how to answer that, so I just nodded.

"Okay. Let's prophesize."

Relief washed over David's face. "Right." He sat up, clasping his hands in front of him. "So where should we . . ."

I got out of the chair and attempted to sit as gracefully as I could on the floor. "Here," I said, holding my hands out.

After a pause, David sat across from me, folding his long legs. But he didn't take my hands. Instead, he stared at them like he'd never *seen* hands before. "It probably *will* only work with Saylor," he said. "Surely you and I have held hands before. In PE, playing red rover or something. And nothing happened then."

I thought back, trying to remember if I'd ever held hands with David Stark, but nothing came.

I opened and closed my hands at him. "Maybe we did, but that was before I got all superpowered, so it doesn't matter. Now come on."

Still, he sat there, hands clenched in his lap. "We hugged!" he exclaimed, lifting his head. "In your car, when we didn't die, and the other night, with the soup. We hugged, and I didn't have some crazy-ass vision."

Neither had I. But I'd had a potential case of the butterflies I was trying very hard not to think of right now. And then I noticed the red flush creeping its way up David's neck and wondered if he was trying to squelch the same thing. "That was just a hug, and we were both fully clothed."

He shot me a weird look, and the flush on his neck got redder.

"I mean our—our skin didn't touch," I hurried on, and now, oh God, I was blushing, too. "So maybe this thing needs skin-on-skin contact. Or hand-on-hand. Or . . ."

Frustrated, I reached out and grabbed his hands. "Please shut up and think future-y thoughts."

"I wasn't the one talking," he reminded me, but before I could give any kind of comeback, I felt the low buzz of electricity start between our palms. It was nothing like that first night with him and Saylor, the power of it nearly blowing us out of our chairs. But it was there. Weak and full of static, like a TV channel that was trying to come through.

David closed his eyes and I did the same. Our hands were warm, and as David's fingers tightened on mine, a picture began to form behind my eyelids. There was a flash of white, another of red, and I thought I could hear screams again, but they were so faint, I wasn't sure. More red, and stairs. A bunch of greenery crumpled on the ground, and silver—

Suddenly, the picture was gone, and David wasn't holding my hands. When I opened my eyes, I saw him standing across the room, next to his bookshelf.

"What is it?" I asked, rising to my feet.

Shaking his head, he turned back around, and his face wasn't so much pale as it was gray. When he still wouldn't answer, I grabbed his arm.

"Remember what you said to me about how I had to start saying 'dead'? Well, you have to start saying things, too. Namely, important things, no matter how dumb you think they are."

He turned to face me, and his mouth opened and closed a couple of times. "I saw you, in a white dress. You were lying on the steps, at Magnolia House, bleeding. And I . . . I saw you die."

Chapter 32

I only *thought* I'd taken Cotillion practice seriously before. Now that I knew what the night was really about, I was nearly fanatical in getting everything right.

That Thursday afternoon, Saylor was MIA at Cotillion practice. She hadn't said where she would be, only that she needed me to be in charge. So I walked up and down the stairs of Magnolia House and did my very best not to imagine myself lying dead on them. Like I'd told David that afternoon, Blythe and Saylor had both said that boy Oracles could see what *could* happen, not necessarily what *would*. Of course I *could* die the night of Cotillion. We'd always known that. But I wasn't going to, because that night was going to go off perfectly, no matter how many times I had to correct the girls' placement. Where they were standing was important since Saylor and I were trying to create an easy exit should stuff go badly.

But the third time I snapped, "Move three steps to your *left*, Mary Beth!" she whirled on me.

"Oh my God, Harper, it *doesn't matter*. You don't have to pick on me just because I sat next to your boyfriend at a movie."

It was almost like the air had been sucked out of the room. Or maybe that was from everyone trying not to gasp all at once. Ryan and I hadn't talked about Mary Beth and the movies, or David and the jacket. I think both of us were willing that entire evening away. He'd come over a couple of evenings, and we'd sat in the entertainment room my dad had set up in the basement, watching movies and occasionally kissing, but things still felt fragile and awkward between us. *Nine more days*, I kept reminding myself. *Nine more days, and all of this is over.*

But now here was Mary Beth, throwing it in my face. Bee moved closer. "You sat where with who?" We were practicing in our dresses today, and Bee looked like a seriously pissed-off bride as she stomped to my side. "You went to the movies with Ryan?" she asked Mary Beth.

Bee was one of the sweetest people I knew, but she was also super scary when she got angry. It didn't help that she was over six feet tall in her heels.

Mary Beth went a little pale. "No!" she bleated. "I-I sat next to him after Harper ran out to hook up with David Stark."

Now everyone did gasp, and David, who was in his usual spot, slouching behind a paperback book, sat up.

Bee turned confused eyes on me. "You and David . . ." She trailed off, and I looked around, wondering where the hell Saylor had gotten off to.

"No," I told Bee. "I ran into him. Literally." Pitching my voice lower, I added, "And you know why I've been spending time with David."

She nodded, but didn't look particularly reassured. From his spot in the corner, David called, "The only hooking up Harper did was with a pint of crab bisque. She ran into me, I spilled soup, and then I gave her my jacket. Like a gentleman. That's all there was."

He pulled his feet up onto his chair, propping the heels of his Converse on the edge of the seat, and disappeared behind his book again. But Mary Beth only narrowed her eyes at him and then turned back to me.

"Whatever. Everyone knows that you and David have been flirting since, like, third grade, and all those mean articles are his way of pulling your freaking pigtails. And you have *Ryan Bradshaw* for a boyfriend, and it's like you don't even care!"

The other girls were all circling around us now, like this was some bizarre game of Duck-Duck-Goose, and I could feel my face flaming. The only thing I hated more than a scene was people getting involved in my personal stuff, and this was both.

"You don't know anything about me and Ryan," I told Mary Beth, trying to keep my voice calm.

"I know that all he is to you is another . . . achievement." Mary Beth seemed close to tears now, her voice tight and squeaky. "Look at the way you treated him Saturday night. You just ran out of the theater. No explanation, no apology. And then you show up two hours later wearing David's jacket?"

My hands were shaking, and I realized I was balling them into fists. Afraid I'd wrinkle my gloves, I yanked them off, trying not to pop any of the buttons as I did. "I saw someone I needed to talk to. And I don't have to explain myself to you, Mary Beth."

"Who did you need to talk to that badly?" She was only a few inches taller than me, but Mary Beth drew herself up to her full height. Her hands were clenched in front of her, gloves wrinkling.

Bee was at my elbow now, her brows drawn together, confusion and suspicion obvious on her face.

"Just this girl," I said, hating the words the second they were out of my mouth. Why hadn't I thought of an excuse? Something that sounded the least bit plausible?

Maybe it was because I was tired of making excuses. Tired of lying to everyone about everything. Even Bee, who I'd let in closest of all, still didn't have any idea about what was really going on.

"It was a scholarship chick," David piped up from his corner. He was standing up now, shoving the book in his back pocket. "Harper and I are up for the same scholarship, and I'm gonna be honest, I was trying my best to suck up. Pres—Harper here ran out to talk to her, too. Hence spilling the soup." He folded his arms across his chest. "Now can we please stop being crazy and get back to prancing around a mansion in wedding dresses?"

Next to me, I felt Bee relax a little. It was a plausible story, and at that moment, I could've kissed David. Well, no, not really. I was in no way thinking about kissing David Stark.

That seemed to put an end to it, and I was about to tell the girls to start from the top again. But before I could, Mary Beth pressed her lips together. It was like I could actually feel her steeling herself for what she was going to say next. "You're exactly like your sister, Harper." The words came out fast, almost like she was afraid to say them. "You act like you're perfect, but inside, you're totally screwed up."

I'd been punched and stabbed and slammed into a bathroom wall. None of that hurt nearly as bad as Mary Beth's words. I felt them everywhere, rattling my teeth, pounding into my bones. I half expected to look down and find myself covered with bruises.

I felt an arm go around my shoulders. Bee's fingers dug into the exposed skin of my upper arm. "Mary Beth," she said, her voice shaking a little, "I don't know what the hell has gotten into you, but that was *so* out of line."

"Seriously," Abigail and Amanda muttered together. They wore identical frowns, two pairs of brown eyes glaring.

"In fact," Bee continued, pulling me closer, "I think you should leave now."

"Happily," Mary Beth said, kicking off her heels and pulling a pair of sneakers out from under the little sofa by the door.

"Are you okay?" Bee asked once she was gone, and I made myself smile, even though I could feel how shaky it was.

"Fine," I told her. "Mary Beth has had a thing for Ryan for a million years, and she's jealous. It's . . . it's no big deal."

Bee wrapped me in a quick hug, her collarbone pressing against my chin. "It is a *big* deal. Everything she said was so freaking offensive. The stuff about your sister, and David . . ."

She trailed off. Over her shoulder, I could see David, his face concerned, lips thin. I hadn't run out on Ryan to go "hook up" with David, but hadn't there been . . . something? Wasn't that nearly as bad as if I had kissed him?

"And you and Ryan are good, right?" Bee pulled back, a slight crease between her brows.

"We're great," I said, and David suddenly turned away, pulling his book out of his back pocket. The stairs rose behind him, and all I could think was, *He saw me dead there.* I needed to get out of this dress. I needed to get out of Magnolia House.

"I think I'm gonna go ahead and go home," I told the girls.

Most of them nodded sympathetically, but I saw a gleam in some eyes. Of course. Harper Jane Price was about to have a nervous breakdown in front of them. Who wouldn't want to see that?

"Let me drive you," David said, but I shook my head even as Bee glared at him and said, "I'll drive her."

"I can drive myself," I told them, and when they both went to protest, I help up my hand. "Promise. I . . . need a break."

I think Bee would've kept arguing, but I told her I would text her as soon as I got home and headed for the door before she had a chance.

I got behind the wheel of my car, meaning to head home. But when I got to the turn for my house, I went left instead of right. There was someone I needed to talk to.

Chapter 33

I DON'T KNOW what Ryan was expecting when he opened the door, but me basically launching myself at him was probably not it, if his "Whoa!" was anything to go by.

I stood in his front door, dressed in my Cotillion gown, my arms locked so tightly around his neck that I was holding my elbows, toes dangling off the ground. After a beat, he wrapped his arms around my waist.

Ducking my head, I pressed my cheek to his neck, wanting to breathe in the safe, familiar scent of him, wanting to climb inside his soft gray T-shirt, wanting to *hide* in him.

"Harper, are you all right?" he asked, and I shook my head, pressing closer.

He gave a sighing laugh, breath brushing my ear. "Well, whatever it is, it'll be okay. Actually, wait." Ryan set me back on my feet, looking me up and down, appraising. "Are you running away from a wedding? Because that might be less okay."

I swatted at him with a watery chuckle. "This is my Cotillion dress, thank you very much."

His hazel eyes went wide. "Ah. I thought I wasn't supposed to see you in that."

Waving that away, I stepped past him and into the house. "Oh, who cares?"

I walked down the hall to Ryan's room. His parents would still be at work, so we could safely hang out in what was normally a forbidden zone.

"'Who cares?'" Ryan echoed, following me. "Who are you, and what have you done with my girlfriend?"

Ryan's room used to be his brother Luke's. It couldn't have been more different from David's room. No maps of Middle Earth, for one thing, and not many books. There was a flatscreen mounted to the wall, and a gaming station. Ryan had been in the middle of some basketball game, but he crossed the room and turned the television off.

"So do you want to talk?" he asked, sounding a little unsure. "Or are you here so we can . . ."

He trailed off, but his gaze slid behind me to his bed.

"Talk," I said firmly, sitting on the edge of the mattress. "For one thing, it takes too long to get this dress off and back on."

That made him smile and took a little bit of the disappointment out of his eyes. "Okay. Can I at least do this?"

Sitting next to me, Ryan took my face in his hands and lowered his mouth to mine. Even as I reached out to clutch the front of his T-shirt, I was thinking of that first kiss on the swings at the park. The way my heart had leapt into my mouth, how every hair on my body seemed to stand on end.

It was only natural that Ryan's kisses didn't make me feel like that anymore. We'd been together for two years now. Those kind of sparks only belonged in new relationships, didn't they?

Or was Mary Beth right? Was I holding on to Ryan because he was another *thing* for me to have? Another achievement on Harper Jane Price's list of accomplishments? 4.0 GPA, SGA President, Homecoming Queen, Haver of Best Possible Boyfriend.

"Um, Harper?"

Ryan pulled back, his hands falling from my back. His eyes were kind of hazy, but he was starting to frown.

"What?"

"It's customary to kiss back when a guy is kissing you."

Ugh. I'd done it again. "Sorry," I said, ducking my head in my best attempt to seem apologetic. "I was thinking."

Sighing, Ryan sat back. "Of course you were."

"You're right. Things are weird right now," I said. "It'll be better after Cotillion." That was becoming my mantra. Problem was, I wasn't sure if that was actually true. Whatever was going to happen at Cotillion, Saylor said it would change things. Would it be for the better?

Ryan reached out and took my face in both hands, a mix of exasperation and love on his face. "You always say that," he said, his thumbs tracing my cheekbones. "It's always going to get better someday. Sometime in the future, things won't be so crazy." Leaning forward, Ryan dropped a kiss on the tip of my nose. "But the thing is, Harper, we can't *see* the future. So how can you have any idea if it's going to get any better?"

Irony, thy name is Ryan.

"Do you like Mary Beth?" I asked suddenly. One of Ryan's pillows sat next to me, and I pulled it to my stomach.

Ryan rocked back from me, his hands lifting from my face to hover somewhere in the air around my shoulders. "Where did that— No. I mean, I like her, but not . . ."

"Right," I said, twisting my hands in my skirt. It wasn't that I didn't believe Ryan. He wasn't a bad liar like David, he just . . . didn't. Ever, as far as I could tell. But there was something kind of unsure in his voice, something that lodged under my skin.

"Do you like David?" Ryan asked, dropping his hands to his thighs.

"No," I said immediately. "We're maybe not as hostile as we used to be, and he's finally backed off on the paper thing, but that's it as far as we go."

But I kept thinking of sitting across from David at Miss Annemarie's, the way he'd said Mary Beth wasn't me. And the more I thought about it, the more confused I felt, which sucked since I'd come to Ryan's specifically to stop feeling so confused. To feel *normal*.

Yes, David and I were closer now than we had been. But that was only because he was the only person other than Saylor who knew the whole truth. Of course I'd feel the odd warm fuzzy for him. So there was an obvious solution here.

"Hey, you wanna help me with something?" I asked Ryan, rising to my feet.

He quirked one auburn brow. "Is it the buttons on that dress? Because if so, then yes, very much so."

It was flirty and jokey and I should find it charming and not slightly irritating. I reminded myself of that as I smiled back. "Not exactly. It's research."

The corners of Ryan's mouth turned down and he flopped back on his bed. "Now that sounds like a great, sexy time right there," he told the ceiling.

"It's going to be fun," I insisted, sweeping a pile of *Sports Illustrated* magazines off his desk chair and turning on his computer. "It features death and destruction and other things boys like. It'll be like *Hard Fists*, only more . . . historical."

Ryan was still lying on his bed, arms folded behind his head. He laughed. "Oh, man, *Hard Fists*. I hate that you missed it. There was this one part where this dude killed another dude using, shit you not, a ladle, and Mary Beth said—"

He broke off, and I pretended to be really involved in finding the perfect search engine. "So what kind of death and destruction research?" he said, finally.

"This king, Charlemagne. He had a bunch of knights who died fighting a—" I broke off, suddenly realizing that I couldn't exactly get into all the Oracle stuff. "A bad guy," I finished lamely. I'd read everything I could on Charlemagne's Paladins on the internet, but there was hardly a mention of Alaric. Still, it couldn't hurt to look again.

I rummaged around on Ryan's desk, sifting through more *Sports Illustrated*s, a bunch of loose change, and a stack of video games. "Don't you have a notebook or some paper or something?"

By now, Ryan had shifted on the bed, turning so that his feet were braced on the headboard. He was tossing the mini basketball that sat by his bed on the wall above. Catching it, he tilted his head. "You're seriously going to do homework."

I paused, my hand still resting on a video game, the box reading *War Metal 4*. "It's not really homework. More like an . . . extracurricular project. I thought it might be fun if you were more involved in the stuff I do."

"Why?" Ryan asked, tossing the ball again. "It's not like you're all that involved in the stuff I do."

He didn't say it accusingly, and didn't even seem that put out by it. It was just a fact. "I cheerlead at your basketball games," I reminded him.

He shrugged. "You were doing that before we even started dating. It's no big deal, Harper, I'm just saying we don't have to be all up in each other's business." He gave the basketball another thump before grinning at me. "Unless it's in the carnal sense."

This time, I didn't even try to hide my irritation. "You spend too much time with Brandon," I muttered, and Ryan gave a bark of laughter.

"Right, because he knows what the word 'carnal' means. But please . . . don't keep trying to fix us, Harper. We're not broken."

But the thing is, we felt broken. Really broken. And the scary thing was, I wasn't sure how we'd even gotten here in only a month. I'd been so busy worried about saving David, saving Cotillion, saving *myself*, that I hadn't noticed my relationship was also in need of a hero. Could I fix that, too?

Ryan kept thumping the basketball behind his bed and I watched him, my Cotillion dress crumpled and uncomfortable, and thought about the scariest question of all: Did I want to?

Chapter 34

WHEN I got to school the next morning, Bee was waiting for me in the parking lot. Leaning against her car, blond hair whipping in the wind, she frowned as I walked up to her. "You never texted me last night, and I called you like a hundred times."

It took me a second to remember that I'd promised to text her, and why. Oh, right, the ugly scene at Cotillion practice. "Ugh, I'm sorry. I went over to Ryan's last night, and I left my phone in the car."

Bee pushed away from her car, tugging her knit hat a little farther down over her forehead. "Are you guys okay?"

The words "Of course!" immediately leapt to the tip of my tongue, but I bit them back. Bee deserved better than that. "We're trying to be."

Kids were walking past us and up the stairs into Wallace Hall. I caught a glimpse of Mary Beth's reddish hair before she disappeared into the building. Bee must've seen her, too, because she paused on the steps. "Mary Beth had it totally wrong yesterday. You and Ryan are perfect together, and you know that."

"Are we?" I heard myself ask, and Bee's head jerked up like I'd smacked her.

"What?"

"It's only . . ." I thought about last night, sitting in Ryan's bedroom, me on the computer, him tossing his basketball, sitting four feet apart, but feeling like there was an ocean between us. "I love Ryan, but—"

"There are no buts," Bee said, taking my hand. "You said it yourself. You love him." She shrugged. "That's all that matters."

"You're right," I said, even though I wasn't really sure that she was. And when she added, "Besides, you guys have to get married, and then Brandon and I will get married, and we'll all live next door to each other, and our kids will play together . . ."

She was smiling, and when she bumped my hip with hers, I knew she wasn't totally serious, but I couldn't make myself smile back. I wasn't an Oracle, but even I knew that future was . . . wrong.

Bee lowered her head. "You know, I was thinking last night. Don't get me wrong, your lessons with Saylor are really awesome. I mean, the other day, when she taught you how to disarm someone with a knife? Even *I* wanted to learn that."

I smiled at the memory of last week, Bee sitting in the grass of Saylor's backyard, her long legs stretched out in front of her, cheering me on as Saylor put me through my paces.

"And I get why you're keeping it a secret," Bee went on once we were inside the school. The burnt-hair smell of the ancient heaters assaulted my nose, and the squeak and click of hundreds of shoes filled my ears. "But . . . Harper, if it's making people think you and David Stark have something going on, is it worth it? I mean, do you even *need* any more lessons? You looked pretty freaking skilled the last time I watched you."

"After Cotillion," I told her, giving her my favorite saying. "I have a couple more lessons, and then I'm totally giving it up. Trust me."

But once again, there was that niggling thought. Even if I did manage to keep Blythe from doing her crazy spell and save the town, what would happen then?

No. One day at a time.

Bee nodded, but she was still chewing her lower lip. "Okay. So, hey, since we don't have Cotillion practice today, wanna hit up the Dixie Bean after school?"

A pair of freshman girls walked by, their arms linked tightly. They were laughing, heads close together, and something about them made my throat ache. "I have to meet Saylor today."

Bee's face fell a little, so I hastily added, "Do you want to come with me again? I think today we're learning this cool move that knocks people out. You know, like that *Star Trek* thing." I pinched the air with my hand, hoping Bee would laugh.

She just shook her head. "That's okay. I think the twins are free, so . . ."

"Oh." I dropped my hand. "Right. Well, y'all go to the Dixie Bean. Put extra whipped cream on your mocha for me."

She smiled at that, but it didn't reach her eyes. We made our way to our lockers. "I suwannee," I joked. "Next year? I am so going to be one of those stereotypical seniors who stacks her schedule with easy classes." As I said it, I tried to push away the image of me bleeding out on the steps of Magnolia House. I *would* have a senior year.

"But I guess that's the thing with junior year. Between college stuff, and regular school, things are so—"

"Really busy right now," Bee filled in, switching her backpack to her other shoulder. "I know. And it looks like things are about to get busier for you." She inclined her head toward my locker, or rather, to the pale purple sheet of paper taped there.

That color paper only meant one thing. The headmaster wanted to see me.

"What?" I said dumbly, ripping the paper from my locker.

"It can't be bad," Bee offered. "I mean . . . you're you."

My hand was trembling a little as I pushed the piece of paper into my coat pocket. "Yeah, he probably wants to talk to me about SGA stuff. See you at lunch?"

Brandon came through the front doors then, whooping Bee's name, and I never got a reply.

Turning away, I headed for the main office, Headmaster Dunn's secretary waving me through when I held up the little piece of purple paper. The office smelled like coffee and leather, and the walls were covered in all of his various diplomas and awards for education.

The headmaster himself was a short, squat man with droopy green eyes and a fringe of reddish hair circling his bald head. I took a seat in the chair opposite his desk, and gave him my best

Harper Jane Price smile. "You wanted to see me, Headmaster? Is this about SGA?"

In a way, it was.

His face folded with concern as he leaned over his desk. "Harper, I understand that you're very committed to this school and to your studies. But perhaps you've overextended yourself."

"I . . . what?" The leather chair squeaked under me as I sat up straighter.

He pulled out a manila folder and began paging through its contents. "According to your teachers, your grades have been slipping. And you've been tardy to class . . . let's see . . . three times in the past few weeks?"

Okay, so yes, I had gotten a B on my last history test, and I turned in one paper—*one*—late in English. As for the tardies, the first time had been after the janitor's closet with David. The second had been because I thought I felt that David's-in-danger feeling, but actually, I just hadn't eaten breakfast. The third time had been because David texted me that he'd seen some weird dude lurking outside the school, but it had been the new lawn guy.

Not like I could tell Headmaster Dunn any of that. "I had female troubles."

But even that, the Gold Standard Excuse to Give to Male Teachers, didn't work. Headmaster Dunn went on like I hadn't said anything. "I think it's possible you're suffering from stress."

"*I am not stressed!*" My fingers dug into the sides of the chair, clutching so hard I was surprised I didn't tear a gash in the leather.

He might have believed me if the words hadn't come out in a hysterical shriek.

As it was, he heaved a huge sigh. "In your best interest, Harper, I'm removing you from the SGA."

"You're . . . you're what?"

"Also, I'm going to advise Coach Henderson to give you a break from cheerleading until next semester."

"But it'll be over next sem—"

Headmaster Dunn's jowls wobbled as he shook his head. "And I think the Committee for Academic Honesty can do without you, at least until Christmas."

Now I was making high-pitched whimpering sounds.

I watched him write down and subsequently cross out every single activity I did for the Grove. Future Business Leaders of America? Gone. Key Club? Gone. Annual Christmas bake sale chairperson? Crossed through *twice*.

"There," he said with satisfaction once he was done erasing my entire life. "Now see? You'll feel so much better."

"But . . . college," I said weakly. I didn't care what Saylor said. I could still do that, right? How could I *not* go to college? "They'll see that I dropped out of all this stuff my junior year, and they'll think I can't follow through, and all I do is follow through, so—"

"Harper," he said sternly. "You are bright and talented and driven, and any college would be lucky to have you. But as your principal, it's my job to guide your academic pursuits. And I think all these things you do here at the Grove are getting in that way of that."

He ripped the paper in half, the sound making me wince.

"But now you're free. Concentrate on your classes. That will do more to get you into a good school than all the extracurricular activities in the world."

I stood up, my legs numb. All I could do was nod.

"And, Harper," he added when I opened the door, "maybe take some time for yourself now, okay?"

Chapter 35

THE DAY before Cotillion, I sat on Saylor's sun porch, staring at a textbook.

Today's lesson involved the history of the Ephors and ancient Greece, even though I'd thought our last session before Cotillion might involve more fighting and training. But Saylor said it was important for me to conserve my strength, hence the studying. The day felt pleasant and fallish, and the sunlight was warm between my shoulder blades as I studied.

"This," Saylor said, pointing to a picture of a stone fort at the edge of a cliff, "was the home of the Ephors. Or was. I have no idea if that's where they're still operating from."

I ran my finger over the imposing building. It was huge and vaguely medieval-looking. There were even bars on the windows, and below, the Mediterranean, so blue it almost hurt to look at, crashed against a rocky shore.

"It's . . . beautiful doesn't seem like the right word."

"It's not," Saylor agreed, taking another sip of lemonade. "It's awe-inspiring and terrifying and lovely to look at, but not beautiful."

There was a wistfulness in her voice, and I glanced up. "You miss it."

It wasn't a question. Saylor's eyes were practically misty as she looked at the photograph.

"It was all I knew for a very long time. And don't get me wrong, Pine Grove is very nice, but it's not . . ." She trailed off, her fingers brushing the edge of the page. Then she cleared her throat and sat up a little straighter. "Anyway, that's the seat of the Ephors. And how many are there?"

Sighing, I leaned back in my seat. "Five. They used to be elected by the Greek people, but now they choose their own successors. And they pass their power on via super creepy kissing, just like Paladins."

Saylor frowned. "That's not exactly how I'd put it, but yes."

When I didn't say anything, Saylor reached out and closed the book. "You seem distracted today."

There was absolutely no humor in my laugh. "Kind of have a lot on my mind right now, Miss Saylor."

"David told me there was an issue at Cotillion practice yesterday. Something with you and Mary Beth?"

A breeze swept through the open door of the sun porch, making the wind chimes ring softly, and even though I wasn't that cold, I wrapped my arms around myself. "It wasn't a big deal. But what was you not being there supposed to accomplish exactly?"

Leaning back in her chair, Saylor folded her arms. "Yesterday was actually another training lesson for you. I wanted to see how you did leading the girls by yourself."

I snorted. "Oh, well, everyone turned on me and started

snarking about my boyfriend and David, so that went super great."

"What about David?" Saylor asked.

"Let's just say it hasn't escaped anyone's notice that we're spending a lot of time together, and people have the wrong idea, and . . . " I trailed off. "Anyway, I can fix it."

Before Saylor could reply, David suddenly appeared in the doorway, leaning his head out. "Say— Oh. Pres. Hi."

"Hi," I replied, turning all my attention back to my book. But he walked onto the sun porch, standing in front of me. "Is everything okay? After yesterday?"

I lifted my head then. David's outfit today was another winner: a shrunken black V-neck sweater over a bright purple collared shirt, with blue and violet plaid pants. I didn't even know where one purchased plaid pants. Still, looking at him, I smiled. Say what you would about David's wardrobe—and I'd said a lot over the years—he was always a hundred percent committed to it.

"It was fine," I told him. "I went over to Ryan's and we worked things out, so . . . yeah, right as rain. Except for saving both of our lives and this entire town, of course." I thumped the book in front of me.

David blinked a couple of times, the effect slightly owlish behind his glasses. "Oh, good. Not about us maybe dying, but you and Ryan. That's . . . that's good."

"It is," I said, rubbing my eyes. I felt like I hadn't slept in years.

Silence fell and it lasted a second too long before David turned to Saylor and said, "Anyway, wanted to let you know I was home."

"Anything to report?" Saylor asked, and even though I wasn't looking at him, I knew David rolled his eyes.

"Nope. No one tried to kill me, I've had no bizarre visions of the future, and now I plan on making myself some pizza rolls. We good?"

"Go," she said, waving a hand at him.

But there was affection in her voice, and her eyes followed him out the door.

"You love him," I said, and she swung her gaze back to me.

"I do." She smoothed her hands over her thighs, flattening imaginary wrinkles from the linen.

"Even though he's not your family."

Saylor laughed, a surprisingly husky sound. "Don't you love people who aren't your family, Harper Jane?"

"Of course I do. But you love him for more than the whole Oracle thing. You love him because he's David."

Saylor sighed, looking behind her. The sun was starting to go down, and her backyard was filled with soft golden light. Even in November, things were still green and blooming.

"Yes," she said at last. "I love him because he's David. That boy can be a pain in the backside, don't get me wrong, but he has a good heart. And he's actually handling this a heck of a lot better than I thought he would. Look at him. Whole life turned upside down, and he's in there making pizza rolls." She gave a fond snort. "He's a good boy. So, yes, I love him, whether he can see the future or not."

My throat felt weird, so I opened the book again, flipping pages and trying to focus on the words in front of me. *Ephors were said to have magical powers of their own, but many people thought they were simply draining that power from the Oracles themselves and—*

"Harper, do *you* care about him?"

Closing my hand around my glass of lemonade before it could plummet to the patio, I shook my head. "David?"

"He was the boy we were speaking of, yes," Saylor answered dryly. "And not just because he's the Oracle, but because he's David."

I made a big show of resituating my lemonade glass on the table, wiping stray droplets from the book. "Of course I don't," I said, even as my heart hammered in my ears. "You've seen the two of us together. All we do is argue."

"Passionately," Saylor said.

"There is nothing . . . *passionate* about me and David. I've spent most of my life despising him and while I'll admit that this—this situation has made me appreciate him a little more, there's nothing going on between us."

I made myself meet her eyes, which wasn't easy, seeing as how just thinking about him was making my skin feel weird and too tight.

"Nothing going on," I repeated, but Saylor only squinted at me.

"Do you know, if it weren't for your respective positions, I'd hope you were lying to me. I'd hope you felt the same way about David he's felt about you all these years."

I couldn't keep myself from snorting. "You want me to loathe him?"

Saylor wrinkled her nose. "Is that really how you think David feels about you?"

I couldn't have this conversation right now. Not when there were about a million other things going on that were way more important than feelings.

"Please don't tell me he's only been writing horrible articles about me because of a secret crush," I said, getting out of my chair and going to stand by the window. A cardinal flew into the birdbath, a bright splash of red against all the green. Something about that bright red bothered me, reminding me of . . . something. Something in David's visions. There had been red in that, a wave of it. Blood? The thought made me shudder.

Saylor came up behind me, watching the bird, too, and I suddenly remembered the other thing she'd said. "What do you mean that you'd be happy if we liked each other were it not for our 'respective positions'? Is Paladin-Oracle romance frowned upon or something?"

She sighed. "There's nothing expressly in the rules about it, but it's generally acknowledged not to be the best idea. The relationship between Paladin, Oracle, and Mage is complicated enough without dragging the heart into it. And there's always the chance that personal feelings can interfere with duty."

The late-afternoon sun shone on her silver hair as I looked over at her. Saylor was still staring into the backyard, but her eyes were far away.

"Miss Saylor," I said slowly. "The spell. What if . . . what if Blythe's right and it just powers him up? No crazy times or power twisting his brain or any of that?"

Saylor kept staring in the backyard. In the fading light, I could see some of her fuchsia lipstick had bled into the tiny wrinkles around her mouth. "If that's the case, it would be a miracle. The Ephors believed—I believed—there was a reason Oracles were almost never male. They're . . ." She sighed. "It's an ugly word, but they're aberrations. And if Blythe does this spell on David, he'll be every bit as lost to us, do you understand me? That much power, it will burn him up and eat him alive until he's not David anymore, but a powerful, dangerous creature that absolutely must be put down."

David's dream. Both of us crying, something in my hand, him dying because of me . . .

Goose bumps had broken out over my whole body, and they had nothing to do with the cold. "I understand."

Chapter 36

ACROSS TOWN, my friends were all at Bee's house, putting on their dresses together, laughing and doing each other's makeup. I imagined them stepping into their white shoes, slipping on gloves, while I got ready by myself. I'd told Bee that Mom wanted it to be just us, a kind of mother-daughter bonding thing. Really, I just wanted to be alone.

Once I was done, I turned to stare into the mirror. The dress was every bit as beautiful as it had always been, but it was a smidgen too big. I'd lost weight these past few weeks. And then there was my face, pale even under the makeup. One way or another, everything would change after tonight.

The door opened behind me, and Mom walked in. As soon as her eyes landed on me, she drew in a soft breath. "Oh, Harper."

I fiddled with my pearls. "It looks good, right? I wasn't sure about these sleeves, but with the gloves . . ."

Mom crossed the room in a few strides and rested her hands on my shoulders. "It's better than good. It's beautiful."

And it was. Or it would've been if I could stop thinking of it as the dress I might die in. The dress I would be wearing when I screwed this whole thing up and got everyone I loved and everything I knew blown off the map.

I swallowed those thoughts down, trying to smile. "You look amazing, too," I told Mom. She was wearing a soft pink dress that brought color to her cheeks and made her dark eyes shine. Tears sprang to my eyes, and I turned around to hug Mom before she could notice.

"I'm so proud of you," she whispered against my temple.

I gave a watery chuckle. "Why? All I'm doing is walking down some stairs and trying not to spill punch on my dress."

But Mom shook her head and pulled back. "No," she said, holding me at arm's length. "Not just for Cotillion. For the girl— no, the woman—you've become."

Now I didn't have to worry about hiding tears. We were both a little weepy.

"I'm sorry for being so overprotective these past few weeks," Mom told me. She smelled like Mary Kay makeup and hairspray, and I hugged her again.

"I'm sorry, too," I told her, and nothing had ever been truer.

There was a soft knock at the door, and when Mom and I turned, Saylor was standing there. She was already dressed for Cotillion, too, wearing a navy dress, with a white rose corsage pinned to the bodice.

"Saylor?" Mom asked, confused.

Saylor met my eyes, and I nodded.

Satisfied, Saylor walked into the room and reached into her

handbag. She pulled out the little pot of lip balm. "Hillary, don't you look lovely?"

Saylor's smile was bright as ever, and her accent seemed thicker than normal. "Where did you find that dress?"

I could tell Mom was still a little puzzled, but manners trumped confusion. "Nordstrom," she answered, brushing a hand over the skirt. "I think it's supposed to be a mother-of-the-bride dress, but I guess that's appropriate."

She gave a nervous little chuckle, and Saylor laughed, too. "Mine is the same. But that color . . . here, let me get a closer look."

And then she touched Mom's hand. The scent of roses wafted over me as Saylor held on to Mom and looked deep into her eyes. "You are going to stay home tonight, Hillary. You and Tom both. You don't feel well, and you can't bring yourself to ruin Harper's special night. Tomorrow, you'll wake up and you'll be so sorry to have missed it, but you'll know it was the right thing to do."

Mom swayed on her feet a little, and I gripped her other arm. But after a moment, she gave a faint nod. "I don't feel very well. I think I'll stay home tonight."

Saylor gave her hand a pat. "Good girl. Now go on and change into something more comfortable."

Mom didn't walk out of my room so much as float. "Thank you," I said to Saylor, even though watching my mother leave made my heart twist painfully.

But Saylor was still staring out the door. "Harper, if Blythe's spell goes badly tonight, it won't matter that your parents aren't actually at Magnolia House."

"I know." I looked around my bedroom, wondering if this was the last time I'd see my purple bedspread, or the silver and cherrywood jewelry box that had been my grandmother's.

"Everyone in this town is in danger if—"

"*I. Know*," I repeated. "And I know that my aunts will still be there, and my friends, and my boyfriend."

Turning back to the mirror, I pinched my cheeks in a last-ditch effort not to look quite so much like death. Honestly, white really is a difficult color for anyone to wear. "But I had to do something."

I thought Saylor would argue that, too, but she just sighed and sank down on the edge of my bed. "Don't we all."

"Have you been to Magnolia House yet?" I asked. "Any sign of . . . anything?"

She shook her head. "Everything is as it should be at the house, but Blythe is here."

The words sent a shiver racing through me. "How do you know?"

"I felt my wards giving way this afternoon," Saylor said, glancing up as she rummaged in her handbag. "I don't know how she did it, but it has to be her."

"What could she even be planning?" I asked, going to sit next to Saylor. "Is she just going to march into Magnolia House and start her mojo?"

Saylor shook her head. "I don't know. She'll need to be

protected from you while she's attempting the ritual, but she doesn't have a Paladin on her side. And the ritual itself is surprisingly simple. It won't take her long."

Dr. DuPont, shoe sticking out of his neck, suddenly flashed through my mind. That had been six weeks ago. Six weeks to completely reorder my entire life.

And possibly end it.

"Hired assassins then maybe? Disguised as cater waiters?"

"That's a possibility," Saylor acknowledged with a nod. "Keep an eye on them."

Crossing over to my dresser, I picked up my lip gloss. I wasn't forgetting that tonight, at least. "I will," I said, swiping on a coat of Coral Shimmer.

Saylor watched me in the mirror. "Of course, there's always the possibility she'll try to kill you before she starts the ritual. That would probably be the easiest thing to do."

My heart sank, and the hand holding the lip gloss trembled. "Well, yeah, there's that."

Rising from the bed, Saylor came to stand behind me, her hands on my shoulders. "You can do this," she told me. "I know you can."

"I have been rocking the training pretty hard," I admitted, and Saylor tightened her grip.

"I've known you since you were a tiny little girl, Harper Jane Price. You are driven, and smart, and sharp, and there's no other Paladin I'd rather have fighting for David tonight than you."

It was all I'd ever wanted her to say. Okay, so I hadn't exactly wanted the Paladin part, but Saylor Stark praising me about any-thing was good enough for me. Reaching up, I took one of her hands and squeezed it.

"Are you ready?" she asked as the doorbell rang downstairs. Ryan.

"As I'll ever be."

Chapter 37

THE GRAVEL and shells crunched under Ryan's tires as he pulled the car up to Magnolia House. My heart thumped steadily in my chest as I stared at his headlights. How many times had I looked at this house and thought it was the prettiest place in the world? How many times had I pictured myself living there, sweeping down those wide front stairs in a Scarlett O'Hara gown?

Now staring at it, all I could think was that not only would I never live in Magnolia House, but that I might actually die there. Tonight. I tugged at my gloves. They were damp and wrinkled, and I realized my palms were sweating.

I was so busy fiddling with the row of pearl buttons, trying to get the stupid gloves off, that I didn't notice Ryan watching me until he reached out and began undoing the buttons himself.

"Here," he said softly. His fingers were surprisingly gentle as they pulled the buttons through their little loops, and for the first time in a long time, something swelled in my chest as I watched him. It wasn't love. Or at least, it wasn't the boyfriend kind of love. But it was warmth and affection and this . . . I don't know, gratitude.

Ryan was a good guy. He always had been. Once he'd finished half the row, he tugged at each finger until the glove slid off my hand. "Thanks," I said as he handed it back to me. One hand free, I went to work on the other glove myself, even though I could feel his gaze like an actual weight on the curve of my neck.

"We're done, aren't we?" he asked. I raised my head, the left glove still half on, half off.

For a second, I thought about pretending I didn't know what he was talking about. Maybe if I smiled at him and made a joke about the gloves, I could stop this from happening. But did I want to? Was there room for Ryan in my life—short as it might be—now?

I knew there wasn't.

But even more, I wasn't sure there had ever been room for Ryan. Not really. Not the way he deserved. Still, I couldn't make myself say anything.

Ryan wasn't stupid. He knew what my silence meant. His throat worked, and his eyes were shiny. "Well, we had a good run of it," he said, broad shoulders shrugging inside his tux jacket. He looked the handsomest I'd ever seen him, like he was meant to wear formal wear every day of his life.

I laughed, but it sounded sad. "You make it sound like we're getting divorced."

He laughed, too, dashing at his face with the back of his arm. "Hey, we've been together nearly our entire high school lives. That's, like, twice the length of a lot of marriages."

Smiling, I reached out and took his hand. "I love you, Ry."

Sniffing, he nodded toward the house. "I know that. But I'm

not an idiot, Harper. There's someone in there you wanna be with more than you wanna be with me."

I actually recoiled at that. "W-what are you talking about?"

Ryan rolled his eyes. "Harper, you and David Stark have been circling each other since kindergarten."

My mouth suddenly felt dry, and I busied myself taking off my glove. "David and I . . . maybe we have ended up being friends after all, and I guess we have some stuff in common—"

"He gets you, Harper. That way you throw yourself into everything you do, he does that, too. And he's a walking encyclopedia like you, and I bet he doesn't even play video games—"

"I like *War Metal 4*," I insisted, but Ryan shook his head.

"It's okay, Harper. I actually feel kind of . . . good. You know, doing the noble thing, stepping aside in the face of True Love . . ."

He was trying to joke, but my throat suddenly went tight. If Ryan had any idea what was really going on between me and David, that it was so much more complicated and so much worse.

"Ryan," I said feebly, but he shook his head.

"It's okay," he repeated even though he sounded a million miles from "okay." "Just go."

I felt like there was more I should say. We might have only been together for two years, but Ryan had been a huge part of my life.

But in the end, I just nodded again. It was better like this. So with one last little wave, I got out of the car and walked into the house.

Saylor was hanging her coat in the front closet when I walked in. "Where are your gloves?"

I stared at her. "Seriously?"

She rolled her eyes, exasperated. "You sound like David. And while I know there are"— she glanced around us—"more pressing matters at hand right now, it's still important that you look the part. Now I'll ask you again, where are your gloves?"

Adrenaline had made me jittery, and my hand shook slightly as I gestured back out the door. "I left them in Ryan's car."

Saylor lifted an eyebrow. "And is Mr. Bradshaw coming inside?"

"I-I don't think so. We broke up."

Closing her eyes, Saylor rolled her lips inward. "Was tonight the best time for that?"

Anger flared up in me. "I don't know. I'm not sure there is a best time for your boyfriend to dump you."

"You and Ryan broke up?"

Bee had just walked in the front door, Brandon a few steps behind her.

"Kind of?" I said before shaking my head. "No, not kind of. We broke up, yes."

I don't know what kind of expression people make after they've watched a puppy get stomped, but it had nothing on Bee's face in that moment. "Right before Cotillion?" she asked, shocked. "You broke up with your boyfriend half an hour before the most important night of your life?"

Taking a deep breath, I picked up the hem of my dress, moving closer to Bee. "First off, this is not the most important night of our lives. There are going to be lots of important nights. And secondly, he actually broke up with me, and it's . . . it's okay."

"It's so not okay," Bee said, her dark eyes watery. "You can't possibly be okay. Harper—"

Behind me, I could hear the kitchen door opening. A couple of men in black pants and white shirts came through, carrying a small table between them.

I met Saylor's gaze. The cater waiters. They didn't seem particularly assassin-like, and they weren't even looking in this direction. But then, Dr. DuPont hadn't seemed scary either until he'd had a scimitar at my neck.

"We'll talk about this later," I told Bee as there was another bustle from the kitchen. The door swung open again, and this time, my Aunts Martha and May swooped in. May was carrying a giant silver punch bowl, while Martha had a ladle tucked under her arm.

"I am older than you, Martha," May insisted. "It is not right that you're making me carry this all by my lonesome."

"You are two minutes older," Martha replied, "and that punch bowl hardly weighs a thing. Besides, Mother left it to you, so it's *your* responsibility to carry it."

May grumbled at that, but then Martha saw me, raising the ladle in greeting. "Oh, Harper! You look so pretty! May, doesn't Harper look pretty?"

"I can't see her over this stupid bowl," May muttered, staggering toward the table the waiters had set up.

Despite everything pressing down on me, I laughed. "Where's Aunt Jewel?"

"She's wheeling the cooler of punch in," Aunt May said, finally getting the bowl situated in the center of the table.

Right. The punch. I thought again of David's vision, the wave of bright red washing over everything. "Where's David?" I asked Saylor, and she nodded upstairs.

Maybe he had some valuable, punch-y insights.

Bee was still standing in the doorway, her arms folded. "Why do you need to see David?"

I opened my mouth, but nothing came out. Thankfully, Saylor covered for me. "With Mr. Bradshaw and Harper's sudden and unfortunate situation, Harper will need an escort. I always bring David as a spare just in case these things happen."

It was probably the last thing Bee wanted to hear, but at least it made sense. I turned away before I could see her scowl, and headed up the stairs to David.

Chapter 38

WHEN I walked into the bedroom, David was standing in front of the window. His tux jacket lay crumpled on the bed, and his bow tie hung around his neck. From the look of his hair, he'd been pulling at it, and one hand was in his pocket, jangling some loose change.

"Nervous?" I asked, and he spun around.

"Are you—" he said, and then he saw me. "Oh. Wow."

I'd had that reaction from a lot of people. Mom, Ryan, the saleswoman at the bridal shop. But hearing *David* say it, seeing *David's* eyes go wide, made me suddenly self-conscious. I had to stop myself from twisting the silk skirt in my hands, and Ryan's words rang in my head.

Harper, you and David Stark have been circling each other since kindergarten.

And maybe we had. But it's not like any of it mattered anymore.

So I put my shoulders back and walked over to David. "You've seen the dress before."

"It looks different tonight—" David said, but I just kept talking.

"Any sign of . . . well, anything?"

Shoving his hands back in his pockets, David turned to look out the window. "No. But . . . I can feel it. She's here. Or close by."

I could feel it, too. An awareness shivered along my skin, like I was being watched. For all I knew, Blythe was already in the house, waiting around a corner.

"Do you want to see if you can have a vision?" I asked, offering him my hand. He took it, but this time, there was no spark, no frisson of electricity. His hand was warm and soft in mine and he absentmindedly ran a thumb over my knuckles. Now there *was* a spark, but I didn't think it had anything to do with our powers. Still, I'd had a boyfriend up until about ten minutes ago, and things were way too screwed up to start pulling romance into it now.

And added to the fact that I might have to kill David one day . . .

I pulled my hand back from his, moving a little bit away. "Well, speaking of visions, the one you had with me and Saylor. Do you remember all the red in it?"

He screwed up his face, thinking. "Yeah. A bunch of red stuff, really bright. At first I thought it was blood, but it's the wrong color."

Leaning against the giant four-poster bed, I clasped my hands behind my back. "Can I say something insane?"

Snorting, David turned his gaze back out the window. "Tonight would be the night for it."

"I think . . . I think it's my aunt's punch. In the vision."

David frowned. "That sugary stuff that makes your brain hurt? I . . . yeah, I guess it was that color red."

"Do you think it means anything?" I asked, looking out the window with him. More cars were pulling up now, and I could hear the soft murmur of voices as people began milling around downstairs. Soon all the girls would come up here to huddle together in one of the other bedrooms, waiting for Cotillion to start. Would Blythe wait, too?

"I doubt it," David said, and at first, I thought I'd spoken my question out loud. But, no, he was talking about the punch. "If shit goes down, it seems likely the punch will spill, right?"

I didn't want to think about shit going down, people running and screaming, my aunt's punch sloshing to the floor.

"Ryan isn't coming," I told David. His head jerked up, but I didn't elaborate. "So you'll have to escort me. Which is probably for the best since it'll keep me close to you for . . . whatever."

"Right," he said, and then his lips lifted in something close to a smile. "Whoever would've thought we'd end up going to Cotillion together?"

I smiled back. "That? *That's* what's bothering you about this night?"

His laugh was low and husky, but nice, and I suddenly wished I'd spent more time getting to know David instead of always competing with him. Somehow, in these past six weeks, we'd become friends. It might've been nice to have him as a friend all along.

I heard the discordant sounds of the band starting up

somewhere downstairs, and I glanced at the delicate silver and diamond watch around my wrist. "Damn," I muttered. "I guess it's time to get started."

David started pacing again, hands still in his pockets, practically vibrating with nervous energy. I remembered when that used to annoy me. Now, all I wanted to do was wrap my arms around him and tell him everything was going to be okay. I wanted to rest my cheek against his collarbone, and have him tell *me* we were going to get through this. But the music was getting louder now, turning into a recognizable song.

"I'm going to go see where the other girls are and check things out one last time," I told him. "Escorts need to start lining up on the stairs in"— I checked my watch again—"about ten minutes."

David stopped pacing, dropping his head into his hands with a sound somewhere between a laugh and a groan. "God, what is the point of being able to see the future if you can't actually *see the future?* I keep . . . it's like digging through sand. I can't see anything,"

"Hey," I said, pulling one of his arms down. "It's okay. You know what Saylor said. The closer you get to eighteen, the clearer the visions are going to get."

He looked at me, eyes wild. "Harper, I saw you die. I saw you in that dress, bleeding to death on those stairs." He pointed viciously out the door. "So don't tell me it's going to be okay."

I swallowed hard. "Saylor said not every single one of your visions comes true. This one won't. I won't let it."

I must've sounded braver than I felt because David gave me a tiny smile. "You would be too stubborn to die."

"I am, trust me."

We stood there, staring at each other. I didn't even realize we were holding hands until I turned to go and had to disentangle myself.

I was already to the door when he called, "Harper."

"Wha—" was as far as I got, because in a few long strides, David crossed the room and pulled me into his arms. I was so stunned that it hardly even registered that he was kissing me until . . . oh. *Oh.*

This kiss didn't make my stomach flutter; it made my skin sing. It made me raise myself up on tiptoes so I could kiss him back harder. It made me want to kiss him anytime, anyplace, even if we were in the middle of Main Street.

I tangled my fingers in his hair, and his hands gripped the silk around my waist before sliding around my back, holding me so tightly that it should have hurt. But it didn't, not even the littlest bit.

When we broke apart, we stared at each other, dazed and breathing hard. "I just . . ." He took three more quick breaths. "I needed to know."

"Oh God," was all I could manage to say. This was what was between me and David Stark? This was what seventeen years of snarking and fighting and competing had been covering up?

His eyes dropped to my lips. "I think we should do it again, though. To be sure."

He barely got the last word out before I was pulling his mouth back down to mine. Any idea I'd had that maybe it had been the shock, or the fact that it was my first kiss with someone who wasn't Ryan since ninth grade, flew right out the window.

This time, I nearly shoved him away when the kiss ended. "This," I panted, pressing a hand to my abdomen, "is really inconvenient right now. We— No!"

David had been moving closer to me, but froze as I held up my other hand. "Okay, so now we know. And we will deal with that later. Provided we don't die."

He shook his head, like he was trying to clear it. "Now that I know, I really, really don't want to die."

The smile that broke out over my face had to be the goofiest, giddiest thing ever, and I quickly tried to suppress it. Tonight was about being a stoic superhero type, not a flustered teenage girl. I cleared my throat. "Me neither. So let's make sure that doesn't happen, okay?"

He took another step closer, but I was already moving toward the door. "Wait here until it's time to go to the stairs. Keep an eye out for Blythe, and . . . stay."

And then I made myself walk out of the room. Shutting the door firmly behind me, I leaned back against it and blew out a long breath. This was absolutely the last thing I needed. I had been single for all of fifteen minutes, I had an insane tiny witch person trying to kill me, and she was going to attempt a spell that might take David away from me for good. Now was not the time to feel all swoony and weak of knee.

Still, I couldn't stop smiling as I walked onto the landing, peering down at the room below. It was nearly full now, and I noticed nearly everyone had a cup of Aunt Jewel's punch. It was the weirdest thing to me how everyone openly acknowledged that it was terrible, but kept drinking it anyway. Manners in action, I guess.

Scanning the crowd, I looked for anyone who seemed out of place, but these were almost all faces I recognized. There was no sign of Blythe, no sign of anything out of the ordinary.

"Harper?"

Miss Annemarie stood at the top of the stairs, an empty punch cup in her hands, a faint pinkish mustache on her upper lip.

"Miss Annemarie," I said, straightening up. "What are you doing up here?"

She placed her cup on the little marble-topped table on the landing. Downstairs, I could hear the string quartet playing something stately and elegant. "Looking for the little girls' room. The one downstairs has a line you wouldn't believe."

There was a small powder room off the main landing, and I walked toward it. "It's right here," I told her, opening the door.

"Oh, goody," Miss Annemarie said. And then with a shove way harder than any octogenarian should be able to give, she pushed me inside.

Chapter 39

I STUMBLED over the hem of my dress, and tripped, smacking my head painfully against the low sink. Stars exploded in my vision, and I heard the door slam behind me. Other than a thin crack of light around the doorframe, it was totally black, and only Miss Annemarie's heavy breathing told me she was right behind me. I heard the whisper of something swinging at me and flopped onto my back, kicking out blindly.

There was a clink of metal and a soft grunt of pain, and then the bathroom light blazed on. Miss Annemarie stood over me, searching the floor for the knife she'd dropped. "Dear me," she said softly in the same tone of voice she used when she spilled tea.

"Miss Annemarie!" I gasped. "You? *You're* the assassin?"

She glanced over at me, her eyes cloudy. "Have to kill Harper Price," she said, almost conversationally. And then, spotting the knife wedged behind the toilet, "Ah!"

Her girth made it hard for her to bend down, and I crouched there against the far wall, watching her struggle. All my Paladin instincts were urging me to rush forward, pin her to the floor, and snap her neck. But . . . this was Miss Annemarie. She wasn't a Paladin, she was just an old lady. An old lady who wanted to kill me, but still.

I got up slowly, sliding up along the wall, but as soon as I was on my feet, she reared back up, one meaty fist swinging for my head. I dodged it easily, grasping her hand in mine. "Miss Annemarie!" I said again, and it was like she couldn't even hear me. The look on her face was dazed, dreamy. She looked like . . . she looked like Mom had this evening.

Mind control. A shudder ran through me. So that's how Blythe was going to get rid of me. By sending the last person I'd expect to—

And then I looked closer at the pink stain over her upper lip. Punch. She'd been drinking Aunt Jewel's punch.

As had nearly everyone downstairs.

Oh my God.

Blythe had gotten her job at the university by making a mass mind-control potion, slipped into their potluck lunch. She'd done the same thing here, only with my Aunt Jewel's punch, and suddenly that part of David's vision made perfect sense.

It also meant I was perfectly effed.

Armies of cater waiter assassins I'd been prepared for. Some hired thugs, sure. But people I knew and loved, all turned against me? I couldn't kill those people. I couldn't even *hurt* those people.

Miss Annemarie jerked her head toward mine, trying to headbutt me, but I'd perfected that move. I ducked, and then reaching out with my right hand, tried the thing Saylor had taught me. I pressed right above Miss Annemarie's carotid artery, and she dropped like a stone.

I did my best to haul her inert body out of the way, and flung the door open. There was no murmur of voices downstairs now, no violins. Everything seemed deathly quiet, and when I eased out of the bathroom and peeked over the landing, I saw everyone just . . . standing there. Arms at their sides, abandoned punch cups on the floor. What I didn't see were any white dresses.

I checked my watch. Of course! While I was fighting Miss Annemarie in the bathroom, the other girls had probably gone upstairs. And they wouldn't have had any of the punch since red juice plus white dress equals disaster.

Moving as silently as I could, I crept down the hall to the bedroom where we'd been told to assemble. The door was closed, but when I opened it, I was greeted by a sea of white dresses. "Harper!" Amanda and Abigail cried, and I waved my hand.

"Shhh!" The girls all stared at me, but everyone went quiet. "Look, there's been a little delay," I said, trying to keep my voice low. "First of all, has anyone in here had the punch?"

"Do we look stupid?" Mary Beth asked, narrowing her eyes. Her cheeks were nearly as red as her hair. "You and Miss Saylor both practically threatened to kill us if we touched the stuff."

Breathing a sigh of relief, I pointed at them. "Wait here."

Dashing down the hall, I ran to the bedroom where I'd left David. He was putting on his jacket when I opened the door. "Am I late?" he asked when he saw me standing there.

Without answering, I grabbed his hand, tugging him out of the room.

When I got back to the girls' room, I practically threw him

inside. "All of you stay in here until I come back," I instructed. "Don't let anyone in, and don't let anyone out."

"Harper," Bee said, moving forward, but I stopped her with a hand.

"Not now, Bee."

"But—"

"Seriously!" I snapped. "I'll be . . . I'll be right back."

Something flickered across her face, but I shut the door before I could put a name to it. I had way more important problems now. Namely that I didn't know what to do next. I had to keep Blythe from David, but that meant I had to find Blythe. She was obviously here, but where? Should I just stand guard over this door, or should I make my way downstairs, fight it out?

And then the choice was made for me. There was the pounding of feet on the stairs, and suddenly, people were swarming the landing, all headed for me. The knife Saylor had given me rested cold against my thigh, but the first person to leap at me was my Aunt May, and I couldn't even think about using it.

Aunt May, my sweet Aunt May, who taught me how to knit, who bought me a piece of candy every time we went to the store, jabbed a cocktail fork at my eye. I ducked, my back still against the door, and then Mrs. Green, the children's librarian, reached down and tried to tug at my ankle. I shook her off, but even as I did, someone else was grabbing my hair, and another hand closed on my wrist, and I was fighting and kicking, but there were so many of them, and they had me backed up against the door.

"Harper!" I heard someone cry from inside the room. I

thought it was Bee, but I couldn't be sure. More hands were on me now, and someone had a pie server nearly at my throat.

I shoved it away, trying to close my fingers around that spot that had worked on Miss Annemarie. I had to get to Saylor. I had to find Blythe. I had to get out of this before I was killed with some elaborate cutlery.

"Bee!" I shouted through the door, Dr. Greenbaum's nose crunching under my elbow. "Is the door locked?"

"Yes!" came her muffled reply. "But, Harper—"

I would have to hope it held. One thing I knew for sure was that Blythe wasn't upstairs. I'd been in all the rooms, and she wasn't in the crush of people surrounding me. Taking a deep breath and muttering, "I'm really sorry about this," I pushed both arms out as hard as I could, fists clenched.

The three people nearest to me fell back, stumbling into the people behind them. I heard someone cry out as they tumbled down the stairs, and I prayed with everything in me that it wasn't one of my aunts. I let every Paladin instinct I had take over as I pushed the crowd back, back, farther down the stairs. There were lots of them, but not a one had my powers. I tried not to look at faces as I whirled and kicked, as I flipped people over my shoulder, as I spun and knocked people off their feet.

Finally, a clear path opened up and I sprinted down the stairs. I heard footsteps behind me, but I didn't turn around. "Saylor!" I screamed. "SAYLOR!"

I ran through Magnolia House. Somewhere in the fight, my dress had gotten ripped, and I nearly tripped over the hem again as I pushed my way into the kitchen.

Saylor was there, up against the counter. Brandon lay at her feet, and there was a rolling pin in one of her hands. The other lay across her abdomen.

"That young man attacked me," she said, her face the color of oatmeal.

"It's the punch," I told her, locking the door behind me. "She put a mind-control potion in the punch, and . . . Saylor, I can't kill people I know. People who don't even know what they're doing."

She grimaced, disappointed in me, I thought. But then she drew her hand back and I saw that it was slicked with blood. For the first time, I saw the knife at Brandon's side. "He got in a good blow before I hit him," she said, her tone surprisingly light for someone discussing being stabbed.

"Saylor—" I said, stepping forward, but she shook me off.

"It's nothing. I have a potion that can heal this right up. David. Is he all right?"

"For now," I said as the kitchen door rattled and shook. "I locked him in with the girls. They didn't drink the punch."

Saylor's mouth wobbled. "One valuable piece of advice, it turns out."

"Can you reverse this?" I asked.

The thumps on the kitchen door were getting louder, but Saylor shook her head. "As long as Blythe is here, they're under her control."

Sighing, I ran a shaking hand over my face. "But where is Blythe? I didn't see her anywhere in the crowd and—"

Pain ricocheted through me, so strong that I felt like I had been stabbed. I bent over, panting, my vision shaking.

No, not my vision. The house. The entire house rumbled and quaked, little bits of plaster falling from the ceiling. "David!" I gasped.

Saylor moved forward, clutching my dress. Her hand left streaks of blood down the skirt. "You said he's with the girls? All of them?"

I nodded, closing my eyes. I could see the sea of dresses in front of me, see David's bewildered face as I'd slammed the door.

"Yes," I said. "All seven of them."

"Harper." Saylor's eyes were huge with pain and fear, her skin paper white. "There were only six other girls."

Chapter 40

THIS TIME, I didn't look or think. I let my fists and feet fly almost independently as I fought my way back up the stairs. These weren't people I knew, these were things standing between me and my duty. The only time I hesitated was when Aunt Jewel came at me with the punch ladle. It killed me to do it, but one quick elbow thrust to her temple sent her sliding harmlessly to the floor. Stepping over her prone form, I swore to myself that I'd go visit Aunt Jewel every single day when this was all over, and make her as many cakes as she could ever want.

The house shook as I moved toward the bedroom. I heard a distant crash, and realized it was the chandelier in the main hall falling to the ground. Light was pouring out from underneath the bedroom door, golden and searing, and all I could hear was the pounding of my heart and the constant repetition of *Too late, too late*.

Throwing my shoulder against the door, I forced it open, and immediately threw my hands up to shade my eyes.

David stood stock-still in the middle of the room, bathed in light, glowing with it. It poured from his fingers, filled his eyes, spilled out of his open mouth. The other girls were all huddled together against the far wall, heads down, while Blythe, clad in a white dress, a blond wig crooked on top of her head, stood on the bed. Her eyes were closed, nose still a little swollen from our fight, and she held both hands open at her sides. Words in a language I'd never heard fell from her lips and seemed to fill the room. Both windows shattered, and I heard high, thin screams.

I launched myself at Blythe, knocking her back on the bed. She gave a grunt as the air rushed out of her lungs, and started to shake. At first, I thought she was crying, but as I rose up on my knees, straddling her waist, I realized she was laughing.

"It's too late!" she yelled as the house continued to shake and sway. "Look at him! He's beautiful!"

David was still standing there, still covered bright light. He didn't look beautiful. He looked beautiful in his stupid sweaters and dumb glasses and unfortunate pants. Now he looked terrifying and unnatural and . . . not human.

As I watched, he lifted one glowing hand toward the girls against the wall. I saw Bee lift her face, saw her wide, horrified eyes.

"No!" I heard myself shout, and then a bolt of light flew from David's fingers, crashing over all of the girls.

The light was blinding, and my blood was churning, and Blythe was still laughing, laughing, laughing in my ear.

Someone grabbed me from behind, yanking me off Blythe. Even as I struggled, all I could think was, *I failed*. All that training, all that trying, and I'd locked David in with Blythe. I'd let her turn him into a weapon. And my friends. Abigail, Amanda, even Mary Beth. And Bee. Oh God, Bee. My attacker had me turned away from the wall, and I was glad for it in a way. I didn't want to see what that bolt of power had done to them.

I reached back, trying to dig my fingers into eyes, but clawed empty air. And then suddenly, there was a thump and I was landing on the ground, hard.

Whirling around, I saw that it had been Headmaster Dunn holding me, and standing over him, hands on her hips, was Bee.

I said her name, confused and relieved. She was okay? But I'd seen David blast her with that lightning thing, seen waves of power crash over her and all of the girls.

Mrs. Catesby, my old Sunday school teacher, ran into the room, wielding the ladle Aunt Jewel had dropped. I braced myself, but then Blythe grinned and said, "Show her what you've got, girls."

Twisting my head to look at Blythe, confused, I almost missed seeing Mary Beth's hand shoot out and grab the ladle. With a neat flip, she used the hook at the end of the handle to catch Mrs. Catesby's ankles and the ladle's bowl at the other end to knock her out. Grinning at her handiwork, Mary Beth brandished the long silver spoon at me. *"Hard Fists!"* she cried, and I could only shake my head.

Two more people, women I recognized from Junior League, raced in. Abigail and Amanda, working together, clotheslined them before spinning and using the inertia of the women's bodies to push them back out of the room.

"Oh my God, we are *ninjas!*" Amanda squealed. "How did that happen?"

They weren't ninjas. They were Paladins. All of them. David had made them Paladins.

David!

As my fellow debutantes kicked the ass of every person who walked through the door, I looked back to the middle of the room. David was on his knees now, no longer surrounded by light. But when he lifted his face to me, his eyes were still bright gold, like coins, behind his glasses.

"David?" I asked, kneeling down with him.

He blinked, and the light faded for a moment before growing bright again. "Pres?" he murmured, and I flung my arms around his neck.

"Oh, you're still you," I breathed. "You're still in there."

"I-I think so," he said. "But—what did I do to them?"

We looked over to where Amanda and Abigail were wrestling with their escorts, and Mary Beth was using her ladle to great effect on the owner of the Dixie Bean.

"You made them Paladins," Blythe said from the bed.

I had almost forgotten about her. She sat in the middle, legs crossed, hands clasped under her chin, grinning like a little kid. "I told you the ritual would work," she said. "You made Paladins, just like Alaric! And this is merely a handful of girls. If you had focused harder and if I hadn't been interrupted"—she glared at me—"you could've made this entire town an army. The whole state, if we tried hard enough."

Breathing hard, David stared at her. His eyes were still filled with light, the effect disturbing. "Why would I want that?"

Giggling, Blythe shook her head. "Oh, if you knew what was coming, you wouldn't ask a question like that."

I stood up, reaching under my dress for the knife strapped to my thigh. I was officially over Blythe. Whipping out the blade, I made my way to the bed, but I only got about three steps when a vise-like grip closed around my wrist.

I glanced back, stunned. "Bee?"

She blinked at me. "I . . . I can't let you hurt her. I don't know why, but I can't."

Mary Beth was at my other side, her fingers tight on my arm. "Me, either. If you try to kill her . . ." She didn't finish, but her hands squeezed tighter. Even Amanda and Abigail were standing by the door, eyes wary.

Delighted, Blythe clapped her hands. "Even better! See, Paladins can't harm their creator. And since I had a hand in turning David into a personal Paladin factory, that makes me a creator!"

"Bee," I pleaded. "Override it or something. I can't let her go."

Everything in Bee's face was anguished. "I really want to, Harper, but I *can't*. Now please put the knife away or I'm going to have to hurt you, and I really don't want to." Tears pooled in her eyes, spilling down her cheeks. "Except I *do* want to. What the heck is going on?"

"It's going to be okay," I told her. "This is what I am. This is what I haven't been telling you, but now you know! And now you're one, too, and we can train together. But let me take care of—"

I didn't finish the words before Bee wrenched my arm,

throwing me off balance. With a well-placed kick to my chest, she sent me tumbling back against the bed. "Oh God!" she cried. "Harper, I'm sorry, I didn't mean—"

"It's all right," I told her, even as I wheezed for breath. "We can fix this."

Blythe got off the bed, her dress bunched up in her hands. "Oh, this is nothing that needs fixing. This is perfect." Her sweet little face practically glowed with excitement. "All these Paladins, and my very own Oracle. Now." Holding out one tiny gloved hand, she crooked a finger at David. "Come along."

His eyes still blazing, David struggled to his feet. "No." The words sounded like they were being forced through broken glass, but he got it out. And then, again, stronger. "*No.*"

Blythe fisted her hands on her hips. "Now isn't the time for stubbornness. I said—"

A thin bolt of golden light shot out from David's finger, striking Blythe in the middle of her forehead. Shrieking, she stumbled back, landing on the little settee at the end of the bed.

"I am not yours to control, Mage," David said in a voice that didn't sound anything like his own.

Blythe slowly rose, staring at David with a mixture of shock and wonder. "Oh," she breathed. "This is . . . unexpected."

David's hand shot out again, and Blythe winced as another bolt of light took her in the chest. "Very unexpected," she said through gritted teeth.

Moving away from the settee, Blythe stepped behind Bee. "Well, if I can't have an Oracle, at least I'll have a Paladin."

Before I could think, she had an arm around Bee's waist. Blythe was so tiny, she barely came up to Bee's shoulder blades. Sticking her head out from behind Bee, Blythe winked at me.

"I think I like this one best," she said and then, almost instantly, they both vanished.

Chapter 41

"Bee!" I cried, staring at the spot where she and Blythe had been. Behind me, David put a hand on my shoulder.

"Pres," he said softly, but I shook him off, leaping to my feet.

"No! They can't be—*she* can't be—"

But they were. She was. My best friend was gone, and I had no idea where Blythe might have taken her. Greece? To the other Ephors?

David reached up, brushing the tears off my cheeks, and I let myself lean into him for a moment. His eyes were still too bright to look directly into, so I focused on his hair, the places where it stood up in peaks and tufts. "If I'd known she'd take Bee, I would've gone with her," he said, sounding like himself again.

I held on to his jacket tighter, the material wrinkling under my fingers. But as I held on to him, I could only be happy that at least David was still here. At least I still had him.

"Whoa," Amanda said, glancing out the door. "What happened?"

David and I walked out onto the landing, the other girls trailing us. Downstairs, the main room was covered in bodies.

"Are they dead?" Mary Beth asked, but I shook my head.

"They were being mind-controlled. Now that Blythe is gone, it's over. Everyone will wake up in a few hours with fuzzy brains and . . . probably a lot of bruises."

We made our way downstairs, stepping over people as we went. It wasn't until we were halfway downstairs that David asked, "Where's my Aunt Saylor?"

"She's in the kitchen," I said, speeding up. "She was hurt, but she said she had a potion to heal it, so hopefully she's okay now."

I moved for the kitchen, but David caught my arm "Harper, there's no such thing as a healing potion."

"What?" I looked up from my skirt. There was a huge splash of red across the front that, thanks to the fruity smell rising up from it, I was pretty sure was punch. My hair was falling in my eyes, and when I went to push it back, I saw another splash of red on the back of my hand. *That* was definitely blood.

The light was beginning to dim from his eyes, but they were still more gold than blue. "She told me that healing is the one thing Mages can't control. Minds, sure, protection, yeah, but healing the human body is way beyond them."

My heart thudded painfully as his hand grabbed my arm tighter. "How bad was she?"

I didn't answer. Instead, I opened the kitchen door.

Saylor was slumped against the cabinets, her eyes closed, her face surprisingly peaceful. Brandon still lay on the floor in front of her, the knife he'd killed her with a few inches from his foot.

And kneeling next to her, shaking and holding one of her hands, was Ryan.

When he saw us standing there, he looked back and forth, his eyes wild. "I . . . I decided to come back because I wanted to see you do Cotillion," he told me. "But when I got here, the place was shaking, and I thought there was an earthquake. I c-came through the back door, and I found her. Brandon—"

Ryan's throat worked convulsively, and I went to him as David knelt down on the other side of Saylor. "I never told her," David said, his voice flat. "I never said thank you for everything she did."

"She knew," I told him, gently prying Ryan's hand from Saylor's. "And she loved you."

"I . . ." He shook his head, and tears splashed onto his black pants. "I should have told her. And she shouldn't have died like this. Alone."

At that, Ryan looked up. "She didn't. I was with her."

His mouth worked again and his hand, still in mine, was ice cold. "That's the thing. I was sitting here with her, and she—she said she hated to do this, and she knew how complicated this would make things for everyone, and then she . . . she . . ."

"She kissed you," I said, not sure if I should laugh or cry.

"Kind of," Ryan agreed. "More like she blew something in me, and I got really cold, and suddenly, I felt like I could . . . I don't know, do stuff. Weird stuff. And I really wanted to find the two of you." He nodded at me and David.

David raised his tear-streaked face to mine. "I feel like now would be a good time to use the F-word."

We spent the next few hours trying to repair some of the damage to Magnolia House. People left in uncomfortable positions were gently moved to the floor. I found my aunts and was relieved to see that with the exception of a scrape on Aunt May's forehead, they were pretty much unharmed.

Finally, I found Bee's parents, slumped at the bottom of the staircase. I went back to Saylor's body, getting the little tub of lip balm out and handing it to Ryan. "You have to put this on your fingers, and then—"

"And then I touch them," he said in a dull voice. "Tell them that Bee is away at cheerleading camp. Be fuzzy on the details."

"How did you know that?"

Ryan seemed to have aged ten years in the last half hour, but there was still a little bit of the sparkle I knew in his eyes as he shrugged and said, "I just know."

"You'll have to do the same to Brandon," I told him, and he just nodded.

That taken care of, we moved to the last task.

All of the girls were gathered back in the bedroom. Their white dresses were streaked with sweat and punch and blood, but they were all yammering excitedly, a couple of them practicing flips and spin-kicks.

"You're sure you can do this?" I asked David, and he nodded, flexing his fingers. A shower of golden light raced along the backs of them.

"Yeah. I hate to, though. I mean, for one thing, it would take some of the Paladin pressure off you. For another, they just . . . they look really happy."

They did look happy. Happier than they'd looked in all of the months prepping for Cotillion. But I couldn't risk Blythe having five girls—six, I thought, my heart aching for Bee—who were willing to fight and die for her.

One by one, David drew the power back from them, until his eyes were bright gold again and he was shaking. That done, Ryan moved down the line with the lip balm, erasing their memories of this night. When he got to Mary Beth, I saw the way his finger didn't so much smudge the balm on as caress her palm, and something in me eased. Maybe Mary Beth would be good for him. And—I glanced at David—hopefully, uncomplicated.

Eventually, they all lay slumped on the bedroom floor, and the three of us stood over them, watching.

"So are we done?" Ryan asked, and it was so close to the words he'd used breaking up with me that I wanted to laugh.

"We haven't even really started," David told him. "The three of us, we're . . . connected. We will be forever, and—"

Ryan held up his hands. "Whoa, what do you mean forever?"

I was exhausted and heartsick and wrung out, and I wanted Saylor here so badly I ached. But she was gone. There was no one left to explain things, to offer guidance. We only had each other.

David reached out and squeezed my hand, and I saw Ryan's gaze drop to it. "That was . . . fast," he said, and David dropped my hand like it was on fire.

"It's not like that," he said, but I shook my head.

Taking David's hand in mine, I held it tightly and faced Ryan. "Actually, it kind of is. And if the three of us are going to work together, Ryan needs to know that."

Ryan looked between the two of us before heaving a sigh that seemed to come from his toes. "I can't," he finally said. "I can't deal with any of this. Superpowers, and Brandon murdering old ladies, and the two of you, I . . ."

He pushed past us. I went to grab his arm, but David stopped me. "Let him go," he said. "Give him time."

I didn't want to. Blythe and the Ephors had Bee, and we had to get her back somehow. We'd need all three of us, working together. But Saylor had let me go once. I had to do the same for Ryan.

The earthquake that hit Pine Grove the night of Cotillion was destined to be a legend. It almost destroyed Magnolia House, and nearly everyone there had some kind of injury, from scrapes, to bruises, to a couple of broken bones. Luckily, no one died. But the house would probably have to be torn down, and no one who was there that night had an especially clear memory of what happened. They all agreed the trauma had probably rattled them all.

Bee's parents were glad Bee had decided to go to cheerleading camp instead of participating in Cotillion this year. No, they weren't sure when she'd be back. Soon. They knew it was soon.

The Aunts mourned the loss of their mother's punch bowl, damaged by falling plaster that night, and Aunt Martha blamed Aunt May for not putting it in a more secure location. Aunt Jewel only knew she never wanted to make punch for Cotillion again, but she didn't know why.

And that Monday, I went to school like nothing had happened. I wasn't surprised to find David in the newspaper room. No one else was in there, and I stood in the door for a while, watching his back as he sat at the computer, typing. "I know you're there, Pres," he said at last.

Smiling, I leaned against the doorjamb. "Could you sense me with your awesome new superpowers?"

He snorted, but didn't turn around. "No, I could actually feel you staring at me."

Wheeling around in his chair, he gave me a truly sad excuse of a grin. "No one's stare is quite as piercing as yours."

When I folded my arms and gave him a look, he sighed. "I knew you'd come. And not because I saw it. I mean, I *did* see it, but . . . " He trailed off, tugging at his hair.

I walked across the room and covered his hands with mine, gently pulling his loose from the top of his head. As I did, he watched me very carefully, and I felt that same fire, the one from the Cotillion, curl in my belly. We held each other's gaze, our hands still tangled up as I stood in front of him.

"You know what's awkward?" David asked, the corner of his mouth lifting.

"Our entire existences?"

Now the grin was real. "That," he acknowledged. "And when you make a big, dramatic gesture because you think you're going to die, and then you—"

"Don't die," I finished for him, and he nodded.

"Exactly. Not that I'm not one hundred percent psyched that we didn't die, but . . ."

"I get it," I told him. "So . . . that's why you kissed me, then? Because you thought we might die?"

"More or less," he said, dropping my hands and turning back to the computer. "It was a heat of the moment thing. I mean . . . you and me, as a couple? Could that even work?"

He typed for a few more seconds, and when I didn't answer, he turned around. There was still the teeniest speck of gold in his eyes, but you had to look for it to know it was there. "Do you . . . Pres, do you want it to work?"

Saylor had said that Blythe's spell could make David dangerous. It could mean I'd have to kill him for his own sake. But he'd controlled it the night of Cotillion. He'd used incredible amounts of power, and he was still here, still David.

The gold dot in his eye seemed to flame brighter for a second, and I felt a little shiver.

Still, I straightened my shoulders and looked into his eyes. "I'd like to try."

David sat in his chair, staring at me for the space of two heartbeats. And then he was on his feet, and his mouth was on mine. It wasn't as intense as the kiss at Cotillion, but it had the exact same effect on me. In fact, kissing David in the newspaper room at seven thirty in the morning, I could almost forget I hated PDA.

He pulled back, giving a breathless laugh. "We're so stupid for doing this."

"It will probably end in murder," I agreed, but we were both grinning. Then David's smile faded. "Have you talked to Ryan?"

I sighed, moving back against a desk. Brushing a few wadded-up pieces of paper off its surface, I perched on top. "No. He's not returning my texts or calls."

"It's a lot to deal with, Pres. Suddenly having superpowers forced on you is rough."

"Is it?" I asked, raising my eyebrows. "I had no idea. Please tell me more, and let me subscribe to your newsletter."

At that, David gave a real laugh, sinking back into his chair. "Okay, now this is the Harper Price I'm more familiar with."

I smiled back at him before looking around the classroom. "So . . . what now?"

David turned around again, propping his head on the back of his chair. "Are you asking me what I've seen?"

"I was actually wondering if you'd had any ideas," I said, shaking my head. "I know this sounds totally stupid, but . . . it's like I keep forgetting you can fully see the future now. That is totally stupid, isn't it?"

Still studying the ceiling, David said, "No. Because I keep forgetting, too. I'll have a dream, and wake up thinking, 'Huh, weird dream.' You know, like I have every day of my life. And then suddenly I have to remember that, no, it might not have been a weird dream. It might have been a-a vision."

"But not everything you see will come true," I said. *We were fighting, but we weren't angry. We were sad. You killed me.* The words spun in my mind.

"That's the whole thing." David dropped his head, looking at me. "The worst part. If not everything you see will come true, how do you know what to do? What's the point of even having your head full of all this . . . this stuff?" He ran a hand over his eyes, and I saw that it was shaking.

Now it was Saylor's words looping through my mind. *That much power, it will burn him up and eat him alive until he's not David anymore.*

I'd spent the past seventeen years thinking David was annoying and mean, but he wasn't. He was smart, and dedicated, and loyal, and completely him. The thought of his powers turning him into someone else, of killing him, hurt too much to even think about.

But I wouldn't let that happen. I knew what Saylor had said, but, hey, I was a Paladin. My job was to protect the Oracle and I'd do that, even if it meant protecting him from himself.

"Anyway," David said, closing the laptop and wheeling his chair over to me, "as for what comes next, Saylor had some kind of in case of emergency spell set up. As far as I can tell, everyone in town thinks she's gone on some kind of extended vacation, and I'm totally fine here by myself."

He didn't sound totally fine, and I took his hand again. "I miss her, too."

David just nodded, pressing his lips together, and I squeezed his fingers. "I don't like the idea of you in that house by yourself."

"It'll be okay," he said. He was wearing a ketchup-red sweater and houndstooth pants. When I glanced down, I saw that, sure enough, he had on one brown sock and one black. He could not have looked any less like someone who would be okay on his own.

I stepped closer, our joined hands between us. "Are you saying that in your usual patronizing sense, or in the 'I can see the future and know how this all turns out' way?"

He grinned at me. "It was definitely more the former than the latter. The whole vision thing . . ." The grin faded. "It's like Saylor said. It needs three of us for me to see clearly. And without Ryan, we're kinda screwed."

"Funny, because Ryan himself is feeling kind of screwed by all of this."

David and I both turned. Ryan stood there in the doorway, chin lifted. He looked like he hadn't slept in days, and I think his hair may actually have been worse than David's, but he still could have been posing for a cologne ad.

"You're here," I said, wondering if the relief I felt was because we had our third part, or just because it was Ryan. Ryan, who may not have been the guy I got all fluttery for, but who had been a rock for me for such a long time.

He gave an easy shrug. "I'm here." Stepping into the classroom, he gave us both a wary glance before closing the door. "So."

"So," David and I echoed in unison.

"The three of us, working together to save the world. Me, my ex-girlfriend, and the guy she dumped me for." His mouth twisted into a half smile. "This has to be the most screwed-up situation three teenagers have ever found themselves in."

"I think I saw an episode of *Gossip Girl* like that once," I offered, and while both boys chuckled, their hearts clearly weren't in it.

"We can do this," I told them, using my SGA president voice. "Is it awkward? Sure. Will it require sacrifice and hard work and probably get even *more awkward*?"

"No doubt," David said, just as Ryan muttered, "Yup."

"But . . . I believe in you guys. And I hope you believe in me. So." I took a deep breath and held out my hands. "Why don't we see what's coming for us next?"

The school was still quiet. Teachers wouldn't start arriving for another half hour, and the janitor who had replaced Mr. Hall was on the other side of the building.

Ryan took my hand and then, with a little more hesitation, took David's. "What's going to happen?" he asked. "Are we all going to stand in a circle and sing 'Kumbaya'?"

David held my eyes for a long moment before rising to his feet. "Not quite," he replied.

And then he placed his palm in mine.

MISS MAYHEM

SPEAK

An imprint of Penguin Random House LLC

375 Hudson Street

New York, New York 10014

First published in the United States of America by G. P. Putnam's Sons,
an imprint of Penguin Young Readers Group, 2015
Published by Speak, an imprint of Penguin Random House LLC, 2016

This omnibus edition published by Speak, an imprint of Penguin Random House LLC, 2017
Copyright © 2015 by Rachel Hawkins

THE LIBRARY OF CONGRESS HAS CATALOGED THE G. P. PUTNAM'S SONS EDITION AS FOLLOWS:
Hawkins, Rachel, 1979–
Miss Mayhem / Rachel Hawkins.
pages cm
Sequel to: Rebel belle.
Summary: "In the sequel to REBEL BELLE, Harper Price and her new boyfriend and oracle
David Stark face new challenges as the powerful Ephors seek to claim David for their own"—
Provided by publisher.
ISBN 978-0-399-25694-3 (hc)
[1. Magic—Fiction. 2. Supernatural—Fiction. 3. Oracles—Fiction. 4. Debutantes—Fiction. 5.
High schools—Fiction. 6. Schools—Fiction.] I. Title.
PZ7.H313525Mis 2015   [Fic]—dc23   2014031151

ISBN 9780147517920
Omnibus edition ISBN 9780451478689

Printed in the United States of America

3 5 7 9 10 8 6 4

For girls and their BFFs, their besties,
their sisters, their soul mates.
For girls creating mayhem, saving the world,
doing their best, figuring it out.
This one is for y'all.

Chapter 1

"THIS IS going to be a total disaster. You know that, right?"

There are times when having a boyfriend who can tell the future is great. And then there are times like this.

Rolling my eyes, I flipped down the visor to check my makeup in the little mirror.

"Is that your Oracle self talking, or your concerned boyfie self?"

David laughed at that, twisting in the driver's seat to look at me. His sandy blond hair was its usual wreck, his blue eyes bright behind his glasses. "Seriously, you have got to stop calling me that."

The visor smacked back into place with a snap as I smiled at him. "But you *are* an Oracle," I said with mock innocence, and now it was his turn to roll his eyes.

"You know which term I was objecting to."

The windows in David's car were down, letting in the breeze as well as the faint smell of beer and the pounding bass coming from inside the Sigma Kappa Nu fraternity house across the street. It was getting late, and there were a million places I would rather have been, but I had a job to do tonight.

Still, I could mix a little business with pleasure. Leaning over the seat, I tipped my face up so he could kiss me. "It'll only take a sec," I promised once we parted. "And besides, this is what we're supposed to be doing."

David's lips were a thin line, and there was a little wrinkle between his brows. "If you're sure," he said, and I paused, hand on the latch.

"What do you mean?"

David pushed his glasses up the bridge of his nose. "This whole changing-the-future thing. Sometimes I wonder . . . like, what if you can't change the future, Pres? What if you're only delaying it a little while?"

My hand fell away from the door as I thought about that, but before I could answer, a loud *bang* from the front of the car had us both jumping.

Two dark-haired guys in polo shirts and pastel shorts chortled as they walked past, their faces washed out in the glow of the headlights. "Nice car, asshat!" one of them shouted before they did some kind of fist-bumping move that made me want to bump my fist, too.

Right into their faces.

At my side, David heaved a huge sigh. "Well, if we're supposed to be fighting evil, I'm not sure guys like that qualify." He turned to look at me, one corner of his mouth lifting and making a dimple appear in his cheek. "Although I am a little more excited about watching you pound them into a pulp now."

I settled back into my seat, fussing with my hair. "Hopefully there won't be any need for that. I'm going to get in there, get the twins, and get out. And you won't be watching anything, since you need to stay in the car."

David scowled. "Pres—"

"No." I turned back to him, the streetlight overhead outlining him in orange. "There's no way those guys will let you in. Because you're . . ."

Wearing an argyle sweater and lime-green shoes, I thought to myself. "A guy."

He was going to argue again, I could tell. That V between his eyes was getting deeper and his knee was jiggling, so I hurried. "You've already done the Oracle thing, so let me do the Paladin thing, and then we can get the heck out of here as quickly as possible, okay?"

Not even David Stark could argue with that, so he gave a terse nod and leaned back in his seat. "Okay. But please make it fast. This place is already starting to have a bad influence on me. I feel the need to buy polo shirts and shorts. Maybe some Man Sandals."

Grinning, I unbuckled my seat belt. "Anything but Man Sandals! Although, not gonna lie, a polo shirt wouldn't be a bad addition to your wardrobe."

David made a face at me and tugged at the hem of his sweater. "This is a classic," he informed me, and I leaned over to give him one more quick kiss.

"Sure it is."

Across the street, a group of boys came stumbling out the

3

front door of the redbrick Sigma Kappa Nu house, one of them breaking away to puke in the azalea bushes.

Charming.

"Abigail and Amanda, the things I do for you," I muttered as I got out of the car, shutting the door behind me.

Pushing my shoulders back, I did the best I could to saunter across the lawn, projecting confidence while also trying not to draw too much attention to myself. That's why I'd picked this dress. Should things get . . . out of hand, "girl in a black dress" wasn't all that memorable of a description.

The door to the frat house was hanging open as I approached, thanks to the puking guy and his friends, so I was able to slip inside unnoticed.

If the bass had been pounding from outside, it was like a physical presence in the house, rattling my teeth and starting an immediate headache behind my eyes.

And the smell . . .

Beer, boy, old pizza, and carpet that probably hadn't been cleaned since they'd built this place back in the sixties.

Ugh. Frats were the worst.

But I was here on a mission, and I switched my purse from one shoulder to the other as I scanned the crowd, looking for Abigail and Amanda's twin blond heads.

A few months ago, I wouldn't have been caught dead here. I mean, don't get me wrong, there are some fraternities worth hanging out with, but Sigma Kappa Nu was not one of them. These were, on the whole, big dumb party boys, and I was not into that. At all.

But back in October, I'd killed my history teacher with a shoe, and everything had changed.

It turned out I was a Paladin, a kind of superpowered warrior, charged with protecting the Oracle, aka David Stark, aka my new boyfriend. Being an Oracle meant that David could see the future, which obviously made him a pretty valuable commodity to a lot of people. And not good people, either. The Ephors were a group of men who had owned Oracles for years, using their visions to get ahead in the world. To predict the outcome of everything from wars to financial investments. Because David was a male Oracle, the Ephors had wanted to kill him—the only other male Oracle had been nowhere near as powerful as the traditional female ones, plus he'd become super unstable. But David had been rescued by his first Paladin, a guy named Christopher Hall, and by his Mage, Saylor Stark.

I hadn't exactly done a bang-up job of protecting David at first—people had died, including Saylor, and David had undergone a spell that gave him stronger powers than ever. Not only did he have much clearer visions, but also, he'd been able to make Paladins, giving the same powers I had to a group of girls at Cotillion. Oh, and did I mention my ex, Ryan, was our new Mage? So, yeah, complicated, but we were all trying to make the best of things.

That's part of why I was here, walking carefully among plastic cups and Ping-Pong balls, dodging puddles of beer. Before she'd died, Saylor had told me there was a possibility of David becoming a danger to himself, that the world-changing, super-intense visions would "burn him up."

Ryan and I had only helped him have two of those big types of visions. The first one, in the newspaper room at our school, had started a fire in a trash can, and short-circuited every computer in there. The second had resulted in David staying home for nearly a week, his eyes glowing brightly, his head aching. After that, I decided we should start small. Besides, it's like my mom always says: Charity begins at home.

What better way to use David's powers than to check on the futures of friends and family, and see if there was anything I could do to help them should those futures turn out not so great?

So far, we'd kept my Aunt May from accidentally using salt instead of sugar in a batch of brownies for the Junior League bake sale (an act that would have gotten her kicked out of Junior League), and we'd saved David's friend Chie from forgetting to save the final copy of *The Grove News* to her hard drive.

And now Abigail. Her future would take a hard left turn tonight when she met some douche-y frat brother named Spencer. They'd date for the rest of Abi's high school career, then she'd marry him instead of going to college. From there, David hadn't been able to see much more, only that Abi's future with Spencer felt "sad," and would lead to her and her twin, Amanda, becoming estranged.

Saving people from future earthquakes or volcanoes seemed daunting—not to mention almost impossible to get people to believe—but keeping a friend from falling for the wrong guy? Oh, that I could handle.

Provided I could find Abigail, of course. A set of French doors opened into a big backyard, and I headed in that direction, hoping to see the twins. As I kicked a crumpled Bud Light can out of my path, my phone vibrated. Pulling it out of my purse, I saw it was a text from David. "This is how I feel about fraternities right now." Underneath was a picture of him pulling the worst face—nose wrinkled, mouth turned down in a huge frown, eyes narrowed. I smiled, unsure of what was funnier: the picture itself or the idea of David Stark taking a selfie.

"Goofball," I texted back before sliding my phone into my purse and stepping outside.

A giant keg had become a sort of fountain in the middle of the yard. Two boys were holding another guy up by his legs so he could attempt the dreaded keg stand, and I sighed, wondering what the appeal of these dudes even was.

And then, thank God, I saw two identical blond heads close together by a cluster of coolers.

"Abigail! Amanda!" I called, making my way over to them. That involved stepping over more beer cans, and at least two unconscious dudes, and I frowned. *Ew.*

The twins both raised their eyebrows at me, surprised. "Harper? What are you doing here?" Abi asked. She wore her signature fishtail braid loose and over one shoulder, while Amanda's hair was pulled back from her face with two little clips. They were both wearing red dresses, so I was glad the hair made it easy to tell them apart.

I gave them my sternest look, propping my hands on my hips. "I should ask the two of you that. Now come on. We're leaving."

This is a secret I learned from cheerleading and SGA. If you act like you're in the right, people will fall in line without really questioning. I'd never bothered to come up with an excuse as to why I was looking for the two of them at Sigma Kappa Nu, and it wasn't like I could say, "My boyfriend has psychic powers, so tonight I'm saving one of you from a terrible future." Instead, I relied on two years of being their head cheerleader to make Abi and Amanda follow me.

And it worked.

They both studied me for a minute. Abi screwed up her mouth like she might argue, but Amanda shrugged and took her twin's arm with a muttered "I'm over this place anyway."

I made my way toward the French doors, pleased. That had gone so much easier than I'd—

A figure suddenly reared up in front of me. "Whoa, whoa, little lady, what's the rush?"

The guy who blocked the doorway looked a lot like my ex-boyfriend, Ryan. Tall, nicely built, reddish hair that was just a little too long. But while Ryan's smile was charming, this guy's was smarmy, and I was not in the mood to deal with him right now.

"We're leaving," I said, smiling but saying the words firmly enough for him to know I meant business. "My friends are ready to go."

"No, I'm not," Abi said, one strap of her red dress sliding off her shoulder. Amanda kind of shook her head, too.

Man, what I wouldn't have given for Ryan and his mind-control powers right about now. But all I had were my powers of persuasion, which *I* thought were still pretty great.

"This place is super gross, Abi," I told her, gesturing around at the crushed cups on the lawn, the stained couches inside, the random depressions knocked into the walls by heads or fists, "and if your parents knew you were here, they'd die. Heck, you're not even related to me, and *I* kind of want to die. Now let's go."

But Frat-enstein over here was still looming in the doorway, arms braced on either side of the frame, a red plastic cup in one hand. "'Super gross'?" he repeated. He pressed a meaty paw over the Greek letters on his shirt, and his blurry eyes tried to focus on me. His cheeks were red, and his nose was kind of shiny. Honestly, what did Abi even see in a guy like this? "Sigma Kappa Nu is the best frat on campus."

I snorted. "Please. Alpha Epsilon is the best frat on campus. You guys are the *biggest* frat on campus, and that's because there's so many of you without the grades to get into decent fraternities. Now get out of our way."

He was blinking down at me, like my words were taking a while to penetrate the haze of beer and dumb that clearly clouded his mind. Then, finally, he slurred, *"You're* super gross."

"Zing," I muttered, turning back to Abigail and Amanda with eyebrows raised. "Can we please go now?"

Amanda nodded this time, thank God, but Abi was still chewing her lower lip and looking at the guy. "It's not even eleven," she said, fiddling with the end of her braid. Now the guy was looking back at her, blinking, and, ugh, this was going to be harder than I thought. "I mean, we could stay for a little while."

Biting back a sigh, I made myself smile at Abi. "No, we can't. Now kindly get out of our way . . ."

"Spencer," the guy offered with a flick of his hair. "And I think your pretty friend is right—she *could* stay for a while."

There was no real danger here, but everything in me ached to go super Paladin on Spencer's fratty butt. And then, thankfully, he gave me the chance.

His hand came down on my shoulder, hard enough that I actually winced. "Hey, there—" was as much as he got out before my fingers curled around his hand, holding him in place while my other hand shot out, heel of my palm smacking him solidly in the solar plexus.

He let out a whoosh of air that smelled like stale beer and sour apple Jolly Ranchers, making me wrinkle my nose even as I hooked my foot around his ankle and sent him crashing to the ground. The dude was built like a tree, so he went down hard, and I didn't give him the chance to get up again. Still clutching his hand, I pressed my shoe to his chest and slid my fingers down to circle his wrist. I only had to pull the littlest bit before he whimpered. And, I mean, I didn't want to break his wrist or anything.

I just wanted to scare him a little bit. It occurred to me that once upon a time I could do that with a mere icy smile or an eye roll. These days, things were a lot more . . . physical.

"When a lady says she's ready to leave," I told him, applying pressure, "she is ready to leave. And you do not get in her way. Is that clear?"

When he didn't answer, I gave another little tug that had him nodding frantically. "Right, yes. I'm sorry, I—I won't do it again."

I tossed his hand down, dusting my palms on the back of my skirt. "I would hope not."

Lifting my head to the twins, I saw them watching me with mouths agape. Luckily, most of the party was still outside, so only a couple of guys—also dressed in the maroon and blue of Sigma Kappa Nu—saw me with Spencer, and they were so drunk that they barely noticed me.

I glanced back at the twins. "Self-defense class," I told them with a little shrug. "Now can we please go?"

Spencer was sitting up now, holding his wrist and watching me with wary eyes, but I saw Abi hesitate before following me out of the room, and I wasn't sure if I'd done my job here tonight or not.

"You're not the boss of us, Harper," Abi said once we were out of the frat house and marching down the front steps toward the street. She'd grabbed her cardigan off the back of a chair on the way out, and was shoving her arms into it, scowling.

Then why are you following me? I thought.

What I *said* was, "I'm just looking out for you. That's what friends do."

"Abi's right," Amanda said, and they both stopped there at the edge of the yard. "We've all known you were a control freak, but this is kind of nuts."

I stopped then, turning to glance between them, wishing their words didn't . . . bug.

It was too close to what David had said when I'd first come up with this idea. "People have to live their lives, Harper," he'd said.

But, as I'd reminded him, what was the point of having

superpowers, superpowers he could actually use now—safely—
if we didn't, you know, use them?

"Ladies," David said with a little wave, and they both scowled
at him.

"What is *he* doing here?" Abi asked, and I rolled my eyes.

"He's my boyfriend. He drove me here, obvs."

The twins were looking at David's car like it might give them
a disease, and while I was irritated, I couldn't really blame them.
David's Dodge was a total clunker, full of dents and dings and
scratched paint, and . . . the truth was, I might have done some
of that damage myself during a car chase last fall, but the point
was that it barely looked drivable. I didn't know why David insisted on hanging on to that thing. He still had his aunt's car, and
while Saylor's Cadillac was of the old-lady variety, it certainly
wasn't in danger of having its engine drop out.

Abi opened the back door, delicately kicking a stack of
books off the backseat and onto the floor. David winced as the
books fell, and the corners of his mouth jerked down as he cut
his eyes at me.

However, when Amanda tossed his ratty messenger bag out
of the way, he twisted to look into the backseat. "Hey," he
started, and then he winced.

I wondered if Amanda had pushed his bag onto something
and broken it—there was no end to the random stuff in David's
backseat—but then I felt my own chest seize up in pain, and
knew we were in for something way worse.

A vision.

But those didn't just pop up the way they used to. David's

powers were under control now. Thing was, David didn't know that me and Ryan were using the wards to keep his powers under control. But it was for his own good. The smaller visions didn't leave him sick and shaking.

Or looking so scary.

"What the hell?" one of the twins squawked from the backseat, and David fumbled with his door handle, shaking his head.

"David," I said, reaching across the car to grab his arm.

Fingers closing around the handle, David shoved the door open, spilling out into the street.

Chapter 2

I WAS ALREADY out of my seat and moving around to him, barely paying attention to the twins, who were climbing out of the backseat.

David fell to his knees, hands pressed to his head. Golden light poured out of his eyes, so bright it hurt to look at, and from behind me, I heard one of the twins make a sound somewhere between a gasp and a breathy scream.

"What is wrong with him?"

There was a part of my mind already on the phone with Ryan, asking him to work his mind-wipe mojo on the twins ASAP, but for right now, David was the only thing that mattered. I didn't know if it was my Paladin powers or the way I felt about him that made my chest hurt, but I knelt down next to him, taking his hand.

His skin was clammy, but he grabbed my hand tight, fingers curling around my palm. "It's all right," I heard myself say, even though the power coming from him was making my teeth ache. I'd only seen him like this once, the night of Cotillion. Right now, light in his eyes, body vibrating, he looked a lot less like my boyfriend, and a lot more like a powerful supernatural creature.

Which, I had to remind myself, was exactly what he was.

But still, he shouldn't have been having visions like this, not anymore.

"We have to go," he said, his voice sounding deeper and echoing slightly, like there were two people talking. "Now. We need to go to them."

I'd never known cold sweat was a thing people could actually feel, but that's exactly what popped out on my forehead.

I held his hand tighter. "Where?" I asked. "Is Bee there?"

David's head swung toward me, and I flinched at the glare.

My best friend had gone missing the night of Cotillion, kidnapped by Blythe and taken who knew where. Of everything that had happened that night, even Saylor's death, losing Bee had been the worst. I couldn't stop feeling like I'd failed her.

"Bee's at cheerleading camp."

Glancing over my shoulder, I saw that the twins were still frowning at us. Well, Amanda was. Abi was just staring at David, shocked.

"Seriously, what is *wrong* with him?" Abi asked, and I winced.

"It's nothing," I said, lifting my and David's joined hands to look at his wrist. I never wore a watch, but David always did, so I checked it now. It was nearly eleven, and I'd promised my parents I'd be home by midnight.

David's vision was already fading. I could feel the power draining out of him, and his breathing was starting to slow, the light in his eyes going dim. "Pres?" he croaked, and while there was still a little echo, he sounded more like himself than like the Oracle.

Sucking in a deep breath through my nose, I forced myself to think. First things first, I needed to get the twins home and dealt with. I could worry about my parents and where David was meant to be taking me once Abi and Amanda were handled.

"Okay," I said, overly bright, as I clapped my hands together and rose to my feet. "Everybody back in the car."

David stood, too, lurching for the driver's side, but I caught his arm and steered him back toward the passenger seat. The twins stood there, arms folded over their chests.

"What the hell was that, Harper?" Amanda asked, and Abi echoed, "The. Hell."

It had been a long night already, and I had a feeling it was about to get a lot longer. I shook my head, shooing the twins back toward the car. "I'll explain later," I promised, even though I had no intention of doing anything of the sort. What I did plan on doing was calling Ryan.

Even though last year I spearheaded the Campaign Against Texting and Driving—I signed a pledge and everything—I was already starting the car when I pulled up Ryan's number and texted, "Meet me at the twins' house. 911."

"Harper," David said, his voice low and rough. "We don't have time. We have to go *now*." I didn't take my eyes off the road to look at him, but I did drop my phone in the change tray under the radio, reaching out to put my hand on his knee.

"It's okay," I said, even though my heart and mind were racing at a million miles an hour.

I had no idea what was going on, but I did know that to handle it, we had to ditch the Not-So-Wonder Twins and hope to God that Ryan had gotten my text, since he didn't seem in any hurry to reply.

But when we pulled up in the driveway, Ryan was leaning against his car outside the twins' house. "What's he doing here?" Abi said from the backseat.

"Don't know!" I chirped, throwing the car into park. "Stay here," I told David firmly, pointing at him in case he wasn't clear how serious I was.

He gave a weak nod and waved his hand, still slumped against the door panel. Maybe this will make me sound like a terrible person, but seeing him like that, much as it worried me, also made me feel kind of . . . relieved. Vindicated, even. This was what Ryan and I were protecting him from, this kind of pain. I knew it had bummed David out that his visions weren't as big as he'd hoped, but surely he could understand that a little disappointment was better than *this*.

I started to open the car door, but before I could, Ryan was suddenly there in the open window, folding his arms on the door, chin resting on his forearms. As always, he looked like he'd just stepped out of an Abercrombie & Fitch catalog, auburn hair curling over his brow, hazel eyes kind of sleepy and lazy, his T-shirt showing off the results of plenty of time in the gym. I could practically feel the twins swoon in the backseat. Ryan used to make me swoon once, too, but now I frowned and waved him back from the door so I could get out of the car.

"What's the emergency?" he asked once we were on the lawn, and I glanced over my shoulder at the car.

"David had a vision, and the twins saw," I said in a whispered rush. "So now I need you to do your Mage thing and wipe their memories, okay?"

By now, the twins were getting out of the backseat, muttering to each other. I heard David's name, and also mine, along with a few words that, were I not so concerned with other things right now, I would have lit into them for. Honestly.

"What kind of vision?" Ryan asked, his brow wrinkling. "About what?"

"It doesn't matter right now," I told him, already making to move back to the car. "Do the mind wipe, and—"

Ryan caught my elbow before I could rush back to David. "It seems like it matters. It's Oracle stuff, which means I'm involved, too. Harper, if he's having visions without us, after all that we did, that's . . . that's kind of an issue."

That was true, but right now, I needed him to erase the twins' memories of tonight so I could get back to David. Luckily, at that minute, the twins wandered up, and I saw Ryan's eyes flick to them.

"We'll talk later!" I called, both to Ryan and to Amanda and Abigail, before hurrying back across the lawn.

David was out of the car, moving to the driver's seat, and I stopped him with a "*Whoa whoa whoa.* What do you think you're doing?"

Under the street lamps, he was looking a little bit better, but not much. There were still shadows underneath his eyes, and he was moving gingerly, like something inside him was broken. But his jaw was set when he looked at me, fingers on the door handle. "I'm driving."

I put my hands on my hips, shifting my weight to one foot. "Um, okay, except you're not?"

Now was not exactly the time to be arguing over who had control of the car, but I was not about to let a guy who looked like his brain might actually start leaking out of his ears get behind the wheel.

But David wasn't budging. "You heard what it—what I—said. I'll lead the way."

Behind me, I could hear the low murmur of voices as Ryan talked to the twins, but I ignored that, focusing on David with my arms crossed tightly.

The twins' street was quiet, the lawns almost identical green squares, glowing in the security lights. Azalea bushes lined the brick walls, and every yard had either dogwood trees or magnolias planted smack-dab in the middle of the grass. "Right, but you could, like, lead the way by telling me where we're going. Like a GPS."

David's eyes blinked behind his glasses, and he shook his head slightly. "Pres, for once, can't I be in charge of some aspect of this whole thing? I'm telling you, I need to drive us there. I'm fine now"—the slight trembling of his hand seemed to make that a lie, but whatever—"so please get in the car."

I thought about arguing with him again, but David was right;

I did tend to put myself in charge of all of these things, but how could I not? Wasn't that my responsibility now that Saylor was gone?

But then I thought again of his visions, and the lies I'd told.

Couldn't I give him this one thing?

Dropping my head, I pinched the bridge of my nose between my fingers. "David—" I started, and he dropped his head, trying to meet my eyes.

"Trust me, Pres," he said. "Please."

The twins were walking toward their house, and Ryan gave me a thumbs-up, so I figured that was settled, thank goodness.

But then Ryan walked over to us and grinned.

"So," he said, opening the door to the backseat. "Where are we headed?"

Chapter 3

"IT'S NOT that I don't want you to come," I explained for what had to be the third time in five miles. "But David and I have this."

From the backseat, Ryan snorted, and when I glanced over my shoulder, he was sitting back, his arms folded, legs spread wide. I'd always hated when he sat like that, taking up too much space, but there wasn't anything I could say to him. That was a Boyfriend Complaint, and Ryan wasn't my boyfriend anymore. Of course, *what* he was now, I couldn't even explain. We'd never been friends, exactly, so saying we were didn't feel true. Maybe we were coworkers.

Which was part of why I didn't want Ryan on this little expedition. He'd never liked the idea of not telling David about how we were limiting his visions, and I was worried that all of the weirdness of tonight was going to make him feel worse, maybe even give him the urge to confess.

"The other day you were bitching—sorry, complaining," Ryan amended, catching my look, "that I wasn't doing enough Mage stuff." He spread his big hands wide. "Isn't this Mage stuff?"

I looked back over at David. His hands were clenched tightly around the steering wheel, eyes on the dark road in front of us. We were driving out of town, in the opposite direction from the college where we'd been earlier, and the houses were starting to be few and far between.

I caught Ryan's eyes in the rearview mirror. "When I said I wanted you to do more Mage stuff, I meant I wanted you to check on the wards Saylor made." David's "aunt" had put up all kinds of magical protection charms over Pine Grove to keep the Ephors from finding him, and we'd told David that they needed to be charged up from time to time.

"And," I added, twisting in my seat, "I think you may want to add wards farther out."

"Sure thing. Should I go ahead and cover the whole state?" Ryan asked, and I rolled my eyes.

"No," David said. "No more wards."

Surprised, I twisted in my seat, the seat belt digging into my hip. "What do you mean 'no more wards'?"

David shook his head, but didn't look at me. "I think the wards are screwing up my visions."

I could hear Ryan shift in the backseat, and willed him not to say anything. Luckily, he didn't, and David continued. "I mean, I had those two big ones, right? The thing about the earthquake in Peru, and then the one about that senator lady Harper likes becoming president. But then . . . nothing. For months now." He was talking faster now, fingers drumming on the steering wheel. "So maybe all the wards Saylor put up to protect me are, like, getting in the way of that."

I tried not to squirm in my seat since it wasn't Saylor's wards getting in his way.

"And now," David added, "the most important thing I've been able to see is that your friend will marry a douche someday. Not earth-shattering stuff."

"Which friend and which douche?" Ryan asked, leaning forward, but I ignored him.

"I happen to think that kind of thing is important, David." And I did. Sort of.

He did look over then, eyebrows drawing close together over the rims of his glasses. We'd started to move out of the city now, fields to either side of the road, and only the occasional streetlight. The green glow from the dashboard lights played over David's high cheekbones, making his eyes look slightly sunken in. "I mean, your friends are important," David said, even though I was pretty sure he didn't actually think that. There was something weird in his voice. "But bigger-picture stuff? Stuff that might actually help . . . I don't know, the world? At least more people than a handful of your friends. Tonight, for the first time in months, I had a strong vision, a clear one that I didn't need any help with. And it was a big one." He glanced over at me. "I saw the Ephors, Pres."

My heart thudded heavily in my chest. "What?"

He nodded and reached over to squeeze my hand. "The Ephors," he repeated, eyes still on the road. It was probably just the reflection of streetlights, but it looked like his eyes were glowing again, and I swallowed hard.

"Although why they've decided to set up shop all the way out here, I don't know," he said, and I jerked my hand back.

"Wait, we're going to see them? That's where you're taking us?"

"That seems like information we should've had from the start," Ryan commented, and when I caught his eye in the rear-view mirror, he was frowning, auburn hair hanging low on his forehead.

"If I'd told you, would you have come?" David asked, turning to glance at me. Now I could tell his eyes weren't glowing after all, but I didn't feel much better.

"Yes," I told him quickly. "But, you know, with . . . weapons. Grenades, maybe."

David shook his head and turned down a dirt road, the car thumping over bumps and ruts.

"There's nothing out here," Ryan offered, leaning up between us. He had his elbows propped on his spread knees, his hazel eyes scanning the road in front of us, the fields of tall grass on either side. "Me and some of the guys used to come out here to drink beer."

"When was that?" I asked, but now it was his turn to ignore me apparently.

"There used to be a house," he told David. "Big ol' *Gone with the Wind*–type place. My grandmother had a painting of it over her mantel. Apparently it was kinda famous or something, but it burned down back in the seventies. All that was left was a chimney. And we threw enough cans at it that I'm not sure much of that was left either."

"What a fabulous use of time," I muttered, and I think Ryan would have had a comment for that had the car not taken a curve in the road right then.

David brought the car to a shuddering halt.

"A house like *that*?" he asked, and Ryan gave a slow nod.

The house in front of us looked a lot like Magnolia House back in town, but while that was just a reproduction of a fancy antebellum home, this seemed to be the real thing. White columns rose from the front porch to a wraparound balcony above, and tall windows, bracketed by dark shutters, stood on either side of the massive front door. Lights glowed in those windows, throwing out long rectangles of gold on the neatly manicured lawn.

"Maybe someone built a new place," Ryan suggested, but his voice was faint. "In the . . . three weeks since I was out here."

"This is the place," David said, drumming his fingers on the steering wheel. "I feel it, don't you?"

I did. I wasn't sure how exactly, but I definitely did. I don't know what I was expecting the Ephor headquarters—if that's what this place was—to look like. I mean, they were an ancient society that started in Greece, made up of people who wanted to control the world, so I don't think I was too far off in imagining that they'd do business in something like a temple, or at least an old building made of stone. It looked like they'd decided to restore some of the local architecture instead.

So I thought I could be forgiven for doubting David. "Are you sure?"

David was still staring at the house, his wrists draped over the steering wheel. "Yeah," he said at last. "That's the place."

As the three of us got out of the car, it was all I could do not to shiver. The house might not have looked magical, but it sure as heck felt like it. I couldn't see any obvious markings, like the wards Saylor had put up around town, but power pulsed off the building in a steady beat that I could almost feel coming up through the soles of my feet. It made the hair on the back of my neck stand up and my teeth ache.

"That's intense," David said, and I glanced at him. Reaching over, I threaded my fingers with his, squeezing.

"Do you have any kind of plan here? Are we just marching in, or . . ."

David squeezed my hand back. "No plan," he said. "I *have* to be here. That's all I know. It's like . . . remember when you told me that if I'm in danger, you can't do anything except save me?"

I nodded. That was part of the Oracle/Paladin bond. Even if an orphanage staffed by kittens was on fire right next to him, I couldn't do anything but save David. So, yeah, I understood how mystical compulsions could make you do things that weren't good for you, but I still didn't like it.

I made myself smile at David. "We got this," I said, even though I had no idea what "this" was. But David and I had handled The Weird before and gotten through it. We could do it again.

Turning his head, he smiled down at me. Well, his lips lifted in something that I think was supposed to be a smile, but he was either too tired or too freaked out to give it his best shot.

I'd take it.

From behind me, I thought I heard Ryan blow out a long breath, but I kept my eyes on the house, waiting for . . . I didn't even know what.

The three of us approached the building cautiously, like we were afraid we'd be rushed at any second. My Paladin senses weren't tingling, so that probably wasn't going to happen, but I still didn't want to take any chances.

The porch steps didn't even creak under our feet although the potted ferns by the door rustled slightly in the night wind. Other than that, there was no sign of movement, nothing happening behind the windows or door, and we all stood there for a moment. I didn't see an intercom button or anything like that, and I wasn't sure if I was supposed to knock. Kick down the door, maybe?

Before I could do either of those things, the door slowly swung open.

"Cool," Ryan said from behind me. "I was starting to think this crap wasn't creepy enough."

David snorted, and when he cut his eyes at Ryan, he looked better. Less pale, for sure. Sharper, almost. "Sorry we got you involved in a Scooby-Doo mystery."

That made Ryan smile a little bit, and he shoved his hands in his pockets, rocking back on his heels. "That is what's happening, isn't it? Which obviously makes you Shaggy." He nodded at David, whose smirk turned into a grin.

"Then you're Fred," he told Ryan. "And Pres here"—he bumped me with an elbow—"is for sure Daphne."

"For sure," Ryan agreed, and I rolled my eyes at both of them.

"Okay, if y'all are done being boys, can we please go in and see what the heck is going on here?"

We walked inside. The house smelled nice, like furniture polish and expensive candles, with a hint of something warm and spicy underneath. Tea, maybe. And it certainly didn't look like a lair of evil. Overhead, a chandelier sparkled, and the wooden stairs gleamed. There were vases of fresh flowers on long, narrow tables, and pretty artwork dotted the walls. It looked like the inside of a lot of these old houses: The outside might be all vintage and historical, but there was clearly some twenty-first-century interior decorating going on.

"Maybe we died?" David suggested. "And ended up in Harper's version of heaven?"

"Well, the Ephors have good taste, even if they *are* evil." I turned in a small circle on one of the lush rugs, glancing up. The house was quiet, but people had to be here.

Bee might be here.

I'd gotten so used to my Paladin senses kicking in when they needed to that it was weird to feel so . . . blank. I couldn't get a read on anything, and not for the first time, I wondered if there was some kind of magic blocking my powers. "If they're evil, why are we here?" Ryan asked, and I had to admit it was a good question. We'd spent last semester trying to hide David from the Ephors, and now we were walking into their . . . house? Headquarters? For a meeting? Still, that didn't keep me from scanning the room for objects that could be used as weapons. There were several pretty hefty candlesticks on the mantel over the enormous fireplace. Those would work.

I turned to ask David more about his vision, but he was studying one of the paintings on the wall. "Whoa," he murmured softly, and I followed his gaze.

"Whoa," I echoed.

The painting depicted a girl in a flowing white gown, her body floating in midair, her eyes bright and golden. On either side of her stood a man, one in armor, the other in a white robe, and kneeling all around the three of them were shadowy figures, their hands outstretched toward the girl. The paint seemed to glow, and I fought the urge to run my fingers over the canvas.

"The Oracle Speaks," a voice said from behind us, and David, Ryan, and I jumped, then whirled around.

A man was standing there, but I had no idea where he'd come from. I hadn't heard his footsteps approach or a door open. He was maybe forty or so, and handsome in the same old-world, expensive way the house was. Blond hair, high cheekbones, really nice suit. Like the house, power seemed to radiate from him, and I rubbed my hands up and down my arms.

But his smile was perfectly pleasant as he gestured toward the painting. "That's what this particular work of art is called. Felt appropriate to hang here."

"You're an Ephor," David said quietly, his hands clenching into fists at his side, and the man gave a slight bow.

"I am. My name is Alexander. And you are the Oracle and, I take it, *you* are his intrepid Paladin and Mage," he said, nodding to me and Ryan. There was a slight lilt to his words, an accent I couldn't quite place. "So good of you to come."

He was acting like he'd invited us here, like we were expected, and I wasn't sure why, but that gave me all of the creeps. Still, although I waited for my Paladin senses to kick in and tell me this guy was bad news, there was nothing. Magic, sure, a hint of power, yes, but none of the chest-tightening, muscle-tensing sickness I felt when David was in danger.

The Ephors had always been the greatest threat to David, so why wasn't I in attack mode? It suddenly occurred to me that they might be doing something to override my Paladin powers. Could they do that? After all, they'd somehow managed to break through the wards so that David could have an all-consuming vision. For probably the thousandth time, I wished Saylor were here to tell me what was going on.

"I'm so pleased to have you here," Alexander said, still smiling that bland smile, one hand extended toward a dim hallway off to the side. "Now, if you'll come with me—"

I was about to interject that we were staying right where we were, but before I could, David stepped forward, looked at Alexander, and said, "You people took a girl last year. Bee Franklin. I want you to tell me where she is."

Chapter 4

"WHAT? IS BEE HERE? Did you see her?" Behind David, I saw my own surprise reflected on Ryan's face.

With a sigh, David turned to me, ruffling his hand over his hair. "No. Or not exactly, but she's . . . close, or . . ." He opened and closed his free hand like he was trying to pull the words out of the air. "Something. I can feel it."

Sensing people's presence wasn't exactly part of David's bag, and I'd certainly never heard him talk about anything like this before. Was he able to sense Bee because he'd juiced her up with Paladin powers before Blythe had taken her?

But David looked back at Alexander, and the Ephor took a deep breath, his brow wrinkling slightly. "All in good time, I assure you," he said at last, and then swept his hand toward the hall again. "First, we need to talk about what occurred this evening."

"The frat thing or David's vision?" I asked, and Alexander's green eyes flicked to me. His expression was blank, but I could still feel magic or power or whatever it was oozing from him, and I made myself hold his gaze.

"They are connected," he said at last, then nodded. "Now, if the three of you will come with me, all will be explained."

"Where are the rest of you?" David folded his arms across his chest. "Aren't there other Ephors here besides you?"

Alexander gave a tiny smile, revealing a hint of teeth. "All in good time."

I thought David might argue with him some more—I knew I wanted to—but instead, he started off in the direction Alexander had indicated.

At my side, I felt Ryan gently take my elbow. "Come on, Harper," he said in a low voice.

The hallway was lit with pretty little sconces covered with tiny burgundy shades, casting pools of warm light on the hardwood, but all I could see in my head was Bee. Bee, laughing with me at cheerleading practice; Bee, handing me lip gloss; Bee, tears streaming down her face as she'd kept me from killing Blythe.

Bee, vanishing right in front of me.

I'd wanted answers about the fight at the frat party tonight, but now, the only thing I cared about was knowing if Bee was here.

Alexander opened a doorway off to the left, ushering us into what looked like some kind of study. The decor here was even more extravagant: antique furniture, Tiffany lamps, carpet that felt lush and deep underfoot.

And three chairs sitting across from a gleaming mahogany desk.

The three of us sat, David between me and Ryan, while Alexander sank into the much larger chair behind the desk. "Well," he said at last, fixing all of us with that smile again. "Here we are. Tea?"

There was a pot beside his elbow, I saw now, steam spilling from the spout, but tea was the last thing on my mind. "No," I said, sitting up as straight as I could. "What we want are answers. Why are we here, what the heck did you have to do with David's vision tonight, and where is Bee?"

Alexander flicked his dark gold hair out of his eyes, frowning as though I had disappointed him. "So we're to skip the pleasantries, I see."

"Pleasantries?" Ryan sat back in his chair, propping his ankle on his opposite knee. "I only came into this thing at the end last year, but didn't y'all try to *kill* David?"

Alexander tilted his head in acknowledgment. "I understand how that may have looked, but we were never trying to harm David, merely to remove his Paladin from the equation."

"Yeah, that's not really helping on the trust front," I said, suppressing a shudder.

Alexander ignored me. "We sent our Mage to perform Alaric's ritual on the Oracle in the hopes that he would not prove as useless as we'd feared."

Alexander turned back to David and spread his hands wide. "And now look at you! Everything we'd hoped for and more. Powerful enough to create Paladins, stable enough to have clear, helpful visions. All in all, the entire process went even better than we'd hoped."

I couldn't help but grit my teeth as I thought of Saylor, bleeding to death in the kitchen. Of Bee, vanishing before my eyes.

But I didn't say anything. If this guy had Bee, I'd hold my tongue for as long as I could.

David had other ideas. "I don't have 'clear, helpful visions' anymore," he said. "All I can see are . . . minor things."

Alexander's pleasant expression didn't falter, but something about him still made the hairs on the back of my neck stand up. Did he know what Ryan and I had been doing?

"You have these powers," he said, waving one hand, "but no idea how to channel them. You're using them for trivial things, like ensuring that Miss Price's friends don't get their hearts broken."

I started. If he knew about that, then surely he knew *why* those were the only sorts of visions David was having. But Alexander just kept going, his voice low and smooth. "With our help, you can reach your full potential, which is all we want for you, David."

On my right, David rubbed his hand over the back of his neck, his shoulders tight. "And I'm supposed to believe that? After you people spent months—no, my whole freaking life— trying to kill me?"

Alexander's green eyes blinked twice, and then he sat up abruptly, thrusting his hand out at David. "Take it," he said, nodding to his palm. "Take it and look for yourself."

David blinked at the outstretched hand, his eyes narrowed behind his glasses. "I can see the future, not read minds."

Alexander's smile widened the littlest bit. "Are you sure?"

Leaning forward in my chair a little, I studied Alexander.

"Who are you? Like, chief Ephor, or head Mage? You clearly have some kind of crazy magic."

Alexander kept his hand outstretched, his eyes on David. "Six of one, half a dozen of the other," he replied, and I wanted to point out that he hadn't given me much of an answer.

I could hear the grandfather clock ticking in the corner, could hear my own breathing, and as I watched, David reached over and very gently laid his hand on top of Alexander's. I couldn't see anything happen when their hands touched, but then David closed his eyes and there was the briefest hint of light behind his eyelids.

And then his hand fell back to his lap. "He's telling the truth," David said, almost wonderingly. "I . . . I don't know how I know, but I know."

I didn't like that. I didn't like it at *all*. How could David suddenly have new powers we didn't know anything about? Saylor had never mentioned anything about mind reading, and, ugh, I was in no way ready to handle a boyfriend who could read my every thought whenever we touched hands.

"There are all sorts of things we can teach you." Alexander sat back, his chair creaking. "All sorts of powers locked away in that mind of yours."

"David doesn't want to learn anything from you people," I said, crossing my ankles.

But David jerked his head to look at me, something like irritation in his face. "I think that's one of those things I get to decide for myself, Pres," he said, and in that second, he wasn't the

Oracle or my boyfriend—he was the annoying guy who wrote mean articles about me in the school paper, the boy who never stopped arguing with me.

"Saylor said—" I started, only to let the words die in my throat. Saylor had told me that David's powers could prove dangerous, and that the Ephors wouldn't care. That his power was the only thing that would matter to them. I didn't think she'd ever told him that, though, and this wasn't a conversation I wanted to have in front of Alexander.

Ryan was looking down, frowning a little, but Alexander only watched me with those green eyes, brows drawn sharply together.

Finally, he folded his hands on the desk, the cuffs of his blue shirt peeking out from his jacket. "The issue as far as I can see, Miss Price, is that neither you nor the Oracle nor your Mage"—Ryan's head came up—"currently have any sort of guidance. With the deaths of Christopher Hall and the woman you called Saylor Stark, any assistance you could have had in protecting the Oracle—"

"David," I interrupted. "His name is David." My voice shook the littlest bit, and I hated that. But I also hated anything to do with these people wanting to "help" David.

Alexander inclined his head the tiniest bit, lips pursing slightly. "As you say. David."

Manners and graciousness dripped off those four words, but I knew when someone was being condescending, and I didn't like it. Maybe that's why my voice was frosty when I replied, "We don't need your assistance. We have things totally under control.

We have a Mage, an Oracle, and a Paladin. We don't need any-one else." It wasn't true, not really . . . I was shaky and tired and completely in over my head. But I couldn't take help from these people. Not the people who kidnapped Bee. As for everything else . . . we'd figure it out as we went.

Alexander's expression didn't change, but a muscle ticced in his jaw and after a long pause, he reached for the teapot at the edge of his desk, filling a delicate china cup. Once he'd taken a sip, he fixed me with that gaze again.

"I'm unsure of how you could control *anything*, Miss Price, seeing as how you are not actually a Paladin yet."

Chapter 5

MY MOUTH went dry. "Excuse me?" I finally managed to croak.

His fingers drummed on the mahogany desk. "Well, you have the powers themselves, of course. That's not in any doubt, as Michael's corpse attests."

"Michael?" I said, confused. Next to me, I could feel David tense, and out of the corner of my eye, I saw that he was sitting up straighter in his chair now.

"I believe you knew him as 'Dr. DuPont'?" Alexander's manner was still casual as he tugged at his cuffs, but there was a hard glint in his eyes.

Oh, right. The history teacher turned assassin who I'd killed. I glanced at Ryan. He'd heard the story—I'd told him everything once he became the Mage—but I knew this was the part he still had a hard time with. It had to be weird, knowing your ex-girlfriend killed somebody, even if it was in self-defense. But he was still watching Alexander, a wrinkle between his auburn brows, his leg jiggling up and down.

Alexander continued, "We don't doubt your Paladin . . .

prowess, Miss Price. But you have not yet earned the right to call yourself by that name."

I didn't like the sound of that one bit, and I crossed one knee over the other as I leaned in toward Alexander. "I gave up a lot to protect David. I lost my best friend, I lied to my family, and I watched a woman I loved and admired die right in front of me. So don't tell me I haven't earned being a Paladin. I've more than earned it, buddy."

"Hear, hear," David muttered next to me, and I felt his hand land on mine on the arm of my chair. I glanced over long enough to smile at him, and across the desk, Alexander sat back in his chair.

"So," he said, nodding at our joined hands, "is that how things are?"

I jerked my hand out from underneath David's, although I couldn't have said why. It was like . . . I didn't want this guy knowing about us. But obviously, it was too late for that.

David shot me a glance that was either pissed or wounded or both before facing Alexander. "What, is that not allowed?"

Alexander gave an elegant shrug, still kicked back in his chair. "It's not officially against any rule *I've* heard of. But it's never been an issue in the past."

Curiosity got the best of me, and I shifted in my seat. "Why?"

Drumming his fingers on the arm of his chair, Alexander looked up, like he was trying to think of the right words. "Oracles are usually very . . . dedicated to their duties. Having constant visions leaves little time for personal relationships."

I thought of how David was when he was in the grips of a vision. I couldn't imagine him being like that all the time. I didn't want to.

When I looked over at David, his face was almost blank, his eyes fixed straight ahead. His foot was bouncing, which meant that he was thinking hard, but about what?

"But what do you mean about Harper not being a Paladin?" Ryan asked. He was slouching again, but he tugged at his sleeves, his eyes never leaving Alexander. "Does that mean I'm not a Mage? I mean, Oracles are born, I got that, but if we were both made into . . . whatever it is we are—"

The Ephor held up a hand. "Every point on the triangle is different, comes with different responsibilities and duties. A Mage, once powers have been transferred, is a Mage, fully and completely. All the knowledge the previous Mage contained is passed on. But a Paladin is a horse of a different color, as it were. Paladins have a sacred duty. As do the Oracle and the Mage, of course, but the Paladin has an especially challenging role. To be sure Miss Price is up to the task, she would have to go through the Peirasmos."

The word rolled off his tongue in a pretty way, but there was power in those three syllables. I could feel it, and even David shuddered a little bit.

"Do you know what that is, Miss Price?" Alexander raised his eyebrows at me, still totally pleasant, and I hated to have to shake my head.

"No."

Alexander made an exaggerated moue of disappointment.

"What a shame. I hoped Miss Stark would have completed that part of your training."

"Things were a little rushed," I told him, scowling, "what with you people and your crazy Mage trying to kill us all the time. We didn't have time for . . . whatever that word was."

"Peirasmos," he repeated. "And in all fairness, Miss Price, we were using the Mage to kill *you*, not the Oracle."

"David," Ryan interjected, and I glanced over at him, throwing him a quick smile.

Now all pleasantness disappeared from Alexander's face, and he sat up in his chair. "Oh, for the love of the gods. Is it like that, too?"

My cheeks flamed red, and I looked away from Ryan, back toward the Ephor. "None of that is any of your business."

Alexander only wrinkled his nose, bracing his elbows on the desk. "Teenagers," he said on a long sigh. "Well, what can one expect, I suppose. In any case." He steepled his long fingers. "When Saylor Stark and Christopher Hall broke away from us, they rejected many of our traditions, it would seem. Which is a shame since the Peirasmos is vital."

"Says who?" I asked, crossing my legs at the ankle. "And why? I mean, I'm clearly a Paladin, I have all the . . . the . . ." I waved my hands in the air. "Superpowers or whatever. What would this Peirasmos change?"

Alexander sniffed, resting his elbows on the desk. "What would they change? For starters, by completing these trials, you get to live. Is that enough of a reason for you, Miss Price?"

It had been a long night. I'd had to go into possibly the

grossest frat house in Alabama, I'd watched my boyfriend go all mega-Oracle, and I'd gotten my ex-boyfriend to wipe my friends' minds; my life being threatened was the icing on a seriously crappy cake.

"So that whole 'Hey, we want to help you and be besties' thing lasted what, five minutes?" I asked. Next to me, I could feel Ryan go tense, and I nudged him with my elbow. I appreciated the chivalry, but dealing with death threats was kind of my area of expertise.

Alexander sat back in his chair, eyes narrowing even as he smiled. "You certainly have enough spark to be a Paladin. I can appreciate that. But let me make myself very clear, Miss Price. We are offering our assistance because you need us, and I think you know that. Work with us, and David stays safe and protected, as well as extremely useful as an Oracle. I think it should be clear by now that our powers are greater than yours. After all, I was able to penetrate your wards with hardly any trouble at all."

"Please don't say 'penetrate,'" I muttered, but once again, Alexander ignored me and kept going.

"You and Mr. Bradshaw here have some of the weight taken off your shoulders. But if you choose not to follow our rules, then you declare yourselves our enemies, and we will spend however long it takes to eradicate all three of you. Should the Oracle die, another will be called. Another Paladin will be created, and another Mage."

Leaning forward, he pressed his palms flat on the desktop. A strand of hair fell over his forehead, marring that whole men's-magazine thing he had going on. "You are expendable to us."

My heart was pounding, my mouth dry. On one side, Ryan was breathing hard, his fingers clenching and unclenching. On the other, David was glaring at Alexander. He wasn't jiggling his foot anymore, and had gone so still it was almost unnerving.

"Then why not kill us all now?" I asked Alexander, trying to keep my voice steady. "I mean, we're all here. It wouldn't be hard."

"Harper, could you not?" Ryan muttered, but Alexander only smiled.

"Because that's not what we want. It's true we can replace you, all three of you, but that's not ideal. Much easier to simply welcome you all back into the fold."

"I am not in your fold, buddy," I said, standing up. "And neither are Ryan or David."

On my left, Ryan rose to his feet, shoving his hands in his pockets. "Damn straight."

But David sat in his chair, his elbows on his knees, hands clasped tightly in front of him. He was looking at the ground, a muscle working in his jaw. "David?" I asked, hating how unsure I sounded.

"It's just . . . Pres, we need help. *I* need help."

"But," I faltered, "you have help. You have me and Ryan."

He nodded, almost too quickly. "I do, and you're great, both of you, but . . . Harper, if my powers could actually be used to help people, if this guy"—he nodded at Alexander—"can help me do that . . . it kind of seems worth it, don't you think?"

I stood there, my stomach twisting, my skin suddenly cold. "Saylor and Christopher gave up everything to protect you from these people. They tried to kill you, David. They took Bee."

"I know," David said, "but, Pres, I looked into this guy's mind. He's not trying to hurt me, and what he said adds up. The Ephors only wanted me gone when they thought I was a crappy Oracle. Now that the ritual has worked and it didn't kill me, they need me again. Hell, maybe . . ." He trailed off, tugging at his hair. "Maybe the *world* needs me. And it's not worth your lives"—he gestured at me and Ryan—"if I'm not doing something important. Plus, I'm . . ." Another hair tug. "I'm sick of running from this. Aren't you?" Behind his glasses, his eyes were very blue, and I could hear the plea in his voice.

"He's got a point, Harper," Ryan agreed, and I turned, surprised.

"Okay, what happened to 'damn straight'?"

Ryan gave one of those easy shrugs, and it was the weirdest thing, seeing such a familiar gesture in such a bizarre setting. "Our job is to protect David, right? If this is what David wants, it seems like we should go with it. If the alternative is us looking over our shoulders forever, this seems a hell of a lot better."

I had plenty of experience getting girls in line, but it seemed like boys were a way bigger pain in the butt. I couldn't believe I was being overruled by my boyfriend and my ex-boyfriend in front of a guy I was already pretty sure I hated.

Still, I wanted to present a united front. "Let's go home and talk about it," I said, smoothing my hands over my skirt. In the soft golden lamplight of the study, I could make out a little stain at the hem. Ugh, Spencer must have spilled beer on me when I grabbed him, and I suddenly felt exhausted. "No decision needs to be made tonight, and, hey, not to be rude, but it's not like either of you have to go through some kind of crazy Greek trials if we say yes."

"Oh, I'm sorry," Alexander said, his brows drawing together with what had to be fake concern. "I don't think I was clear. There's no 'deciding.' You are already in the Peirasmos, Miss Price."

I turned to look at him. "What?"

"The moment I arrived here, the Peirasmos began. It's not a choice you get to make, but rather a duty you *must* fulfill."

If I hadn't been so tired and rattled, I probably could've managed something better than "That's not fair!" But that's exactly what I said, and I sounded petulant even to myself.

Alexander only shrugged. "Has any part of this been fair to anyone?" he asked, and I realized I couldn't argue with that. Everything about this had been unfair from day one, but this seemed particularly awful. I was getting sick of not being offered a freaking *choice* in things.

"The Peirasmos have begun," Alexander continued. "And either you will pass, or you will die."

That seemed like a pretty steep grading curve, and for the first time in a long time, I felt something like real fear. Not the adrenaline spike I got when I was fighting bad guys or keeping David safe, but the scary kind. It was a cold, kind of sick feeling that made me want to go home and put my head under the covers, maybe forever.

But I couldn't do that right now, so instead, I stared Alexander down and said, "That seems kind of stupid. If I fail the trials, I die, and then David doesn't have *any* kind of Paladin, official or not, and how—"

"Ah," Alexander interrupted as he drummed his long, elegant fingers on the desk. "That actually brings me to my next point."

"I wasn't finished," I said, turning a glare on him, but he was already rising from the desk.

"We've made provisions for those circumstances." He lifted a hand and nodded at the doorway behind him. "Thanks to you, David, we have a spare."

I turned, my heart in my throat.

There, in the doorway of Alexander's study, was Bee.

Chapter 6

I'D THOUGHT ABOUT seeing Bee again for so long, but now that she was actually there, standing right in front of me, I felt frozen. Paralyzed.

I think I was afraid to believe she was actually there.

Ryan apparently did not have that fear, though, because he crossed the room in a few strides, swooping her up into a big hug. "Holy crap," I heard him say, and her hands came up to rest on his shoulder blades, hugging him back. Bee was only a few inches shorter than Ryan, so I could clearly see her heart-shaped face over his shoulder. Long blond hair pulled back in a braid, dressed in a simple black T-shirt and jeans, she looked so . . . normal.

"Easy there," she said, and her voice sounded exactly the same. "I like my ribs."

That's what did it for me, hearing her sound so normal, so Bee, and then I was across the room, too, shamelessly using my Paladin strength to push Ryan out of the way and throw my arms around her.

"You're okay," I said, squeezing my eyes against the sudden

stinging there. "You're okay, you're okay . . . wait." I pulled back, held her at arm's length. "Are you okay?"

There were tears in her big brown eyes, but she laughed shakily, nodding. "I am. I totally am."

"Miss Franklin was never mistreated in our care," Alexander said, and it was like I'd forgotten he was there. I turned to look over my shoulder.

"That doesn't exactly make up for kidnapping her," I said, and he gave another one of those rolling shrugs.

"She was not meant to be taken. That was all Blythe's doing, and I assure you, she was punished for it."

Something about the way he said "punished" made my skin crawl, but for right now, Bee was here, and she was fine, and she was smiling at me, and I didn't care what the Ephors wanted, so long as she was here.

But then I remembered what he had said, about how if I died during the trials, they'd made "provisions."

The night of Cotillion, David had transformed all the other girls into Paladins, too. He'd undone the spell on everyone else, but Blythe had taken Bee before then. Which meant that Bee—

"Miss Franklin is a Paladin as well," Alexander said, finishing my thought for me. "She's been with us, training, being very well cared for, as you can see." He gestured to Bee, and I had to admit, she didn't look terrible. Her cheeks were full, her skin was as clear and bright as it had always been, and while there was something in her eyes that I couldn't quite name, she seemed . . . fine.

"Should you fail in the trials, Miss Franklin will be here to take your place as the Oracle's Paladin." He lifted his shoulders. "Easy as can be."

It didn't sound all that easy to me. In fact, it sounded like a lot of BS. There were no Paladin powers racing through me, so I figured the prickling at the back of my neck was good old-fashioned anger.

"So you're using my best friend as my understudy in case I get killed?" I said.

Alexander sat back behind his desk, taking a sip of his tea. "When you put it that way, it sounds a great deal more mercenary than it actually is. We simply want to . . . hedge our bets, let us say." He nodded at Bee. "And Miss Franklin has been very well prepared for this."

When I turned back to Bee, she was looking at Alexander, but her gaze slid to me. She tried to smile, but it was shaky and I reached out to hold both her hands in mine.

"They did tell me about all this," she said, taking a deep breath. "That's why they took me, so that they'd have a . . . a spare, I guess."

"You're no one's spare," I told her, squeezing her hands. Relief and anger warred inside of me, along with a fair amount of confusion. I was so happy to have Bee back, but the last thing I'd ever wanted was for her to get involved in this, too. Bad enough that Ryan had been dragged in, but—

Suddenly David was at my side, taking my hand from Bee's. "What the—" I started, but he only shook his head, pressing his palm to Bee's. I saw his brow wrinkle in confusion, and he glanced over her shoulder at Alexander.

"That mind-reading trick. Why won't it work on her?"

Alexander lifted both eyebrows. "Oh, did I not mention? Once the Paladin begins the Peirasmos, the Oracle is stripped of her—well, *his*, in this case—powers. Can't have you looking into the future to help Miss Price face her trials."

David's hands clenched into fists. "You can't do that," he said, but Alexander only shrugged.

"I already have."

"And I didn't begin anything," I argued, dropping Bee's hands. I noticed Ryan moving a little closer to her as David and I approached Alexander's desk.

"You said that I have to do these things or die. It's not like there was a starter pistol or a ready-set-go that happened, so how—"

"They began the moment I summoned David," Alexander interrupted, giving me a smile that showed too many teeth for my liking. "Congratulations."

"No," I said, shaking my head. "No, you don't get to come here and tell us what to do. We were getting along fine without you."

"Were you?" Alexander rolled his eyes up toward the ceiling as though he were thinking something over. "David was squandering his godlike power while the two of you scrambled to keep the people in your lives from figuring out what had happened to you. You threw up wards around your town to keep people from remembering what happened the night Blythe performed the ritual. You acted like children, hoping pebbles would hold back the sea. And Miss Franklin," he finished, inclining his head toward Bee, "was missing—for all you knew, never coming back. And now we have come to help you."

He kept saying "we," but the house was empty except for him, as far as I knew. But then, as far as I knew, there hadn't even *been* a house here a few weeks ago.

I didn't like it. No, more than that, I hated it. Saylor would have known what to do here. The weirdest thing was that parts of it sounded okay. It sounded *right*. And there was Bee.

"I understand why you hesitate to trust us, Miss Price, I honestly do," Alexander said. "But right now, we are all you have. And believe me when I say we need you as desperately as you need us."

"What for?" David asked, but Alexander only shook his head.

"All in good time. Now, Miss Price, the Peirasmos began as of midnight tonight. There are three trials you will undergo before the end of this moon cycle. The trials may be physical in nature, or perhaps tests of the mind, of your spirit. You will not know when they are coming, and you will not receive any assistance. To do so violates the laws of the Peirasmos, and would be considered a failure of the tests. At the end of the trials, you will be stronger, quicker, better at being a Paladin, and Miss Franklin"—another nod at Bee—"will lose her own Paladin powers and return to life as before. Have I made myself clear?"

"As mud," I muttered, and he frowned again.

"Pardon?"

Waving that off, I took a deep breath. "I get it. I do these trial things, I get better powers, I *don't* die, and Bee gets to be de-Paladined." I looked back at Bee, still standing in the doorway. "Is that what you want?"

She didn't even hesitate, her head bobbing up and down quickly. "Yes. God. Like . . . a lot."

That was it, then. It's not like I'd ever had much of a choice in this thing—"do this or die" is not a choice, let's be real—but seeing the relief on Bee's face was enough to make me feel a little better about all of this. Go through these trials, get even more powerful, *don't* get killed, and Bee gets to be happy? That seemed worthwhile to me.

But that wasn't the only reason I found myself turning back to Alexander and saying, "I guess I'm in." It was that something twisting in my stomach, and I knew it was part nervousness, but more than that, it was a little bit . . . excitement. Look, I'm not saying I didn't feel terrible about this—after all, it was probably going to mean more lying, and definitely more danger, but for the past few months, I'd felt like I was in this weird stasis, waiting for something to happen. And now here it was.

And here was *Bee*.

I took her hand and started pulling her toward Alexander's office door, even as David said, "So that's it? We're leaving?"

"We need to get Bee home," I said. "And I think we've heard everything Alexander has to say." Flipping my hair over my shoulder, I looked at the Ephor with raised eyebrows. "Unless there's some other horrible thing you'd like to dump on us tonight?"

To my surprise, he replied, "No, I'm finished for now."

At least he didn't try to argue that this had not been horrible. That was something.

The four of us made our way back down the hall, me and Bee in front, the boys trailing behind. We weren't even halfway to the front door when David said, "So where did they have you?"

Next to me, Bee twisted to glance back at him. "Here," she said. "But . . . it's like it wasn't here. It was this house, but not in this place."

"But this is the house that was originally here," David said, walking a little faster so that he was right behind us, the toes of his sneakers nearly catching the back of my heels. "He . . . magicked it up or whatever. Are you sure it wasn't here?"

Bee's fingers were clammy in mine when she answered, "I never went outside, but I don't think it was here. Or maybe it wasn't this house." Stopping, she pressed her fingers to her forehead. "It was just a bunch of rooms, like a hotel. I never saw anyone but Alexander, but there was food, and all these books about Paladins and Oracles and—"

"What did the books say?" David asked, and that was enough for me. I stopped in front of the door, my hand already on the crystal knob.

"Okay, look. This has been a weird night. Bee has had a weird few months. Ease up on the third degree, please?"

David's blue eyes fixed on mine, his fingers flexing at his side. "We need to know this stuff, Pres."

Ryan's hand came down on David's shoulder. It was a friendly enough gesture, but it was firm, too. Unlike me, Ryan *could* be firm with David.

"Harper's right," he said. "We can talk about all this later, but for now, let's get Bee home."

"Home," she mumbled, following me out onto the porch in a kind of daze. "God, what do my parents think happened to me?" When she turned to look at me, her eyes were so big that I could see the whites all the way around her irises. "Are they okay? Are the police looking for me?" Her grip tightened on my arm. "Have I been on one of those true-crime TV shows?"

"No," I told her, covering her hand with mine. "No, everyone thinks you were at cheerleading camp. Ryan did a spell." I stopped suddenly, pulling Bee up short. "I . . . should probably explain that."

But Bee shook her head. "No, Ryan's a Mage and does magic. Alexander told me when I was . . . wherever I was." She frowned slightly, tugging her hand from mine and hugging herself. "But I have to be honest, I still don't totally get . . . any of this."

"We'll explain in the car," I told her.

So we did. The entire ride back into town, the three of us took turns explaining how all this had come about, starting with that first night in the school bathroom, ending at the frat party tonight.

By the time we were done, we were at my house, and the car was very quiet except for Bee's breathing.

"That's . . . a lot," she said at last, and all three of us muttered, "Yeah," in unison.

Her fingers were twisted tight in the hem of her black T-shirt as she lifted her eyes to me and said, "Do you think it would be okay if I slept over at your house tonight? I'm not sure I'm ready to deal with my parents yet. Especially since they didn't even miss me."

That would be weird, I realized, and I nodded quickly. "Of course you can, no problem."

David shook his head. "We need to keep talking about this,"

he said, drumming his fingers on the steering wheel. "About what they told Bee, and about how we can prepare for the Peirasmos, and about what the heck *I'm* supposed to do without any powers, and—"

I cut him off with a palm laid flat across his mouth. "Tomorrow," I told him. "Or the next day. For now, let me help Bee. Everything else will wait."

David mumbled something behind my hand, and I rolled my eyes.

"She's right," Ryan said from the back, leaning forward and bracing both his hands on the headrest of my seat. "It's late, we've had a lot to process, and Harper and Bee should have some time to themselves."

With that, he lifted one hand to slap the back of David's seat. "Don't try to come between these two, man, trust me," he said, his voice light and jovial even though I was guessing he didn't feel it. I'd known Ryan long enough to know that tightness in his voice when he was worried about something.

But thankfully David nodded. "Okay. Yeah, you're right, nothing we can do right now. We'll talk later."

With that, he leaned over like he was going to kiss me, only to pause, his eyes flicking toward the backseat.

Scoffing, I reached out and grabbed his face with both hands, planting a quick but firm kiss on his lips. I didn't like PDA, but Ryan and Bee weren't the public, and it wasn't like they didn't know we were dating.

Oh. Wait.

It wasn't like *Ryan* didn't know we were dating.

I looked back at Bee, who was watching me with her mouth slightly open. "Um. That is . . . another thing we should've mentioned," I said, a little meekly, but Bee was already reaching for the door handle.

"One trauma at a time, please."

David winced at that, but it made me feel better to hear a little of the old Bee in her voice. I gave him another quick kiss, this one on the cheek, and then stepped out of the car to stand next to Bee at the edge of my driveway.

Bee watched Ryan and David drive off into the night, and stepped close to me, our arms brushing. "Your life got weird," she said after a long pause, and I thought of Alexander, of everything that might be coming.

"And getting weirder."

Chapter 7

BEE WAS GONE when I woke up in the morning. A note left on my dresser said she'd walked home. Since her house was only a couple of blocks from mine, it wasn't all that weird, but I still wished she'd hung around a little longer. It was like I needed to convince myself that she was okay. But I reminded myself that she definitely needed some Parental Time, and probably wanted to sleep in her own bed.

Mom was already up and making breakfast when I went downstairs, which was surprising. It was Sunday, which meant we went to the earlier church service, then out for breakfast afterward.

"Eggs?" she asked, gesturing to the pan on the stove.

The sight of them made me a little queasy; I'd never been a big breakfast person. So I shook my head and grabbed an apple from the fruit bowl on the counter. "No, thanks."

Maybe it was my imagination, but I could have sworn Mom looked a little disappointed. Tucking her hair—dark like mine, but cut shorter—behind her ear, she turned back to the stove. "Okay. I could also make bacon? Ooh!" She set the spatula down on the trivet I'd made her at summer camp years ago. It was supposed to look like a frog, but something had happened in the kiln to turn it into more of a dark green amoeba. "How about pancakes?"

I glanced at the clock, then back at Mom, still in her robe. "Don't we have church?"

She gave a little shrug, turning back to the stove. "I thought we might skip this Sunday. Spend some family time."

With that, Mom turned back to the stove. The eggs had started to smoke a little, and she heaved a sigh as she scraped them around the skillet.

I frowned. Bad enough that things were weird with David right now. I wasn't sure I could handle family problems on top of that. Maybe Mom wanted us to hang out because she needed to tell me she and Dad were separating, or she was sick, or . . .

I stood up, putting the apple back in the bowl. "Mom, is everything all right?"

She glanced over her shoulder at me. "As far as I know. Why?

The eggs were completely burned now, and Mom made a faint "tsking" sound as she moved the pan off the eye of the stove. My mom was traditional in so many ways—in the Junior League, taught Sunday school, wore makeup even if she was just staying home all day—but she was not the best cook.

"You never skip church," I told her. "Or make breakfast. Or get up this early. So I thought maybe something was up."

Mom dumped the eggs in the trash and put the pan in the sink. "It just seems like I never see you." She crossed her arms, the delicate gold bracelet around her wrist flashing. It had belonged to my sister, and Mom had worn it ever since Leigh-Anne had died two years ago.

When I didn't answer, Mom gave a rueful smile. "I guess missing you is to be expected with as busy as you are, but . . ." She trailed off, her eyes moving over my face. "I worry about you, sweetie."

I crossed in front of the island in the center of the kitchen. "There's nothing to worry about," I said. I thought I sounded pretty convincing, given that I was lying through my teeth. I'd gotten good at lying over the past few months. It wasn't something I was particularly proud of, but I didn't see a way around it. The fewer people I loved who knew about Paladins and Oracles and Ephors and all the other crazy stuff that had taken over my life, the safer they'd all be.

"You've gone through so many changes recently," Mom said, the corners of her mouth turning down.

You have no idea, I thought. What I said was, "Nothing major, though."

Mom's frown deepened. "'Nothing major'? Harper, you broke up with the boy you'd been in love with for years, you started dating a boy we all thought you'd *hated* for years, and you hardly ever spend any time with Bee." For a second, her eyes got slightly hazy, confusion wrinkling her brow. "Where is Bee, anyway? Didn't she go somewhere?"

"She's back," I told her, not having to fake the brightness in my voice. "Remember, she was at cheerleading camp? She got back last night, actually."

Some of the wrinkles around Mom's brow eased. "Oh. Well, that's nice. But Bee aside, I'm still concerned about you and Ryan. You seem happy, but—"

I squeezed her fingers. "I am happy. And Ryan and I still hang out; we're friends. We just don't date anymore."

After a moment, Mom squeezed back. "Okay. But you promise everything is all right?" Smiling, she brushed my hair back from my forehead with her free hand. "You're not going to suddenly dye your hair blue or start piercing things, are you?"

I shook my head with a little shudder. "Okay, the very thought of that makes me want to vomit. No."

Mom laughed a little at that before wrapping me in a hug. "Well, there's the Harper Jane I know."

On Monday morning, I was heading out to my car when Bee's white Acura came roaring up to the curb. She sat behind the wheel, her curly blond hair a cloud around her bright, smiling face, music blaring on the radio.

I smiled back, but something about her grin bothered me. It seemed . . . fake. Still, I made my way out to the car. "You offering me a ride?"

"A ride and coffee!" Triumphantly, she held a Starbucks cup out the window, and I took it, still feeling uneasy. I barely slid into the passenger seat before she was pulling back into the street, her fingers drumming on the steering wheel.

"So did everything go okay with your parents?" I asked, holding the coffee tight to keep it from sloshing through the little hole in the lid as Bee took a corner a little too fast. I almost had to yell to be heard over the music.

"It was fine!" Bee said, and I wished she would take off her sunglasses so I could see her face. "I mean, weird. At first it was like they didn't even recognize me, or it was like they had just woken up or something." She gave a little shrug. "But then it was fine. Like you said, they think I've been at cheerleading camp this whole time."

We were almost to the school now—it wasn't very far from my house—and I put my coffee in the cup holder before reaching out to touch her arm gently. "You're sure you're okay?"

"Are you?" she asked, glancing over at me. I could see her brows rising over the tops of her aviators. "I'm not the one who could have super-dangerous challenges thrown at me at any moment. Although"—the corners of her mouth turned down— "I guess I will be if something happens to you."

"Nothing is going to happen to me," I said with a confidence I definitely did not feel. "I'll get through this, you can go back to being normal, and everything will be like it was before. Well, mostly."

Bee pulled into a parking spot and shut off the engine, turning to face me. She slid her glasses onto the top of her head and studied my face. "Nothing is ever going to be normal again, is it?" Then she frowned. "But it hasn't been normal for you in a long time."

Look, I definitely wasn't thrilled my best friend had been all magicked up, and was now my backup in case I got horribly killed during some supernatural trials. But I had to admit that Bee actually knowing what was going on, being able to talk to her about it and have her understand, felt good. One fewer person to lie to was always a nice thing as far as I was concerned.

"Don't worry about me," I said. "I've had months to get used to this kind of thing."

"That's what all the hanging out with Saylor was about, huh?" she asked, opening her car door. "The karate stuff?"

I nodded. "I'll tell you the whole story at lunch, promise."

We both stepped out of the car and into the bright spring morning. The smell of flowers hung in the air, and the grass sparkled with dew. It was a gorgeous day, and I took a deep breath, feeling a little better. On a morning like this, it seemed impossible to believe that anything bad could happen. I had my best friend back, a new pair of ballet flats on my feet, and a boyfriend heading toward me with a smile on his face and . . . what appeared to be bowling shoes on his feet.

"Where did you even get those?" I asked as he came up to stand beside me, and he held one foot out, turning his ankle.

"Salvation Army. They're cool, right?"

They *did* kind of match his shirt, which I guessed I should consider a win.

I turned to say something to Bee, but she was already heading off toward the school, shoulders held back.

Following my gaze, David nodded toward Bee. "She okay?"

I thought about Bee's bright smile, how fake it had seemed, and I gave an uneasy shrug. "She's not *not* okay, I guess," I finally settled on, and David nodded.

"Kind of the status quo around here."

I couldn't argue with that.

Bee wasn't in any of my classes that day, which wasn't a surprise since technically she wasn't registered for spring semester. Ryan had said he'd meet her at the main office to do the best he could, Mage-wise, to help out with that, but by the time lunch rolled around, I was getting a little worried about Bee. Stepping outside, I scanned the courtyard for her bright hair, but there was no sign of her. Ryan was out there, though, already sitting at one of the picnic tables with Mary Beth and the twins, but there was no sign of Brandon, Ryan's best friend and Bee's boyfriend.

Catching Ryan's eye, I mouthed, "Bee?"

He gave me a thumbs-up, then a little wave, inviting me to sit at his table. Mary Beth glanced behind her, and while she didn't, like, hiss or anything, I could see her eyes narrow. So, yeah, sitting with them was out.

I thought about going back into the building to look for Bee, but she was a big girl, and if she wanted to handle this on her own, I needed to respect that.

Taking a deep breath, I glanced around the courtyard again, and saw David waving to me, so I joined him and his friends from the newspaper, Michael and Chie. The three of them were sitting underneath the big oak tree on the edge of the courtyard, and when I walked over, David jumped up to pull a jacket out of his bag for me to sit on.

"Thanks," I told him, arranging myself on his tweed. Chie and Michael, who'd been laughing when I came over, now sat in silence, paying a lot of attention to their lunch.

Apparently I wasn't going to escape weirdness no matter where I sat.

"I like your necklace, Chie," I said, figuring flattery was always a good tactic. And seeing as how she was wearing a battered army jacket, an oversized black T-shirt, and a pair of leggings that I was pretty sure violated dress code, the necklace was about the only thing I *could* compliment.

But as Chie's fingers trailed over the gold chain, her dark eyes regarded me suspiciously. "I got it at Walmart," she said, almost like a challenge.

I nodded. "They have pretty stuff. Sometimes."

David shot me a look that was part exasperation, part amusement, and I gave a little shrug in response. I was all for making an effort to be nice, but I wasn't going to gush over Walmart. Come on, now.

After clearing his throat, David pulled an apple out of his bag, tossing it back and forth between his hands. "We were talking about what story the newspaper should tackle next." He nodded at his friends. "Chie has this great idea about how few people in Pine Grove actually recycle, and then Michael wanted to investigate allegations that the cafeteria is still using foods with MSG even after the school board told them they couldn't."

I took a long swallow of Diet Coke, hoping that would give me time to think of some reply. In the end, all I came up with was "Okay."

Chie flicked her bangs out of her eyes. She wasn't exactly glaring at me, but I was clearly not her favorite person right now. "What, you don't think those are valid stories?"

Next to her, Michael tugged his sleeves over his hands, his right foot jiggling. He was taller and skinnier than David, something that hardly seemed possible, and his dark hair was thick and shaggy, lying over his collar. In the few months I'd been working in the newspaper room, I wasn't sure he'd said more than a dozen words to me. I got the sense that I might have scared him a bit.

"It's not that," I said to Chie, tucking my hair behind my ears. "But . . . both of those stories seem depressing."

And boring, I thought.

David frowned and drew his knees up to his chest, circling them with his arms. "The news isn't always cheerful, Pres."

"I get that, but . . ." I looked around at the three of them, all regarding me seriously. "This is a tiny school paper read by a few hundred kids. If that. Gotta be honest, when y'all hand those things out, most of them end up in the trash can. Or the recycling bin," I hastily added when Chie's shoulders went up. "But my point is, maybe more people would read *The Grove News* if it were, like, cheerier. Funnier. When the SGA was doing a newsletter—"

"Maybe we should print it on pink paper," Chie muttered under her breath, and David sat up straighter.

"Hey," he said as he pushed his glasses up with one finger. "Harper is a member of our staff now, and she might have a point."

Michael nodded but Chie rolled her eyes and stood up. "David, please. She's on the staff because, for some reason none of us understand, she's your girlfriend. So sorry if I don't exactly feel like taking advice from her." Leaning down, she scooped up her bag and jerked her head at Michael. "Let's go, Mike," she said. "We can let our fearless leader and his first lady debate the principles of journalism without us."

Michael's blue eyes darted back and forth between me and David still sitting on the ground and Chie looming over him. Eventually, he gave a mumbled "Sorry," and the two of them walked back toward the building.

David and I watched them go.

"I'm sorry," I said at last, picking an imaginary piece of lint off my skirt. "I shouldn't have said anything. I mean, she's right. I'm only on the paper to be closer to you."

But David shook his head, his gaze still on his friends. "No, you have every right to an opinion. They shouldn't have been jerks."

Over at their table, Mary Beth and Ryan were laughing. As we watched, she rested her head on his shoulder and he slung an arm around her neck, pulling her in to kiss the top of her head.

"Get a room!" I heard Amanda cry as she tossed a napkin at them.

"It's not like my friends would be that much nicer to you," I reminded David.

The wind was blowing softly through the leaves over our head, and I remembered earlier this morning, thinking what a pretty day this was. It was still gorgeous, but I had to admit, my mood was not nearly as sunny.

Then the toe of David's ugly shoe nudged my thigh. I glanced up and David leaned closer. "Our forbidden passion has transgressed social boundaries, and now we pay the price," he intoned with a somber nod, and I giggled, batting his foot away.

"Shut up."

But David only released his knees and wrapped his arms around me, pulling me sideways. "We shall be shunned!" he continued, squeezing me tight. "Driven from the lands of our birth, forced to wander the wilds—"

I was laughing now, even as I reached down to keep my skirt from riding up my thighs. "You are insane," I informed David, twisting in his embrace.

He grinned at me, and in that moment, there was no gold in his eyes, no feeling of danger. No prophecies or powers or magic. Just us, laughing under a tree in the courtyard.

My laughter faded and I reached up to push a lock of hair off his forehead. "I like you kind of a lot," I said quietly, and David's arms tightened around me.

"You're not so bad yourself, Pres," he said, and I wondered when the nickname that used to annoy me so much had started sounding so sweet.

I was still pretty firmly anti-PDA, but when David kissed me—quickly, but firmly—I decided that every once in a while, it wasn't so bad.

I was still smiling when I saw Brandon come out the front door, Bee right behind him. "Oh, there she is," I said, standing up. I walked quickly toward the sidewalk where they were standing, and only then did I realize how pale Bee had gone, how big her eyes were.

And Brandon was staring at her in obvious confusion.

"Brandon, it's *me*," she said. "Why didn't you wait when I called you?"

He flicked his hair out of his eyes, shifting his weight uncomfortably. "Um, because I don't know who you are?"

Chapter 8

BRANDON WAS BLINKING at Bee, his handsome face scrunched up in a puzzled frown, one hand running over the back of his neck. "I mean, you're pretty hot," he said with a shrug, "so I'd think I'd remember you, but . . . yeah, not ringing any bells."

David had jogged up beside me, and I could hear him blow out a long breath. "Crap," he muttered.

People were starting to stare. There was a group of freshman girls sitting at a nearby stone table, clearly paying a lot of attention to what was going on right now. All three had dark, shiny hair, and I watched one lick yogurt off her spoon before leaning in to whisper something to her friend.

Taking Bee's elbow, I tried to draw her back from Brandon a little bit. "It's okay," I said in a low voice, but she looked at me and shook her head.

"It's not okay, Harper. Mrs. Carter in English didn't recognize me either. That didn't seem like such a big deal, but then on the way to lunch, Lucy McCarroll stopped to welcome me to Grove Academy." She reached out, wrapping her fingers around my wrists, her grip tight enough to hurt. "It's like I never existed." Her voice wavered on the last word, and there was real panic in her eyes. I stood there, helpless, and wondered where the heck Ryan was. This was *his* spell, after all. Maybe there was something he could do, some way to—

"Be a real shame if a girl as fine as you didn't exist," Brandon practically leered, and Bee whirled on him.

"God, shut *up*, Brandon!" She was scared and hurt and frustrated, and I think she only meant to swat at Brandon's shoulder, like she'd done a thousand times before. Trouble was, all those other times?

She wasn't a Paladin.

Her hand connected with Brandon's collarbone, and he went flying backward, tripping over his backpack and landing hard on the grass with a startled yell.

"Brandon!" she cried as I squawked, "Bee!"

If only a handful of people had been watching this scene play out before, I was now pretty sure that every single person in the courtyard was paying rapt attention to what had just happened. I could hear voices not even bothering to whisper. One very loudly asked, "Who *is* that girl?" and Bee visibly shuddered.

David stepped forward, offering a hand to Brandon, who shook it off with an irritated glare before rising to his feet. "What the hell, crazy chick?" he asked Bee, who could only shake her head, and stammer, "I—I didn't mean to."

"Whatever," Brandon said with a dismissive wave of his hand. He was a good-looking guy, all blond hair and cutest-boy-on-the-basketball-team face, but in that moment, his expression was one of the ugliest things I'd ever seen. He brushed past Bee without a word, and when she took a step after him, I pulled her up short.

"Wait," I told her. "We can . . . We'll talk to Ryan, and—"

Luckily, Ryan was already walking over to us, Mary Beth trailing in his wake. "What's going on?" he asked.

"It's your sp—" I started, only to stop when I realized Mary Beth was right there. "Your *spectacularly* dumb friend upsetting Bee," I covered as quickly as I could, then jerked my head toward the building. "Can we go inside and talk for a minute? All of us?"

"About what?" Mary Beth asked, and I practically groaned. I was getting used to the idea of her and Ryan together, but that didn't mean I liked having to factor her into things like this. Right now, my main priority was getting Bee out of the courtyard and somewhere private. Tears were leaking down her cheeks, carrying a fair amount of her mascara with them, and I didn't like the way that table of freshman girls was still watching her.

I nearly had to go up on tiptoes to wrap my arm around Bee's shoulder, but I did it anyway, tugging her close. "It's nothing," I told Mary Beth, then flicked my gaze up at Ryan. "Can we?"

With that, I started pulling Bee toward Nash Hall. Maybe it wasn't nice to let Ryan deal with getting rid of Mary Beth on his own, but that wasn't my problem.

As we walked back into the school, a blast of air-conditioning washed over us, making Bee shiver, and I chafed my hand up and down her arm. "It's okay," I said again. It was becoming my mantra, no matter how untrue it was. Bee only sniffled in response.

"The newspaper room," David said from behind us, and I started steering Bee that way. We were still getting a few confused looks, and I wondered if that was from Bee crying, or from no one remembering who she was.

I was going to *throttle* Ryan. Okay, so maybe it wasn't entirely his fault, and the spell was bigger than he'd thought, but I needed someone to be mad at, and he'd do.

Michael and Chie were in the newspaper room, but when David asked if we could have a second, they cleared out. Chie glared at me as she picked up her bag, but I ignored that. I had bigger things to worry about right now than one of my boyfriend's besties being hostile all the time.

Bee was still shaky when she sat down in one of the rolling chairs at the back counter, and David watched her with a slight frown, taking a seat on top of a desk. I went over to sit by Bee as Ryan walked into the room, closing the door behind him. He leaned against it, arms folded over his chest, the sleeves of his T-shirt tight over his biceps.

"Is there anything you can do?" Bee asked, raising her head to look at Ryan. She wasn't crying, but she was still kind of sniffly, and I got up to go get the box of tissues on Mrs. Laurent's desk.

I handed it to Bee as Ryan sighed and said, "I don't know. This Mage stuff . . ." Trailing off, he opened and closed his hands. "It's like I know how to use it, but it's all instinct or something. Not real knowledge. I can do spells, but undoing them, or fixing them when they get screwed up?"

Reaching up, he scrubbed a hand over his auburn hair. I wondered if that was a habit he was picking up from David. "That I'm not so sure about," he said.

Wiping her nose, Bee shook her head. "My parents remembered me. Not at first, but then after a minute or so, it was like I'd never been gone."

"Maybe that's because they're your parents," I suggested, leaning forward to rest my hand on her knee. Her skin felt clammy and cool. "You'd have a stronger bond with them than—"

"Than with my boyfriend?" she asked, her head jerking up. None of us said anything for a while, and the only sound was Bee's harsh breathing and the rattle of David jiggling his leg up and down on the desk seat.

Finally, Bee wadded up her tissue. "I thought once I was back, everything would be fine. That's all I thought the whole time I was with Alexander. That if I could get back home, this would all be over."

She looked at me then, and I felt a lump rise in my throat. "But it's not, is it? Hardly anyone can remember me, you're a superhero who has to go through these . . . these *things* that might kill you, and if you do die, not only will I have lost my best friend, but I'm stuck protecting *him*." Bee gestured toward David and then added, "No offense."

"None taken," he replied quietly. "Trust me, I'm used to being a pain in the ass."

"You're not," I said automatically, but even as I did, I was remembering how I'd felt when Saylor had told me that my sacred duty was to protect David. I'd told her that I didn't want to screw up my life to save someone else.

Once again, this helpless, choking feeling rose up in my

throat. I wanted to pass the Peirasmos because I didn't want to *die,* obviously, but looking at Bee, who, even though she was more than half a foot taller than me, looked so small and scared sitting in that chair, one knee drawn up under her chin, her eyes still red, I realized there was more than just *my* life at stake.

I hadn't been able to protect Bee the night of Cotillion, but if I managed to survive the Peirasmos, she would be free from all of this.

"We're going to get through this, Bee," I said, and her head shot up. She'd rubbed off most of the mascara with the tissue I'd handed her, but there were still dark flecks around her eyes, and her face was splotchy and damp.

"You can't promise that, Harper," she said, and then, as the bell signaling the end of lunch rang, she stood up, rolling the chair underneath the counter.

"I just . . . I thought you'd all know what you were doing," she said at last, and with that, she walked out of the room, leaving me, Ryan, and David in silence.

Chapter 9

"THAT IS RUDE, Harper Jane."

I glanced up guiltily, lowering my phone back into my lap. "Sorry, Aunt Jewel."

After school, I'd decided to run by The Aunts' house. Bee had gone home early, so I'd gotten David to drive me to my house to pick up my car. After everything in the newspaper room, I hadn't gotten a chance to talk to Bee again, and while I was worried about her, I thought maybe she needed a little space. Plus, I wasn't sure what to say. She was right that Ryan, David, and I hardly knew what we were doing, but it had still stung.

So off to The Aunts' I went. I hadn't done the best job being a good niece over the past few months, and as Mom always reminded me, The Aunts were the closest things to grandparents I had, so I needed to appreciate them.

And that meant that when I went to see them, I shouldn't be messing around on my phone. But I hadn't been able to resist poking around the internet a little bit to see if I could pick up any information on the Peirasmos, especially since The Aunts had been distracted by discussing whether or not Jell-O salad was still a thing you could take to a church potluck. Preparation was the key to any test, after all, and even if Alexander had said that the whole point was for me to be caught unaware, I didn't think that had to mean, you know, going in *completely* blind. But it wasn't like it mattered. Google seemed to think I might have some kind of stomach issue, but there was nothing on the internet about Peirasmos, the trials. I had been fixing to text David to see if he'd found anything in Saylor's books yet, but from the way Aunt Jewel was looking at me, that was no longer an option.

Aunt Jewel was only a year older than Aunt May and Aunt Martha, but she took her role as the eldest sister very seriously. She regarded me now through pink-rimmed glasses fastened on a sparkly chain around her neck. All three of The Aunts were decked out in pretty pastel sweaters, the pale green of Aunt Jewel's almost matching her eyes.

My purse was sitting beside my chair, and I slipped my phone into it.

"Oh, leave her be, Jewel," Aunt May said, not glancing up from her own cards. "The children today need their technology."

"That's true," Aunt Martha said, nodding. She'd been to the beauty shop that morning, obviously, since her steel-gray curls were tight against her head. "I read it in the *New York Times*. People Harper's age are actually in love with those fancy-schmancy phones of theirs. Activates the same chemicals in the brain." Sighing, she discarded a card. "I went to look at one of those phones at the Best Buy, but I couldn't make heads or tails of it."

"You can't make heads or tails out of your cordless phone, Martha," Aunt May said, picking up the card Aunt Martha had put down. All three had skin that still glowed despite their age, and green eyes like mine.

Before they could get into too much of a fuss, Aunt Jewel gave a little smile and said, "Well, I don't think it's her phone Harper is in love with, so much as the boy at the other end of it."

Aunt Martha gave a happy grin at that, tugging at the lace collar on her lavender sweater. "That Ryan sure is pretty."

Both Aunt Jewel and Aunt May gave identical sniffs of disgust. "They're broken up, silly," Aunt May informed Aunt Martha. "Have been for ages."

"Four months," I clarified, getting out of my chair to grab the pitcher of sweet tea on the kitchen counter. As I refilled The Aunts' glasses, I added, "Remember, Aunt Martha, I'm dating David Stark now."

Frowning, Aunt Martha set her cards down and picked up the pack of Virginia Slims by her elbow. "Oh. That's right. Saylor's boy."

I stiffened a little, hoping they wouldn't notice. Just like with Bee's disappearance, there was a spell keeping the people of Pine Grove from knowing what had really happened to Saylor Stark. Bee's spell had clearly held—maybe too well—but Ryan should probably shore up the one that made everyone think Saylor was just on an extended vacation.

Making a mental note to talk to him about it later, I set the pitcher back on the counter and took a seat at the table. I still wasn't allowed to play gin rummy with The Aunts—only once I was officially an adult, i.e., married, would I get invited to that table—but I liked to watch.

"And how are things with David?" Aunt Jewel asked. Her voice was light, but I saw how closely she was watching me. I loved Aunts May and Martha, but I was closest to Aunt Jewel. And while it wasn't like I'd told her anything that was going on with me, I always had the feeling she somehow knew there was more to me and David than met the eye.

But I smiled back and gave a little shrug. "They're good." I thought it would be easiest to leave it at that.

Aunt Jewel nodded, taking a sip of her tea. "Well, that's good to hear. I wondered, since you've looked a little out of sorts lately."

Aunt May and Aunt Martha made humming noises of agreement, and it was all I could do not to roll my eyes. "Just busy," I said. "Spring semester of your junior year is an important time. College applications, all of that."

That got all three of The Aunts' attention. "Ooh, what colleges are you looking at, honey?" Aunt May asked.

Relieved that we were on slightly safer ground, I launched into an account of the top schools on my list. They were mostly all here in the South, and I thought I'd chosen a pretty good mix of big state universities and smaller private colleges. Of course, they were all schools I'd picked out last year, and I felt a little twinge of guilt that I hadn't done more on the college front lately.

Of course, I'd been kind of busy.

Aunts May and Martha smiled pleasantly, but Aunt Jewel asked, "And David?"

When I didn't answer right away, she took one of Aunt Martha's cigarettes, lighting it with a hot pink Bic. "Are y'all looking at the same places? I know you haven't been together long, but it still seems like something you should talk about."

The College Issue was one of those things David and I had trouble talking about. Obviously, going to the same college was a nonnegotiable, and had nothing to do with us being a couple. I couldn't even go that far out of town alone without feeling an aching weight in my chest. But I was convinced we could find a place we both agreed on.

Unfortunately, David never wanted to talk about it, always shrugging and saying, "We'll cross that bridge when we come to it." Problem was, that bridge was rapidly approaching.

To Aunt Jewel, I said, "We're talking about it." And I certainly didn't add that my dream college was a women's school that was completely out of the question, and that no matter how hard I tried, I couldn't help but resent that the teensiest bit. Or that Ryan probably needed to be factored into the equation now.

Closing my eyes for a second, I took a deep breath. One thing at a time. First we'd deal with the Peirasmos, and then I could worry about how to negotiate The College Issue.

Thankfully, Aunt Martha changed the subject, asking if any of my friends were going to be in the upcoming Miss Pine Grove Pageant.

I laughed, leaning back in my seat. "Not that I know of. Most girls at the Grove aren't into that kind of thing." The pageant, which happened every May Day, was held in the town's big rec center, and despite the name, it was open to any girl in the surrounding few counties. As a result, Miss Pine Grove was usually from Appleton or Eversley rather than Pine Grove itself.

The Aunts thought the pageant was tacky and nearly had a collective stroke when my sister, Leigh-Anne, had decided to be in it several years ago.

They'd been even more horrified when she'd won.

So when I said that no one I knew had anything to do with it, I could practically feel them all sag with relief.

"Good girl," Aunt Martha said, just as Aunt May muttered, "Trashy," under her breath.

Aunt Jewel only took a drag on her cigarette and commented, "Oh, like you both don't have *Toddlers & Tiaras* saved on the TV box thingie."

"That is different," Aunt Martha said with a lift of her chin, and Aunt May agreed with a fervid "Very different."

On that note, I decided to head out. I still wanted to run by David's before I went home, so we could go through some of Saylor's books together. I'd thought about asking Bee what books she'd seen, but after today's incident, I thought it might be best to let that drop for a while.

But just as I went to go, my phone rang. Glancing at The Aunts, I shook my purse at them. "May I answer?"

"Go ahead, honey," Aunt May said with a wave, and I smiled, reaching into my bag. It was Ryan, which was kind of a surprise. He almost always texted if he needed to get in touch.

I had barely said hello when he broke in, his voice tight and breathless. "Harper, you need to get over here. *Now.*"

Chapter 10

I MADE IT OVER to Ryan's house in record time—one of the perks of being a Paladin is the ability to drive like a stunt person—and Ryan was already waiting outside the front door for me as I pulled up.

"What took you so long?" he asked, and I noticed that he was the palest I'd ever seen him, almost gray.

Slamming the car door behind me, I hurried up his front steps, nearly tripping over a rocking chair on the porch. "I came as fast as I could," I said, moving past him into the house. "What is it? Is it Alexander? Is it one of the trials?"

That's what I'd thought when Ryan first called, and it had been the scenario I'd spun out in my head on the short drive over. But Ryan seemed okay, if shaken up, and now he shook his head at me, waving a hand toward the front door.

"Upstairs," Ryan said, scrubbing a hand over his hair. "It's MB." Misery was etched in every line of his body, and my heart took a sudden plunge as I started up the staircase.

There was a part of me expecting to see Mary Beth lying on his floor with a scimitar through her stomach or something, so I was actually relieved to see her sitting on the edge of Ryan's bed, seemingly completely okay, if a little . . . spacey.

"Hi, Mary Beth," I said, already trying to formulate a reason for being at Ryan's house. He'd called me to work on a school project?

But she didn't reply. In fact, she didn't even seem to hear me.

I shot a glance at Ryan over my shoulder. He was leaning against the doorjamb, nearly crying, his hazel eyes red.

Kneeling down at the edge of Ryan's bed, I snapped my fingers in front of Mary Beth's face. Her eyes slowly blinked once, then twice, but other than that, there was no sign that she'd heard me. Groaning, I turned back to Ryan. "What the heck did you do?"

The last time I'd seen Ryan this miserable was when he'd missed a free throw at a game against our rivals, the Webb Spiders. Now, like then, he was fidgeting, his arms crossed tightly across his chest. "I don't know. She was still pissed about me ditching her at lunch, so I wanted to . . . fix it."

"Ryan," I groaned, and he held up both hands.

"I know, I know. Anyway, I used some of that lip balm stuff on her. That stuff Saylor had."

Now that he mentioned it, there was a distinct rose scent wafting up from Mary Beth. "You kissed her with it on?" I was pretty sure my eyebrows were in my hairline, and when Ryan looked down at me, he scowled.

"Well, yeah. She's my girlfriend. And that seemed the easiest way to . . . apply it."

Still crouching in front of her, I studied her face. "Maybe

she wasn't meant to ingest it," I mused. "How much did you put on?"

Ryan knelt down next to me, and while he wasn't quite wringing his hands, he was close. "Not a lot," he said, a dull flush creeping up his neck. "I mean, I'm a dude, it would look weird if I slathered my whole mouth in a bunch of rose lip gloss, you know?"

There was nothing funny about this situation, but I couldn't stop a brief smile. Seeing it, Ryan smiled, too, giving a nervous laugh. "I need to go through Saylor's things, see if there's anything else that works for mind control, since I can't keep carrying lip balm everywhere."

"Maybe there's something you could work into an aftershave?" I suggested. "Or that gross boy body spray they're always advertising?"

He sniffed, shoulders rising and falling. "I don't wear that crap," he reminded me, and I nodded.

"I know. Trust me, you wouldn't have lasted long as my boyfriend if you had."

That made Ryan smile again, and he looked over at me with squinted eyes. "What is it you call David? That word he hates?"

"Boyfie," I answered, and Ryan laughed.

"Yeah, *you* wouldn't have lasted long as my girlfriend if you'd said that." He was still smiling, just the littlest bit, but then he looked back at Mary Beth and all the humor left his face. "She'll be okay, right?"

I leaned in closer to Mary Beth. Her eyes met mine, and I could tell she was trying to focus. "Mary Beth?"

Another blink, but nothing else. Next to me, Ryan stood up, chafing his palms against his thighs. "Oh God," he groaned. "I've lobotomized her. I've lobotomized my girlfriend with a— an effing *potion*."

He didn't say "effing," but I didn't bother admonishing him. We were in F-word territory for sure.

Crossing the room in two long strides, Ryan moved to his desk and snatched up the little pot of lip balm. "Screw this stuff," he said, and before I could stop him, he'd opened the window and thrown it out as hard as he could.

Now I shot to my feet. "Ryan!" I said sharply. "So you screwed up using it once. That doesn't mean you won't use it again. And what if someone else finds it?" Moving to the window, I ducked my head out, even though I knew I wasn't going to be able to see it.

"I suck at this," Ryan moaned, dropping his head into his hands as he sat down heavily on the bed. "I screwed up the spell with Bee, and now I've screwed up with MB, too."

I don't think I'd ever heard Ryan admit to being bad at some-thing in his entire life. I wasn't sure he actually *had* been bad at anything in his entire life, now that I thought about it. Things had always come pretty easily to Ryan. It was one of the few things we'd had in common, and now, as I remembered how awful and confused I'd felt when I'd first learned I was a Paladin, I couldn't help but sympathize.

"Hey." My hand hovered over his shoulder as he slumped for-ward, elbows on his knees. Was I allowed to hug him? Even in a totally platonic, comforting way? I wasn't a hundred percent sure, so I did what seemed safest and patted his back a few times before clasping my hands in my lap. "You don't suck. You just don't know all the ropes yet."

Ryan dropped his hands from his face, swiveling his head to look at me. "Is this something where you can know the ropes, Harper? Because I'm pretty sure magic and potions and—and Oracles are always gonna be pretty effing confusing to me."

Considering the fact that I still had no idea when the Peirasmos was starting, that wasn't exactly something I could answer. Instead, I gave him another pat and said, "We'll all figure it out together."

Ryan seemed to sigh with his whole body, his hair ruffling with the long breath he blew out. "You say that all the time. 'We'll work it out.' 'Everything will be okay.'"

Stung, I dropped my hand from his back again. "We will. And it will be."

Ryan straightened, watching me over steepled fingers. "You've never been able to admit that you were in over your head."

I opened my mouth, but Ryan raised one hand. "No, I know you're going to say it isn't true, but it is, Harper. You know it. Only this time, it's not school dances and leadership committees and student government issues you're trying to balance. It's huge, life-or-death stuff, and you're still pretending it's another project. People are going to get hurt."

His gaze drifted to Mary Beth, slumped next to him. "People have *already* gotten hurt."

I moved over to Ryan's bookcase. It held a few sports biographies, but the shelves were mostly stacked with video games and a couple of picture frames. Once they'd held pictures of me and Ryan, but now he and Mary Beth smiled out at me from behind the glass. But in one picture frame, behind a photo of the two of them with their arms around each other on Mary Beth's parents' porch, I could make out a bright turquoise corner. That had been the backdrop for last year's Spring Fling. The theme had been Under the Sea. Ryan and I had gone together. Apparently, Ryan had shoved a picture of them on top of one of the two of us.

I fiddled with the frame now, half tempted to open it and see if I was right. "You think I don't know that?" I said at last, not looking at him. "Saylor Stark died the night of Cotillion. Bee was kidnapped. And now the Ephors suddenly want to be besties, and I'm apparently going to face some kind of trials, but I have no idea what they could be. And if I don't do them, we spend the rest of our lives trying not to get killed."

My voice broke on the last word, and from behind me, I heard Ryan sigh.

"I'm sorry, Harper," he said softly. And then he gave a little huff of laughter. "It's weird, my impulse is to hug you, but I don't know if that's something we can do anymore."

Turning around, I smiled and put the picture back on the shelf. "I know what you mean. But we should probably do without hugging."

Ryan was still wringing his hands in front of him, glancing over at Mary Beth. "It's gotta wear off eventually."

"I'm sure it will," I said, even though I wasn't exactly. Saylor had used that stuff a lot, but I'd never asked questions about how it worked. After she'd died, we'd handed all her various potions and elixirs over to Ryan without thinking. He'd inherited Saylor's skills, but that didn't necessarily mean he knew exactly how to use every little tool she'd had. Not for the first time, I wished that she were here.

Mary Beth's eyes started to flutter a little more, and Ryan was off the bed like a shot, kneeling in front of her. "MB?"

"My head," she slurred, her fingers going to her temple. Her dark red hair swung above her shoulders, and the freckles across the bridge of her nose stood out against her pale skin.

"You're okay," he said, cupping the back of her neck in one big hand. "You're fine." I wasn't sure if he was trying to use magic to convince her of that, or if he was just saying it in the normal, comforting boyfriend sense. In any case, Mary Beth didn't *look* fine. She was still blinking, her face flushed, her gaze muddled.

But it occurred to me that I might want to skedaddle before she came back fully and realized I was standing in her boyfriend's bedroom.

I didn't think that would go over particularly well, so I gave Ryan a little wave and mouthed, "Gonna go." He gave a distracted nod as I walked away.

Once I was outside, I took a minute to dig in the bushes around his house, trying to find the little pot of lip balm (and hoping no one saw me prowling around in Ryan Bradshaw's front garden). I finally felt it behind a camellia bush, and, pulling it out, rose to my feet. Ryan would definitely want the balm again, although maybe he'd be a little more careful with how much he used next time.

Chapter 11

"So, THE MALL?" I asked, starting my car. Bee sat in the passenger seat, her sunglasses on, elbow resting on the open window.

"Yup," she replied. "I need some normalcy."

Bee's second day back at school had been better than her first—fewer of the teachers seemed to think she was new, and Abi and Amanda had totally recognized her, which seemed to cheer her up. Brandon was still keeping his distance, though, and when I'd mentioned his name at lunch, Bee had cut me off with a shake of her head. "I don't want to talk about that."

After school, I'd planned on going home and doing a little more work on college stuff. That talk with The Aunts had reminded me that I'd been meaning to add at least two more schools to my application list. But then Bee had caught up with me and asked if we could have a "girls' afternoon," so here we were, heading toward the Pine Grove Galleria.

"Are you weirded out by Ryan and Mary Beth?" Bee suddenly asked, and I glanced over at her.

"Why would I be?" I asked, and she cut me a look.

"Okay," I acknowledged, turning right so that we could take

a shortcut through downtown, "it's a little weird, sure, but . . . not necessarily the bad kind of weird."

"Mary Beth hardly speaks to you." Bee twirled one long blond curl around her finger, still watching me, and I rolled my eyes.

"She barely spoke to me before except to be rude, so her dating Ryan isn't making much of a difference. And why does this bug you so much anyway?"

Bee shrugged, pulling up one leg so that she could wrap an arm around her knee. "Doesn't bug me. I'm just . . . curious. And an invested party, what with being your best friend and all."

That made me glance over at her. "Ryan, David, and I are all superheroes—as are you, I might add—and it's our romantic entanglements you wanna talk about?"

She laughed a little, more a huff of breath than a real chuckle. "I'm starting small."

"Are you sure things are—"

"They're fine, Harper," she said, and then shrugged, pulling her knee in tighter. "As fine as they're going to be, I guess."

I didn't know what to say to that, so instead of saying anything, I turned up the radio.

We were rounding the main square when Bee suddenly sat up in her seat, pointing to the statue of Adolphus Bridgeforth, one of Pine Grove's founders, that looked out over downtown. "Oh, man, someone vandalized poor Mr. Bridgeforth!"

I glanced over quickly, then did a double take, slamming on the brakes. Someone hadn't vandalized the statue. Someone had gouged marks into the stone around the base.

Wards. Right next to the other ones, the ones Saylor had put up to keep David safe.

My heart pounding, I turned the car so that we were heading toward Magnolia House.

"Harper?" Bee asked, twisting in her seat. "We're going the wrong way."

"Tiny detour," I promised.

Magnolia House, the huge mansion where Cotillion had been held, stood on a shady, oak-lined lane, but as we passed, I was able to see more marks on the wooden columns of the front porch. Another place where Saylor had her wards. They were still there, but now there were new ones next to them.

It had to be Alexander, or whoever he had working for him. But what did those wards do?

An hour or so later, I was the owner of two new pairs of shoes, a dress for Spring Fling, some new jeans, and a gorgeous Lilly Pulitzer skirt. Too bad none of that made me feel much better.

"You're making that face again," Bee said, nodding at me over a rack of cute rugby-striped shirts.

I shook my head, like that would somehow change my expression. I'd explained to Bee about the wards, but they were still on my mind. When Saylor had talked about the Ephors, I'd always pictured them in this more . . . administrative role, I guess. Guys in suits, pulling the strings, not guys with actual powers of their own. But Alexander had somehow managed to blow through the wards we'd put up, and now he was apparently setting up the Peirasmos all on his own. Were the new wards to help him, then? Or could wards, like, cancel one another out?

Adding to my irritation, I'd texted Ryan like five times about it, and had yet to get a reply. Funny how the one time I needed him to step up to the plate, he was missing in action.

"Lots on my mind," I told Bee.

She gave a sympathetic frown. "Nothing new on the trials?"

"Nothing," I said on a sigh. It had been a few days, and I knew we only had twenty-eight days—one full moon cycle, Alexander had said—to complete the Peirasmos, but other than Ryan's false alarm, nothing weird had happened at all.

Which felt weird in and of itself.

Now, I walked around the rack of clothes and looped my arm through Bee's, tugging her out of the store. "Come on. I have an angst only Cinnabon can cure."

When we got to the food court, Bee went off in search of drinks while I grabbed us a couple of cinnamon rolls.

By the time I got back, Bee was already at a table near the carousel, two Diet Cokes in front of her, and she pushed mine toward me as I sat down, along with a pale pink flyer.

"Look what I found!"

I took the flyer from her, raising my eyebrows. "The Miss Pine Grove Pageant?"

Bee took a sip of her drink and nodded. "We should do it."

Blinking, I chewed on the end of my straw and tried to think of the best way to answer that. A group of girls I recognized from school walked by, their arms laden down with bags, and Bee watched them pass with a wistful expression on her face.

But then she shook her head quickly, and turned back to the flyer, tapping it with one manicured nail. "Look at the date."

I did. "May first?" I read, and Bee nodded. "Last day of this moon cycle. Didn't Alexander say that the trials would take up one full moon cycle?"

He had, but all that had meant to me was that we had a nice timeline—almost a month. I hadn't considered what might be happening on any of those days.

"The Ephors are big drama queens, right?" Bee said, still looking at the flyer. "Look at what happened on the night of Cotillion." When she lifted her head, her eyes were brighter than I'd seen them in a long time. "The trials are going to be connected to *you*, which makes me think they'll be at school, or involve the town somehow. Stuff like that since that's, like, your whole wheelhouse."

Bee definitely had a point, and I wasn't sure what bugged me more: the idea of something big going down in front of my whole town again, or that she had had that idea and I hadn't.

When I didn't say anything, Bee gave a little shrug. "And, hey, if I'm wrong, it'll still be something kind of fun we did to-gether. Something normal."

I couldn't help but snort at that. "Okay, Bee, I love you, but the Miss Pine Grove Pageant is far from normal. There is noth-ing normal about parading around in bathing suits and high heels." I didn't add that when my sister, Leigh-Anne, had done the pageant years ago, my parents had practically had a stroke over it. I didn't even want to think how they'd react to *me* want-ing to do it.

Flashing me a look, Bee stirred her drink. "Oh, come on. It'll be fun. And it's not that much different from Cotillion."

It was worlds away from Cotillion, and I started to say that, but then Bee stabbed at her drink and said, "And, hey, maybe more people will remember I exist if I have a big honking tiara on my head."

She was joking, but the words still cut pretty deep, and I chewed on the end of my straw, thinking. I couldn't blame Bee for wanting some normalcy in her life after all that had happened to her. Besides, if she was right that this was when the last trial would happen, best to be prepared.

"It might look good on a college application," I acknowledged. "Showing a broad interest in things."

Bee smiled, her teeth straight and white. "Is that a yes?"

I thought of how The Aunts would react to the sight of another one of their nieces parading around in a swimsuit at the rec center and shuddered. "Do you promise I won't have to sing?"

Bee beamed at me. "Of course not." Then a dimple popped up in her cheek as she narrowed her eyes and added, "Besides, you're supposed to have an actual talent for the talent competition, Harper, and no one could call *your* singing a 'talent.'"

I tossed a balled-up napkin at her. "Ha-ha."

"Sign-ups for this are next week," I told Bee, tapping the flyer. "So you prepare answers about world peace, and I'll brush up on my baton skills."

Bee took the paper and folded it up, putting it in her purse. "Good deal." She glanced up then, her face brightening. "Oh, look, it's Ryan!"

I turned in my chair and our eyes met across the food court. For a second I thought that maybe he hadn't gotten my texts, but then I saw the guilt flickering across his face. I could tell he wanted to bolt, but it wasn't like he could pretend he hadn't seen me.

"Be right back," I said to Bee, then I walked as quickly as I could to where Ryan stood. He already had his hands shoved in his pockets, so I knew what he was going to say before he said it.

Still, I tried. "Did you get my texts?"

"Harper—"

"There are new wards set up around town, and I don't know what the heck they do."

"Yeah, I put them up."

I don't think my jaw has ever literally dropped before now. "What do you mean *you* put them up?"

"Alexander asked me to. It's part of the thing," he said, waving one hand. "The . . . peripatetic . . . peri—"

"Peirasmos," I hissed back. "And what do they do, exactly?"

Ryan's shoulders rolled underneath his shirt. "They just make sure David stays here. Like how Saylor's wards kept other people out, these keep him in."

The hairs on the back of my neck stood up. "Why would Alexander want to do that?"

"I don't know," Ryan admitted. "He just said it had something to do with the trials, and—"

"So Alexander has been in touch with you, but not me? And you . . . didn't bother to tell me?"

"It was literally two days ago, Harper. I was going to tell you, I promise, but . . . look, Mary Beth is weird about me spending time with you, and I'm trying to respect that."

It was one of the biggest struggles of my life not to roll my eyes at him right that second, but I managed admirably.

"I understand," I said, "but I've spent the past few days jumping at shadows over this thing. If you know anything about Paladin stuff, you have got to tell me. Especially about stuff that could be dangerous to David."

Ryan heaved a sigh, shoving his hands in his back pockets. "I'm trying, Harper. I seriously am, but—"

"This isn't easy on any of us," I reminded him, but Ryan shook his head.

"No, it's not, but you have to admit, it's a little easier on you and David than it is on me."

I looked up at him. "How do you figure that? David's visions make him feel like his head is splitting open, I'm worried about him, worried about me, and you, and Bee—"

Ryan leaned closer. "Look, I didn't say it was a freaking cake-walk for y'all, but at least you have each other. When you get your weird"—he waved his hands in the air around me— "Paladin feelings or David gets one of his visions, you can tell each other. David knows exactly what's going on with you, and you know exactly what's going on with him. You don't have to lie, either of you."

On the other side of the food court, the carousel was starting up again, the sound of tinkly calliope music filling the air. A little girl was tugging her mother toward a purple painted horse, and as I glanced over at them, I caught a glimpse of two blond heads making their way through the crowd.

Abi and Amanda. *Shoot.*

Grabbing Ryan's elbow, I tugged him into the little hallway where the bathrooms and water fountains were. "I understand that this isn't easy for you," I said once we were out of sight. "It isn't easy for me, either, and if you'd like a list of all the reasons why, I could make that for you. With annotations."

Ryan flicked a glance at the ceiling that wasn't quite an eye roll, but it was pretty close. Still, I kept going, tightening my fingers in the crook of his elbow. "You can't not tell me things, Ry. This whole . . . thing. None of it will work if we're not honest with each other."

Ryan looked down at me, his auburn brows raised. "Really? You wanna play that card when we've been lying to David about his visions since day one?"

I shook my head. "That's different. That's for his own safety."

Ryan blew out a deep breath. "You can keep saying that, Harper, but we can't keep lying to him. This Alexander guy is already promising David he can help him, but he doesn't *need* help. He couldn't have strong visions because *we* kept him from having them."

He reached out and covered my hand still resting on his arm with his own, his fingers curling around mine and squeezing. "We have to tell David the truth."

"Tell David the truth about what?"

Chapter 12

MARY BETH stood there, arms folded, mouth pressed into a tight line. As much as I hated myself for it, the words "This is not what it looks like" actually came out of my mouth, and from the way Ryan's eyes practically turned into hazel lasers, I could tell that he hated me for saying it, too.

I won't get into the details of all that happened next. Have you ever seen teenagers fight embarrassingly in public? It basically went like that. There was yelling and tears and Ryan trying to hug her while she yelled things like, "Don't touch me!"

Honestly, I tried to leave, but they were both blocking the entrance to the hallway, so in the end, I just stood there by the water fountains, wanting to die of humiliation. I mean, people were looking at us. Lots of people. And if Mary Beth hadn't finally ripped off her necklace, thrown it at Ryan's feet, and stormed off, I think a mall cop would've shown up, and then I would have had no choice but to change my name and leave town—heck, leave *Alabama*—forever.

Ryan didn't try to follow her this time. I guess once someone has thrown jewelry at your face and hollered about forgetting you exist, you sort of figure that ship has sailed. Instead, he squatted down and picked up the necklace, then stayed there, the chain dangling from his fingers, thumbs pressed against his eyebrows.

Bee came around the corner, arms full of bags, her eyes widening when she saw Ryan crouched on the ground and me standing right behind him, worrying my thumbnail with my teeth. As soon as I realized what I was doing, I made a disgusted sound and dropped my hand, wiping it on my skirt. I must've picked that up from David; he was always doing stuff like that.

Raising her eyebrows at me, Bee jerked her head toward Ryan.

"Mary Beth" was all I said, and she nodded.

As if his new ex-girlfriend's name was some sort of magic word, Ryan stood up abruptly, dropping the necklace into his pocket. "Well, that's effing great," he said, scrubbing his hands over his face.

Of course, he didn't actually say "effing," but it didn't bother me.

Tentatively, I laid a hand on his shoulder. "At least you don't have to worry about lying to her anymore?" I offered. We were still standing in the cramped little hallway, my hip almost right against a water fountain, and beyond us, people were still milling through the food court. Of all the places to go through a breakup, it was definitely low on glamour.

Lifting his head, Ryan looked at me. I'd known him almost my whole life. He was the first boy I'd ever kissed. The first boy I'd done . . . other stuff with, too. But in that moment, his handsome face drawn tight, he could've been a stranger.

"Whatever," he said, the word flat and heavy all at once.

I winced like he'd slapped me. Okay, maybe I hadn't been all that sympathetic to his issues with Mary Beth, but honestly, how did he think it was going to turn out? David and I were all tangled up with him, and there was no getting out of that. I was sorry he was hurt, but if he hadn't gotten involved with her in the first place, then none of this would have happened.

I think I might have actually said some of that, and probably ruined any chances I had of Ryan and me ever being friends again, but luckily, Bee stepped forward. Putting the shopping bags down, she laid her hand on Ryan's arm.

"Hey," she said, her voice warm and sweet. "Would you mind giving me a ride home? Harper drove us here, and she has to run back up to the school."

I didn't, and for a second, I frowned at her, confused. And then she gave me a little nod.

"Sure," Ryan said, his voice still blank, and as he turned to go, Bee looked over her shoulder at me, mouthing, "I'll talk to him."

That was good. Bee and Ryan had always gotten along, and if anyone could bring him back around to Team Harper, it was Bee.

I watched them walk off, then gathered up the shopping bags Bee had left with me and trudged out to the parking lot.

To my surprise, David's car was parked outside my house, and when I came in, Mom glanced up from the couch.

"There you are. David's in your room. Said the two of you had some kind of school project to work on?"

"Oh, right," I said, hanging my purse on the coatrack by the door next to my dad's truly heinous University of Alabama jacket. "Totally forgot, I was out shopping with Bee."

"Hope my American Express isn't smoking," Mom joked, and I pulled a face behind her back. I had indulged in a fair amount of retail therapy today.

As I jogged up the stairs, Mom called, "Door open, please!" and I rolled my eyes even as I called back, "Yes, ma'am!"

My parents had gotten pretty lenient with me and Ryan, I guess because they'd had a long time to get used to him. But something about David had made them hypervigilant on the propriety front, which was ironic, seeing as how me and David weren't . . . doing those things yet. I mean, we wanted to, and it's not like the subject hadn't come up, but the timing had never been right, and now with the trials and the Ephors, I wasn't sure when exactly things would get all consummated.

Certainly not now while my parents were downstairs, though. Gross.

When I pushed open my door, David was sitting in my desk chair, spinning idly. He stopped when he saw me, holding up his phone.

"So apparently you and Ryan caused a scandal at the Pine Grove Galleria today?"

Groaning, I dropped to the end of my bed. "It's already on Facebook?"

"Yup." He was looking at me from over the rims of his glasses, eyebrows raised. It was a familiar expression, and I'd always thought it was cute, but today, I wasn't sure what it meant, exactly.

With an exaggerated wince, I leaned back and put my hands

over my face. "That is so embarrassing. Almost as embarrassing as your shirt."

I heard the chair creak and then felt something nudge my knees. When I lifted my hands, David was leaning over me, his hands braced on either side of my head. There was still some space between us, but if my parents had walked in right then, well, let's just say David probably wouldn't have been allowed in my room anymore.

I didn't care. I let my hand rest on the back of his neck as he nuzzled the underside of my jaw.

"I happen to like this shirt."

"You happen to like all sorts of ugly things," I reminded him, even as I closed my eyes and let him dot kisses along the side of my neck. "That shirt, your car, like ninety-nine percent of your shoe collection—hey!"

I broke off laughing and rubbing the spot he'd poked on my ribs. "No fair," I said, lifting my head to give him a quick kiss. "You know I can't poke you back."

Smiling, David eased off me and sat on the floor. I slid down, too, sitting next to him and linking our hands as we both leaned back against my bed.

"So you aren't mad or jealous or weird?"

"I'm always weird," he acknowledged with a twist of his lips. "But mad or jealous? Nah. What's Ryan got that I don't have? I mean other than height and fabulous hair and cheekbones carved from granite."

I laughed and shook my head, tugging at his hair. "I like this. Most of the time."

David's lips brushed mine, briefly again, and I know I said I wouldn't do anything with my parents right downstairs, but I'd be lying if I said, in that moment, I didn't want to.

There were times things with David were weird—and I don't mean the Oracle stuff. We'd spent all our lives arguing, so this sudden shift to coupledom had been a tough transition in some ways. But when it was only the two of us, hanging out alone, we almost felt normal.

He pulled back again, returning to his chair. "Anything else happen at the mall?"

"I might have figured out at least one of the trials," I told him, handing over the flyer. "Same date as the last night of the moon cycle. Seems like a possibility, at least."

David's eyes scanned the paper. "They do seem to like picking big events for maximum damage, don't they?" he murmured. He glanced up at me then, quirking an eyebrow. "Will you twirl a baton?" he asked. "Please promise me a baton will be involved. And, like, huge hair."

I swatted at him. "You know I despise pageants. But I'm doing this for the greater good. And, hey"—I shrugged—"maybe it will make me look even more well rounded on my college applications."

"Well, as long as that's the only reason," he said with a shudder, and a little sizzle of irritation buzzed through me.

"It's not like the pageant is that big of a deal," I told him. "And Bee wanted do it."

That wiped the smirk off his face. Brows drawing together,

he shifted so his elbows rested on his knees. "How is she? After the other day?"

I picked up one of the throw pillows from my bed, tugging at the embroidery. "She's . . . okay. Obviously still shaken up and trying to come to terms with all of this."

David nodded, then reached up to scratch his shoulder through his ugly T-shirt. "I'm sorry," he said.

I looked up, surprised. "What do you have to be sorry for?"

He frowned, clasping his hands in front of him. "If I didn't suck so much at being an Oracle, maybe I could've found her earlier, you know?"

I dropped my gaze from him, watching my fingers as they traced over the little flower on the pillow. Aunt Martha had made this for me. Or had it been Aunt May? One of them. And maybe if I stared hard enough at the stitches, David wouldn't see the guilt on my face. If I hadn't messed around with his visions, could he have seen Bee?

David sat back in my chair, and it creaked slightly. "And of course now, I'm completely useless."

There was a bitterness in his voice I hadn't heard in a long time, and I set the pillow back on my bed, getting up to go to him. "Hey," I said softly, brushing a hand over his jaw. The stubble there was rough against my fingers, and when David looked up, I moved my hand to the back of his neck. "Just because you can't see the future right now doesn't mean you're useless."

One corner of his mouth kicked up in a smile. Or a grimace. "I guess I could make a dirty joke about what uses you might have for me," he said, and I rolled my eyes, letting my hand drop away from his neck.

"What I *meant,*" I told him, going back to sit on the edge of my bed, "is that David Stark the person is worth a lot more to me than David Stark the Oracle."

Snorting, David crossed his feet at the ankle. "Yeah, well, David Stark the person just annoyed you. He didn't ruin your life."

There it was again, that bitterness I definitely didn't like. "Could you not say stuff like that?" I snapped. "I think I can decide who and what ruins my life."

Downstairs, I could hear pans rattling as Mom started dinner, and Dad's low voice talking on the phone. David glanced toward the door and heaved a sigh.

"I'm sorry, Pres," he said before standing up. "I'm embracing my inner emo, I guess."

I stood up, too, crossing the room to wrap my arms around his waist. "Well, that would explain the T-shirt."

He smiled then, a real smile, and after he kissed me, I said, "Why don't you stay for dinner? I don't like the thought of you in that big house alone."

David's expression didn't change, but I could feel his hands tighten on my waist. Then he shook his head and stepped back. "Thanks, but I'm not great company tonight. Besides, I have some stuff I need to work on for school."

I was going to ask what stuff exactly, but David was already picking up his bag and heading for the door. I walked him down, stopping so that he could say good night to my parents, and then followed him out to where his car was parked in the driveway. He opened the door and threw his satchel inside before turning back to me, that familiar wrinkle between his brows. "Sometimes I wonder what would happen if I just drove out of town, you know?"

His tone was casual, but something about those words made goose bumps break out all over my body. "You can't," I told him, my voice stiff. "I mean, right now, you literally can't since Alexander had Ryan put up all these wards, but—"

Shoving his hands in his pockets, David leaned forward a little. "What? Why?"

"I don't know," I confessed. "Apparently the one time Ryan decided to take the initiative, it potentially screwed us over."

With a groan, David tipped his head back. "It would be awesome," he said, "if people would stop doing things that affect me without, you know, asking how I might feel about those things."

I swallowed hard.

David tilted his head back down and gave me a steady look, his hands still in his pockets. For a moment, I thought my guilt must show clearly on my face.

But he didn't ask me anything about his visions. Instead, he studied me and asked, "If you could do it all over again, don't pretend that you never would have gone into the bathroom that night."

I blinked, thinking about Bee. About Saylor and the Cotillion and all the lying I'd done to my family.

Smiling as best as I could, I raised up on tiptoes and kissed him. "Of course I would have."

Chapter 13

"So THIS IS a thing that's happening?" David asked as he sat against the fence in my backyard.

Pulling my hair up into a high ponytail, I sighed around the rubber band in my mouth. "Yes," I mumbled. "And if you mock it, I'll never ask you to come back."

"No mocking," David replied, laying his arms on his upraised knees. His wrists looked bony underneath the cuffs of his (both ugly and seasonally inappropriate) plaid button-down. "You're going to train for whatever trials the Ephors may have coming your way by . . . spinning a baton? Because I was honestly kidding about that earlier."

Hair secured, I propped my hands on my hips. "It's not like I can practice dagger swinging or karate kicks in the backyard. But baton twirling is totally socially acceptable, and it lets me both work on my agility and wield what *could* be a weapon." I gave the baton a few experimental twirls, and David laughed.

"Your ability to multitask is truly extraordinary, Pres."

He looked back at the book he had spread open on the grass, and I tossed the baton up, catching it easily. "What are you reading?" I asked, and he raised his head, sunlight flashing off his glasses.

"Still looking through some of Saylor's books for stuff about the Peirasmos."

"Anything?" I asked, but he shook his head.

"Not yet. But Saylor had a *lot* of books."

I kept twirling, but watched him out of the corner of my eye. "And you? You feeling okay?"

"Sure," he said, the word clipped off and sharp in his mouth. He didn't look up at me, and something in my stomach twisted.

"David," I said, and he sighed, tapping his pen furiously against the page.

"It's just irritating, that's all. Being completely useless, power-wise. If I could just see something . . ." He broke off with a frustrated noise. "My visions might have been stupid before, but at least I could have them." Shaking his head, he leaned back against the fence. "No idea why everyone is working so hard to protect me when I'm not exactly worth much."

It was the second time he'd said something like that, and I still didn't like it. Part of that, I knew, was the guilt. But warding him had been for his own good, I thought again. To keep him safe and keep him . . . well, *him.*

But I'd tried to ignore how that was making David feel, especially when he was all alone in Saylor's house, with nothing but his own thoughts to keep him company. David was a smart guy, and ever since I'd known him, he'd had a bad tendency to overthink things. I knew he'd been sitting there at night, brooding over all of this.

Now, he tipped his head back and studied the sky, bright blue through the oak leaves overhead. "I'm trying to help by going through all these books, but nothing there is all that helpful, and I . . ." Trailing off, he pushed his hands under his glasses, scrubbing his face. "If something happens to you during all of this, Harper—"

I set the baton down and walked over to stand in front of him, catching his chin in my fingers and tilting his head up to look at me. "Nothing is going to," I told him. "We got through Cotillion, and we'll get through this, too."

David's eyes were nearly as blue as the sky above, and as they searched my face, I could tell he didn't believe me. But he dropped the subject, picking up the baton I'd laid down on the grass.

"I'm still having trouble wrapping my mind around you twirling this thing in a *pageant*," David said, idly toying with it as he stood up.

I took it from him with a skeptical frown. "It's a traditional choice," I admitted. "And my Paladin skills mean that I'm weirdly good with it."

David laughed at that. "Seriously? Thousands of years of knowledge and training have resulted in the ability to spin a baton?"

"Yup," I replied. "Check this out." With that, I tossed the baton from hand to hand, spinning it furiously as I did. The metal rod slid easily through my fingers, and I realized that in the right circumstances, this thing could actually be a pretty impressive weapon.

But I hoped that the right circumstances never occurred.

Braining someone with a baton was not on my agenda any time soon.

Tossing the baton high in the air, I added a backflip before coming down solidly on both feet and catching the baton with one hand. I used the other hand to give a little wave, and David looked at me with a grin.

"Okay, now you're showing off."

"Little bit," I admitted, glad that we were talking like normal people again. I tossed him the baton.

"Maybe you should start carrying one of these things," he mused as he inspected it.

He looked at the rubber end over the top of his glasses, squinting slightly, and I leaned over and smacked a kiss on his cheek. That was one of my favorite David faces.

"I'll stick with my dagger," I told him as he let the baton drop back on the grass.

He laughed. "I think the baton would be a little less conspicuous."

I shook my head. "No way. And then I'd have to join the marching band as a majorette to make up an excuse for carrying it around all the time." With a dramatic sigh, I tipped my head back to look at the sky. "And I've already had to join the paper and now I'm going to sign up for a pageant . . ."

David closed his notebook. "Admit that you kind of like the paper."

Wrinkling my nose, I shuddered. "No. It is a necessary evil."

But I couldn't stop smiling a little bit, and David pointed at me. "Aha! You do like it! In fact, you *love* the paper."

"Do not!" I insisted, but he was fully dedicated to teasing me now.

"You love the paper so much you're thinking of studying journalism at college instead of poli-sci."

"Ignoring you," I said in a singsong as I scooped my baton off the grass and started twirling it again.

David sat back down on the grass, wrapping his arms around his knees as he watched me. "It's too late. I know your secret heart."

Feeling better, I kept spinning the baton, tossing it and catching it, watching the sunlight glint off the silver. I was still practicing when the back gate opened and Bee walked inside, also dressed in a T-shirt and shorts.

"Have you come to mock with David?" I asked, and she shook her head, a few tendrils of hair coming loose from her own ponytail.

"I actually thought we should join forces on our talent. Do some kind of dual baton thing. Especially if I'm right about the pageant being one of the trials."

"That was Bee's idea?" When I glanced back, David was sitting up a little straighter, his eyebrows raised. "I thought you put that together, Pres."

Irritation bubbled up in me, which was probably stupid, since what did it matter whose idea it had been? But I didn't like the sharp, interested way David was looking at Bee. He was thinking . . . something. I wasn't sure what, but the wheels were clearly turning.

I shrugged, sweat rolling down my spine. The late afternoon

was getting warmer, and I was about to suggest going in when Bee held out one hand. "Here," she said, nodding toward the baton. "Let me try."

The baton was a little slick with my sweat—more from the warmth of the day than from any real effort—but I tossed it to her.

The baton turned end over end in the air, but before it had even completed one full rotation, Bee had launched into a forward handspring unlike anything I'd ever seen her do in cheerleading. Heck, Bee had been so bad at jumps that it was sort of a joke. She'd always said it was because she was too tall, but apparently that wasn't a problem anymore.

Bee was a blur of motion, and then the baton was in her hands before rising back into the sky. Another series of easy, effortless flips, and she caught it again, beaming at me triumphantly.

And then from the fence, I heard David breathe, "Holy crap. She's better than you."

Chapter 14

"Okay, well, let's not go that far," I joked, and Bee stepped up beside me, frowning at David.

"No, I'm not," she said, but David was already standing up, shaking his head.

"No, no, I didn't mean, like, *better* better," he said as he shoved his hands into his back pockets. "I just meant . . . you're good. It's one thing to know you're a Paladin, but it's another to see it in action, I guess."

David was still watching both of us, eyes bright behind his glasses. "What if . . ." He stopped, holding up both hands even though neither Bee nor I had said anything. "Hear me out," he added, and I knew that whatever was going to come next was not going to be something I'd like.

"Okay, so if Harper fails the Peirasmos, you become my Paladin, right?"

Bee shifted her weight, looking at David like he'd started speaking a foreign language. "Harper can't *fail* the trials," she said, and I noticed her fingers tightening around the baton. "She'll die."

"I know that," David said. "But is there any way she could maybe, I don't know, opt out? Let you take over?" He lifted his hands. "Not that I want *you* to die, obviously."

The words hit me square in the chest. "You don't want me to be your Paladin?" I asked, and David's gaze swung to me.

"Don't you get it?" he asked. "It's *perfect*." David was practically bouncing on the balls of his feet, his blue eyes bright when they looked over at me. "This is the solution to everything, Pres. *Bee* can be my Paladin, she can do this"—he waved one hand in the air—"Peirasmos thing, and we can just be us."

He was smiling so big, looking happier than I'd seen him look in a long time, and all I could do was stare at him, suddenly cold despite the warm afternoon.

"But . . . Bee doesn't want to do those things." I turned to her, pushing a stray strand of hair off my forehead. "You have powers, and that's awesome, but this is my problem. I'm not going to foist it off on you to make my life easier."

David blinked rapidly, like I'd smacked him in the face. "Pres," he said, shaking his head again, "we're not talking about making Bee do anything she can't do."

Now the cold was fading, and I felt something hot and angry rise up inside of me. "She was kidnapped," I said, gesturing toward Bee with my baton, "and she just got back, and you want her to go through something that might kill her?"

He frowned, eyes darting to Bee. She was still standing there, arms folded over her chest, watching the two of us. Even though we were talking about her, I had the sense that she wanted to stay out of this.

"Of course I don't, but I don't know why you're being so stubborn about this. If Bee can be my Paladin, that makes things less complicated for us."

"And totally screws up her life," I argued. "My life is already screwed up, so we might as well leave things the way they are."

Tugging at his hair, David tipped his head back to look at the sky. "Or maybe you *like* doing everything in the whole freaking world."

"Like?" My voice got louder. I wasn't shouting, not yet, but we were getting close. "No, I don't *like* having to do all of this, but that's the way it goes. Sorry that I won't throw my best friend away so you can have a regular girlfriend. Not that *you* could ever be a regular boyfriend, so what does it even matter?"

"Everything okay out here?"

I turned to see my dad sticking his head out the back door. His expression was fairly mild, but I saw the grip he had on the doorknob.

Taking a deep breath, I made myself smile. "Yup!" I called brightly. "Practicing for debate club!" I gave Dad a little wave, but he jerked his head, beckoning me over.

Hiding a sigh, I jogged away from David and Bee, up the porch steps and into the kitchen.

It was cooler in there, the air-conditioning nearly making me shiver. "Harper Jane, I know you're not in the debate club," Dad said as he walked over to the island.

I tried very hard not to fidget as he braced his hands on the counter and fixed me with a look, his eyes as green as mine. He was wearing a polo shirt and khaki shorts, plus there was a slight sunburn on his balding head, so I guessed golf had been on the agenda earlier.

"It's nothing," I told him with a little toss of my head. "Typical me-and-David stuff."

Dad frowned. "You never yelled at Ryan like that."

"Sure I did," I said, even though when I thought back, I realized that was a lie. "You just never heard me. And seriously, Dad, this is no big deal. Promise."

Another lie. I was furious, nearly shaking with anger at the idea that David wanted me to offer up Bee like some kind of Get Out of Paladin Life Free card. And if there was a part of me that didn't necessarily like giving up control, well . . . I could think about that later.

Now, I just smiled at Dad. "I'm going to head back out there now," I said. "I promise not to bean David with my baton. But if I do, luckily I know a good lawyer."

Dad rolled his eyes, but I could tell he was trying not to smile. "I'm a tax attorney, honey. You murder someone, that's on you."

I grinned back, then thought of Dr. DuPont, my shoe sticking out of his neck. What would my dad think if he knew I already *had* killed someone? That I was about to go through some kind of tests that might end with me killing more people? Or someone killing *me*?

When I went back outside, David and Bee were sitting near the fence, talking. As I approached, whatever conversation they'd been having died, and David nodded at the house.

"Is your dad going to kill me?" His thin shoulders hunched forward, one ankle crossed in front of the other.

"Not today," I said with a cheer I didn't feel.

David's eyes met mine, and I could tell there was more he wanted to say. This argument wasn't over yet, and that made me feel a weird combination of sad and frustrated. Why couldn't he see that this was the best way to handle things?

Leaning down, David grabbed his bag. "So I'm gonna head home," he said. "See you tomorrow, Pres?"

"Yeah," I told him, walking over and slipping an arm around his waist before going up on tiptoe to press a quick kiss against his lips, willing him to let this go, to let us be okay.

He kissed me back, but when I pulled away, that wrinkle was still between his brows. "See you tomorrow," I said, ignoring the wrinkle. "Don't forget, we have an assembly bright and early, and I want to see you in the front row."

Nodding, David smiled the littlest bit. "Got it. See you then." He waved to Bee, then let himself out the back gate.

After he was gone, I turned back to Bee. "So you want to work on more baton twirling?"

A wide grin split Bee's face, and overhead, the sun filtered through the leaves, leaving pretty dappled shadows on her skin. "Or we could practice something else."

With that, she lunged at me.

Instinct took over, and I dodged, dropping to sweep my leg underneath her feet. But she was quick, and leapt away from my kick with a laugh.

And then it was on.

In a weird way, it was like we were back in cheerleading

practice. Bee and I had always been a great team, and nothing had changed. Every punch she threw, I countered. Every kick, I matched. And when she caught me by my wrist, flipping me over her back, I actually laughed at the sheer *fun* of it. Not only did I have my best friend back, but I finally had someone who could train with me, who could let me release my abilities to their full extent.

When Bee and I were done, we were both sweating and breathing hard, but we were also smiling, so much that my cheeks ached.

We sat on the grass, and from beyond the fence, I could hear a car driving down our street. The wind rustled through the leaves overhead, and birds were singing. It could not have been a more perfect spring day, but I couldn't help the little chill that went down my spine. It wasn't the sense of dread and pain that came when David was in trouble—it wasn't nearly intense enough for that—but I frowned anyway.

"Bee," I ventured, "you know what David said . . . I'd never want you to do that for me. I wouldn't ask you to."

She glanced over at me, the breeze blowing wisps of blond hair into her face. "I know that, Harper. But I would. If you needed me to."

I shifted on the grass, scratching a spot behind my knee. "Bee, I know this isn't something you really want to talk about, but . . . when you were with Alexander, did he train you?"

I couldn't tell if the look in Bee's eyes was wary or embarrassed, but in either case, her gaze slid away from me and she

117

gave a little shrug. "Sort of. There was a room there with these dummies I could kick, but no weapons."

"Makes sense," I muttered, then leaned closer to her. "And you never saw anyone but Alexander?"

She shook her head. "That girl who took me, Blythe. She was there at first, but she was gone within a day or two. Other than that . . ." Trailing off, she shaded her eyes, studying a bright blue bird perched on our privacy fence. "It was just him."

I frowned and settled back against the tree trunk. "I don't get it. The Ephors are supposed to be this . . . group. Like the Illuminati or something. Why is he the only one who seems to be in charge of anything?"

At that, Bee looked at me, resting her cheek on her raised knees. "Maybe he's an overachiever," she suggested, and that dimple appeared in her cheek again. "*Maybe*," she added, "he's the *you* of the Ephors and doesn't like delegating."

I bumped her with my own raised knees. "I guess that's possible, but still, it seems weird, right?"

With a long sigh, Bee leaned her head back, the sunlight and the leaves casting shadows on her face. "What about this isn't?" she asked.

She had a point.

For a while, we were silent, both lost in our thoughts, and I was actually a little startled when Bee said, "I feel sorry for him."

"Alexander?" I asked, wrinkling my nose, and she shook her head.

"David. Having powers you don't really get, people trying to kill you, people trying to keep you safe, and not being able to do anything about any of it. I mean, it's not easy for you or Ryan, either," she added, tucking a loose strand of hair behind one ear, "but y'all get to be *active* instead of waiting for other people to fix things."

Stretching out my legs, I let my head drop back against the trunk, too. "I never thought of it like that, exactly. Is that what y'all were talking about earlier?"

Bee unfolded her legs, mimicking my posture. "Kind of. He was apologizing for asking me to do the Peirasmos. Said he's spent a lot of time trying to come up with solutions, and that one just occurred to him before he really thought it through."

I definitely felt better about that, but it was still a little weird to think of David and Bee, like, sharing confidences and stuff.

"I don't think there is a solution to all of this," I told her, and Bee looked over at me.

"That's . . . depressing."

I laughed, but it sounded a little forced. "It's not so bad," I said. "Once David gets his powers back and under control, I'm sure having a future-telling boyfie will be the best, plus I get to be a ninja, and that's always fun—"

Bee reached out and laid a hand on my shoulder. "Harper," she said, and I recognized her "don't give me that BS" look. It was something about the way she tilted her head down, making me meet her eyes.

"Okay," I conceded, crossing one ankle over the other. "It sucks. It sucks a lot. But it's the way things are, and there's no way to change it."

Her hand fell away, fingers playing in the grass between us. "If David did just leave . . ."

I sat up, looking at her more sharply. "Did he mention that to you, too?"

She didn't look up, using one nail to split a blade of grass. "A little, but apparently there are wards keeping him here for the time being?" Now she lifted her gaze. "What would happen if he broke them?"

Surprised, I blinked at her. "I . . . don't know, honestly. I guess it would hurt him, or do something bad."

It was a little embarrassing to admit that I knew so little about something so major, but Bee only gave a slight hum and split another piece of grass.

Chapter 15

I GET THAT most people think that school assemblies are totally boring, and they're not always wrong—if I never have to sit through another meeting on selling wrapping paper to raise money for the Grove, it will be too soon—but I was actually looking forward to Friday morning's. Maybe it was because I got to speak before it started, and I always enjoyed things like that, especially now. There was something comfortingly normal about walking up to the podium and speaking confidently to the other students, even if it was only about upcoming service projects and the Spring Fling. It reminded me that there were still things in my life I controlled.

Or maybe I was psyched because I got to talk about the dance. In any case, I sat in the folding chair next to Lucy McCarroll, the sophomore class president. I'd dressed nicely today, wearing a yellow-and-green Lilly Pulitzer dress Mom had gotten for me on a shopping trip to Mobile. Headmaster Dunn made his remarks first, reminding us about upcoming ACT dates and not to leave litter in the parking lot and to remember that "after last year's unfortunate incident with farm animals in the band room," senior pranks were expressly forbidden. It may not have been a display of great manners, but I scanned the bleachers in front of us as he droned on. I spotted Bee almost immediately, sitting next to Ryan, and I smiled.

She grinned back, giving me a little wave, and then leaned over to say something to Ryan. His gaze flicked toward me, but I couldn't read his expression. Apparently the Mary Beth incident was still an issue. Which was fine, since the whole defacing-the-wards-and-not-telling-me thing was very much an issue as far as I was concerned. So I let my gaze move away from him, searching out David.

Who was . . . not there.

I spotted Chie and Michael talking to each other on the very top bleacher, clearly not listening to Headmaster Dunn. So where was David? He always sat with them, and if he wasn't there, then I'd expect him to be next to Bee and Ryan. I'd told him I was going to speak this morning, and, hey, even if I hadn't, assemblies were mandatory.

There was no tightness in my chest, no sense that anything was wrong with him, but still, it was weird.

I racked my brain, trying to remember if I'd seen him this morning, all while studying the note card in my hand like I was going over my remarks. Okay, yes, he'd been in the parking lot, wearing some atrocious shade of green. So where—

Lucy's elbow nudged my ribs, and I realized the gym was quiet, Headmaster Dunn waiting expectantly by the podium.

Shoot.

Rattled, I stood up, smoothing my skirt down over my thighs with one hand while the other clutched my note card. I usually breezed right through things like this, but right now I was unsettled. When I stepped up to the podium, the microphone released a shriek of feedback as I adjusted it, and I winced, tucking my hair behind my ear.

"Sorry about that," I said with a pained smile. "Anyway, um, good morning, Grove Academy. As you know, I'm Harper Price, your SGA president, and I wanted to mention a few upcoming—"

It hit me like a brick.

One moment, I was fine, albeit nervous; the next, I was gasping and clutching both sides of the podium, my entire upper body in a vise. I could feel sweat break out all over me, prickling at my hairline and my spine, and when I managed to open my eyes, I saw that Bee had risen to her feet and was already moving toward me.

"Harper—" Headmaster Dunn said, laying a beefy hand on my shoulder.

I gritted my teeth, my knees feeling weak and watery, adrenaline racing through me, alarm bells going off in my head.

No, wait. Those weren't in my head.

It was the fire alarm.

Easing me out of the way, Headmaster Dunn faced the six hundred or so students in the bleachers. "All right, kids," he said easily enough, but I saw the furrows around his mouth deepen. "You know the drill. Orderly line, out the main doors and into the courtyard."

It was a drill we ran at least twice a semester, and Headmaster Dunn's calm baritone voice kept everyone from panicking as they began to file out of the bleachers.

Everyone but me.

I stood there, waiting until the last person disappeared through the big double doors, and then I turned, heading for the back doors of the gym. Those were the ones that led to the main school buildings, and that, I knew as surely as I knew anything, was where David was.

Headmaster Dunn's hand on my arm stopped me.

"Whoa there, Miss Price," he said with a friendly smile. "Wrong way, sweetheart."

"I need to get my bag," I said lamely, and he shook his head.

"You know the rules," he said, his thick eyebrows drawing together. Under the gym lights, his bald head gleamed. "Way more important that you get out okay than that your stuff makes it. Come on."

There was no thinking. I drew back the arm he was holding, fast enough that it surprised him, throwing him slightly off balance. I saw his eyes go wide for a second, and his mouth made an almost perfect O shape as he stumbled.

A knee to his outer thigh had him dropping lower, and then, with his hand still clutching me, I drew back my free arm and elbowed him in the temple, hard.

He dropped like a sack of rocks, eyes rolling back in his head, and trust me, I felt *super* bad about it.

But David came first, and every cell in my body was urging me to get to him, get to him *now*.

Alarms were still going off, and as I entered the main building, I could smell smoke, acrid and bitter.

Heart racing, I made my way to the English hall, where the journalism lab was. He was there, I could feel it, and underneath all my worry, all my Paladin senses going crazy, there was this little flicker of irritation.

I'd told him I was speaking this morning, told him I'd wanted to see him, and instead, he'd skipped the assembly to do stuff for the paper. It shouldn't have been as annoying as it was, but for whatever reason, it seriously bugged me. I did stuff that was important for him, right? I'd joined the stupid paper, and—

I rounded the corner, and all of my anger vanished. One entire end of the English hall was in flames. I don't know what I'd expected, but that was definitely not it. It seemed to be pouring out of the janitor's closet at the end of the hall, and for a second I froze, watching flames lick up against the walls, consuming the banners SGA had hung for the Spring Fling, racing along posters, flickering in a huge pool underneath the closet door.

My heart hammered against my ribs, my stomach twisting, and I felt legitimate panic surge through me, even underneath all my "David's in danger" feelings. The classrooms—

Were empty, I remembered with a wave of relief. The assembly had seen to that. But as I made my way farther down the hall, I couldn't help but think that if they *hadn't* been, if there had been students trapped in there, I wouldn't have been able to save them. Not until I knew David was safe.

It was a disturbing thought, and I made myself shove it away, trying to focus on what was happening.

There was another smell mixed in with the smoke, a heavy, chemical odor, and I wondered if some of the cleaning products had exploded or something. And then I looked again at that spreading pool of flame, and with a sudden jolt, I realized that it wasn't spilled bleach or ammonia. It was gasoline.

Someone had set that fire on purpose, and I thought I had a pretty good idea of who.

Of course, none of that mattered right now. Right now, the main thing was getting to David. Throwing an arm over my face, I ran to the journalism lab. The fire was only a few yards or so away, and the doorknob was already warm to the touch as I twisted it.

My eyes watered as I scanned the room, but there was no sign of David.

Still, he had to be here. I felt it. "David!" I called, rushing in and bumping into a desk. It screeched across the linoleum, and I called again. "David!"

And then I saw his messenger bag propped against the door of the darkroom.

Several years ago, some parents whose kids had been super into photography had donated the funds to have the darkroom installed in the newspaper lab, but hardly anyone used it anymore.

Except David.

The little light over the door was on, showing that it was in use, but I ignored that, flinging open the door to stare at David, who whirled around to glare over the top of his glasses.

When he saw it was me, the glare lessened a bit, but he still didn't seem thrilled. "Pres, you know you can't open—"

Then he stopped, lifting his nose. "Wait, are the alarms going off? Is that smoke?"

Without answering, I reached in, grabbed him by the sleeve of his ratty sweater, and tugged him out of the darkroom.

I could already hear the wailing of sirens as I pulled David through the empty halls of the school, heading for the doors that led to the courtyard. He was safe now, so I didn't feel like my chest was in a vise, but my stomach still churned. The English hall hadn't totally gone up in flames, but the damage was going to be huge. We'd probably have to move classes out of there for the rest of the semester, a thought that made me feel angry and sad and sick. My *school*. The place I'd spent so much of my time trying to make perfect. But since I couldn't even begin to process that right now, I turned to David.

"Why were you in there?" I asked over the various sirens, and David pushed his glasses up the bridge of his nose.

"I forgot that I had some photographs I wanted to develop, and the assembly seemed like a good time to get them done."

Now that David wasn't in imminent danger of becoming charcoal, I whirled on him right there by the front doors. "I told you I was speaking this morning."

He frowned, folding his arms over his chest. "Yeah, but just about the dance, right? You already told me everything you were going to say."

It was the worry getting to me, I think, the worry and the knowledge that my school had been attacked and pretty seriously damaged. I couldn't freak out about all of that right now, but I could snap at David. "So you didn't care?"

He blinked at me. "Are we seriously going to do this here?"

He was right; now was definitely not the time, but if I could have shoved him out the door, I think I would have. Instead, I opened it and steered him toward the steps. "Go to your car. I'll meet you there in a minute."

David ran a hand over his sandy blond hair, ruffling it. "You're going back in there?" he asked, and I nodded.

"I knocked Headmaster Dunn unconscious, so I should probably deal with that."

His eyebrows lifted up into his hairline, but he didn't say anything else, jogging down the steps toward the group of students milling around on the grass.

I darted back inside, running back for the gym, trying to tell myself that it wasn't that big of a deal that David hadn't come to the assembly. I was probably just mad because it had put him in danger.

But then, as I rounded the corner back toward the gymnasium, I realized: If this *was* one of the trials, why on earth would the Ephors put David in danger? They said they wanted him.

Unless this was all a trick, and I was right about Alexander being evil.

Man, I really hoped I was right.

When I got back to the gym, I was surprised to see Ryan there, kneeling next to Headmaster Dunn, who was trying to stand.

"You okay, Headmaster?" Ryan asked, easing a hand under the man's elbow. "You seriously whacked your head on that podium."

Ryan could annoy the ever-living heck out of me, but right now, I was so grateful, I could have cried. Somehow, he must've known I'd need him, and I smiled at him as I came to help him get Headmaster Dunn to his feet.

"It's these gym floors," I said. "Super slippy."

But then Headmaster Dunn looked at me, his expression dark, his face nearly purple. "Gym floors?" he repeated. "You *hit* me, Miss Price."

Panicked, I looked at Ryan, who was staring back at me, confused. He gave a tiny shake of his head, and I could smell the rose balm in the air. He'd used the mind-wipe stuff, so why wasn't it working?

"Young lady, you are coming to my office right now," he continued, shaking his head as though he couldn't believe he was saying those words. *I* couldn't believe he was saying those words.

I'd already told David to meet me at his car so we could get to Alexander's and find out what the heck had happened. If I went with Headmaster Dunn now, I had a feeling I'd be in his office for a while. They'd have to call my parents. Oh God, or the police. Or my parents *and* the police. Honestly, what was the point of having someone who could do mind-wiping magic if the freaking mind-wiping magic didn't work?

Two choices stared me right in the face. Either I stayed here and I dealt with this, or I took off for my car and got to David and Alexander. If I did that, maybe I could get some answers about why one of the trials involved nearly killing David, and why Ryan's magic wasn't working.

I took a deep breath and blurted out, "Headmaster, I'm sorry about all of this, and I promise there's an explanation." Behind him, Ryan was already shaking his head and mouthing my name. "But I . . . I have to go."

And with that, I took off running.

Chapter 16

We took David's car out to Alexander's and spent most of the drive in silence. I wondered if I should text my parents, but I figured the school had already called them. *Later*, I thought, turning my phone off. Whatever was happening, we'd get to the bottom of it, and soon this whole unpleasant morning would be wiped away, either by Ryan's magic or by whatever Alexander could do.

"If this is a trial," David said, lifting one hand so he could push his glasses up his nose, "why put me in danger? That seems counterproductive."

"Who knows?" I replied. "In case you forgot, they're insane killer people who sent crazy witches to murder you last year, so we shouldn't be that surprised when they do, you know, crazy murderous things."

My heart was still pounding, an intense mix of irritation and fear shooting through me, and I focused on the green fields flying past, trying to calm my temper.

My school. The place I worked so hard to make nice and safe, and they'd used it as one of their . . . their testing grounds. They'd damaged it, set it on fire, could've freaking *destroyed* it for good.

That was so seriously not okay.

Next to me, David drummed his fingers on the steering wheel. "I read Alexander's mind, Harper. He didn't want to hurt me, I could feel it."

"Maybe you were wrong," I answered, but he shook his head as he turned the car onto the dirt road leading to the house.

"I'm just saying, hear the guy out before you go in there guns blazing."

Twisting in my seat, I faced David. *"Hear him out?* Even if he set the Grove on fire?"

David didn't answer, but kept watching the road, and I flopped back into my seat with a huff.

"Well, if they did set it, they must have kept an eye on you and known you weren't where you were supposed to be."

I didn't exactly hear David sigh. It was more like I *felt* it, a shiver of irritation that ran through him. "I'm sorry I wasn't at the assembly," he said in the most even tone known to man. "But I had something I needed to do, and I didn't think you'd mind."

"Something you *wanted* to do," I countered, and I got the sense he was counting to ten in his head.

"Let's focus on the task at hand, okay?"

"Fine by me."

When we pulled up to Alexander's, the late morning sun was playing on the windows, making them sparkle, and I was struck again by what a pretty place this was. Had this been what the original house looked like, or had Alexander—or a Mage, I was guessing—made it to suit himself? In any case, I liked it.

Too bad the person inside was a total jerk.

The car was barely in park before I was out of it, heading up the front steps with David close behind.

"Should we knock?" David asked, and I glared at the big wooden door in front of us.

"Oh, I'm going to knock," I told him, and gave the door a vicious kick. Even if the magic on this place kept me from being able to break in, kicking it was still pretty satisfying.

But the door flew open with a splintering crack when the flat of my foot hit it. David stepped back with a muttered "Whoa," but I was already moving into the house.

"Alexander!" I called. "Hey! Anybody home?"

"There's no need for screaming, Miss Price," Alexander said, appearing on the landing. He was wearing another suit, this one black, and smiling pleasantly at me like I hadn't just kicked in his front door.

"I disagree," I told him. "I usually feel pretty screamy when someone attacks my school."

His brows drew together as he made an exaggeratedly puzzled expression. "Did I not tell you that the trials would be coming up very soon? Or are you confused as to what the trials entail?"

"Actually, yes, I am confused," I said, my heart still pounding. Even though David was safe now, I could still feel a sort of residual ache in my chest. "Because I expected someone to come after *me*. I didn't think you'd put my entire school in danger."

Alexander gave one of those little smiles I hated so much.

"Well, if we let you face the expected, that would hardly serve the point of going through trials, now would it?"

"You could have hurt innocent people," I told him, my face hot. "You could've killed them. You could have made our school a smoldering pile of ash, and all for what? For some test?"

The smile vanished from Alexander's face. "Not some test, Miss Price, I assure you," he said, coming down a few steps, his shoulders rigid. "The most vital test a Paladin can face. And, in case this has not been made perfectly clear, I do not give a tinker's damn about your school or the people in it. The main purpose of this exercise is to test whether or not you are an adequate Paladin for the Oracle. You passed that test today—quite well, I should add."

"Are you going to give me a gold star?" I asked, and from behind me, I heard David's warning: "Harper."

"No," I said, turning to face him. "You should be angry, too. What is the point of putting your Oracle in danger to prove that your Paladin knows her stuff?"

At that, Alexander sighed, straightening one of his cuffs. "Mr. Stark was never in danger," he told me. "The situation was closely monitored, I assure you. Had you failed in your task, the Oracle would not have come to harm."

I didn't even know where to start with that, so I latched on to something else he had said. "Monitored by whom? And I smelled gasoline, so what's up with that? Can't you just, like, magic up some fire?"

Alexander flicked a strand of hair from his forehead, and I got the feeling he was rolling his eyes at me, like, in his soul. "The details of how we conduct these tests is not your concern."

I moved closer, my shoes tapping on the hardwood. "You keep saying 'we,' but I gotta be honest, I'm only seeing *you*. If you're going to do stuff like set a building full of kids on fire, I'd kind of like to talk to your supervisor."

"Harper," David said again, but Alexander held my gaze.

"As far as you are concerned, I am the alpha and omega of the Ephors, Miss Price. You do not dictate the boundaries of our tests, and there is no one you can talk to above me, I assure you."

I shook my head and said, "School should be off-limits. Period."

"Hmm," Alexander said, narrowing his eyes and tilting his head. "I see. So when you protect the Oracle from people who may want to hurt him, there will be places in this world that are off-limits? When some despotic ruler learns there's an Oracle in the world, ripe for the taking, if he approaches you at, say, your family's home, you'll simply inform him that this is not one of the agreed locations where an Oracle may be in danger?"

Faltering, I shook my head. "No, it's . . . it's not like that, but if it's only for a *test*—"

"The tests are meant to assess your readiness for real-world situations, Miss Price," he said sharply, all trace of that lazy elegance gone from his voice. "If you cannot be ready, then you cannot be a Paladin. This is not a hobby or an extracurricular activity."

I wanted to argue that, but nothing I could think of seemed

to work. He was right, and, ugh, I hated that so much. Still, I could at least try to get him to fix some of this mess.

"Fine," I said. "You've made your point. Now if you could please"—I waved in his direction—"rustle up some magic or whatever so that my principal forgets that I hit him and my parents don't freak out, I'd appreciate that. Ryan's Mage skills are apparently on the fritz."

But Alexander gave a tiny, elegant shrug. "They're not 'on the fritz.' They're gone for the time being."

"What?" David asked, coming up to stand beside me, his sneakers squeaking on the hardwood.

"Gone," Alexander repeated. "A simple ward I myself was able to create to keep Mr. Bradshaw from using his magic to assist you. It isn't as though that particular use of magic benefited the Oracle."

I swore I could feel my heart skip a few beats. Next to me, David scoffed, throwing up one hand.

"It benefits me plenty. Him helping Harper would help *me*. So let him do his mind-wipe thing, and let's—"

"No," Alexander said, his voice icy. He began to walk down the stairs, footsteps silent on the thick carpet. "Miss Price needs to learn that you cannot magic your way out of every obstacle. You hit your principal to save the Oracle. That's what you should have done, but now there must be consequences. Being a Paladin means accepting the consequences that come as a result of doing your duty."

Seriously afraid I was going to throw up, I clenched my

hands. "So you chose to set one of the trials at my school, and now I'm probably going to be expelled, and there's nothing I can do about it?"

Alexander sniffed, coming to the bottom of the stairs. "You're a clever girl, Miss Price. I'm sure you'll think of something. The Mage's powers do not exist in order to make things more convenient for *you*."

Please, I thought, but wouldn't let myself say. *Please don't tell him.*

Alexander's eyes remained on mine, and while I didn't think he could read my mind, I had a pretty good idea that he knew what I was thinking.

But that didn't stop him from saying, "We removed his powers because he was using them to stifle the Oracle's visions. An instruction *you* gave him, I believe."

The hall was so quiet I could hear my own heart racing, could hear David suck in a surprised gasp. "You were doing what?" he asked quietly, and I turned to face him.

My clothes still smelled like smoke, which was probably why my eyes were stinging as I said, "We were trying to help you."

But David was shaking his head, backing away from me. "You used Ryan to keep me from having visions?"

"No," I said, walking toward him. The sun coming in the big front windows had turned his hair lighter, lining him in gold. "No, you still had visions, but not ones that were big enough to hurt you."

I could see David's throat working, and I hated the way he was looking at me.

From behind me, Alexander gave a sigh. "Well," he said, "it would appear you two have some things to discuss."

I looked back, and he was already heading up the stairs again. "And, Miss Price," he added before turning back to flash a wolfish smile, "congratulations. You're one step closer to being a true Paladin."

Chapter 17

WE LEFT Alexander's house in silence, me trailing behind David. He jangled his keys in his hand, his jaw set, shoulders forward. I knew that look. That was David's thinking look, and I had no doubt exactly what he was thinking about now.

Guilt is such a weird feeling, a combination of sad and sick that I was getting too used to feeling. I'd had Ryan set up the wards to block David's visions because I'd thought it was the best thing for him—I still thought that, if I was being honest—but I knew I should have talked to David, should have tried to make him see that it was only because I wanted to keep him safe.

I slid into the passenger seat without a word, still lost in my thoughts, and David started the car, heading back out toward town.

David's fingers were curled tight around the steering wheel, so tight that his knuckles were turning pale.

"I'm sorry," I told him, rubbing my eyes. "I . . . I should have told you what Ryan and I were doing. And I wanted to. I was *going* to, I promise."

"When?" he asked, a muscle working in his jaw.

I didn't have an answer for that, not really, and I didn't think "eventually" was going to cut it.

And then, David suddenly jerked the wheel, pulling the car off the road, gravel and dust flying up in a cloud behind us as he came to a stop right past the "Welcome to Pine Grove!" sign.

Throwing the car in park, David opened his door and got out, walking a little ways away.

I watched him pace for a few seconds before getting out of the car, too.

"I don't know what else you want me to say," I told him, leaning one elbow on the open door. "I'm sorry I wasn't honest with you, David, I genuinely am, but part of my job is to protect you, and that's what I was doing, okay?"

David had his back to me, and didn't turn around as he tipped his head to look at the sky.

"All that time, I thought I was a crappy Oracle. But it was *you*. You keeping me from being what I'm supposed to be. And the fact is, if you'd left me alone, I might have been able to help you before this whole thing even started." He shook his head, a quick, angry series of jerks.

It was weird, how quickly guilt gave way to anger. "Did you hear the part about how I was doing it to keep you from going insane? Did you look at any of those Oracle pictures back at Alexander's?" I flung my hand back in the direction of the house. "Not sure if you noticed, but none of them exactly looked like people anymore, David. They were . . . things."

David glanced over his shoulder at me, hands low on his hips, elbows jutted out to the side. "But I *am* one of those 'things,' Harper. And you made a decision for me that you had no right to make. And by making a decision like that without talking to me, you pretty much treated me like a *thing,* didn't you?"

It had been a very long day, and my head was still spinning with everything that had happened, so it took me a sec to say, "No, *right*? This is part of what being a Paladin means. Keeping you safe, making hard decisions—"

The lines around his mouth looked deeper than normal and he waved a hand between us. "Hard decisions you didn't bother letting me in on. Because why would you? This is what you do, Harper, you . . . freaking steamroll everybody. You decide it's the best thing to do because it's what *you* want to do."

Slamming the car door, I walked over to David, the tall grass brushing my ankles. "That's unfair, and you know it."

David watched me warily. "Is it? What about all the stuff you had me do for your friends? Saving Abi from meeting that guy—"

I blinked, feeling his words like a punch to the gut. "That will make her life better," I snapped, but David threw his hands up, looking at the sky again.

"Will it? You don't know. You don't ask people what *they* want."

I opened my mouth to argue, but he held up a hand. "Don't start on the Paladin duty thing again, please. If you want to argue that you were doing what was best for me as an Oracle, fine, whatever. But that's not all I am to you, and you didn't take that into consideration at all." He shook his head. "Pres, you have to admit, us being an *us* has made things more complicated."

I wasn't sure how my heart could be fluttering and sinking all at once, but that seemed to be what was happening, and I wrapped my arms tight around me.

"It's made things better, though," I said. "Or has being my boyfriend only been a chore for you?"

David rolled his eyes, looking back up at the sky again. "No, of course not. I'm just saying that maybe . . . maybe we should rethink some stuff."

"Rethink?" I repeated. This could not be happening. I could not be getting dumped by David Freaking Stark on a country road in the middle of nowhere.

But behind the disbelief was another emotion.

Anger. Lots of it.

"Let me get this straight," I said, holding out one hand. "I made a call to keep you from having visions that would burn your brain up, and you dump me for it?"

David dropped his head to look at me, eyes slightly narrowed. "I didn't say I was dumping you, I said—"

"No," I interrupted. "That's what 'rethink stuff' means, David. And it means you're letting the Paladin/Oracle thing get all tangled up with everything else we are."

David laughed, but there was no humor in the sound. "It's already all tangled up, Pres. It always has been, and it's making both of us crazy."

Now David's arms were tight across his chest, too. "You can't quit being my Paladin, and I can't quit being an Oracle, but maybe until all this is sorted with the Peirasmos and Alexander and Bee—"

"What does Bee have to do with this?" I asked, shading my eyes against the sun. It was warm out here by the side of the road, and I could feel sweat on my forehead, behind my knees. My stomach ached, and my chest hurt. From the pained look on his face, I thought David might be feeling something similar.

"She's wrapped up in this, too. Which, let me remind you, is another thing that I *might* have been able to see coming if you hadn't screwed around with my powers. Maybe I could have looked for her, or we could've brought her back sooner."

I stepped closer to him, wishing I could at least poke him in the chest or something. I'd have to settle for saying all the hostile stuff I wanted. "Are you suggesting that what happened to Bee was my fault?"

A car drove by, sending up a cloud of dust, and David glared at me. "You know I don't think that."

But I did. That was the problem. If I'd told Bee the truth from the beginning, if I'd been faster at Cotillion, if I'd tried to do something to keep her from even *going* to Cotillion.

If I hadn't been so scared of my boyfriend turning into a monster that I'd kept him from using powers that maybe could've seen her.

Could've saved her.

"Harper," David said, his voice quieter now. "Why can't you admit that you can't do everything?" He sounded so much like the David Stark I'd fought with for all those years that it was hard to believe I'd kissed him just yesterday. That I'd loved him.

"You can't let go of anything, can you, Harper? You can't admit that maybe some things are too much for you. You can't be Homecoming Queen, and Paladin, and SGA president, and my girlfriend—"

I spun away from him, heading for the car. "Yeah, well, we can go ahead and strike one of those from the list, no problem."

With an aggrieved sound, David caught my elbow, pulling me up short. "I don't want to break up."

I stepped back, shaking my head. "Too late."

With that, I stomped back to the car, my throat tight, my eyes stinging.

David was still standing a few feet from the car, one hand at his waist, the other rubbing his mouth as he watched the traffic. Then, after a moment, I saw his shoulders rise and fall with a sigh, and he walked back to the car.

When he slid back in the driver's side, he didn't even look at me, starting the car and staring straight ahead.

I took a deep breath, wishing it hadn't sounded so shuddery. So that was that. We were done. Less than six months as a couple, and now it was over.

Maybe David was right and it was for the best.

We didn't say anything else until David pulled up in front of my house.

"Both your parents are home," he said, the car still idling.

"Probably because the school called them, and I'm about to be grounded for the rest of my life, if not imprisoned."

"Right," David said on a sigh, drumming his fingers on the steering wheel. "Do you want me to go in with you, try to explain?"

I was going to cry. I could feel it in my throat, which suddenly seemed so swollen and painful I was surprised I could breathe. And the last person I wanted to see me cry right now was the boy sitting next to me.

"No," I said. "I need to deal with this on my own."

"Pres," he said softly. In the dim light of the car, I could make out the freckles across the bridge of his nose, see the slight wobble of his chin, and I fumbled with the door handle as tears filled my vision.

"We'll talk tomorrow," I said, getting out of the car as quickly as I could and slamming the door behind me.

I didn't look back.

Chapter 18

"WOULD IT HELP if I apologized again?"

I was sitting between my parents in Headmaster Dunn's office on Monday morning, the leather of the chair sticking to my thighs underneath the white linen skirt I was wearing. I was all in white today, down to the thin ribbon headband in my hair, hoping to project an air of innocence, but so far, it didn't seem to be working.

Headmaster Dunn still had an angry purple bruise on his right cheek, and the top of his bald head was red with anger, a vein pulsing steadily there. I'd never seen Headmaster Dunn angry before. God knows I'd never given him any reason to be before today, and for the first time, I got that—as a principal—he was pretty scary.

"Martin, you know this was very unusual behavior for Harper," my dad said, resting his ankle on his knee. "And we don't understand it any more than you do."

"I panicked!" I insisted, wondering if going all wide-eyed would be taking the innocence thing too far. "There was a fire alarm, and—"

"And your boyfriend was trapped in the newspaper room," Headmaster Dunn said on a sigh, and I startled.

"What?"

Reaching for a pen, Headmaster Dunn looked at me over the top of his half-moon glasses and said, "David Stark came to see me this morning, saying that you'd saved his life on Friday."

"Oh" was all I could manage. I'd been punched and kicked and attacked with knives, but I wasn't sure any of those things hurt as much as hearing David's name. When I'd gotten in on Friday afternoon, I'd had my parents' complete and total freak-out to distract me from the fact that David and I were no longer together. The school had called, of course, and told them about both the punching *and* the running off, so I'd had to spin a story and fast. It was the same one I'd told Headmaster Dunn during this meeting—freaked out, had a panic attack, acted in a Wildly Inappropriate and Uncharacteristic Manner—and while I was still grounded for the time being, at least they'd stopped yelling.

But later that night, lying in my bed, all I'd been able to think about was David's face, the way his voice had cracked when he'd said, "Pres?" And then on top of that, there was the worry. Breaking up sucked no matter what. Breaking up with a person who you had a mystical and lifelong bond with? Yeah. I'd been awake most of the night wondering what this would mean for us on the Paladin/Oracle side of things. And would this have any effect on the trials? It wasn't like I could quit being David's Paladin, or quit going through with the Peirasmos, but at the moment, I didn't even want to see David, much less go through more crap like what had happened Friday.

"Harper?"

I was so lost in thought that I hadn't noticed Headmaster Dunn talking to me.

"Yes, sir?" I asked, sitting forward in my chair a little bit.

He heaved another one of those sighs, his watery green eyes flicking between me and my parents. "I could have had you arrested, you know." He tapped the end of the pen up and down on the desk. "Charged you with assault."

My stomach dropped, and I clenched my suddenly sweaty fingers in my lap. "Yes, sir," I said, as meekly as I could manage.

"At the very *least* I could have you expelled." The pen was tapping faster now, and next to me, I heard both of my parents suck in a breath. When I looked over at Mom, she had her legs tightly crossed, fingers linked over her knees. Like me, she was mostly in white, although her pants were houndstooth.

Headmaster Dunn sat back in his chair. "*But* since this was extremely uncharacteristic of you, and you were doing it in the service of helping your fellow students, I'm not going to do either of those things."

I let out such a deep breath that I'm surprised I didn't sag in my chair. "*Ohmygoshthankyou,*" I said in a rush and then stood up, reaching across the desk to shake his hand.

Headmaster Dunn flinched back, and Mom tugged at the hem of my skirt. "Sit down, sweetie."

As I did exactly that, Headmaster Dunn added, "You're not getting off scot-free, though, young lady. I expect you to dedicate at least a hundred service hours to the school before the end of the year." His gaze flicked past me and toward the door; he was no doubt picturing the English hall. It was still standing, but the smoke and water damage were bad enough that classes had been moved into the cafeteria for the time being. "Lord knows we'll have plenty for you to do," he said on a sigh, and I stood up again, this time not reaching for him.

"Thank you," I said again. "I promise, nothing like this will happen again, and I'm going to do a *totally* great job helping out."

Headmaster Dunn gave a snort and went back to tapping his pen. "We'll see about that."

Once we were back in the main office, I turned to both my parents, giving them my best smile. "See? It all worked out."

Dad shoved his hands in his pockets, rocking back on his heels. He had this way of looking at me where he sort of tucked his chin down and raised his eyes. He'd looked at Leigh-Anne like that, too, and it was always a sign that we were in trouble.

That was clearly still the case now, since his voice was firm when he said, "Just because you managed to avoid expulsion doesn't mean you're in the clear with us, young lady."

Mom reached out, setting her hands on my shoulders. "We're still worried, sweetheart. You have not been yourself for . . ." She looked up toward the ceiling. "Months, it seems like. And if you're having panic attacks so severe you assault your principal—"

"It wasn't assault," I said quickly. "It was an instinctive reaction so that I could help people."

Mom was still watching me, a deep crease between her brows, and I gave her my best "I've totally got this" smile.

I could tell she wasn't buying it, though—that crease only got deeper—so I hurried on, adding, "So I should get to class, and I promise we can talk more about this after school. Or after I get back from the pageant sign-ups."

Mom frowned at that. "Pageant sign-ups?" she repeated, and I nodded.

"Miss Pine Grove. Bee wanted to do it. Anyway, we can talk later, love you!" I gave her a quick kiss on the cheek, did the same to my dad, and then skedaddled out of that office as quickly as I could, leaving my parents' shocked expressions and the smell of burned coffee behind me.

The rest of the day was kind of a blur. The fire had everything all discombobulated, so classes were meeting in different locations. I had English in the gym, and Mrs. Laurent had sent all of us an e-mail that newspaper would now meet in the computer lab near the math hall. I hadn't seen David all day, and assumed he was avoiding me. That was . . . good. I wasn't ready to face him, not yet.

But when I got to the temporary newspaper lab and realized he wasn't there, I got worried. Even if David was lying low between classes and at lunch, he'd never miss newspaper.

Chie and Michael were working on computers in the back, and I tried to keep my voice as casual as I could. "Have either of you seen David?"

Chie shook her head, dark hair swinging around her jaw. "He's not in school today." She looked over her shoulder at me, the light from the computer monitor glowing in her eyes. "Did it take you this long to notice your boyfriend's missing?"

Okay, so David hadn't told his friends we'd broken up. I hadn't told mine either, except Bee.

Nodding, I gave a little shrug and backed up from them. "Sure, but I thought he might still show up for this class."

Neither Chie nor Michael replied, and I went over to one of the empty desks, sitting down with my bag. I had no idea what to do here without David. I usually worked with him, going over articles, suggesting layouts, throwing away any unflattering pictures—yearbooks are forever, and no one deserves to have certain shots preserved for eternity—but without him I felt sort of . . . lost.

And still worried.

Mrs. Laurent was nowhere to be seen, so I pulled out my cell phone and moved to the very back corner of the room. It smelled like dry-erase marker back there, and weird as it seemed, I kind of missed the hot ink smell of the old newspaper lab.

Ducking my head down, I dialed David's number quickly, and when he picked up after the third ring, I turned to face the wall.

"Pres," he said, and I closed my eyes for a second, willing myself not to sound all shaky and teary.

"Hi," I said as brightly as I could manage. "Skipping school today?"

On the other end of the phone, I could hear him blow out a long breath. "Thought it was a good idea, yeah," he replied. "And I've been meaning to spend some extra time with Saylor's books."

Frowning, I tried to decide how I felt about that. On the one hand, I was glad he was getting some research done. Saylor had tons of old books, and we'd barely scratched the surface of Oracle/Paladin knowledge. On the other, there was something about the image of him in that house, going through Saylor's things, that twisted my heart.

"Have you found anything?" I asked, and he sighed again. I pictured him with his phone jammed between his shoulder and his ear, an enormous tome spread out before him. I could hear the rattle of pages, and figured my mental image wasn't too far off.

"A few things," he said. "Not much, but at this point, I guess anything is better than nothing."

"Right," I agreed, and then, before I could stop myself, added, "You could bring some of the books by my house later if you wanted. We should, um, make sure we're both prepared for whatever comes next. Especially since that first trial was so intense."

There was silence on the other end of the phone, but only for a few heartbeats.

"Sure," he said at last. "After school?"

I glanced around. Chie was still facing her computer, but she wasn't typing anymore, and I got the feeling she was trying to listen.

Lowering my voice, I said, "I have pageant sign-ups, but after that, yeah. If my parents aren't home, you can use the extra key to let yourself in. It's—"

"I remember where it is," he said, and in the ensuing pause, I imagined him tugging at his hair.

Could we do this? Still act as Oracle and Paladin and pretend our hearts weren't breaking every time we talked? Sitting there in the computer lab, surrounded by people who were David's friends, I wanted to wish we'd never even tried to be together. That we'd made a mature decision that things were too complicated as it was, and that dating would make it worse.

But that would mean wishing he'd never kissed me the night of Cotillion. Wishing we'd never laughed together and held hands and all the other things that I already missed.

I wondered if David was thinking that, too, but in the end, he murmured, "See you then," and hung up.

Chapter 19

THE AUDITORIUM at the rec center smelled like floor polish, upholstery cleaner, and that indefinable old-building smell. In this case, I thought the smell might be the bitter tinge of humiliation. So many major events in town happened at the Community Center, and I wondered how many lives had been ruined on that stage? In Leigh-Anne's grade, there had been a girl named Sydney Linnet who'd puked during her eighth-grade graduation. And at least one kindergartner wet his or her pants every year during the Christmas pageant. I'd suffered the sting of defeat on that stage in sixth grade when David had beaten me in the spelling bee.

And now I was about to be humiliated all over again.

"You know we're not walking to a guillotine," Bee said, linking her arm with mine. "Besides, you *like* being in front of people."

"I like *talking* in front of people," I said, bumping her hip with mine. "Being in charge, directing things, not . . . performing."

"Fair enough," she said, glancing around the auditorium. "Is that the only thing making you look like you missed being valedictorian by a half a point?"

I tried to smile at her, but I know it didn't look right. "I was just thinking."

Bee puckered her lips briefly, brows drawing together. "About David?"

Sighing, I nodded, and Bee gave me a quick squeeze. "Look, I get that breakups suck, but . . . I mean, doesn't this make things a little easier? Now it's more like you're coworkers."

"Coworkers who are magically bound to each other. Forever," I reminded her, and Bee's big brown eyes blinked. "And, not to mention," I added, "my *other* ex is also a Magically Bound Coworker. I'm permanently tied to two guys I used to kiss."

Bee blew out a long breath. "Yeah, okay, that does make it tougher than a regular breakup. But . . . what were you going to do for the rest of your lives, anyway? Were you assuming that you'd always be a thing, and, I don't know, get married, have little future-telling babies?"

"It doesn't work like that," I said, meaning David's Oracle powers, but Bee nodded and said, "Exactly. Look at me and Brandon and you and Ryan, and Mary Beth and Ryan . . . your parents may have met in high school, Harper, but for most people, it doesn't work like that. You and David were probably going to break up at some point."

"I guess I could always ask him," I tried to joke. "See if he knew this was coming."

There was no way to explain to Bee how fast everything had been, how complicated. For people dealing with a guy who could see the future, we sure hadn't spent much time thinking about it. We'd always been focused on the present, on getting through one day, and then the next . . .

And look where we'd ended up.

I turned back to the stage, where a girl was practicing what might have been a modern dance routine. There were a lot of jazz hands happening, and a costume that was way too short. She'd probably learned to dance at the Pine Grove School of Dance over by the highway. Mom had sent me and Leigh-Anne to the Pine Grove Performing Arts School for our dance classes, since, according to her, the performances at PGSOD were too risqué.

As I watched the girl onstage stick her leg up behind her ear, I had to acknowledge Mom might have been right.

Then I tried to picture myself in that girl's place. Me. On-stage, in front of the whole town, doing a "talent," twirling that stupid baton. Taking a deep breath, I pushed my shoulders back and made my way down the slight incline to the stage. There was a long table set up just in front of the first row of seats, and a woman sat behind it, stacks of paper in front of her.

"Miss Plumley?" I asked, Bee trailing beside me. The woman turned around, pushing her glossy dark hair out of her eyes with manicured nails. A ridiculously huge diamond sparkled on her left hand, nearly blinding me as it caught the lights from the stage, and I remembered hearing that Sara was engaged to Dr. Bennett, a new dentist in town.

Sara Plumley had been friends with Leigh-Anne when we were growing up, even though she'd been a few years older than my sister. Still, she'd gone to our church, and when Leigh-Anne had been on the cheerleading squad her freshman year, Sara had been a senior.

She'd also won Miss Pine Grove several years back, and now she seemed to be the main force keeping the pageant going.

When she saw me and Bee, Sara gave a good-natured eye roll. "Oh, for heaven's *saaaake*, Harper," she drawled. "Do *not* call me 'Miss Plumley,' please, not when I'm only a few years older than you. It's always Sara."

Her accent was so thick that it came out "Say-ra," and I smiled, hugging her when she stood up.

"Okay, fine, Sara, then."

"That's better," she said with a wink. Then she looked up at Bee.

"Beeee, darlin', how *are* you? Didn't your mama say you were at some sort of . . ." Her face clouded for a second. "What was it again? A camp?"

"Cheerleading camp," Bee said quickly, and I hurried on before Sara could ask any more questions.

"So how is all of this going?" I nodded up at the stage, where a handful of girls were milling around.

Sara gave a wave of her hand. "The Lord is testing me, as usual. I swear, I would rather wrangle kittens than try to get a bunch of teenage girls to follow instructions, but what can you do?"

Her brown eyes narrowed slightly, taking in the two of us. "Are you girls here to volunteer? Because I am not gonna lie, I could use some help, especially from someone as organized as you, Harper. From the way I heard it, you practically ran Cotillion back in the fall."

She shook her head, glossy waves falling over her shoulder. "Of course, not even you could hold off a freaking earthquake. What a mess."

That was one word for it. But I smiled at Sara and shook my head. "Actually, we're here to sign up. For the pageant."

Sara's heart-shaped face wrinkled in a frown. "Well, that's real nice, honey, but sign-ups were last week. You know I love you, but I can't let you join up this late. It wouldn't be fair."

I bit back a smart reply. There were maybe twenty girls in the whole pageant, so it wasn't like me and Bee joining up was suddenly going to tip the whole thing into chaos. But snapping at Sara wasn't going to get me anywhere, and Aunt Jewel always said you gathered more flies with honey than vinegar.

So I put on my most honeyed smile and let my own accent drag out a little as I simpered, "I knooow, I'm *so* late. But to be honest, I wasn't sure if I'd have time to do the pageant this year, and then I was dusting Mama's curio cabinet. You know, the one right by our front door?"

Sara nodded, a little hesitant, and I decided it was time to lay it on thick. "And I saw Leigh-Anne's picture in there, from back when she won, and I . . ." I let myself trail off before biting my lower lip. "I felt like it was something I needed to do. I've followed in her footsteps in so many things, and the Miss Pine Grove pageant seemed like the final piece."

It was loathsome and heinous and probably made me a bad person, taking advantage of Leigh-Anne's death. But being a Paladin sometimes meant doing things like this, no matter how yucky I found it. If Bee was right and the last trial was tied to this pageant somehow, I sure as heck was going to be in it.

And yucky or not, it worked, because a sheen of tears suddenly appeared in Sara's eyes. She looked up at the ceiling, dabbing at the skin under her eyes with those French-manicured nails. "Oh, honey," she said, her voice thick. "You are exactly right. I don't know why I was fussing about deadlines and sign-up sheets."

She pointed one of those sharp nails at us. "But promise me that neither one of you is planning on singing 'The Greatest Love of All' or 'Hero' as your talent. If I have to hear either of those two songs again, I will eat a gun."

When Bee and I shook our heads, Sara gave a relieved sigh and handed us sign-up forms. "Fill these out and get them back to me by next Monday. That's the next rehearsal."

"We can't rehearse today?" Bee asked, gesturing up at the stage. A girl I didn't recognize—she either went to Lee High, the big public school on the other side of town, or was one of the girls from a neighboring county—was tap-dancing like her life depended on it.

But apparently Sara had already broken enough of her rules today, because she gave a very firm shake of her head. "Absolutely not. Not until your paperwork is sorted out."

"That's fine," I said quickly. I needed time to prepare myself for pageant practice anyway. Just coming in here had been weird enough. But, hey, if my trial ended up being public humiliation, at least I'd given the Ephors a heck of a setting.

Agreeing with Sara made her happy, because she flashed that super-white smile at me again. "Good. So are y'all gonna do the Festival, too?"

I wrinkled my nose. The Azalea Festival was the big fair on the outskirts of town. We had it every spring, along with the pageant, a giant bake sale, and this thing where people drove around looking at old houses with girls in hoop skirts out front.

The fair was like any carnival—rides, fried food, cheesy games, and oversized stuffed animals. I'd never been that crazy about it, even as a kid, but I'd always gone. The last few years, it had been a double-date thing with Ryan, Bee, and Brandon, and I'd kind of been looking forward to skipping it this year.

"Ooh, I hadn't thought about that!" Bee said, slipping her arm through mine again. "We ought to go tonight." Her brown eyes were warm when she looked down at me and added, "It might cheer you up."

I was pretty sure a cheesy town fair couldn't cheer up anyone, but, hey, I was already doing this pageant. *In for a penny, in for a pound*, I thought, and smiled back at her. "Sounds great."

Chapter 20

WHEN I GOT HOME, David's car was parked against the curb, and I took a deep breath.

My parents were still at work, so David must have used the extra key like I'd told him to.

He was already in my room when I came up, standing at my desk, fiddling with his phone.

"Hi," I said, and he glanced up quickly, fumbling to put his phone in his pocket.

"Hi."

I inwardly cringed. This was ridiculous. A few days ago, he had been my boyfriend. In fact, the last time he'd been in this room, we'd done a fair amount of making out, and now I was standing in my own room, feeling awkward and . . . oh dear Lord, was I blushing?

Shaking my head, I tossed my bag next to my desk and put on my most no-nonsense voice to ask, "So what's up?"

David blinked behind his glasses. There were circles under his eyes, and I wondered if he was still having trouble sleeping. I could ask him that, right? I mean, that was Paladin/Oracle business, not girlfriend stuff. And the more I focused on Paladin stuff, the easier it was not to feel angry or hurt or any of the other things I'd been feeling since that afternoon in his car.

But just to be on the safe side, I didn't mention it, and instead sat down backward on my desk chair, folding my arms on the back and resting my chin on top of them.

Clearing his throat, David gestured to my bed. "Can I sit?"

"Sure," I said with a wave of my hand, trying not to remember how the last time he'd sat on my bed, I'd been sitting with him, my arms wrapped around his neck, our lips—

Nope. Nope, nope, nope, not thinking kissing thoughts.

But I thought maybe David was thinking them, too, especially since his neck was red and he wasn't quite meeting my eyes.

He sat down on my purple comforter and pulled an enormous book from his messenger bag. "I think I might have found something."

I should not have been disappointed. Of course he came over to talk business. That was good. Hadn't he promised to keep looking for more information about the trials? So, yeah, not disappointed at all. Pleased. Proud. Happy things like that.

"There isn't much," he said, opening the book on his lap and flipping to a page marked with a yellow sticky note. "Apparently they wanted to keep it pretty secret."

"Makes sense," I observed, twisting one of my rings. "Isn't the element of surprise the whole point? See how quickly you can think on your feet without getting killed?"

David glanced up at me, his lips quirking. "Basically, yeah. But here"—he tapped the page—"there's a story about a sixteenth-century Paladin, another girl—er, woman—like you, who went through her Peirasmos. It seems like the trials themselves are geared toward the particular Paladin. So, like, the first one was specific to you because of . . . the school, I guess."

Taking a deep breath, I stood up and walked back to my desk chair, bracing my hands on the back. "Thanks for this, David."

He gave an uneasy shrug, shoulders rolling underneath his gray T-shirt. Wait, David was wearing a T-shirt? A regular one without, like, a dragon on it or an ugly pattern? Then I took in the rest of his outfit. Jeans, and regular jeans at that, not those super-skinny ones he liked so much. Even his shoes were plain sneakers.

"Was there a fire at the argyle factory?" I asked, nodding at his clothes, and hoping that didn't come out too mean. I wasn't sure if snarkiness was something we could still do, or if it came off as too flirty now.

David frowned at me, brow wrinkling before understanding dawned. "Oh, right. Yeah, I, uh, threw something on this morning."

I was probably reading too much into David's wardrobe. We all had days when fashion seemed beyond us, right? Surely his dull clothing didn't mean he was . . . bummed or anything. Why should he be? He was the one who had done the dumping, not me.

There was a sudden stinging in my eyes that I blinked away,

turning to study the calendar on my desk like it was the most important thing in the history of creation. "If you wouldn't mind, could you leave the book with me? I want to read a little bit more."

I'd been aiming for "breezy," but my voice was so tight it sounded like I was choking.

And then I felt a warm weight on my elbow. Glancing down, I saw David's fingers curled there against my skin, and I let out a slow breath.

"Pres," he said, his voice every bit as tight, and I turned to look at him.

His eyes were very blue, and the freckles across his nose stood out against his paler-than-normal skin, and all I wanted to do was tuck myself against his chest and breathe in that familiar smell of soap and printer ink that David carried on him.

Then I shook myself. No. He had called things off, and a girl had to have some pride.

I stepped back so that his hand fell from my elbow and folded my arms across my chest. "Thanks for your help," I said again, and this time, there was no choking feeling in my throat. "But you should probably go now. My parents will be home soon, and they'll freak if you're in my room with no one else here."

"Right," he said, turning away quickly to grab his bag off the floor. "Good. Well, um. I hope it helps."

"I'm sure it will," I told him, forcing a smile.

I picked up the book instead of turning to watch him go. I'd just opened it when my phone buzzed. It was Bee.

"Azalea Festival? When do you wanna come over?" I glanced at the book on my bed, and then at my phone.

"Be there in fifteen."

"Are you sure you're okay?"

It was already the third time Bee had asked the question, so for the third time, I gave her the same answer.

"I'm great!" Earlier, when she'd answered the door, I'd said it with a sincere look in my eyes. Then when we'd come up to her room and she'd asked again, I'd tossed it over my shoulder as I flipped through the latest issue of *US Weekly*. Now, I didn't even look up, pawing through my purse for mascara.

From behind me on her bed, I heard Bee heave a sigh, and I fought back one of my own. It wasn't that I wasn't thankful for her concern. I was, honestly. But I didn't want to talk about David to her or to anyone else right now. It was all . . . yucky. Stressing over the trials, worrying about David being an Oracle, dealing with Bee being back—happy as that last thing was. Thinking about the breakup was too much on top of all of that, and for now, I wanted to pretend it wasn't happening. That shouldn't be so hard, right? I mean, David and I had gone years and years practically hating each other. Surely, it wouldn't be that tough to downshift to not being in love.

Too bad my eyes stung as soon as I thought of the word "love."

I located my mascara and did my best to act like all the blinking I was doing had everything to do with makeup application and nothing to do with David Stark.

"I'm super excited about the fair tonight!" I chirped, and Bee met my gaze in the mirror.

She sat up, tossing her own magazine back onto her night-stand and frowning. "Okay, now I know you're not okay, because you are never 'super excited about the fair.'"

"What are you talking about?" I scoffed, sliding the mascara wand back into its tube. "There are rides and lights and cotton candy. You have to be some kind of Nazi not to like cotton candy."

Bee's brown eyes narrowed. "And there's also the smell of manure and dudes who wear trucker hats, and more chewing tobacco than you can spit at." She waggled her eyebrows. "Get it? Spit? Because chewing—"

Holding up a hand, I stopped her before the thought could make me any more nauseated. "I got it. And you're right, I'm not a fan of those things." With that, I turned, bracing my hands on the little vanity. Bee's room had been the envy of every girl we knew . . . when we were eight. For some reason, she'd never got-ten around to redecorating, and while I definitely understood the allure of a canopy bed, it was always a little weird seeing all six feet of Bee on a pink swiss-dotted bedspread.

"What I am a fan of," I continued, crossing my ankles, "is spending time with you. I need a good girls' night."

Bee's eyes darted away from mine.

"What?" I asked.

"Don't get mad," she said quickly, "but I sort of asked Ryan if he wanted to come with?"

For a second, all I could do was blink at her. And then, when

I actually went to talk, my voice was way too high. "Ryan?" I all but squeaked.

"I didn't mean to," Bee replied, rising to her feet. She was fiddling with the ends of her hair. "I was talking about the fair, and he mentioned that he wasn't sure he was going this year because he and Mary Beth had planned to go, but obviously that's not happening, and then he looked so bummed and I felt bad for him."

Last year, Ryan and I had gone to the fair with Bee and Brandon. I could practically still smell the popcorn and sugary-sweet scent of candy apples. Could remember Ryan's hand warm in mine. It hadn't been a great night or anything—Bee was right, the fair wasn't exactly my fave—but it had been normal.

I tried to imagine walking around the fair tonight with Ryan, not just my ex but a freaking Mage, a walking, talking reminder of how weird my life had become.

Disappointment has a taste, I swear. Something kind of bitter in the back of your throat that you can't quite swallow. It seemed like I was tasting it a lot these days.

But now I smiled at Bee and said, "Oh no, I totally get that. No worries."

Bee tilted her head, watching me. "Are you sure?"

"Yeah." I waved one hand. "Ryan and I are okay for the most part, and it might be nice to do something with him that's not crazy-superpower related."

Bee nodded, her hair bouncing. "That's what I thought!" she said, and there was something about the brightness of the words that had me looking at her a little more closely.

"Bee," I said slowly, resting one hip back against the vanity, its lace skirt brushing my calves. "You're not thinking about *Parent Trapping* us, are you?"

Rolling her eyes, Bee flopped back onto the bed. "This Paladin thing is making you paranoid. I only want everything to be normal."

So did I. A lot. But the thing was, it was never going to be. And it was like every time I thought I'd achieved some kind of normal, there was some new wrinkle thrown in, some curveball I had to adjust to. "Excellent multitasker" might have been one of the skills I'd listed on college applications, but it was getting harder and harder to do.

Maybe tonight could be a start, though. If eating cotton candy with Ryan and riding a machine that had been put together by scary dudes for like twenty bucks would make Bee happy, I'd give it a shot.

Chapter 21

THE FAIRGROUNDS were set up on this big field the town had especially to host the festivities every year, about a fifteen-minute drive from Bee's house.

There was a little bit of weirdness when Ryan came to pick us up, since I had no idea where to sit. Once upon a time, I would have sat with him in the front, but now that felt too couple-y. Especially since we were both technically uncoupled now. So I surrendered the front seat to Bee, sitting in the back and trying to pretend that this wasn't all super awkward.

Once we were parked, I followed Ryan and Bee from the "parking lot"—another field with a few orange cones and pieces of twine marking off spaces—and wrinkled my nose at the smell of horses and hay.

"Remind me why we're doing this again?" I said to Bee.

She was walking a little bit ahead of me, and she smiled as she turned to look at me, flipping a handful of hair off her shoulders. "Because it's fun," she insisted, hanging back to loop an arm through mine.

April in Alabama is usually pretty close to full-blown summer. Hot, humid, all of that. But it was nice now with the sun going down, the breeze cool enough to make me glad I'd grabbed a light cardigan before I'd left. In front of us, the fair sparkled with brightly colored lights, the sound of music and screams greeting our ears.

Stopping outside the main gate, Ryan shoved his hands in his pockets and rocked back on his heels, a broad smile splitting his handsome face. "Now we're talking," he said happily, and I couldn't help but smile, no matter how awkward this felt.

In that moment, I would've given anything to be able to slip my hand into Ryan's and lean against his shoulder. Not because I wanted him to be my boyfriend, but because he was good at that, being a shoulder to lean on.

Instead, I hugged myself, walking toward the booth to pay.

Once we were inside, the three of us kind of stood in the midway, unsure of what to do first.

The fair was, as usual, way too crowded, and I was a little too out of sorts to deal with things like the smell of farm animals and too many people. Still, I was doing my best to pretend this was the Best Night Ever, so I smiled at Bee and looped an arm through hers.

"What should we ride first?"

But Bee was not that easily fooled. "It's okay, Harper," she said, patting the hand I had resting on her forearm. "I know you hate every second of this."

"I don't!" I argued, but that lasted all of five seconds before I let my arm fall back to my side. "Okay, I do, but it's honestly not as bad as I remembered. I mean, they banned smoking! So that's something."

Laughing, Bee rolled her eyes at me. "At least you're trying," she acknowledged.

At my other side, Ryan nudged my elbow, nodding toward the shooting gallery amid the carnival games that lined the center of the midway.

"You wanna try out one of those?" he asked.

I almost laughed and shook my head. I had never been a fan of those types of things, and honestly, how many giant stuffed animals does a girl need? But then Ryan grinned down at me and nudged me again. "Come on, I wanna see your Paladin skills in action."

That was right. Along with increased strength and speed, I had some seriously excellent accuracy now and, like any girl right out of a breakup, I saw the appeal of making things explode.

I approached the booth, going to pull five bucks out of my pocket, but Ryan waved my money away. "No, this is on me. Harper Price, shooting things? Totally worth it."

Rolling my eyes, I smiled anyway. "Shooting balloons with a bright yellow plastic gun," I reminded him. "Not exactly superhero stuff."

He flicked his auburn hair out of his eyes. "I'll take what I can get."

So for the next ten minutes or so, I shot the heck out of some balloons with a dart gun. And to be honest, it was fun. Not just the shooting things—although I have to admit that was a lot more enjoyable than I'd ever thought something like that could be—but the joking and laughing with Ryan and Bee. It felt so good not to worry about Oracles or Ephors, or if a vision was suddenly going to come out of nowhere, making me have to lie to everyone around me.

Part of me felt guilty about that, like having fun wasn't allowed.

But then I reminded myself that David was the one who had broken things off, David was the one who had chosen the Paladin over the girlfriend, and if I wanted to have a good time with my best friend and my ex-boyfriend, I was more than allowed.

After the shooting gallery, we went in search of other games that might test my and Bee's Paladin skills. That thing where you throw balls into goldfish bowls, more dart games, even an archery booth with foam-tipped arrows—I did them all, grinning at the surprise on the barkers' faces when I hit target after target, laughing with Bee as she struggled to hold all my stuffed prizes.

Finally, when we'd hit pretty much everything we could, we headed away from the carnival games..

"Can I stand next to Bee so people think I won all those for her?" Ryan asked, making us laugh.

"No need to feel emasculated," I reminded him as Bee handed yet another one of her prizes to a passing kid. "You did win the basketball thingie."

"Only because you let me," he reminded me, and I shrugged.

"What can I say, I'm a good friend."

Ryan stopped, turning to face me. The lights overhead brought out the red in his hair, and once again, I was forced to acknowledge that he *was* handsome. Maybe he didn't make my stomach flutter anymore, but there was something nice about feeling this way about him now. Like I actually saw him for the person he was—loyal, stubborn, easygoing—and not the trophy he used to be for me.

"You are a good friend, Harper," he said. "And I kind of like being your friend."

"Same," I told him, smiling.

Over his shoulder, I caught Bee watching us with an expression I couldn't read. Probably thinking more *Parent Trap* thoughts, I decided, and went over to take more of the fluffy animals from her hands.

"Stop," I told her in a low voice, joking, but she gave me a sort of wan smile in return, handing her last prize, a bright green stuffed frog, to a little boy in an Auburn Tigers T-shirt.

Once we were out of prizes to hand out, we made our way to the food trucks. "Did all that winning work up a hunger for something super caloric?" Bee asked, tugging at the hem of her light pink blouse.

Look, I'd love to tell you I was totally disgusted by the fried food on display, but A) some of those trucks were raising money for various charities and schools, and B) deep-fried Oreos were sent from heaven to prove God loves us.

"Yes, please," I told Bee. "Preferably something covered in powdered sugar."

She laughed at that again, and started tugging me toward the cotton candy machine. As we made our way down the midway, I bumped into someone, and I turned, an apology already on my lips.

The man I'd bumped was wearing stained jeans and a Lynyrd Skynyrd T-shirt, so nothing unusual for the fair, but there was something about the way his eyes focused on mine that had the words dying on my lips.

"Paladin," he said with a little nod, and a jolt went through me. It wasn't the feeling I got when David was in trouble; this was just normal fear, slithering through me, making food the last thing on my mind.

The crowd swallowed the man, but I stood still, making Bee turn to look at me with a little frown. "Harper?"

"Something's wrong," I told her. "It's . . . I think it's a trial."

Chapter 22

BEE REACHED OUT, squeezing my hand. "I'll come with," she said, "whatever it is."

But I shook my head. "No, you heard what Alexander said. If anyone helps me, I'm disqualified."

Which I was pretty sure meant "dead," even though Alexander hadn't spelled it out that specifically.

I could see a white circle forming around Bee's lips as she pressed them together, but in the end, she nodded. "Okay. But is there anything I can do?"

"Leave," I told her immediately. "You and Ryan get out of here, and if you see anyone we know, try to get them to leave, too." The last trial had involved fire, after all. There was no telling what might happen this time, and the fairgrounds were full of people. Kids.

"Will do," Ryan said, already taking Bee's elbow and pulling her away. I turned from them, heading in the direction the man had gone. My heart was pounding, palms slick with sweat, and with every step I took, my knees seemed to go more watery. The colored lights that had seemed so pretty when we came in now cast weird shadows, making me jumpy as I kept pushing my way through the crowd.

I couldn't see the man who had called me Paladin, but I somehow knew where to go, walking down the midway before turning left, then taking a right. All the rides on this side of the fairgrounds were crowded, lines of people waiting to get on the Ferris wheel or ride something called the Galactic Centipede. But one attraction was completely deserted, almost like there was a bubble around it, making it invisible to the rest of the people here.

The Fun House.

Sighing, I studied the dark building with its garish green door. "Of course," I muttered, visions of possessed carnies dressed as clowns filling my head. I didn't have a weapon, and I'd worn low sneakers tonight, so my footwear wouldn't be of any use.

Glancing around, I looked for anything I could use, but the only thing I saw was a couple of corn dog sticks, batter still clinging to the ends, stamped in the dirt. Um, no, thank you.

Then I glanced to the right, dozens of bobbing balloons catching my eye.

Perfect.

The guy running the balloon dart attraction was too busy flirting with a redheaded girl I vaguely recognized from the pageant sign-ups today to notice me sneak up alongside the booth and snatch a few darts from the side. Their tips weren't all that sharp—that had to be a lawsuit in waiting—but I figured they'd do in a pinch. And when I saw a deserted spork lying on the ground, I grabbed that, too, grimacing as I wiped it off on my jeans. Desperate times clearly called for desperate measures.

Heading back to the Fun House, I saw that it was still deserted, people walking by it like it wasn't even there.

Taking a deep breath, I slid the darts into my pocket, keeping the spork in my hand.

"Okay," I muttered to myself. "Let's do this."

The Fun House had never been one of my favorite parts of the fair. I'd only gone in it once when I was about nine. Leigh-Anne had gone with me, holding my hand the whole time, pointing out how silly we looked in the distorted mirrors, giggling about how fake the lime-green skeleton dangling from a doorway was. Afterward, she'd told me I was obviously the bravest third-grader in the state of Alabama, and we'd gone to get another cotton candy as a reward.

I kept that memory in mind now as I slowly made my way through the deserted Fun House. It was eerily quiet, the only sound the creaking boards underneath my feet and my own breath sawing in my ears. What exactly was going to happen here? Were more brainwashed people going to jump me? Ugh, fighting off frat boys had been terrible, but fighting off carnies? Yeah, I definitely wanted to take a pass on that.

There were a few lights scattered here and there, but it was still dim enough that I had trouble making out the room I was in. Or was it rooms? I felt like I'd gone through a doorway, but I wasn't sure.

I turned left, only to run into a wall, but when I turned back the way I'd come, there was a wall there, too. Disoriented, I turned again, passing through a door narrow enough to scrape my shoulders.

I was in a bigger room now, but it was even darker, and I wiped my free hand on the seat of my pants, wishing my heart weren't thundering in my ears.

From the corner of my eye, I saw something move, and I whirled around, spork raised high, only to drop my arm immediately when I saw who was standing in front of me.

My parents were wearing the same clothes I'd seen them in earlier this evening, Dad in his sweatshirt and jeans, Mom already in her pajamas. They had their arms wrapped around each other, their eyes huge and faces almost gray.

"Harper!" my mom screamed, and I rushed forward, the spork falling from my suddenly numb fingers. Not my parents. The school had been bad enough, but if Alexander or the Ephors hurt my parents—

I reached out, but instead of grabbing my parents, my hands hit hard, cold glass. One of the mirrors. Confused, I stumbled back, only to watch Mom and Dad vanish, my own reflection staring back at me. I looked as gray and panicked as they had, my hair coming loose from its braid, my lips parted with the force of my breathing.

Another movement, and I spun again, this time seeing Bee across the room, still in her T-shirt and jeans. Even though I'd told her to leave, I practically sagged with relief when I saw she was there. "It's some kind of illusion thing," I told her. "Making me see things, and—"

My words broke off in a shriek as something suddenly thrust through Bee's right side. I saw the glint of light on metal, the circle of red that began to spread across her shirt, her mouth open in a silent scream.

"Bee!" I practically threw myself across the room, only to come up hard against another mirror. Now Bee was gone, and I could only see myself again.

Panting, I turned in a circle, looking all around me. Earlier it had seemed like there were two mirrors, but now it was like the entire room was lined in them, reflecting dozens of me, all terrified, all confused. And then I wasn't in the glass anymore. It was my parents again, crying out for me even though I couldn't hear them. It was Bee, a sword through her back; Ryan, lying in a pool of blood like Saylor at Magnolia House; my aunts, their eyes blank, their minds not their own. Even Leigh-Anne was there, dressed the same as she was that night we'd gone through the Fun House all those years ago. She was pale, but smiling like she always had been, and for some reason, that hurt the most.

Swirling pictures of people I loved, scared or hurt or dead, appeared over and over again until I wanted to put my hands over my eyes and curl up on the floor. I'd been prepared to fight someone, but this? This was more than anyone could handle, superpowers or not. The room seemed to have gotten colder, so cold I was shaking, and I felt like my mind was going to snap.

A glow filled the room, coming from somewhere at the end

of the corridor, and when I made myself open my eyes, I saw that there was one more horrible vision for me to take in.

David floated a few feet ahead of me, but I knew it wasn't actually David. It was another illusion. But it didn't feel fake. It felt entirely too real, watching him as he looked down at me, his face blank, his eyes nothing but glowing orbs.

Then suddenly *I* stood in front of me. I wasn't dressed like I was tonight—jeans, T-shirt, cardigan—but in a dress. A white one that looked like my Cotillion dress, but couldn't be, since I'd burned that thing. It had still had splashes of blood on it, and every time I'd looked at it, I'd remembered what happened to Saylor, how although I'd saved David that night, I'd lost so much else.

The me in the mirror was standing right behind David, and she was crying. Of course, the me *not* in the mirror was crying now, too, because I'd seen what was in the other me's hand.

A knife.

Not any knife, but a dagger, the blade shiny and bright, the hilt intricately carved. Somehow I knew that this was a ceremonial dagger, something special.

Something only used on one occasion.

I watched golden light spill from David's fingertips, his eyes, his mouth. I watched the me in the mirror step closer to him, one hand going to his hair, the hair that he always tugged and pulled when he was nervous.

The Harper in the mirror was tugging his hair now, too, but only to pull his head back.

The blade caught the light, almost sparkling and looking strangely beautiful.

It came to rest under David's chin, and I looked at myself in the mirror, feeling a jolt as the other Harper's gaze met mine. Her eyes were bloodshot and wet, but her expression was firm as she watched me.

"Choose," she said and, with one quick jerk of her arm, drew the dagger across David's throat.

Chapter 23

Just like that first night, the door to Alexander's house swung open the second I was on the porch, and I walked right in, making my way down the hall and toward his office.

Alexander sat behind his desk, a steaming cup at his elbow, a huge book spread out in front of him. Music was playing in the background, something soft and vaguely sad on piano that I thought might be Chopin. Even though it was past eight o'clock, and he was the only one here, Alexander was wearing another one of those beautiful gray suits, his tie cinched in a tight Windsor knot at his throat.

He glanced up when I came in but didn't seem particularly surprised to see me. "Ah, Miss Price." Gesturing to the teapot at the edge of his desk, he raised his golden eyebrows. "I'm assuming the latest stage of the Peirasmos went well, then. Tea?"

"He'll die, won't he?" I asked, and Alexander blinked once. Twice. Then, sitting back in his chair, he laced his fingers over his chest. The ring he wore on his pinky glimmered in the lamplight.

"Everyone dies, Miss Price," he said mildly. "I know American schools are said to be woefully lacking, but it seems this is a fact you would have learned at some point in your educational career."

I was seriously not in the mood for this tonight, so I folded my arms and glared at him.

Finally, with a sigh, Alexander sat back up, the chair creaking slightly. "It's true that Oracles seem to have a short shelf life."

"I don't mean it like that," I said, coming to sit in the chair across from the desk. The music switched to something full of violins, the sound scratching over my frazzled nerves. "I mean that if he fully does the Oracle thing, he won't be David anymore. The Oracle part of him might keep going forever, but the David part, the part I . . . care about. Know. That part will be gone, won't it?"

Alexander lifted his hands in an elegant shrug. "That is part of it, I'm afraid."

I shook my head. David might not have been my boyfriend anymore, but that didn't mean that I was willing to let him get all super magicked up and then forget about him. All I could think of was David in fifth grade, his hair a lot blonder, but his scowl just as fierce when I'd beaten him in the spelling bee. David, one corner of his mouth lifting as he'd called me "Pres." David, sitting too close to his laptop and leaning over it in a way that made my neck ache in sympathy as he worked on the school paper.

David, the night of Cotillion, crossing the room to kiss me.

Alexander sat forward again, bracing his elbows on the desk and pressing his fingers together. "This seems to be another part of your training Miss Stark has neglected. You see the Oracle as a person. It's high time you started seeing him as a vessel."

"David is a lot more than his powers," I argued, but Alexander was already shaking his head.

"He's a boy, Miss Price," he said, and while the word "boy" didn't exactly drip with disdain, it didn't sound much like a compliment either. "A boy with powers he hasn't even begun to understand. Clearly they are greater than *you* understand. Are you saying that you'd rather David be your prom date than a being with the powers of gods in his veins?"

With a *tsk*ing sound, he fixed me with those green eyes. "You think we only want to use him, but his entire existence is an exercise in being useful, Miss Price. You're meant to protect him from those who would wish to hurt him, not from himself. Not from who he is."

I thought of what I'd seen in the Fun House tonight, remembering the blank look in David's—no, not David's, the *Oracle's*—eyes in that vision. "Even if it means killing him?"

Alexander didn't say anything for a long time, and I couldn't make myself look up and meet his eyes. I had never been a coward, but after admitting that, I didn't feel much like being the tough girl right now.

Finally, he said, "Is that what you saw tonight?"

I sat up a little in my chair. "What, you guys didn't make me see that?"

Sighing, he leaned back. "We engineer the scenario, not the specific visions. This test was meant to be psychological in nature. You saw the things that you fear the most, not things that will necessarily come true. Being confronted with one's worst nightmares is both a way of testing your mental fortitude and seeing where your heart lies. If one of your fears is David dying—"

"Not just him dying," I broke in. "Me *killing* him."

Alexander inclined his head slightly. "Even so. If that's one of your fears, that seems to prove that you are the woman for this job."

For a moment, I saw something flicker in Alexander's eyes, but he looked back at his desk again before I could tell what it had been.

And then he said, "I know you care about the Oracle, Miss Price, but the more you deny what he truly is, the more hurt you'll be in the end. It will be easier if you accept it now."

His voice was tight, and he didn't lift his head to look at me, but there was a note in his voice that almost sounded like sympathy.

Curious, I sat forward a little bit. "What was the last Oracle like?"

Alexander sniffed and dropped his pen in a little brass cup that held about five more pens. It clinked against the side as he said, "She was obedient and functional and performed her duties as was required."

That was it, but I saw that flicker again, and how white his knuckles were as he laced his fingers on top of his desk.

"Did you know her?" I asked. "I mean, obviously you *did*, but, like, the actual her? Or was she always all Oracled up?"

Alexander kept his gaze on me, but I had the feeling he was almost looking through me. "Like most Oracles, there was a period early on where she was more human than Oracle, and, yes, I did know her during that time."

I'd been so focused on keeping David away from the Ephors that I'd never spent much time wondering how they worked. They were the bad guys, and that had seemed like the only important thing to know. But now I wanted to know a lot more. "Where did y'all keep her?" I asked. "And when did you become an Ephor? Do you apply for it like a job? And that guy tonight, the one who talked to me. Was he an Ephor?" He cut me off with a brisk shake of his head.

"The gentleman tonight was one of your own townsfolk, temporarily magicked into service. As for the rest, my affairs are none of your concern. My point is this, Miss Price. David is an Oracle. He can never *not* be an Oracle. Perhaps your friendship has kept him more . . . average for the time being. But you'll never be able to keep him from becoming what he *is*. A being whose sole purpose is to tell the future."

I had the sleeves of my cardigan tugged over my hands, and I suddenly pushed them back with disgust. I was not going to be a sleeve-pulling weirdo. Sitting up straighter, I pushed my hair back over my shoulders and faced Alexander.

"I don't want that, though," I told him. "I want to protect *David*, not some freakish thing with glowing eyes who only speaks in riddles or prophecies."

Alexander took a deep breath, nostrils flaring slightly. The music was off now, the scent of tea still heavy in the air.

Looking in my eyes, he smiled, the first genuine smile I think I'd ever seen from him. But it was sad, and his voice was low when he said, "Miss Price, they are one and the same."

Chapter 24

"HARPER!"

Sara's sharp tone snapped me out of my thoughts, and when I blinked at her, she made a sweeping gesture with one hand.

"It's your turn to walk." Clipboard propped on her hip, bright fuchsia lips clenched, Sara did not seem like my biggest fan at the moment, and I shook myself slightly, stepping forward and completing the circuit around the stage as quickly as I could.

Which was apparently not what Sara wanted, since her lips somehow got even thinner. She twirled her glossy dark hair and said, "It's not a race, Harper. And this is Miss Pine Grove, not Cotillion. You can remove the broom handle from your backside. Walk lightly. Float." She demonstrated, but whatever she was doing looked a lot more like prancing than walking. Still, I nodded and murmured something about doing better next time.

But that only made Sara glare and announce that the pageant was practically here. "There are hardly any next times left, Harper!" she all but shrieked, and I had a sudden, satisfying vision of using my Paladin powers to boot her perky little butt all the way to the back of the auditorium.

Taking a deep breath, I closed my eyes and tried to stop the orgy of violence currently unfolding in my mind. It wasn't Sara's fault that I currently hated everything. The night at the fair was a week ago, but the vision of slitting David's throat still had me rattled. Alexander had said that the second trial was about facing my worst fears, that what I saw there wouldn't necessarily come true, but that didn't make me feel any better. Especially when I thought of what David had once told me—that he'd had a dream of the two of us fighting. That we weren't angry but sad. And on top of that, I could still see Saylor's worried expression when she'd told me that David could one day become a danger to himself as well as to everyone else.

So, yeah, I had a lot on my mind, and almost none of it revolved around making Sara Plumley happy with my walk. Plus, I still had one more trial left to go, and with the way the previous two had gone, I was pretty much expecting this last one to make my house blow up or something. It seemed like with every trial, I was losing a little bit more and, if I were honest, I wasn't even sure what I was doing this for. Being David's Paladin didn't seem so great when he wasn't even David anymore.

"Are you listening to me, Harper?" Sara asked, and this time, I thought of clobbering her with my baton.

"Yes, ma'am!" I called as brightly as I could, taking immense satisfaction from the way her brows drew close together. The "ma'am" implied "old," which was clearly not okay with Sara, but it was also polite, which meant there was nothing she could do about it.

Honestly, not enough people know how to use good manners as a weapon.

But that thought wiped the smile from my face. If only good manners would be an effective weapon in whatever it was Alexander had coming next. After the fire, I'd been prepared for all the trials to be like that, dangerous and destructive. But then the Fun House had been a psychological thing, and, for my money, that had almost been worse. I wasn't sure I'd ever get over not only the vision of David, but also seeing my mom screaming.

Seeing Bee with a sword thrust through her stomach.

That's what would happen to her, I reminded myself, if I didn't get through whatever this last trial was. Maybe not any time in the near future, but as I'd learned, being a Paladin was a dangerous business. I had to pass the Peirasmos, not just for me, but for Bee.

But thinking of Bee reminded me that I hadn't seen her in a while. I'd driven her to pageant rehearsal, but I hadn't seen her in at least fifteen minutes. That was weird. Like me, she'd decided to stick with the baton twirling, and Sara always made us go last. She had a pretty rigorous schedule for talent practice: singers first, then musicians, then the "athletic talents," like dance or, yes, baton twirling. Jill Wyatt was playing the accordion right now, and she was the last of the musicians to go (although calling what Jill did "music" was charitable). We'd be up soon, but Bee was nowhere in sight.

I made my way off the stage, nearly bumping into Amanda as I did. "Sorry," I said, and she shrugged it off.

"Someone needs to sneak something into her Slim-Fast before the pageant," Amanda muttered, nodding toward Sara, and I snorted.

"Agreed."

Like me, Amanda was dressed casually in jeans and a T-shirt, but tottering around on the heels she'd wear on the night of the pageant, and she nearly stumbled now as she went to cross one foot over the other.

I caught her elbow, steadying her, and she flashed me a quick grin. "Thanks."

"No problem."

Amanda and I were pretty much the same height in our heels, so she looked me in the eyes as she said, "It's intensely weird that you're doing this thing, you know. Me and Abi can't figure it out."

"Bee wanted to," I told her as one of the girls from Lee High hustled past us to practice her walk onstage. "And as Bee go, so goeth my nation."

That made Amanda smile, and she jerked her head toward the wings. "I hear you. I'm only here because Abi insisted."

I was smiling as I glanced over to where Amanda had gestured, only to feel my smile freeze when I saw who Abi was talking to.

Spencer. The frat guy who would, according to David's vision, one day ruin her life. But we'd stopped her from hooking up with him. Ryan had even wiped her memory so that she didn't remember *meeting* him. So what the heck was he doing here?

"Who's that guy?" I asked Amanda, and she gave an extravagant eye roll. "Oh my God, the love of my sister's life, apparently. Everything is all Spencer all the time with Abi."

My stomach churning, I watched as Abi leaned closer, letting one hand rest on Spencer's chest. He was grinning down at her, tucking her hair behind her ear, and while he didn't look quite as gross as he had the night of the party—not having roughly a twelve-pack of beer in your system will do that to a guy, I guess—I still was not a fan.

Neither was Amanda, if the way she looked at them was anything to go by.

What if you can't change the future, Pres? What if you're only delaying it a little while?

David's words echoed in my head, making me clench my jaw. That couldn't be true. If you couldn't change the future, what was the point of being able to see it?

From the front of the auditorium, Sara called, "Harper!"

Amanda grimaced in sympathy. "Seriously, some kind of mood stabilizer, right in her caramel Slim-Fast," she said. "It's happening."

Sighing, I headed back out onstage. Sara was indeed drinking a Slim-Fast, with a bright green bendy straw poking out of the top of the can. "Can you do me a favor?" she asked. "Go and see if you can find some crepe paper. Pink, preferably. In the closet by the stairs."

I wanted to tell her to get her own darn crepe paper, but instead, I gave a forced smile and said, "Sure thing!"

The closet by the stairs was in the back of the rec center, down one of the hallways underneath the stage, and I rolled my eyes as I made my way down there, still holding my baton.

Of course there would be crepe paper. Streamers, probably. Before you knew it, Sara would have a balloon arch up, and then my humiliation would be complete. I almost hoped whatever was going to happen would happen before the pageant got started, so no one would have to see me in this stupid leotard, twirling a baton under freaking crepe-paper streamers.

The supply closet was next to the staircase, and I saw the door was slightly ajar. My mind was still full of crepe-paper streamers, balloon arches, and the looks of horror sure to be on The Aunts' faces, when I tugged the door all the way open.

But the closet wasn't empty. There were people in there. Two of them, and I rolled my eyes, wondering who the heck would pick a supply closet in the rec center for romanc—

And then I saw the girl's blond hair, saw the tall auburn-haired boy kissing her, and realized what I was looking at. *Who* I was looking at.

Bee and Ryan.

FOR A LONG MOMENT, it was like my brain refused to process what it was seeing. Bee. Ryan. Bee and Ryan, their mouths pressed together, Bee's hands clutching his shirt at his waist, Ryan holding the back of her head. I mean, I saw all of that, but it was like I kept trying to tell myself I wasn't seeing what I was seeing. That she was, I don't know, giving him mouth-to-mouth or something. That it wasn't even Bee, but Mary Beth in a blond wig. That I had finally snapped and was having some kind of psychotic break.

But no. No, that was my best friend and my ex-boyfriend, and they were full on *making out* in the supply closet at the rec center.

I guess the natural thing to do would have been to freak out and start yelling like I was gunning for a spot on a tacky talk show, or maybe to quietly close the door and pretend I'd never seen anything, but I didn't do either of those things.

Instead, I just stood there in my stupid leotard, hand on the doorknob, and said, "Oh."

They broke apart, Bee's Salmon Fantasy lip gloss smudged on both her mouth and Ryan's, and if I hadn't been busy trying to keep my stomach from plummeting to my feet, I guess there would have been something funny about the way they both gawked at me with big eyes and equally shocked expressions.

"Damn," Ryan muttered, while Bee nearly leapt out of his arms.

"Harper," she said, but I shook my head. My face hurt, and I realized it was because I was giving them another one of those big fake smiles I hated.

"It's fine," I said quickly. "So super fine. I mean, we've been broken up"—I waved my hand between me and Ryan—"and you and Brandon are broken up, and Ryan and Mary Beth are broken up, and wow, there has been a lot of breaking up going on lately, I just realized that. I guess that's the perils of trying to date in the middle of a supernatural crisis, right? Right. Anyway, I'll let y'all get back to . . . that."

I shut the door with shaking hands and turned away, walking back toward the auditorium, my baton clenched tightly in one hand. My eyes were stinging, and I almost bumped into a Styrofoam tree propped against the wall. Dimly, I heard the door open from behind me, and Bee called my name again.

I didn't stop walking, but when she caught my elbow, it wasn't like I could shake her off. I turned to see her watching me with big eyes. She'd wiped some of the gloss off her mouth, but there was still a faint salmon smudge on her chin.

"Harper, I am so sorry I didn't tell you," she said, her hand squeezing my arm.

"It's fine," I said, but voice was shaking, and Bee sighed, stepping a little closer.

"It's not, I know it's not. But I promise, it hasn't been going on for very long."

For some reason, it hadn't even occurred to me that it had happened before at *all*. Like I'd thought the kiss I'd seen had been their first or something, which was stupid. If they had already reached the "sneaking around" stage of things, this had obviously been going on for a little while.

"How long?" I asked, and Bee's brown eyes slid away from mine. My stomach was still rolling, and I tried to tell myself it was the smell of the rec center, all furniture polish and industrial carpet cleaner, making me feel sick.

"The night at the fair," she told me, and I remembered now that Ryan had dropped Bee off last.

"We were both kind of freaked out by everything that went down that night, and it . . ." Tears spilled over Bee's lower lashes, and she scrubbed at them with the back of her hand. "It just happened. I didn't mean for it to, and I swear to God, I never looked at Ryan like that while y'all were dating."

The thing was, I believed her. Bee had always been loyal, the best best friend a girl could have. It wasn't jealousy that was making me want to cry. Ryan and I were more than done, and while things with me and David were not all that simple right now, there was still no one else I'd rather be with. So it wasn't the actual kissing bugging me, it was the secrecy of it all. Bee had always told me everything, but she'd been keeping this a secret from me. I got it, but I didn't like it.

"If you want us not to see each other anymore, I'd totally understand," Bee said, and then Ryan came up behind her, laying one hand on her shoulder.

"I wouldn't," he said, looking at me, but I was still staring at his fingers curled over her shoulder. Since the night of the fair, she'd said, but that had been just a week ago.

There was a lot of intimacy in the way Ryan's hand lay there at the crook of her neck.

"Ryan," Bee said, but he shook his head, a muscle working in his jaw.

"I was okay with Harper and David," he said, "so Harper can be okay with me and you."

"I am okay with you. Both of you," I replied, but the words came out too fast. I thought of me asking David if we were okay, how quickly he'd answered me and how fake his answer had sounded. I guess I sounded every bit as fake, if the matching frowns on Bee's and Ryan's faces were anything to go by.

But for now, I didn't care; I needed to get out of here.

"Seriously," I told them as I turned to hurry back down the hall. "It's fine. So super fine."

Luckily, neither of them followed, and I managed to get to the dressing room, shucking off my leotard like it was on fire. I threw my clothes back on, and hurried out the back door of the rec center before anyone could see me. I'd e-mail Sara and tell her I'd gotten sick or something.

Getting into my car, I pushed my hair back with hands that were still trembling. I needed to talk to someone, but I sat there in the driver's side, the air-conditioning raising goose bumps on my skin, and racked my brain for someone I could talk to. Not David; things were still tense with us, and I was afraid that I wouldn't be able to explain why Bee and Ryan were weirding me out so much without him thinking it was a jealousy thing. But if I couldn't talk to David, and I couldn't talk to Bee, who *could* I talk to?

When the answer came, I felt a wave of relief wash over me.

It only took a few minutes to drive to Aunt Jewel's, and when I got there, she was outside watering her roses, dressed in a pretty light green top that seemed to have some kind of bird on it, and matching polyester slacks. As soon as I pulled up, she turned the hose off and waved me inside.

"Well, isn't this a nice surprise?" Aunt Jewel led me into the living room, and I flopped on the flowered sofa while she went into the kitchen to get us something to drink.

I fiddled with the hem of my dress, and when Aunt Jewel came back in, I blurted out, "I have something to tell you."

Aunt Jewel had leaned down to hand me a glass of iced tea, and she froze in place, the glass halfway to me. "Oh, Harper Jane," she said on a sigh. "You're not in trouble, are you?"

I was, of course. In lots of trouble, and I almost said answered yes. But then I realized Aunt Jewel thought I was in *that* kind of trouble.

"No," I said quickly, taking the tea before she spilled it. "No, no, no. Not even a little bit."

Breathing a sigh of relief, Aunt Jewel pressed her hand to her chest, right over the painted hummingbird on her sweater.

"Well, thank heaven for that at least." She squinted at me, leaning a little closer, and I picked up the scent of Estée Lauder perfume and the slightest hint of baby powder. "But if you're not in the family way, why do you look so sick?"

I didn't know I did look sick, and when I pressed both hands to my cheeks, Aunt Jewel clucked, sitting next to me on the couch. "I've thought you looked peaked for a few weeks at least. You aren't doing too much at school, are you?"

The tea was cold and sweet, and I gulped nearly half of the glass before setting it back on its coaster. "It's not school, Aunt Jewel. Or it is, but not the way you're thinking. Last year, during the fall, something . . . something happened to me."

She was squinting at me now, reaching down to pick up the glasses suspended on a glittery chain around her neck. Once they were on her nose, she settled deeper into the sofa and said, "What, exactly?"

It all spilled out then. All of it. The night of the Homecoming dance, Mr. Hall, killing Dr. DuPont, learning what a Paladin was, David being an Oracle, all the training with Saylor, Blythe, how there hadn't been an earthquake the night of Cotillion. How that had been me. How Ryan could do magic, and I'd made him do a spell that had wiped everyone's memory.

When I was done, the living room was very quiet. I'd drained my tea during my confession, but Aunt Jewel hadn't touched hers. The ice was melting in it now, leaving a dark ring on the coaster in front of her. I could hear the grandfather clock ticking in the main hallway, but that was the only sound.

Aunt Jewel heaved a sigh, and I waited for her to tell me I was insane or to say she was calling my mom.

Instead, she got up and patted my knee. "Come on, baby girl. We've got somewhere to go."

Chapter 26

I FIGURED AUNT JEWEL was taking me home. Or maybe driving me all the way up to the psychiatric hospital in Tuscaloosa.

So when she pulled into the parking lot of the Piggly Wiggly, I was both relieved and confused.

"The grocery store?" I asked as Aunt Jewel attempted to squeeze her massive Cadillac into a teensy parking space.

I winced as one of the side-view mirrors clipped the car next to us, but Aunt Jewel didn't seem too concerned.

"I think better when I'm shopping, and you have given me a lot to think about."

I was fairly certain my mouth was hanging open, and I imagined my eyes popping out like something in a cartoon. "Aunt Jewel, I just told you that I have superpowers. That my current boyfriend is an Oracle, and my ex-boyfriend is more or less a wizard. And you want to do a little shopping? I'd hoped you wouldn't freak out, don't get me wrong, but I expected *some* freaking out."

Heaving a sigh, Aunt Jewel gathered her pocketbook in her arms and faced me. "Harper Jane, I am nearly eighty years old. I have lived through a world war, buried two husbands, and when I was eighteen, I told my parents I was going to a church revival, but I actually spent a weekend in Biloxi with a traveling salesman. In other words, young lady, I understand that weird crap—Lord forgive me—happens. Now get out of the car and stop overthinking things."

So a few minutes later, I found myself stepping into the overly air-conditioned, overly Muzaked store, trailing behind my aunt.

I pushed the buggy for Aunt Jewel while she scanned the shelves of the Piggly Wiggly, occasionally squinting at the yellow legal pad she'd pulled out of her purse. She had just put a bunch of bananas in a little plastic baggie and laid it in the buggy when she said, "So David can see the future."

"Shh!" I hissed, glancing around us. This time of day, the Pig was mostly deserted, but I still couldn't be too careful. "Aunt Jewel, that is a private topic."

But she tsked at me and lifted her glasses to her nose, the sparkly chain winking in the fluorescent lights. Over the sound system, Whitney Houston wailed about finding the greatest love of all inside herself.

I trailed Aunt Jewel into the coffee and cereal aisle. "Yes," I said as quietly as I could.

"Hmm." Aunt Jewel picked up a can of Cream of Wheat. "How far into the future?"

I stopped, startled. Weirdly, I'd never thought of that before. It wasn't like David was seeing spaceships or intergalactic wars. "I don't know," I told her. "We never tried that much, I guess."

Aunt Jewel took that in with a little nod before adding a package of coffee to her groceries, along with some nondairy creamer. "Okay. Well, how often does he see the future? And is it only his future, or yours, or everyone in the whole wide world's? Because it seems to me that that would be a lot going on in one brain. I know that Stark boy is bright, but I'm not sure anyone's mind could handle all that information."

"That's exactly what I thought!" I exclaimed, our buggy squeaking to a halt. "But apparently me trying to keep him from seeing too much means that I'm controlling or whatever, and—"

I broke off, aware that Aunt Jewel was watching me. "Oh yeah," I added, a little sheepishly. "I, uh, I may have done some things to be sure he couldn't have very strong visions. But it's only because I was trying to keep him safe, which is supposed to be the whole point of this thing."

Sighing, Aunt Jewel wrapped her fingers around the edge of the buggy and tugged it out of my grip, wheeling it in front of her. As she took the handle and steered us down the Asian and ethnic food aisle (which contained some ramen and spaghetti sauce), she glanced over at me. "Don't fret, honey. It seems like you and David have taken on more responsibility than most children should."

"We're not children," I insisted, but Aunt Jewel only laughed.

"Of course you are. You're barely seventeen, and you still have a whole other year of school to get through. That makes you a child as far as I'm concerned."

When she turned back to me, her blue eyes were soft and she

smiled. "But then you'll always be my baby, even when you're forty years old with babies of your own."

It was a sweet thing to say, but it still hit me squarely in the chest. Aunt Jewel must've seen it, because her smile faded. "Oh. Except you can't have babies, can you? Not if you have to run around protecting David. Doesn't exactly seem like a child-friendly environment."

I shook my head, but it wasn't like I'd thought much about all of that. I'd thought about college, sure, but that was as far as I'd let myself go. Thinking about all the other stuff—marriage, kids, a career—had been too hard. Too scary, too *much*. I wasn't proud of the whole head-in-the-sand thing I'd been doing, but I hadn't known what else to do.

When the buggy stopped this time, it was Aunt Jewel's fault. She stopped there in front of a row of Chef Boyardee, frowning. "And David is your boyfriend now, but what if you break up? Or find someone else?"

I put a couple of jars of spaghetti sauce into the buggy. "We already broke up," I told her. "But bringing someone else into this would be a disaster. It was hard enough dealing with Ryan and Mary Beth." I thought again about Bee locked in Ryan's arms in the closet, her lip gloss smeared on Ryan's face. "Not that they're an issue anymore, I guess."

I'd told Aunt Jewel about Ryan's powers, but I'd left out the part with him and Bee. I wasn't quite ready to get into that just yet.

But now Aunt Jewel was frowning at me, her eyes bright over the tops of her glasses. "How did Ryan even get involved in all this?" she asked. "How did he get . . . powers or magic or what-ever you want to call it?"

"Saylor passed them on to him after Brandon stabbed her," I answered without thinking.

The box of pasta in Aunt Jewel's hand tumbled to the floor, the container breaking open and penne spilling everywhere. But she didn't even seem to see it. "Saylor Stark was murdered?"

Oh. Right.

A stock boy rounded the corner and, seeing the mess, jogged off, probably to get a broom. I scooped Aunt Jewel's purse up out of the buggy and took her gently by the elbow.

"Maybe we should shop later."

"Yes," she said faintly, giving a nod. "M-maybe that's for the best."

Fifteen minutes later, we were at Miss Annemarie's Tearoom, huddled in one of the corner tables and drinking chamomile. Aunt Jewel's pot of tea was half empty by the time she took a shuddery breath and said, "All right, Miss Harper Jane. I take it back. You are not overthinking this. I don't think anyone could overthink such a thing—goodness."

Pressing a shaking hand to her lips, Aunt Jewel shook her head. "And you've been dealing with this all alone."

"Not alone," I told her as I poured us both another cup. "I have David and Ryan. And Bee. Bee knows." I left it at that, rather than explaining Bee's new Paladin powers and her kid-napping and sudden reappearance. Aunt Jewel had had enough shocks for one day. We could always get into that later if needed.

"But no adults," she said, dumping a few sugar cubes into her cup. "And all of you running around, breaking up with each other, getting together, breaking up again, getting together with different people."

I thought about telling her about Alexander, but since I still hadn't made up my mind how to feel about that, I decided I could skip it for now. "I know, things are complicated, and the dating stuff probably doesn't help."

But Aunt Jewel only shook her head, the cubic zirconias in her ears winking. "You're children," she said again. "That's what children do, make things messier than they have to be."

I thought of Ryan and Bee in the closet, her lipstick on his face, his eyes daring me to say I didn't want them to be together.

Yeah, things were messy, all right.

Miss Annemarie stopped by the table, smiling down at the two of us. "Harper! I've seen your mama and your aunts in here, but I haven't seen you in forever!"

"I've been busy with school," I said, not adding that I'd been avoiding her since we'd tried to kill each other at Cotillion. It was still bizarre to look into her face and remember her coming after me with a knife.

After Miss Annemarie had gone back to the kitchen, promising to make some of her crab bisque, Aunt Jewel turned back to me, her eyes rheumy but sharp behind her glasses.

"Sweetheart, if anyone can handle all these responsibilities, it's you. I've never known such a determined little thing in all my life. Did you know, when you were about two, your daddy built you and Leigh-Anne a sandbox. And every day, you'd toddle out there and try to build you a castle, and every day, your sister would knock it down."

Clucking her tongue, she took her glasses off, letting them dangle down the front of her shirt. "I loved that little girl, but Lord, what a pill she could be. Anyway, all those times she knocked down your castle, you never once cried. Never complained. You jutted that bottom lip out and got back to work. You never quit, even when that would have been the smartest thing to do."

Somehow, I didn't think that was supposed to be a compliment. But I was still about to thank her when Aunt Jewel reached across the table and took my hand. "You are trying to be too many things to too many people, Harper Jane."

Aunt Jewel's fingers were cold, the skin papery, but she held me tight as she added, "And I think one day, one day soon, you're gonna have to *choose*."

Chapter 27

"YOUR LEOTARD is ugly."

I looked down at the little girl standing next to me. She came up to right above my elbow, but I was pretty sure that a solid foot of that was hair. The rest of her was covered in a sea of pale blue ruffles, so I wasn't sure how she had any room to talk about what was ugly.

Still, being mean to kids is never okay, so I made myself put on a smile. "That's not very nice," I told her, but the little girl shrugged.

"It's very true."

In front of us, another girl about the same age as this devil spawn standing next to me was practicing her "dance" on the stage. It mostly seemed to consist of some awkward shuffling and a few waves, and every now and again she'd glance down to where her mom was doing a much more enthusiastic version of the same dance in the front row.

I sighed and shifted my baton to my other hand. Normally the Little Miss Pine Grove portion of rehearsal was over by the time we got in, but Sara was running late today, so we were stuck waiting for the younger girls to finish. Which apparently *also* meant we were stuck getting harassed by second-graders.

"It's the sleeves," the girl next to me said, looking me up and down. There was something weird about the way she talked, and when she opened her mouth to yawn, I realized she was wearing those little fake teeth they use to cover a missing tooth or two.

Seriously, pageants were the *weirdest*.

"Well, I like the sleeves," I told her, tugging at the material in question. I'd used Leigh-Anne's old majorette uniform, a sparkly green number that was a little too big for me. Aunt Jewel had sewn on some sleeves for me to give it "a little flair." Apparently, to Aunt Jewel, "a little flair" meant a metric ton of sequins and fake jewels, so every time I threw the baton, my arms clattered.

"You shouldn't like them," the little girl told me, "because they're ugly."

"Okay, thanks, got it," I replied through clenched teeth.

"Get lost, Lullaby League," Abi said, sauntering up, and the little girl stuck her tongue out at us before heading down the aisle toward the front of the stage.

Abi's gaze slid over me. She was wearing a simple black dress, since her talent was playing the piano. Looking at her, I wished I hadn't begged my mom to let me quit lessons when I was twelve, because piano seemed like a totally unembarrassing talent. A thin gold chain winked around her neck, and when Abi noticed me looking, she grinned, lifting the necklace up. "Isn't it pretty? It's from Spencer."

That name made me want to shudder—a reminder that we

might have been wrong about David's visions, that we *couldn't* change the future. And if that was true, what was the point of all of this?

Abi misread my expression, clearly, because she scowled at me, letting the necklace drop back to her chest. "Okay, Harper, enough with the judge-y face. Just because you're boyfriend-less for the first time in, like, ever, it doesn't mean you can't be happy for other people."

"I am," I said, and the words might have been convincing had I not seen Bee walk in. She was practically running—worrying about being late, I guess—and while it's not like she was wearing a sign that said, "I was making out with Ryan!" I couldn't help but remember them locked together in the closet. She looked . . . suspiciously glowy.

Abi glanced over at Bee, and when her gaze swung back to me, both eyebrows were lifted. "Where were you at lunch today?" she asked.

I'd hid out in the library like a weirdo because I hadn't wanted to face Bee or Ryan yet. I'd thought about hiding in the temporary newspaper lab, but when I'd walked past, David had been in there with Chie and Michael. As I'd sat on the floor in the back stacks of the library, I'd reminded myself that a few months ago, I would've died before being one of those people who *hid* during lunch. Lunch was primo socializing time, after all, but with Bee and Ryan being . . . Bee and Ryan, and me and David being *not* Me and David, I hadn't known what else to do.

It was an icky feeling.

Bee's eyes met mine across the auditorium, and her smile

faded. This was ridiculous, not talking to her in the middle of everything that was going on, but I . . . couldn't. I still didn't know what to say. I had no right to be jealous, not of Bee for being with Ryan, and not of Ryan for taking Bee away from me. Abi was right; just because I was alone, that didn't mean everyone else had to be, too.

Turning away, Bee headed for the little stairway that led to the backstage area, undoubtedly to change, and I breathed a little sigh of relief.

One that, unfortunately, Abi saw. "So y'all are fighting?" she asked. "That's what Amanda thinks. Is it about Ryan? Amanda said she saw Bee getting a ride home with Ryan after school yesterday, and—"

"Oh, shut up, Abigail," I heard myself say. "I try to do nice things for you, like save you from a dude who will ruin your life, and all I got for my time was a ruined pair of shoes and a dress that still smells like beer, and now you're with him anyway, *and* you're giving me crap, so honestly, why do I bother? Why do I bother with *anything*?"

I hadn't realized that my voice was getting so loud, but from the way Abi blinked at me, I thought maybe I'd gotten close to shouty on that last bit. But I *felt* shouty. All I ever did was try to help, try to make things *better,* and it seemed like I was failing all over the place. Sure, I'd gotten through the first trials, but I was wearing a leotard in the rec center, I had no boyfriend, things with me and my best friend were intensely weird, and I'd been insulted by a munchkin wearing fake teeth.

There was only so much a girl could take.

Except apparently the universe wasn't through screwing with me, because when Abi glanced toward the back of the auditorium, I saw someone standing in the doorway.

David.

"I . . . I'm sorry for the yelling," I told Abi, ignoring her when she asked, "What did you mean about Spencer?" and moved up the aisle toward where David still hovered.

It was stupid to feel embarrassed, but David seeing me in my leotard left me feeling weirdly exposed, and not because of all the skin on display. The old David would have watched me with twitching lips before making some kind of annoying joke about how I clearly had a future in leading parades. But now, it was like he wasn't seeing the costume. He was wearing a long-sleeved shirt in a shockingly nonoffensive shade of blue that brought out the color of his eyes.

Holy crap. His *eyes.*

When I looked closely, I could see light glowing there. Not brightly, but still there and not a reflection.

With a sigh, David whipped off his glasses, replacing them with a pair of sunglasses that he had hanging in the front of his shirt. "I'm guessing you can see it?" he asked, and I stepped closer. Behind me, I could hear the stereo system blasting "Yankee Doodle Dandy," so I knew the little kids were still practicing.

Momentarily distracted by that, David gazed past me before shaking his head slightly. "This place is—"

"It's a total freak show," I confirmed. "But we can worry about that later. Why are your eyes all . . . like that?"

Reaching up, David ruffled his hair. "They just are, okay?"

"That is like the least acceptable answer in the history of un-acceptable things, most of which, I should add, involve your wardrobe," I told him, folding my arms and trying not to notice the clatter of plastic gemstones. "David, what's going on?"

For all that his eyes were freaking me out, I wished I could see them right now. I could read a lot in his face—the tightness of his mouth told me he was going to be stubborn about this, the tugging at his hair meant he was nervous—but his eyes would've told me more. How freaked out *he* was, for example.

"I've been trying some things," he said, and I blew out a breath that ruffled my bangs. A few days ago, I'd thought about how much I didn't like him alone in that house, obsessively going through Saylor's things. Hadn't I thrown myself into time with Bee and pageant practice to distract me from our breakup? What had David been distracting himself with? It wasn't like he could see the future anymore, after all. Alexander had seen to that.

But if that was the case, why the heck were his eyes Oracled out? Again, I remembered him in the Fun House, floating in front of me, his eyes nothing but that golden light.

My knife at his throat.

Pushing that image away, I leaned in closer. "What kind of things?"

He'd tugged his sleeves over his hands. The music had stopped now, and I could hear Sara calling for all the Miss Pine Grove girls, but I kept my gaze on David. "What. Kind. Of. Things?" I re-peated, and David looked straight at me. Even through the dark lenses of his glasses, I could see the twin sparks of light there.

"Visions," he said in a low voice. "Alexander's spell doesn't work anymore."

That startled me so much that my baton nearly slipped from my suddenly numb fingers. "What?" was all I could manage, and David's mouth turned down at the corners. For the first time, I noticed that he looked even thinner, paler. Almost like he was fading away right in front of me.

"I don't know why or how," he continued, "but the other night, I . . . I saw something."

I opened my mouth to ask what, but David held up a hand before I could. "It wasn't clear. It was like before, when my visions were all muddled and cloudy. But I think . . . I think with *help* . . ."

It was my turn to hold up a hand. "Even if Ryan and I did try to help you have a vision, Alexander would know, right? He'd . . .Who knows what he'd do? That could disqualify me from the Peirasmos. It could kill me. Or you, or—"

But David shook his head. "This will work," he insisted. "And think about it—if I can override his powers, maybe I could override . . . I don't know, *everything*. Maybe this could end. If Alexander doesn't have any power over me, he doesn't have any power over you either."

It was tempting. *Really* tempting. But if David was wrong . . .

Like he could read my mind, David reached out and took my hand. His skin on mine felt familiar and good, and I fought the urge to let my fingers curl around his.

"Pres," he started, then moved in closer. "*Harper.* Trust me."

Behind me, Sara called my name, and I thought of what this would mean. I'd have to talk to Ryan, of course, and Bee, too, probably, since this affected her. The four of us—my two ex-boyfriends and my maybe-ex-best-friend—would have to work together.

It would be scary and hard and, if David was wrong, quite possibly fatal.

But in spite of all that, I squeezed David's hand and nodded.

Chapter 28

I'M SURE there have been more awkward car rides than the one we took out to the golf course to have David's vision.

I mean, Aunt May once told me a story about a funeral where the limo company screwed up and sent the same car for her cousin Roderick's wife and his mistress, and they had to ride to the cemetery together. That was probably worse than this ride.

But not by much.

Ryan had agreed to drive since he had the biggest car, a nice SUV his dad had bought for him last year when the basketball team had managed not to come in dead last. But even with all that space, I still felt cramped, even though it was just me and David in the backseat. Apparently the weirdness between us took up a lot of space. Bee rode up front with Ryan, and she'd done a decent job of trying to keep small talk going, but after getting monosyllabic answers from most of us, she'd given up, and now we drove in silence.

Bee and I still hadn't talked about that afternoon at the pageant, which, to be honest, was fine by me. Nobody can repress better than a good Southern girl, and I wondered if the best thing to do was to forget any of that had ever happened. So Bee and Ryan were a thing. So she hadn't told me.

That was . . . fine. No big deal at all. I certainly wasn't watching the two of them, waiting to see if their hands touched or if they glanced at each other the way they had that afternoon. And I definitely hadn't spent a lot of time wondering if, no matter what they'd told me, there hadn't been a spark of something there before.

No, definitely not wondering any of that.

Next to me, David felt like he was strung so tightly that he nearly vibrated, and I couldn't blame him. There was this bizarre vibe in the car, like something bad was coming, but that could have been all the tension. Still, when Ryan made the turn onto the highway out to the country club, I almost told him to turn back. Which would have been dumb, of course. I'd promised David we could do this, but if I was being honest, I didn't expect anything to happen. Alexander had taken David's powers from him, and no matter how much David thought he could somehow overcome that, I didn't have particularly high expectations. If anything, this felt more like a favor we could do for him.

That thought in mind, I laid my hand on David's leg, trying not to notice how he flinched when I first touched him. But then he glanced over at me, his blue eyes bright behind his glasses, and he linked his fingers with mine. It had been a while since we'd touched, and I was surprised by how good it felt to have his hand in mine, even if it was only for a second.

The big stone and wood sign announcing the Pine Grove Country Club was lit up, but everything else was dark as we turned down the winding drive. Ryan rolled down his window, waving a card in front of a sensor, and the gate slowly swung open. Technically, the club closed at seven, but since Ryan's dad owned the place, he could come and go as he pleased. And if his dad asked him why he'd been out at the club on a Wednesday night at ten, Ryan could always say he'd been cleaning the pool or something. That's what he'd said on the nights we'd come out here after hours—memories I didn't want to dwell on right now.

From the almost embarrassed way Ryan's eyes met mine in the rearview mirror, I didn't think he wanted to stroll down memory lane either.

We'd decided to come here for a couple of reasons. One, in all of David's readings, he'd realized that the past Oracles were always having visions in nature-y places like caves or forests. There were a few woody places around Pine Grove—there was a reason the town was called what it was—but since none of us were in the mood to tramp through underbrush and risk snake bites, ticks, and God knew what else, we'd chosen . . . civilized nature. Plus it was a nice, private space still in town, but not too close to anything else, just in case this got out of hand.

The country club was a pretty building made to look like an antebellum mansion, and as we drove past it, spotlights on the tall white columns, giant tubs of azaleas by the front door, David snorted. "I feel like I should start humming 'Dixie.'"

"Have you never been out here?" I asked, and he shook his head.

"Saylor came out here for lunch sometimes, but it's not exactly my scene."

There were still shadows under his eyes and his nails were bitten almost to the quick, but in that moment, there was enough of the old David in his face to make me feel a little better about what we were about to do. David's powers still scared me, and for all that he wanted to use them to the best of his abilities, I thought they scared him, too. And with the Peirasmos still going on, what if him doing this . . . violated that somehow?

I didn't want to think about what the repercussions of that could be, but I felt like this was something I owed David. He was asking me to have faith in him, and the least I could do was try.

Ryan's SUV drove silently over the asphalt lane winding its way to the golf course. We'd decided to attempt this on the eighth hole. Well, Ryan had decided, pointing out that that part of the golf course was hidden from the main road by a hill, plus there was the lake to one side, and trees to the other.

Once the car was parked, we piled out, and for a moment, we all just stood there, looking at the fairway.

"We're really going to do this," Ryan said, his hands in his pockets.

At his other side, Bee nodded. "We have to." She looked over her shoulder at me, tucking a strand of hair behind one ear. "Right, Harper?"

I nodded without thinking. "Right. So let's get started."

All four of us tromped down the hill, and once we were near the eighth hole, I gestured for us to sit. We did, forming a semi-circle with David in the middle, Ryan and me on either side of him, Bee across from us. Overhead, the moon was high, reflecting on the pond. I could hear frogs croaking and the occasional chirp of bugs, but there was no breeze. The night was still and warm, almost too warm, but I still felt chilled.

I think David felt the same sense of wrongness. "Maybe this is a bad idea," he said in a rush, and a sudden whoosh of relief shot through me. *Yes, let's go home,* I thought. *Forget this whole idea.* Again, I saw David like I'd seen him in the Fun House—his skin glowing, his eyes pure light.

My dagger at his throat.

But that was the girl thinking, not the Paladin. It wasn't my responsibility just to keep him safe; I needed to make sure he could do everything he was meant to do, fulfill his destiny as an Oracle. And that meant having visions.

So I reached out and took his hand. To my surprise, Ryan reached out and took David's other hand.

"It's what we came here for," I said softly.

David turned to look at me, his eyes already bright. The light cast strange shadows on his face, emphasizing his cheekbones and the dark circles underneath his eyes. "And if it goes wrong—"

"It won't," Ryan said, his voice firm. "Me and Harper are here, and it's . . ." His eyes met mine over David's shoulder. "It's going to be fine."

It was the first time since all of this had happened that I honestly felt like that might be true. It was nice, going through one of these with everyone. Even with the oddness that was Bee and Ryan, I felt better having her here.

Reaching over with my free hand, I took Bee's and gave it a quick squeeze before letting go and taking Ryan's other hand.

"Ready?" I asked both boys, and they nodded.

There was a feeling in the air, a slight electric tingle that I recognized but still hadn't quite gotten used to. My hair felt like it was crackling over my shoulders, and on the other side of David, I heard Ryan suck in a breath.

David closed his eyes, but I could see the glow brightening behind the thin skin of his eyelids, and his hand shook in mine.

The electric feeling in the air got stronger, almost uncomfortably so, and I opened my eyes to see the flag stuck by the eighth hole snapping like there was a breeze, but the air was totally still.

Frowning, I held David's hand tighter. The flag waved again, then stopped, almost like it was frozen. Another ripple, but there was something off about it, something unnatural.

"Harper!" I heard someone cry. I thought it was Bee.

And then I didn't hear anything else as the world shattered apart around me.

Chapter 29

THERE WAS a sound like something tearing, and I felt David's hand fall from mine, but I couldn't see anything. Nothing except this bright golden light, so bright that I had to turn my face away, covering my eyes and crying out. Underneath me, the ground rumbled, and I felt like my whole body was about to shake itself apart.

It was still so bright that I could barely see, but I held my hand over my eyes and I could make out David on his feet off to one side.

There was a sound like wind or the ocean roaring in my ears, and I gritted my teeth against the hammering in my head. I'd seen David have visions lots of times now, had seen Blythe's ritual take him over the night of Cotillion, but this was something totally new. Something terrifying.

I caught movement out of the corner of my eye, and saw that the little pond next to the fairway was roiling, waves splashing onto the reeds by the shore, its entire surface practically bubbling. Bee followed my gaze, her eyes huge. "Harper!" she called out, but I only shook my head, my attention focused on David.

He was standing up straight, his arms rigid at his sides. At some point, his glasses had fallen off, but that didn't matter since his eyes were just glowing orbs now.

David stared at me, and I waited for him to do his normal thing, spouting out a direction or a specific event we needed to beware of.

But he didn't say anything at all. He kept looking at me, and I felt everything inside me go very cold. It was like what I'd seen in the Fun House, that same amount of power and that . . . I don't know, *lack* of David. He wasn't a person; he was a thing, just like I'd always feared.

The longer he stood there, saying nothing, but with power rolling off him in waves, the colder I felt. He'd broken through whatever it was Alexander had done to him. What did that mean? And what the hell was he *seeing*?

But David just watched me, the light burning and hurting. Still, I wouldn't look away. I couldn't.

"What exactly do you see?" another voice shouted. Ryan.

He moved closer to me, the wind or whatever the heck it was blowing his shirt away from his body as he looked at David, one hand lifted against the light. "Give us something here, man."

David's bright gaze swung to Ryan, and I saw Ryan flinch against it, but he still stood there, his shoulders back, his eyes trying to stay locked on David's face.

"Harper, what's going on?" Ryan shouted, lifting one hand to shade his eyes. "Why isn't he saying anything?"

I could only shake my head, and then there was this feeling, almost like a surge of power. I felt my hair blow back, and swore

I saw the ground ripple. Bee gave a little scream, and when I turned toward her, I saw a small section of grass was on fire.

Bee rushed over to it, stomping out the small flames with her booted foot.

David's eyes swung to me, but they weren't his eyes, not even a little bit. He didn't say anything, but I could feel something happening. He was seeing something, something to do with me. I couldn't say how I knew it. It was more like I felt it, this certainty that whatever vision he was locked into, it involved me.

I thought again about my knife at his throat, the bright red of his blood when I'd jerked my arm, and felt my stomach roil.

There was another pulse of power, and the ground shuddered, a crack springing up a few feet away from me, snaking through the earth, sending up clumps of grass and red dirt. It was close enough to Bee that she had to scramble backward, tripping as the ground gave way underneath one shoe.

"David!" I screamed.

The power went out of him all at once, and he sagged to the ground so suddenly that neither Ryan nor I had a chance to catch him. David fell in a heap, and all three of us moved forward, but I got to him first, resting my palm against his cheek. "David? David, wake up."

His eyes slowly blinked open, still bright, but nowhere near as blinding, and without thinking, I gave a soft cry of relief and leaned forward to kiss his cheek.

"See?" I told him. "You're fine, it's all fine."

But it wasn't, and all four of us knew it. That much power . . .

It felt like everything Saylor had warned me about, and I could see just how much it had taken out of David.

If I'd thought the ride to the golf course was awkward, that was nothing compared to the ride home. David sat on my left, his knees drawn up tight, his head resting against the window. I was holding his glasses, and he kept his eyes closed the whole way back. I could still see the light burning behind his eyelids, though, and his whole frame shook with occasional tremors.

"Should we take him to Alexander's?" Ryan asked.

"No," David replied. His voice sounded so thin and weak that it broke my heart. "I want to go home."

"Fair enough," Ryan said, and I reached over to hold David's hand. He curled his fingers around mine again, but this time they felt cold and clammy, and all I could think of was him standing there on the grass, light and power pouring out of him.

David's house was dark as I let us in, and even though he seemed a lot better than he had in the car, I kept my arm around his waist as we walked up the stairs. His room was, as usual, kind of a wreck, and I kicked clothes out of the way, clearing a path to his bed. That was also cluttered, but with books, and when I swept them all to the floor, David winced at the thump.

"Be careful with those, Pres," he said, and I was happy to hear him call me that. Happy that he finally sounded like the David I knew and not some kind of mystical bigwig.

Now that we were alone, I had to ask. "David, what did you see tonight?"

When he turned to look at me, there were still dark circles underneath his eyes, and the hollows under his cheekbones seemed deeper. There were little pinpricks of light at the center of each of his pupils, and I had to try very hard not to shudder at that.

He shook his head, rubbing a hand over his mouth. "It wasn't anything," he said at last. "A jumble of stuff." He glanced up at me, brows lifted. "Alexander's spell must have worked in some way."

He was lying.

There was no doubt in my mind. I had known David Stark most of my life, and I knew that look, knew from the way his lips twitched that he wasn't telling the truth.

I didn't press him—tonight had been rough enough on him—but I decided I would do a little truth-telling of my own.

"I had a vision, too, you know," I said, crossing my arms over my chest. "The night of my second trial. I saw you like that, the way you were tonight. I . . . I saw me with you." I couldn't add the part about what I'd done to him in that vision. I wanted to, but the words were too awful, and I couldn't seem to say them. Instead, I said, "The me I saw in the vision, she looked at me. She told me to choose."

David blew out a very long breath, his shoulders sagging a little. "You've had a lot to choose between," he said, reaching out with one hand and idly pushing his desk chair in a slow circle. "Your regular life, or life as my Paladin. Me as a person or me as an Oracle." He glanced up then, the tiniest smile lifting one corner of his lips. "And of course the most important choice of all—plaid or paisley?"

I laughed, but it sounded a lot like a sob. "As if."

Sitting gingerly on the edge of the bed, I reached out and took David's hand, pulling him closer to me. As soon as he did, he wrapped his arms around me, pulling me in tight for a hug. He wasn't shaking now, and I buried my face in the crook of his neck, breathing him in. I knew this was definitely not something we were supposed to do anymore—we were in boyfriend/ girlfriend territory for sure with this kind of hug—but it felt so nice, and I'd missed it so much that I couldn't make myself stop. Not when every time I closed my eyes, I still saw him as the Oracle, not the boy.

"I'm sorry," he choked out, and I let my hands drift up and down his back.

"Sorry for what? You didn't do anything wrong tonight. We knew it might go like this, and—"

But he shook his head and pulled back. "No. I don't mean for tonight. I mean, I am sorry for that. I know it was scary. But I'm sorry for all of it." His hands came up to cup my face, fingers cold against my skin, but I leaned into him, resting my forehead against his.

"I'm sorry I told you we should take a break. I liked you for such a long time," David continued, making me huff out a laugh even as I reached up to curl my fingers around his.

"Even when I was beating you in spelling bees?"

David closed his eyes, a smile lifting his lips. "Especially then," he told me, his hand cupping the back of my neck. "And I feel like I finally got everything I ever wanted, and I screwed it up."

"You didn't," I promised him. "I mean, it's not like any relationship between the two of us was going to run smoothly. Making the shift from mortal enemy to boyfie was bound to be difficult."

He huffed out a laugh, opening his eyes. "I told you not to call me—" he started.

I kissed him.

It was stupid, probably. I never wanted to admit that Alexander was right, but if David couldn't be saved and he would eventually be that glowing, powerful creature all the time, I'd only get my heart broken.

But maybe it was too late for that, anyway.

"Pres," David said softly when we parted. "Is this, like, the absolute worst time in the world to tell you I love you?"

I wasn't sure if it was a laugh or a sob welling up in my throat, but I nodded. "Pretty much, yeah."

"We suck at timing, don't we?"

"We do."

And then David smiled. "Good thing we're so good at kissing."

He kissed me again then, and again, sitting on the edge of his bed, our arms twined around each other.

After a long while, David lifted his head, his fingers playing along the back of my neck. "Choose," he mused, and I shook my head, letting my hand rest on the back of his neck, too.

He sighed, his breath ruffling my hair, and I tightened my grip on him. "I choose you," I whispered. "I choose you, David. No matter what."

David wanted to argue. I knew him well enough to know

that, to understand that that was why his mouth quirked down, why his eyebrows drew together, why he said "Pres" one more time.

But then I kissed him, really kissed him this time, and there was no more arguing.

There were hardly any more words at all.

Chapter 30

"ALEXANDER WANTS to see us." I have to be honest, those were not exactly the words I wanted to hear from David after everything that had happened the night before, but when he came up and found me at lunch, that was what he blurted out.

I was eating in the library again, thinking that after a few more days like this I'd have to buy an all-black wardrobe and stop combing my hair, so when David suddenly appeared in the stacks, my cheeks flushed bright red, and I felt weirdly nervous.

As a result, it took a minute for what he was saying to sink in. When it did, I stood up, dusting my hands on my pants—I'd taken to wearing pants more often at school on the offhand chance that something Peirasmos related could happen—and crammed my half-empty water bottle back into my bag.

"Did he say what it was about?" I asked, and David gave me that look from underneath his brows. There were still little pinpricks of light in his eyes, glowing brighter in the dim library, and I noticed he still had sunglasses hanging from the collar of his shirt.

"Pretty sure there's only one thing it could be about, Pres. He has to know about last night."

Again with the blushing. I knew David was referring to the vision at the golf course, but I remembered the way Alexander had looked at the two of us when he'd figured out what we were to each other. What if he wanted to talk about . . . the other thing that had happened yesterday?

The same idea had apparently occurred to David, because it was his turn to go pink, his eyes dropping to the floor. "I'll meet you by your car after school?" he asked, and I nodded.

I could barely concentrate on anything else for the rest of the day, and when Bee found me as I made my way out to the parking lot after the last bell, she had to call my name more than once.

It was another beautiful sunny day, and Bee looked just as beautiful and sunny herself as she jogged toward me in a lime-green shirt and white jeans. "Hey," she breathed when she caught up with me. "Are you okay?"

"Yeah," I said with a quick nod, even though I felt anything but. The weirdness between me and David, knowing that Alexander was waiting . . . It was a lot on my mind, almost too much for me to focus on the fact that things with me and Bee weren't exactly the best right now. But then she reached out, laying a hand on my shoulder, and looked down into my face.

"Are we okay?"

Taking a deep breath, I shook my head. "Probably not?" And then I smiled, a little shakily. "But we will be."

Now it was Bee's turn to take a deep breath, but she smiled back at me, squeezing my shoulder. "Good. That's . . . good."

I wanted to stay and talk to her longer, but I could already see David standing by my car, so with a little wave at Bee, I made my way toward him.

"How?" It was the first thing Alexander had said to us when we walked in the door, and he seemed determined to repeat it now. We were in his office, but for once, he wasn't sitting behind the desk. Instead, he was pacing, a hank of hair coming forward to fall over his forehead.

David and I stood on the rug like a couple of kids called to meet the principal, and I wondered why I felt so guilty. David could do whatever the heck he wanted with his visions, and while, yeah, it had gotten a little scary there for a second, it wasn't like anyone had been hurt. Besides, he'd proven exactly how powerful he was, and that seemed like something we should actually be pretty pumped about.

"Was it from one of the books your Mage kept?" Alexander asked, almost frantic. His tie was loose, one cuff of his shirt unbuttoned where it peeked out from underneath his jacket sleeve. "A . . . a ritual or something that you found and decided to experiment with."

"There wasn't a book," David told him, jamming his hands into his back pockets. "I just . . . I felt like if I tried, I could have a vision, and I did. It was cloudy and . . . I don't know, murky. Like they used to be before Blythe did the ritual."

Alexander stopped pacing, coming to stand in front of his desk with both hands braced on the edge. "But you *did* see something?"

David kept his hands in the pockets of his skinny jeans, his shoulders tight. After a moment, he nodded, and Alexander dropped his head with a deep sigh.

I'd never seen Alexander look anything besides 100 percent with-it and together, but now, he wiped a hand across his mouth, and I could swear he was shaking. There was also something about the way he was looking at David that I definitely did not like.

"It's impossible," he said. "Even with the ritual Blythe performed, there's no way you should . . . No one has ever overcome the removal spell I did on you. *Ever.*"

Next to me, David gave a familiar shrug. "Well, I did." He said it as a challenge, and as I watched, David pushed his shoulders back, meeting Alexander's gaze head-on.

"What was it you saw?" Alexander asked, and David flexed his fingers. I was waiting for that answer myself, but if David wouldn't tell me, I knew he wouldn't tell Alexander. And sure enough, after a pause, he shook his head.

Alexander stood there, his hair still messy, his gaze fixed on David's face, and while his expression didn't change, it was like I could see the gears whirring in his head. I sometimes felt that with David, too, that I could sense all that was going on beneath the surface, and it was weird to have the same feeling watching Alexander.

Then he straightened up abruptly, fixing his tie and tugging at the unbuttoned cuff with a sniff. "The Peirasmos is cancelled," he said in a tight voice, and I blinked, caught totally off guard.

"What?"

"There's no need for it anymore," Alexander continued, and when his eyes met mine, they were hard chips of pale green ice.

But I'd faced a lot of scarier things than one pissed-off snooty guy, so I met that cold gaze and asked, "Why? A few weeks ago, this was so important that if I didn't do it, I'd *die,* and now you're telling me, 'oh, no big, totes cancelled, everyone go on your merry way!'"

Alexander stood ramrod straight, his fingers still on the cuff of his shirt. "I do not know what 'totes' means in this context, but I assure you, no one is 'going on their merry way,' Miss Price."

With that, he crossed over to his desk, pulling open a drawer and yanking out an ancient-looking binder of some kind, the leather cracked and peeling. As he smacked it on top of his desk, he glanced up at the two of us.

"You may go now," he said, lifting one long-fingered hand to more or less shoo us away.

I stayed right where I was, hands on my hips. "Um, I will not be shooed. What is going on here?"

"What is going on," Alexander replied, bracing both hands on his desk to look up at me, "is that our Oracle is more powerful than I'd guessed, and now I have to rethink some things. Which I can do much better without you standing there yammering at me."

I was pretty sure I'd never been accused of "yammering" in

my life, and I was about to *show* Alexander what real yammering was, but David tugged my elbow, pulling me toward the door. "Let's get out of here, Pres."

I followed him through the house, and as we got close to the front door, a loose board tripped me, the tip of my shoe catching its lip. David paused, but I gave him a little wave, saying, "I'm fine, no worries." But as I looked back at the board, I noticed it wasn't the only one that was loose. There were a couple that were warped and not fitting flush against the floor anymore. That was weird. As was how . . . unshiny the hardwood looked. And when I glanced at the wall, I could see wallpaper peeling in the corners. Even the paintings seemed less glowy than before.

Maybe whatever magic Alexander had used to make this place was fading. Or maybe it looked worse in the afternoon sun. I had no idea, and at the moment, my brain was so full of thoughts, I couldn't stop to consider that.

We paused on the porch, David's hands thrust into his pockets, my own dangling limply at my side. I had no idea what I wanted him to say. We weren't fine. No matter what had happened last night, we weren't back together, and none of the issues between us had been solved. I knew that, and from the slump in his shoulders, I think he must have, too.

"Guess you don't have to do the pageant now," he finally said. The afternoon light was turning his hair a dark gold, almost the same color as Alexander's. I could hear the hum of insects, the soft whisper of the breeze through the tall grass, and all I wanted to do was step back into his arms like I had yesterday after the golf course.

But I stayed where I was on my side of the steps, watching David. "I guess I don't," I agreed, "but I might as well at this point. I think Sara Plumley might actually murder me if I dropped out."

That made him smile, but it didn't reach his eyes, and I felt a million unsaid words sitting between us.

"Pres, about last night—"

"If you say you're sorry," I interrupted, "I'll murder *you*. Not that I can, of course, but I could try."

This time, his smile was genuine, but there was something sad in it. "I wasn't going to. I was going to say . . . Look, it's not like I can say it didn't change things, exactly, but . . ."

My chest hurt, but it had nothing to do with any Paladin powers.

"But it's still easier when we're not together," I finished, and David sighed, his eyes searching the horizon.

"It's not easier," he said, and I heard the slight catch in his voice. "But it's still the best thing we can do."

He turned to look at me then, and I wasn't sure if it was the sun on his glasses or that glow that still wasn't going anywhere. "I meant everything I said last night. Every word. But—"

"We need to stay Paladin/Oracle and lose the whole boyfie/girlfie thing," I said, and David's lips twitched.

"Still the worst word."

I smiled at him even though nothing in me felt all that smiley. He was right, I knew that. But that didn't mean I had to like it.

And then he turned to me, taking my hands in his and searching my face. "Even if the Peirasmos is over, that doesn't suddenly make things right, you know? There could still be people want-ing to take me, you'd still have to deal with Bee and her Paladin powers, I could turn into . . . Pres, look into my eyes."

I knew he didn't mean that in a romantic way, and sure enough when I looked closer, I could see the dots of light there in his pupils.

"That's not going away," he told me. "And I have a feeling that every time I have a vision, they're going to get bigger and brighter. You keep saying you don't want me to go with Alexan-der because he'll turn me into a 'thing,' but . . . Harper, I think that's going to happen anyway."

"It's not," I said, shaking my head. "I know that if we—we work at it, and try to—"

"Harper." He squeezed my fingers tighter. "It's going to happen."

Stupid as it was, I heard myself blurt out, "You can't know that."

But of course he could. Of course he *did*.

I stepped back, letting my hands fall from his. "That's what you saw, isn't it? Last night at the golf course."

"Part of what I saw, yeah," David said, turning away and heading down the porch steps.

I stood where I was, and despite the warmth of the late spring afternoon, I suddenly felt very cold. "What was the rest?" I asked.

He didn't answer.

Chapter 31

THE NIGHT of the pageant was hot and muggy. Mom and Dad still didn't quite get why I even wanted to do it, but they came anyway. "I missed Cotillion," Mom had said as she'd carried my baton out to the car, my costume in a garment bag draped over one arm. "I won't miss this."

Without Ryan's powers, there was no way to keep my parents from coming, although, trust me, I'd been trying to find an excuse. Of course, now I guessed that didn't matter so much. Alexander had said that the Peirasmos were over, but you couldn't blame me for not trusting the guy. He'd looked plenty freaked out the last time I'd seen him, and I'd thought he'd sounded sincere. But then I remembered Cotillion and the Ephors' flair for the dramatic. It would be just like them to make me lower my guard, only to attack when I was unprepared.

That wasn't going to happen.

So by the time we got to the rec center, I was already pretty tense.

So was Sara Plumley. Granted, she wasn't worrying about the boy she loved possibly turning into a mystical being, but from the way she was running around shrieking, you would think something a lot more dire had happened than one girl running a little late.

"Harper!" she barked at me as soon as I walked backstage. "I thought you weren't coming!"

"It isn't that big of a deal," Bee said, walking in behind me. "She was—"

"What if she hadn't been here?" Sara near-shrieked. "One girl missing creates a hole in the choreography!"

With that, she stomped off, clipboard in hand, heels clacking, and as soon as she was gone, Bee and I burst into giggles.

"Maybe we should have told Sara about Cotillion," I said, hanging up my talent costume. "It might have put things in perspective."

I'd meant to make Bee laugh, but instead, she frowned. And when she reached out to take my hand, I realized she was shaking.

"Hey, are you all right?" I asked, stepping closer.

Bee smiled brightly, and something in my stomach twisted. I knew that smile. I'd made that smile before. That was the smile of a girl desperately trying to fake it.

"What—" I started, but then the lights blinked twice, signaling that it was almost time for the pageant to start.

"That's our cue!" Bee chirped, and then she was out of the dressing room, leaving me to trail in her wake, confused.

We gathered in a straight line toward the back of the stage, and as the curtain went up, music blared from the sound system. I was between Bee and Rebecca Shaw, which made me feel about three feet tall, but that was actually okay. The fewer people noticed me as we launched into our supremely cheesy dance routine (one that involved smiling too hard, thrusting our arms out, and the occasional pivot) the happier I was.

As I thrust out one hip, I shot a look at Bee out of the side of my eye. Honestly, the things I did to be a good friend.

The dance portion mercifully over, Sara emerged from the wings. Her dress wasn't quite as sparkly as the contestants' were, but she was still wearing her Miss Pine Grove sash and tiara from five years ago.

Pushing her dark glossy hair back off her shoulders, Sara smiled out at the audience. "Good evening, y'all!" she drawled, the words nearly echoing throughout the room. When there was no reply, she tilted her head a bit, that bright smile stretching even further.

"I said good evening!" she called again—and I guess once head cheerleader, always a head cheerleader, but I resolved right that second to never, ever be Sara Plumley. In fact, I might turn in my uniform first thing Monday morning.

After the audience gave her the response she wanted, Sara beamed harder, taking a sip from the water glass on the podium, leaving a bright red lip print on the rim. "All right, folks, we're going to go ahead and get started," she announced. "First we'll give y'all a chance to meet these lovely ladies before proceeding to the talent portion and then the evening gown competition. And before we leave tonight, one of these very lucky girls will be Miss Pine Grove."

There was a round of applause for that, and I bit back a sigh. The whole night seemed to stretch out in front of me, and I suddenly wondered what David was doing tonight. Was he sitting all alone in his room, listening to that whiny music I hated? Was he thinking about me?

Rebecca Shaw had completed her circuit of the stage and answered the judge's question—the ever-so-original "What would you do if you won the lottery?"—but I hadn't heard Rebecca's answer. I assumed it was something equally original, like "Give it all to charity." It wasn't until she slid back into place next to me that I remembered I was next.

I broke off from the rest of the line, walking to the front of the stage as Sara rattled off my name, age, and who my parents were. The lights nearly blinded me and my smile felt frozen on my face as I walked, but I tried to keep my head high and my shoulders back.

The Aunts and my mom and dad were sitting in the front row, and seeing them, my smile felt a little more natural. But then, in the row behind them, I could see David.

What was he doing here? My eyes met David's, and it might have been the lights, but I was sure that his eyes were glowing faintly behind his glasses. Not only that, but his whole body was drawn up tight in his seat.

Maybe he was weirded out from seeing me after the last time we'd talked, but I wasn't sure. What I was sure of was how my heart thudded painfully against my ribs when I saw him.

I was so distracted by worrying about that that I almost

walked right past the microphone. It was only when I heard Sara hiss, "Harper," that I stopped, disoriented. There was the squeal of feedback as I grabbed the mike stand with unsteady hands.

From behind the podium, Sara winced, but she kept that bright smile on her face as she chirped out, "Harper, your question from the judges tonight is: If there was one thing in your life you could change, what would it be?"

I swallowed, my eyes still on David's. In the audience, I could hear the rattle of programs and someone unwrapping a hard candy. The lights were still too bright, and I was suddenly afraid that I might actually be sweating.

But my voice was calm and sure as I answered, "Nothing."

When I didn't elaborate, Sara gave a nervous laugh. "Not a single thing?"

David was watching me, sitting up straighter in his seat. The auditorium was full of people, but in that moment, I felt like we were the only people there. "No. I wouldn't change anything. Not one bit of it. I mean, don't get me wrong, not everything in my life has been . . . easy. There's a lot that's been harder than I ever thought it would be, and there may have been times I've wished things were different. But that doesn't mean I'd ever want to change it. No matter what."

My words echoed through the room, but they were only for David, and when he smiled, I smiled back, feeling almost lightheaded with relief. Until I'd said the words, I hadn't realized they were true, but now that I knew, now that I was sure, there was nothing I wanted more than to climb down off this stage and go find David and make things right between us.

But then Sara gave another one of those laughs and said, "Well, all right, then, Harper. Thank you for your answer."

Dismissed, I made my way back to the line of girls, taking my spot beside Bee. She glanced down at me, and something strange passed over her face for a minute. Pursing her lips slightly, she studied my face before turning to the front again.

The talent portion was next, and as the girls all raced off to the dressing room, I hung back in the wings. Could I just leave? Maybe I could tell Sara I'd gotten sick. The last thing she'd want was one of the girls puking all over her stage, so I was sure she'd let me go.

I wanted to go out in the audience and find David, grab him, and get the heck out of here.

But then Bee stopped beside me, taking my elbow. "Harper? Come on, we need to get changed."

"I'm actually thinking I might leave," I whispered, leaning in close as Rebecca dashed past me in a pink tutu. "I don't feel so great."

Frowning, Bee studied my face. "You can't leave in the middle of the pageant."

With a light laugh, I shrugged. "Why not? You can stay, obviously. To be honest, I'd much rather watch you win from the audience."

Bee reached out, her fingers closing around my elbow. "No," she said firmly. "You can't leave."

I stared up at her, surprised. "Bee, I know you wanted us to do this together, but it's not really my thing, and I need to talk to David—"

Her fingers squeezed tighter. "I thought y'all broke up."

Shaking off her hand, I stepped back. "We did. Kind of, but that's not—Bee, are you honestly mad at me because I don't want to finish the pageant?"

The lights backstage outlined her in soft blue light, her dress twinkling and shimmering in the gloom. And then I realized she was trembling.

"Bee?" I asked, and then it hit me.

Pop Rocks exploded in my stomach, racing through my veins, my whole chest tightening.

Gasping, I leaned forward, one arm banded around my waist. "I have to go," I said, panicked. "David—"

But Bee only grabbed my elbow again, and now she wasn't so much trembling as shaking. "No," she said, her voice wavering. "You have to *stay*."

I tried to shake out of her grip again, but she was holding on too tight, and my Paladin powers were no help against hers. "Something is wrong with David," I told her, reaching out to pry her hand from my arm. "That's a lot more important than a freaking pageant, Bee."

Looking up, our gazes met, and just like that, I understood. Bee wasn't holding me so that I wouldn't leave the pageant. That wasn't what this was about.

Tears pooled in her big dark eyes. "I'm sorry, Harper," she said. "But I can't let you go."

Chapter 32

I FROZE. If it had been anyone else, I wouldn't have hesitated. But this was Bee. I couldn't just start swinging fists.

But apparently Bee didn't have any reservations on that front. Placing her hands firmly on my shoulders, she shoved, hard.

It was enough to send me stumbling backward, and I heard a delighted gasp from behind me. "I told you what pageants were like," someone said, but I was already regaining my footing and taking off after Bee.

I stumbled over cables in the dim light, barely able to make out the blue sequins on her dress flashing as she dodged behind one of the curtains.

One of the stage managers gave a startled cry as she pushed past him, and he may have used a four-letter word when I did the same.

Bee was right against the back wall of the theater now, a giant fake oak tree blocking her path.

She turned to face me, wearing an expression I'd never seen before. One that, to be honest, I never would have thought Bee was even capable of. She was practically snarling.

"I trusted you." It was the only thing I could think to say, the only words that seemed to be pounding inside my head, and they hurt coming out of my mouth. They hurt maybe more than anything else I'd ever said. This couldn't be happening. I couldn't have been wrong. Not about Bee.

"Trust me now, Harper," she choked out in reply. "This is the only way."

I reached out and yanked a branch off the fake tree. The crack was probably loud enough to be heard in the audience, but I didn't care. "By letting the Ephors take David? That's what this is about, isn't it? You're working for Alexander."

Bee reached out and did the same with another branch, and we stood there facing each other, fake branches clutched in our hands, both of us breathing hard.

"I'm not working for them," Bee said, her fingers tight around that branch. "It isn't about Alexander or any of that, Harper, I swear, but you can't go to him. I can't let you."

"He's in danger," I cried, my chest seizing even as I said the words.

Nodding, Bee gripped her branch harder. "He might be, yeah. But I promised him I'd let him do this."

The words landed harder than her blows had. "What?"

"I promised David," she said, and I felt like my head was spinning. "He knew you'd never let him leave, knew you'd fight to keep him here. But this—" She clutched the branch harder, and I saw tears start to pool in her eyes. "This is what's actually best for him." Her voice had turned pleading now. "Please, Harper, don't make me do this."

Out onstage, I could hear Sara announcing the beginning of the talent portion of the pageant. The stereo system was blasting some kind of terrible smooth jazz, but even that couldn't drown out the rush of blood in my ears as I faced down Bee. I knew what she meant. We were both protecting David, albeit in different ways. My Paladin instincts weren't going to quit until the threat—Bee—was eliminated. Bee wouldn't stop until she'd fulfilled whatever vow it was she'd made to David.

"Nothing bad is going to happen to him," Bee said.

"That's a lie," I cried, "because I wouldn't feel like this if he were going to be fine."

Bee shook her head, hard enough that her blond hair began to spill out of her updo. "It's the only way."

With that, she swung the branch at me. I raised my own, blocking her blow. Whoever had made the fake tree had done a darn good job, because even though I could feel the reverberations all the way down my arms, the branch didn't break.

Throwing my weight behind it, I pivoted the branch in a wide circle, trying to disarm Bee, but she was prepared for that. She'd planted her feet, and while she grimaced, she kept her hold on the branch, and then, with a sharp stabbing motion, managed to drive me back.

"The only way for what?" I asked. "For him to run away and get caught by Alexander and the rest of the Ephors, who will kidnap him and turn him into their personal fortune-teller?"

I gritted my teeth, hands nearly numb with how tightly I was holding on to my weapon, and let myself be led backward. That had been one of Saylor's lessons: Let them think they have the upper hand. Bet on their overconfidence giving you a window of opportunity.

"No," she replied. "It's the only way for any of us to have a normal life again."

Bee pushed forward with her branch and I stepped back, my high heel catching on the velvet curtain a little.

And then suddenly I was blinded by bright lights and I heard a big intake of breath, like a bunch of people had gasped all at once. What the—

In front of me, Bee hesitated for a second, her head swinging to the left.

Oh. Crap.

We were onstage.

As I looked out into the audience, I saw my parents tilt their heads to the side, faces wrinkled in confusion. Next to them, Aunt Jewel raised one hand to cover her mouth.

Aunts May and Martha were still eating lemon drops, seemingly unconcerned that their niece had just torn down the curtain and appeared onstage with her best friend, both of us swinging giant fake branches.

The music was still playing, something from *Swan Lake,* and I remembered Rebecca in a tutu.

She was frozen at the corner of the stage now, staring at me and Bee, one arm still raised over her head, her feet in second position.

Then, with a grunt, Bee swung at me again, the branch connecting with my thigh. The pain helped me focus, and I turned back to her, parrying with a vengeance. My blow caught her on the ribs, and as she staggered back, she cried, "Just let it happen, Harper. I promise, it's for the best."

I gave one quick glance to the audience, my eyes searching for David. But his seat and the ones around it were empty, and my stomach was jumping, my chest still so tight I could hardly breathe.

With a snarl, I launched myself at Bee. "That's what Blythe said, too. That the ritual was for the best, and look what it did to you. Can you honestly"—I sucked in a breath as Bee's branch grazed my knuckles—"say it was for the best?"

I wished now I'd picked a looser dress. The tight sheath skirt made it hard to maneuver quickly, and Bee's dress was a lot more voluminous, giving her a freedom of movement I just did not have.

We stumbled across the stage, the music from *Swan Lake* still blasting through the auditorium, our arms a blur of thrusts and swings and blows. Bee's hair had completely fallen by now, and her long blond curls swung around her face as we fought. Her face was blotchy with tears and sweat, and I knew mine was, too.

"Let him go!" Bee yelled again, and this time, when her branch hit me square in the chest, I fell to my knees. Even over the music, I could hear a gasp from the audience.

Pressing one hand against the stage, I tried to catch my breath. My body ached from David being in danger, and I could feel every one of Bee's hits. I'd only ever fought another Paladin like this—seriously—once, the night I'd killed Dr. DuPont. I realized then that every cell inside me was crying out to kill Bee.

That she was the thing standing between me and David. But for once, my mind was overriding my instincts.

No matter what my duty, no matter that she had lied to me and led us to this, this was Bee, and I couldn't kill her. Not for David, not for Pine Grove. Not for anything.

She swung the branch down in an arc toward my head, probably hoping to knock me out.

I reached up with one hand and caught the wood in my palm. The shock of it jarred all the way down to my shoulder, but I used the branch to leverage myself back into a standing position. Gripping Bee's branch as hard as I could, I looked into her tear-streaked face.

"I'm sorry," I gritted out, and then I swung.

I pulled back at just the right moment, the branch glancing off her temple instead of crashing into her skull. But it was still enough to make her eyes roll back, and Bee slumped to a sequined heap on the floor.

At that exact moment, the music cut off, and for a long moment, all I could hear were my own ragged breaths and the thundering of my heart in my ears.

And then, from the auditorium, Aunt May said, "Ooh, performance art!" and started to clap.

Hers was the only applause, though, and as I looked out at the audience, I saw my parents sitting like they were frozen in their seats, their mouths open in identical Os of horror. It was a sea of pale, shocked faces as far as I could see.

Another pair of hands began clapping loudly. As I watched, Aunt Jewel rose from her seat, her tall form sparkling slightly from the sequins on her dress. "It's part of the show!" she said loudly, still clapping and giving me a nod. "Performance art!"

Her words slowly started to penetrate the rest of the crowd, and there was the slightest smattering of applause, but for the most part, everyone was still gaping at me, and I felt sick to my stomach.

The sick feeling increased when I looked down and saw Bee, slumped there on the stage, her temple already swelling, black and blue.

But I couldn't worry about that right now. Not when something was happening to David.

Nodding at Aunt Jewel in thanks, I dropped the branch and ran.

Chapter 33

My instincts were leading me outside, and as I ran backstage, I dodged the other girls, all of whom were blinking at me. "What was that?" Abi asked, her hand closing around my elbow, but I shook her off, making my way to the back door that led to the parking lot behind the rec center.

I pressed down hard on the bar, but the door wouldn't budge. The tightness in my chest was getting worse, my blood and heart racing, and I tried again, even harder this time.

But whoever had sealed this door had done a darn good job, and when I squinted at the bar, I saw crude runes scratched into the metal.

My whole body went cold.

Those were wards. A Mage had put those there.

"Harper," Ryan said, panting, and I turned to see him standing beside me. His tie was loose, his cheeks flushed, and he'd shed the jacket he'd been wearing earlier.

"Can you undo this?" I asked, gesturing to the door. "We've got to get—"

"To David, I know. But . . . Harper, let him go."

I'm pretty sure my mouth actually fell open. "You're in on this?"

He winced. "Don't say it like that. Like we're not on the same side."

My chest was so tight it was a wonder I could breathe, but I managed to say, "If you did these"—I pointed savagely at the wards—"then we are *not* on the same side, Ryan. Not even remotely."

Ryan's gaze swung to mine, his face pale. "We both want what's best for David, right? Harper, this is what's best."

Tears spilled down my cheeks all over again, and I wiped at them. "Then why is my chest on fire? Why do I know he's in danger, Ryan?"

When he didn't answer, I kept going. "Did Bee talk you into this? Did she tell you she was doing this to save David? Because that wasn't her call to make. Or yours." I hit my breastbone with my fist, but that was nothing compared to the pain there. "It was *mine.* You lied to me, both of you lied, and—"

Ryan crossed the space between us, one warm hand coming down on my forearm. "David didn't want to tell you. He knew you'd never let him go. That you *couldn't* if it was dangerous. So he . . . he asked us to help, and what were we supposed to say?"

I didn't know how to answer that. They were supposed to be loyal to me? Supposed to tell me what David had planned?

From the stage, I heard music start up again and I stood up fast enough to make me dizzy.

Looking back toward the stage, I couldn't see any sign of Bee and I ducked back down beside Ryan, hissing, "She's gone. Bee."

Ryan sighed, scrubbing a hand over his face. "You didn't hit her that hard," Ryan said. "And my magic fixed the rest."

I stared at him, confused. "Your magic doesn't work."

"After the vision at the golf course, it came back," Ryan answered, and I nearly squawked.

"And you didn't think this was worth telling me?" I hissed, but before Ryan could answer, there was a loud pop, followed by a hiss.

The lights overhead flickered once, twice, then went out altogether.

"That cannot be good," I whispered, and when the entire building began to shake, the screams of the audience filling my ears, Ryan muttered, "The hell?"

We crouched in the darkness, my skirt pooling around my legs, my heels wobbling slightly. I could hear Ryan breathing hard and could nearly feel the fear vibrating off him.

"Take the damn wards off the door!" I whispered. It was too dark to see him, but I could tell from the change in his breath that Ryan was looking at me. "I'm not supposed to," he answered, and honestly, I could have slugged him.

"Look," I said, leaning in closer to him. "I'll forgive you for this, and I'll even forgive you for stealing my best friend."

"I didn't—" he started, but I cut him off.

"I figure I owe you a couple of things after nearly getting you killed last year. And for . . . other stuff."

Ryan didn't say anything, and even though I knew this was not exactly the best time to get into this, I felt like it was now or never. "We should've broken up a long time before we did. I should've . . . I don't know, set you free or whatever. But we'd been together too long, and I didn't know how, and I nearly kissed David while I was dating you."

At that, Ryan gave a sharp intake of breath. Miserable, I continued. "I know, I know. I am a terrible person. But I promise nothing happened between us until after we broke up. I mean, it was like ten minutes after we broke up, which I still don't feel great about, but—"

"Harper." Ryan grabbed my elbow, his fingers digging into my skin. "First off, I think Bee and I might have made a mistake about letting David go. Secondly, we have no idea where David is right now, and seeing as how it is more or less our sacred duty to protect him, that's kind of an issue. And third, I kissed Mary Beth before we broke up."

For a moment, all I could hear both of us breathing and the rush of blood in my ears. "You what?" I was proud of how non-shrieky I managed to sound, considering how shrieky I felt.

"I kissed her. That night at the movies."

The same night I had almost kissed David. I had spent all these months feeling terrible about that, and the whole time, he had been making out with Mary Beth Riley? Seriously?

I jabbed my finger in the general direction of Ryan's face. "You are so lucky we are busy right now, because if we weren't, you and I would be having a major discussion about this."

Ryan snorted and swatted at my hand. "Why? Didn't you just say we should have broken up earlier?"

"Yes! That doesn't mean it was okay for you to cheat on me."

"You had been cheating on me way before that, Harper," he hissed, and I gave a squawk of outrage.

But then he raised up on his knees, whipping out a pocket knife and scratching at the marks. The door gave with a creak, spilling Ryan out into the parking lot. He glanced over his shoulder at me.

"Harper?"

Outside, the wind was blowing hard, reminding me of the night we got Bee back from Alexander's house. Just like then, there was this almost overpoweringly electric feeling in the air, racing along my nerves and making my hair stand on end.

The parking lot was full, and several car alarms were blaring. Underneath the sodium lights, Ryan's hair was orange, his skin pale.

"This is bad," he said, his gaze darting around.

Shooting him a glare, I bent down and grabbed my skirt in both hands, ripping the little slit in the side until the dress was open to my upper thigh. I wasn't going to let the skinny skirt get in my way again. "Yes, Ryan, that's been established."

Ryan shook his head. "No, Harper, I mean . . . this is not just run-of-the-mill bad. I can feel something. There is major magic happening out here. Scary magic. It's like . . ." Trailing off, he shook his head and looked at me. "We shouldn't have done this," he said, and it wasn't the cool spring air raising goose bumps on my arms.

"We have to find David."

Chapter 34

My parents had driven me, so I turned to Ryan and said, "Car!"

He was still standing there in his white button-down and khakis, looking around with a pained expression. "It wasn't supposed to go like this," he muttered, and I grabbed his shirtfront, forcing him to look in my eyes.

"It *is* going like this, though," I said, "And we need to find David now. Before it gets worse."

I remembered the wards Alexander had had Ryan put up, wards that were meant to keep David in town. We'd never tried to break a ward before; I didn't even think that was possible, but if that was what David was doing now . . .

From somewhere in the distance, there was a loud boom, and both Ryan and I flinched.

"He can't leave town," I said to Ryan. "It's not that simple. Did he not bother to explain that to y'all?"

Dazed, Ryan shook his head. "He said he had to leave, that it would be better for everyone if he did."

Looking down at me, Ryan's eyes seemed to focus. "Harper, I

think whatever he saw that night at the golf course scared the hell out of him."

I remembered what I'd seen in the Fun House. If David had seen that, if Alexander was wrong about the Fun House only showing me my worst fears . . .

"We have to get to him," I told Ryan, dropping my hands from his shirt. "And . . ."

My words trailed off. Why did we have to get him? If the wards were going off, he was already gone, and this was pointless. But I could still feel that ache in my chest, telling me that he was in danger, that we at least had to *try*.

"We're wasting time," I told Ryan, scanning the parking lot. I could still hear people leaving the rec center, and I sent up a quick prayer that my parents wouldn't worry too much about me.

Ryan took my elbow, pulling me in the direction of his car. As I hopped into the passenger seat, he glanced at me from the corner of his eye. "Bee," he said, and I held up a hand.

"We can talk about her later, but for now—"

"No, I mean Bee is heading this way," Ryan said, nodding out my window.

I turned and sure enough, there she was, a knot on one side of her forehead, but other than that, totally fine.

"We can't take her," I said to Ryan, even as he clicked the button to unlock the back doors. "She'll try to stop us, she'll—"

"No, I won't," Bee replied, sliding into the backseat. When she looked at me, her expression was pleading. "I had no choice, Harper, but now that he's gone—"

"We don't know that," I snapped back, even though she was

probably right. Whatever the three of them had planned, it had worked.

"Where do you want to go?" Ryan asked me, and I closed my eyes, taking a deep breath and trying to sense where David was. Just outside of town, I thought. Close, still. I could find him, I could talk to him, I could get him to see that this wasn't the solution.

"Head toward the city limits," I told Ryan. "He'll be going for the highway; we might be able to catch up."

Ryan started the ignition, pulling out of the parking lot.

"When?" I asked as we left the rec center. "When did y'all put this whole plan in motion?"

There was a pause, and I could see Ryan catching Bee's eye in the rearview mirror. "Four days ago," he said, and I racked my brain, trying to remember what had happened four days ago.

We'll think of something, David had said, and I guess he had. Too bad he'd never thought to let me in on this.

"So he comes to you, says he wants your help leaving town," I clarified, and Bee leaned forward, sticking her head between our shoulders.

"Yes. He chose the night of the pageant because he'd thought you'd be distracted, and he'd hoped that it wouldn't . . . I don't know, trigger your Paladin senses or whatever."

She looked at me, and I could see the whites of her eyes around her dark irises. "He didn't think it would be dangerous."

The car rounded the square just as Adolphus Bridgeforth exploded in a shower of sparks and stonework.

All three of us instinctively ducked, and when a large piece of marble bounced against the hood of Ryan's car, denting it, he gave a groan.

I wanted to remind him that this was all his fault, his and Bee's for deciding to handle this without me, but then I remembered how much Ryan loved his SUV, and decided that would be adding insult to injury.

"Well, clearly it is," I said through clenched teeth, and Ryan took his eyes off the road long enough to flash me a panicked glance.

"What's happening?"

"Those wards Alexander had you put up, genius. Either David did some kind of crazy spell himself to get rid of them, or this is what they do when they're broken." Either option seemed possible at this point, and then something occurred to me.

My hand flew to my mouth, stomach clenching. "You put the wards where we'd put the other ones." I looked at Ryan and saw the same realization dawning on his face.

"We put hundreds of wards on Magnolia House."

I turned my head east, in the direction of the huge mansion where we'd had Cotillion, and saw a faint orange glow in the sky.

Without a word, Ryan turned the car that way.

Magnolia House was on fire. Cotillion hadn't destroyed it— although it had come pretty freaking close—but this . . . this had finally done it.

We sat in the car for a while, watching flames lick out of the windows, racing along the white wood, wrapping the huge pillars out front in fire.

"How?" Bee asked, and the words almost stuck in my throat.

"Alexander put up different wards," I told her. "To keep David here. But they . . . they didn't work." One of the upstairs windows suddenly burst outward in a spray of glass. That was the bedroom where I had kissed David for the first time, finally understanding what had been between us for all those years.

"We need to get to him," I said, even though I hated to do this. "Alexander. Maybe he can stop David."

I didn't think that would actually work. I could actually feel David getting farther away from me, a steady pulse beating behind my ribs like a second heartbeat.

I'd failed.

The one job I'd had was to keep him safe, and I hadn't been able to do that. Saylor had told me that one day, I might have to protect David from himself, but I'd never thought it would be like this. I'd imagined him having too many prophecies, burning up his mind. Never running from town—from *me*—and leaving this kind of destruction in his wake.

Silently, we drove out of town and onto the dirt road where Alexander had set up headquarters.

I waited for the house to loom out of the darkness, its windows glowing, but the closer we got, the darker it seemed to get. Frowning, I sat forward in the seat, squinting into the inky blackness.

"Where is it?" I said, then glanced over at Ryan. His hands were so tight on the steering wheel, it looked like he could snap it right off, and from the back, I heard Bee take in a sudden sharp breath.

"Harper," she said softly. "Look."

Chapter 35

THERE WAS no house left.

It was like Ryan had described that first night, just a charred and broken chimney rising from tall grass, a few stray cinder blocks littering what appeared to be an empty field.

Alexander sat on one of those blocks, his head in his hands. His hair was a mess, his tie dangling limply from his fingers, and it looked like one sleeve of his jacket was singed.

"Holy crap," Ryan murmured as he stopped the car, and I laid a hand on his sleeve.

"Let me go by myself, okay?" I wasn't sure why, but this seemed like something that should be between me and Alexander.

I thought both Bee and Ryan would argue that, but neither said a word, and I opened the car door, stepping out on shaking legs.

I took a few steps forward, my high heels crunching on stones and broken glass. My dress snagged on a tall weed, but I kept walking. Overhead, there was no moon, but the sky was full of stars.

And smoke. Not much of it—we were still a few miles outside

of town—but I could see the bright glow in the distance and took in a deep breath at the thought of Magnolia House burning.

At the knowledge that my parents were probably frantic and looking for me.

Alexander only lifted his head when I was a foot or so away, and when he did, his face looked . . . broken. His eyes were bloodshot, circled in lines, and when he smiled at me, it was one of the scariest expressions I'd ever seen.

"Is this what you wanted, then?" he asked, his voice hoarse. My chest was still aching, telling me that wherever David was, he was in danger, so I shook my head. I had never wanted David to belong the Ephors, but I hadn't wanted him to leave, either. Especially not like this. If he had known . . .

Maybe this was what he'd seen that night at the golf course? Our town burning, me standing in a deserted field with Alexander? It was difficult to speculate about what David had known or not known.

"I didn't have anything to do with this, believe it or not," I told him, coming to stand in front of him. "This was David's doing. He . . . he didn't want to go with you, but he knew he couldn't stay here." The words stuck in my throat. I hated them. Hated that as I said them, I knew David had done the right thing. Or at least the best thing he could think of.

Not that I thought this would last very long, of course.

Staring down at Alexander, I said, "I'm guessing you'll report back to the rest of the Ephors and drag him back."

"There are no more Ephors," Alexander said, his voice dull. "Only me."

I'd never thought surprise could actually knock you on your butt, but I swear I rocked back on my heels. "What?"

Still looking at the ground, his tie wrapped around his hand, Alexander gave an entirely humorless huff of laughter.

"It's flattering to know I fooled you, Harper Price, it truly is." He looked up at me, his green eyes sharp despite the obvious devastation there. "What a Paladin you would have made."

"I am a Paladin," I answered without thinking, and he smiled again. This time, there was something like fondness in it, and to be honest, I think that freaked me out more than the whole sardonic-in-the-face-of-destruction thing he'd had going on.

But then he looked back at the tie in his hands, heaving a sigh. "We can't last without the Oracle, you see. Her—or in this case *his*—power feeds ours. We're all very, very old men, no matter how dapper we appear." He gestured to himself, and I thought it would probably be mean to point out that he wasn't exactly rocking it on the dapper front right now.

"Without the Oracle, we wither. We *die*. It's why we were so desperate to find him."

Bee and Ryan still stood by the car, watching, and I gave them a little wave to let them know that I was all right. Then, clutching my skirt in my hands, I sat down on a cinder block next to Alexander, watching him carefully.

"The Peirasmos?" I asked, and Alexander heaved a sigh, grinding the heels of his palms into his eyes.

"Had you completed them, the trials would have increased your powers enough for me to use you if I had to. Ephors gain most of our strength from the Oracle's magic, but the Paladin and the Mage help as well. Not enough, not *nearly* enough, but some."

I took a deep breath. "That's why you stripped Ryan's powers. It wasn't so that he couldn't help me. It's because you were draining his . . . his Mage energy or whatever."

With another one of those humorless laughs, Alexander nodded. "Indeed. All of this had been an elaborate ploy to keep myself alive, and"—sitting up, he placed his hands on his knees, the headlights from Ryan's car winking off the heavy gold ring on his pinky finger—"you see how well it has gone for me."

"So the house was an illusion?" I asked, and Alexander shook his head.

"It was real enough. Created by magic, yes, but real."

My head hurt. My *heart* hurt. And while I wasn't sure how it was possible, I was pretty sure my soul hurt.

"If you were dying or . . . fading, how did you get enough power to set all this up?"

Alexander looked down again. His normally shiny shoes were covered in dust, and he poked at a loose stone with the toe of one. "Blythe proved useful."

They were only three words, but they sent a finger of ice down my spine. I hadn't liked Blythe—I'd hated her for taking Bee—but the idea that Alexander had killed her to take her magic . . .

Shaking his head, Alexander chuckled. "God, what a mess this is. And to think, all we wanted was to have things back the way they should've been. The way they've been for millennia. A powerful Oracle at our side, a brave Paladin, a crafty Mage. Now we have nothing."

The night was warm, but I was nearly shivering now, wrapping my arms around myself. "Will you go after him?" I asked, and Alexander looked off into the distance. It was probably just my imagination, but I could swear his cheeks looked more hollow, the lines around his eyes deeper than they were when we started talking.

"There's no point," he said. "I won't last long enough to find him, and whatever he did to blow through my wards seems to have drained the last bit of magic from me."

He smiled that ghoulish smile. "So you see, Miss Price? I am just a sad old man now. You are just a pretty girl in a silly dress. Your friends are now simply your friends. Oh, you'll all retain some powers for a while, but they'll fade over time, and all will go back to the way it was."

His smile turned fierce, almost a grimace. "Isn't that what you wanted?"

It had been. I'd spent all this time trying to make my life resemble what it had been before, trying to convince myself that I could balance it all. Paladin and SGA president, Oracle and boyfriend, family and duty. Now I had what I wanted, but as my chest ached and I thought of David, speeding off into the darkness, the cost seemed so high.

Placing his palms flat on his thighs, Alexander heaved himself to his feet, and I heard the creak of his knees. "I suppose this is my cue," he said, and I stood up, too.

"Harper?" Bee called, and I held up a hand.

"So this is done?" I asked Alexander. "My powers will . . . go away, and Bee's and Ryan's will, too?"

"Oh, it's very done," he assured me. "For you, for your friends, for David, and most certainly for me."

And with that, he fell to the ground, his eyes open.

Unseeing.

Chapter 36

"Do you have David's jump drive?"

I glanced up from my desk to see Chie standing in front of me, a sheaf of papers clutched to her middle. I hadn't thought there was anyone in all of Pine Grove who looked as wretched as I did, but she was coming in at a close second. Her dark eyes were huge and bloodshot. Apparently she hadn't been sleeping either.

Shaking my head, I murmured, "I don't know what you're talking about," but then she nodded at the bag by my feet. David's bag. I'd found it in Saylor's house that last night. There hadn't been anything else of his, other than a couple of sweaters too not-ugly to bother taking, I guess.

Maybe I'd taken those, and maybe they were hanging in my closet right now. I wasn't admitting anything.

But I'd been using David's bag since he'd left, not caring what anyone thought. Ryan had done one of his Mage tricks, convincing everyone David had taken an early acceptance at some college up North, so no one questioned my whole grieving-girlfriend thing.

Chie was watching me with an unreadable expression as I

pulled the bag into my lap, and as I rifled through it, she said, "I miss him a lot."

Her voice was soft and quiet and it made me look up at her. There was no universe in which I'd thought Chie and I could ever be friends, but seeing my own loss reflected in her face felt . . . good. Or at least comforting.

I'd been keeping my stuff in the main part of David's satchel, but I hadn't looked through the little pockets. That's where I found the jump drive, there in one of the tiny pouches inside the front flap.

It was the same bright blue as The Doctor's TARDIS, and looking at it made my eyes well up. Still, I handed it over to Chie and watched her make her way over to one of the computers in the back.

It was bizarre how . . . normal everything felt. Ever since Homecoming, I'd been wishing for normalcy, trying to shove my anything-but-ordinary life back into the box where I'd lived my actual ordinary life. And now everything *was* normal again, and I hated it.

Opening my notebook, I did my best to outline a story I wanted to write for next week's edition of *The Grove News*. It was about the chemicals they use to keep the lawns so green, and I thought it would make Chie happy.

It would've made David happy, too, probably.

For two weeks now, I'd been waiting for some feeling, some idea of what was going on with him or where he might be. I had that same faint sense that I'd always had, a weird awareness of him, but all it told me was that he was far away from me.

And moving farther.

I was so involved in sketching out my idea for the story that I was almost startled when Chie suddenly appeared in front of me again, holding out the drive. "Thanks," she said, and when I took it back from her, she hesitated for a second. I glanced up and saw her chewing on her bottom lip, watching me cautiously.

"You should look at that," she told me, gesturing toward the bright blue stick still in my hand. "I didn't read it," she went on to add quickly, "but it seems like there's something on there for you."

I almost went to one of the computers in the back and plugged it in then and there, desperate to know what David had left for me. Was it an explanation? Or a clue to where he'd gone?

But I was afraid it might not be either of those things, and I couldn't stand the idea of bursting into tears in here, in front of these people who were trying to be nice to me, but weren't really my friends.

No, there was only one place I wanted to read this. And only one person I wanted with me.

"You're sure?" Bee asked, her hand on my shoulder.

We were sitting in David's house, at the computer in his bedroom. I still had a key to the place, although with Saylor dead and David gone, none of us had any idea what to do with it. But for now, it sat like it always had, most of David's things still in his room.

Including his computer.

Nodding, I plugged in the drive and clicked on "Open."

It took me a minute to find what I was looking for. I was scanning the various documents looking for my name, so the first time I saw it, my eyes actually drifted over the file meant for me. It was Bee who leaned forward and tapped the screen, saying, "I think it's this one."

Egregious Felicitations.

With a choked laugh, I shook my head, murmuring, "You idiot."

Bee gave my shoulder a quick squeeze, and then went to sit on David's bed, leaving me alone with the computer.

I opened the file. *Pres*, it started, and then the tears were on my cheeks, splashing onto the desk. *I know you're going to say this is dumb, and I know you won't understand. Which is why I asked Bee and Ryan for help. Don't get me wrong, I like fighting with you, but there are some things you just can't argue. This is one, and I hope you'll come to accept that.*

I have to leave Pine Grove. I have to leave Alabama, and I have to leave you. After tonight, that's all completely clear to me. This whole situation is so effed up (hope you appreciate my discretion there), and it's clear to me now that the only way to un-eff it up (do I get bonus points for that one?) is to take myself out of the equation. Without me, you, Bee, and Ryan can just be you, Bee, and Ryan. Not Paladins or Mages. People. With your own lives.

It's like you said at that time at Cotillion practice—you want to be a good woman who chooses the right thing for everybody. Well, so do I. (Minus the woman part, obviously.)

Have a good life, Pres. I love you. Always.

D

I read the note two more times before closing the document and turning away from the computer.

Bee sat on the edge of the bed, watching me, her long blond hair caught in a braid over one shoulder.

"Well?" she asked.

"You did the right thing," I said, even though the words hurt, hitting my heart like broken glass. "You were the Paladin I couldn't be, I guess."

At that, Bee stood up, her skirt swishing across her knees as she crossed the room to stand in front of me.

"No," she said, shaking her head vehemently. "I wasn't his girlfriend, so it was an easier choice to make."

When I didn't say anything, Bee sighed, folding her arms across her chest. "So what do we do now?" she asked me.

I got out of David's chair, picking up his bag, but leaving the jump drive in his computer. When I walked out into the hall, Bee followed me, and we stood there, looking back into David's room. There was a steady ache in my chest, and I had no idea if it was some residual Paladin thing—if David was in danger, but too far away for me to feel that normal crushing, burning sensation—or if it was just my heart breaking all over again.

I wrapped my fingers around the doorknob and turned back to Bee.

"We go back to normal," I said, letting the door click shut.

Bee gave a little snort at that, looking around at Saylor's house, still strewn with books about Oracles and magic and history, all these weird, incongruous things tucked alongside the china figurines and ugly paintings.

"Can we do that?" she asked, and I made myself walk down the stairs, my eyes on the front door.

Have a good life, Pres.

"We're going to try."

Look for the thrilling conclusion!

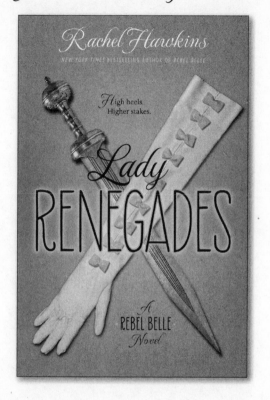

JUST AS Harper Price starts coming to terms with her role as David Stark's battle-ready Paladin, protector, and *girlfriend*—her world goes crazy all over again. Overwhelmed by his Oracle powers, David flees Pine Grove and starts turning teenaged girls into Paladins—and these young ladies seem to think that *Harper* is the enemy David needs protecting from. Ordinarily, Harper would be able to fight off any Paladin who comes her way, but her powers have been dwindling since David left town, which means her life is on the line yet again.

"HAWKINS'S NOVEL does not disappoint in this final addition to the Rebel Belle trilogy. Funny and sassy, Harper is the perfect combination of strong heroine and Southern lady."

—*VOYA*

Rebel Belle Acknowledgments

HUGE THANKS to Jennifer Besser for loving this weird little book first, and to my agent, Holly Root, for not blinking an eye when I said the words "it's like *Legally Blonde* meets *The Terminator*!"

I'm also massively grateful to Ginny Bakkan, Hunter Chapman, Ashley Parsons, Andrea Poole, and Rachel Waters for sharing everything they knew about debutante balls with me. Sorry I took your memories and covered them in Hawaiian Punch and violence, but such is the risk of being friends with a writer! Thanks too to Jennifer Sauls for coming up with the perfect tagline!

Thank you as always to my mom, who signed me up to be an Azalea Trail girl when I was six and had a special dress made just for the day (even if a fever kept me being an Azalea Trail girl in what I like to refer to as the Most Tragic Thing That Ever Happened to Me). Mama, no one is as rebellious and belle-a-licious as you, and I love you.

Hugs and snuggles and kisses to John and Will for being the best little family a girl could have, and for understanding when I locked myself in the dining room during our vacation to Scotland so that I could finish this book. There are not many men who would be patient when a visit to the Loch Ness Monster is on the line, but y'all didn't complain once.

And lastly, huge, obscene, downright embarrassing amounts of gratitude to my editor, Arianne Lewin, who helped me knock this book down to its foundations and rebuild something much more befitting a Queen Bee like Harper. You may be a New Yorker, but you will always be an honorary belle to me, and I am so, so thankful that I get to work with you!

Miss Mayhem Acknowledgments

WRITING A BOOK involves a fair amount of mayhem, and I'm lucky enough to have a bunch of fabulous mischief-makers on my side.

Thank you to my amazing editor, Ari Lewin, who gets me and my books so very well, has been such a champion for me and Harper, and never minds when I send her pictures of People I Find Attractive. You are a rock star, and I love making books with you!

Thanks, too, to the amazing Katherine Perkins, who is so smart I'm a little afraid of her, and whose notes on this book were insightful and encouraging and sharper than Harper's favorite high heel.

This is the sixth book that I've been lucky enough to thank Holly Root for, and I could fill up six more books just explaining why I feel so fortunate to have her as my agent. Everyone should have a Ninja-Angel like Holly on her side.

Massive thanks to the people at Penguin who have done so much for me and my books and who make me so grateful to shout "TEAM FLIGHTLESS BIRD!" on the regular. Special thanks to Anna Jarzab and Elyse Marshall for being both amazing at their jobs and just amazing humans in general.

Thank you so much to all of my readers, especially the Rebel Belles on Tumblr who have embraced Harper, Bee, David, and Ryan and made such lovely things to go along with the books. Best Readers Ever!

For me, these books are about the power of ladies and the special bond that is Lady Friendship, and I am, as the kids say, #blessed to have so many wonderful ladies in my life. I have to single out one of those ladies in particular, Julia Brown, for all her encouragement when I was working on *Miss Mayhem*, and for the ridiculous amounts of Happy she's brought into my life. Lady Bros 4-Ever.

As always, all the love to my family. Y'all are the reason I get to make up things for a living, but you've made the world I live in an even better place than all the worlds in my head. I love you.